THE STORIES
THAT ARE GREAT
WITHIN US

Library and Archives Canada Cataloguing in Publication

The stories that are great within us / edited by Barry Callaghan; introduction by Matt Shaw.

ISBN 978-1-55096-360-1 (pbk.)

1. Short stories, Canadian (English). 2. Toronto (Ont.)--Fiction. I. Shaw, Matt, 1982-, writer of introduction

PS8323.T67S77 2013 C813'.0108358713541 C2013-905115-5

Composition and Design by Michael Callaghan. Typeset in Big Caslon and Trajan fonts at the Moons of Jupiter Studios. Cover painting "Night Ride, 1970" and french flap painting "Tour de Force, 1987" by Charles Pachter, used by permission of the artist. Back cover photo by Yvonne Vaar, used by permission of the photographer.

Published by Exile Editions Ltd ~ www.ExileEditions.com
144483 Southgate Road 14 – GD, Holstein ON, N0G 2A0.
Printed and Bound in Canada by Imprimerie Gauvin in 2013.

The publisher would like to acknowledge the financial support of the Canada Council for the Arts, the Government of Canada through the Canada Book Fund (CBF), and the Ontario Arts Council for our publishing activities.

Conseil des Arts du Canada Canada Council for the Arts Canada ONTARIO ARTS COUNCIL CONSEIL DES ARTS DE L'ONTARIO

Canadian Sales: The Canadian Manda Group, 165 Dufferin Street, Toronto ON M6K 3H6
www.mandagroup.com 416 516 0911

North American and international distribution, and U.S. sales: Independent Publishers Group, 814 North Franklin Street, Chicago IL 60610 www.ipgbook.com toll free: 1 800 888 4741

FOR

GREG GATENBY

INTRODUCTION

Matt Shaw

In praise and condemnation, Toronto is a city of neighbourhoods. Uptown, downtown, midtown; Corktown, Leaside, Parkdale, Don Mills, Yorkville, Forest Hill, and Liberty Village; Malvern, Moore Park, Agincourt; the Junction, Weston, the Annex, Chinatown, Little Viet Nam, Beaches; Lawrence Heights, Regent Park and the Village; Ward's Island, Centre Island and Hanlon's Point; Earlscourt, Cabbagetown; Rosedale, Riverdale, Islington and Lambton; Corso Italia, Little Portugal, the Distillery and Little India; Runnymede, Swansea, Humbermede and Mimico; the markets – St. Lawrence and Kensington; the Kingsway, Willowdale, Jane and Finch, Hogg's Hollow; Rexdale, Downsview and Old Mill (there are now over 160 designated areas within the Greater Toronto Area).

However one defines their borders, permeable and impermanent as they are, there are more neighbourhoods in Toronto than there are countries in the world. For inhabitants, these named and unnamed slivers, rectangles and oblong plots evoke a sense of place or shared identity – for outsiders, they are hazy as mirages. At worst, they appear impenetrable and unwelcoming. Those with community associations help the casual visitor by marking their street signs or bus stops. Some are preceded by reputations. Others are evocative of cultures, landmarks, histories or flavours. The rest are known mostly to those who live there.

Their arrangement seems haphazard yet their composition is complex: coloured by immigration, race and faith; rendered mutable and immutable by zoning, property valuations, bylaws and political wards; topographies veined with ravines and ancient underground rivers; swaths of bungalows, skyscrapers, projects and the omnipresent condominium – neighbourhoods in the sky in which it is possible to know the people next to you only by the sound of the television or the slapping headboard.

It is fitting, then, that these stories exist alongside one another as neighbours – each concerned with its own life, history and dreams, each occasionally peering out the window at one another. They live intensely and privately yet in concert with those who share the city with them, a cross-section of the writers and literature of modern Toronto since the early 20th century, when the Toronto of today was born. Together they map much of modern Toronto's streets, landmarks, history – charting the matter-of-factness of a public consciousness often accused of narcissism while suffering, paradoxically, under the "anxiety of influence," the shadow of some larger, more glamorous and international city.

As Carl Sandberg and E.B. White memorialized Chicago and New York, Toronto stands here as terrain and as character, muse, history and tableau. Tourists might recognize the sights they have seen – the Bloor Viaduct, the CN Tower – and plan their next stop. In this cubist continuum of stories, excerpts, non-fiction and art, history jostles with the present. The future is warily considered. Views combat. The city is in the eye of the beholder. From the skyline, the city becomes a flatland forest, a city of not enough parks but thousands and thousands of big trees; the view is dizzying. There is much to see.

Like strangers arriving to parts unknown, we ask many questions of this place as we find our way and learn its customs. What constitutes a Toronto writer, anyway? Must Toronto itself be the subject of a Toronto story? Can outsiders write Toronto stories? And how much does the subway cost? All fine questions. The city never answers.

Go, *flâneurs*. But, let's be clear: this is not a dutiful and comprehensive catalogue of all the honest writers who, as honest citizens, have told their stories about Toronto.

There is no map here.

In lieu, one encounters moods, visions, concerns and obsessions. Mayoralty is in short shrift; this city is governed by the muse, Gwendolyn MacEwen. Relentless storyhounds Joe Fiorito, Alice Boissonneau and Hugh Garner trawl the thoroughfares and back alleys, uncovering the truth of the city's dispossessed and disenfranchised. In its public spaces, unlikely companions sit together and argue their views – Joe Rosenblatt with Margaret Atwood, Lisa Foad with Janice Kulyk Keefer, Christine Miscione with R. Murray Schafer, Helen Weinzweig with M.T. Kelly, Katherine Govier with Ludwig Zeller; Greg Kearney and Linda Griffiths with David Cronenberg and Norman Snider; Sang Kim with Nina Bunjevac. A three-man band of kazoos, umbrellas, musicals saws and clarinets warbles on the sidewalk. Cars honk. Blazing long-legged women in spiked heels strut their runway stuff. Glenn Gould plays on the keyboard in his head. Crowds swarm the monuments of Michael Snow, Charles Pachter and Sorel Etrog, on their way to diamonds and rinks.

Yet, a sense of community emerges from the apparent disorder of this city. Chronologically, and there is a kind of chronology, these stories begin, as they should, with Morley Callaghan – young, well-read, determined, "stubborn and alone," as Alistair MacLeod has put it, staking Toronto's first claim to literary greatness in the 1920s and 1930s. Callaghan sets the tone: writing of strange fugitives – writing from Toronto the Good, of all places, writing North America's first urban gangster novel – as Hugh Garner reports on the lives of a staid, Protestant town, the Anglo-Saxon slums of Cabbagetown and the Ward. These inhabitants buckle under the nauseating smell of slaughtered hogs and labour in tanneries and garment factories while Jarvis Street socialites summer in High

Park – the same tennis set that wealthy Mazo de la Roche, friend of the Masseys, savages with psychological grotesquerie.

Time passes, and the city's voices multiply as individuals pour into its neighbourhoods – the immigrant experiences of Irish, Italians, Jews; Eastern Europeans; and the urban First Nations peoples; influx of Carribbean and African, Indian, and East Asian cultures; and more, from all reaches of the globe. The worldly and weary voices of Austin Clarke, Michael Ondaatje and Dionne Brand swell alongside Timothy Findley and Anne Michaels. The rhetoric of Robertson Davies is overdubbed with jazz; the high Anglican tonalities of "Massey culture" mingle with the rough vernacular of prostitutes, gamblers, hustlers and horse racers. And always there is music: blues, Ravel, Thelonious Monk and, of course, Glenn Gould – variations on a theme by B.W. Powe and Susan Perly. On the subject of losers, there are Toronto's sports teams; the gritty knockout punch of Billy Tabb in "The Chiseller"; the Sultan of Swat himself, Babe Ruth (who hit his first home run in the waters off Toronto Island's Hanlan's Point in 1914); and the best blind goaltender the Maple Leafs never drafted. Marginalized gay and lesbian cultures begin to blossom, while First Nations peoples, in Joseph Boyden's "Painted Tongue," remain on the fringes, the city an enigma to the end. Violence flares, with racism, alienation, paranoia and profound anxiety. All, finally, is observed through the wry eye of the city's most ubiquitous citizen, a raccoon.

These stories tell, in part, the story of a place. Yet, despite their familiar landmarks, they derive their strength not from Toronto's *terra firma* but the *terra incognita* of each character's experience. The story tellers are intelligent, anxious or personable. Self-concerned with their own matters, they wittingly (or not) and willingly (or not) find themselves citizens of a republic. They are entirely themselves: the deadpan daring of Barbara Gowdy, the laughter of Leon Rooke. The sonorous Michael Ondaatje or Anne Michaels. The guiling and contemplative Sheila Heti, big-hearted Paul Quarrington and Steven Hayward. And throughout, the probing visions of Gwendolyn MacEwen. Where else might one find, cheek by jowl, such talents as these?

It has been said that there are only two kinds of stories: a stranger coming to town or a hero embarking on a journey. In a city where nearly everyone is from somewhere else, we encounter both. Austin Clarke's Calvin, a black man from Barbados, arrives in Toronto to earn his small piece of the urban dream, a Ford Galaxie. The young narrator of Barry Callaghan's "Our Thirteenth Summer" comes of age discovering that his Jewish neighbours, who he has never thought of as any different from himself, are very much "the other" – people from a culture beyond his own and who see him as a threat. It is the eponymous Russian cousin, in David Bezmozgis' "Natasha," who arrives to enlighten Mark Berman to more worldly pleasures and sorrows, while the narrator of Sang Kim's "When John Lennon Died" stands alone at the precipice of his own epiphany. We are struck by the verisimilitude of recognizing in our neighbours our own yearnings and fears, even as we stand in awe of the strange human life, civilized and brutal, that lives among us.

It can be said that a city has no presence until it exists in our imagination. This Toronto's streets can be walked, its landmarks photographed. It teems. It's real. And yet a city is in part merely a reflection of its residents. It is you.

To amend Julio Cortázar: *The only true exile is the writer who lives in his own city.* In *The Stories That Are Great Within Us,* we are reminded that in a place of three million citizens, we find as many visions. This is merely one, curated by its native son and resident exile, Barry Callaghan: novelist and poet and reporter, ,not just a man about town but, like Clarke, Atwood, MacEwen, Michaels, Govier, Fiorito, and his father, Morley, a chronicler of his city. *The Stories That Are Great Within Us* may not be your vision. You may disagree. *But what a vision it is!*

In *this* city, neighbourhood borders collapse. What remains is a wild pastiche of styles and subject. These voices dare to be themselves, to be great. Through them we are certain that, like St. Petersburg, London or Berlin, Chicago or New York - Toronto *exists.*

These stories are like streetcars, sparking as they trawl the city, a cacophony of voices carrying beyond the lake long after the city itself dissolves to the horizon. Toronto *is.*

He awoke sighing and talking to himself the way sleepers do when they leave the private country of their sleep. "Where are we going?" he murmured. "Toronto. Unless you have some other place in mind."

—GWENDOLYN MACEWEN

THE SPHINX IN TORONTO

LUDWIG ZELLER

SHORESIDE

GWENDOLYN MACEWEN

You walk along the lakeshore late at night and head eastward from Sunnyside Baths which is a naked castle whose towers guard nothing but themselves, or an Eastern pavilion filled with dark musicians and dancers, along Sunnyside beach and the kids' park with its paper dinosaurs and green and purple monsters gloating in the moonlight, down to the shore where you stoop and find white pebbles almost as thin as communion wafers which you send skimming and skipping across the black water as the silver sliver of the moon skims across the sky. The lake is deliciously, hellishly cold and you think of the thousands of swimmers of times gone by who shed their clothes in the great pavilion and shivering and ridiculous in their navy blue swimsuits ran across the burning sands to the scathing water. Now the fervent voices of the summer people carry all the way up to High Park, from the rides at the amusement park, from the ghosts of the Ferris wheel and the roller coaster which lifted them shrieking and squealing to heaven. Farther on is the Palais Royale where the big bands played their brassy satin music and dancers danced until they dropped...

from KING LEARY

PAUL QUARRINGTON

The brothers of St. Alban the Martyr started putting together the boards. They were usually a quiet bunch, but they got even quieter, all of them rushing around with hammers in their hands and nails sticking out of their mouths. The only thing us lads heard from them was pounding out in the playing field, pounding and the occasional grunt. I personally thought the monks were crazy, and I'll tell you why: they laid out the boards in a circle. A huge and, as far as I could tell, perfect circle. I even asked Brother Isaiah about it. He just grinned and fastened his strange eyes on my left shoulder. "Have ye not known?" he asked me. "Have ye not heard? It is he that sitteth upon the circle of the earth that bringeth the princes to nothing." That's the kind of answer I used to get from Brother Isaiah. So anyway, they laid out the boards in a circle, and around the beginning of December they raised them. The monks took the old horses off the cart. It took the horses and sometimes six or seven brothers to raise each section of board. The weather stayed pleasant for a week or two, the sun all biting and bright even though the trees were naked as firewood. We all waited; the monks prayed.

On Christmas Eve the temperature fell about forty degrees. The brothers rushed out with buckets and hoses. They stayed out there all night, and to keep themselves amused they sang. They sang strange songs with words I didn't understand. All night long the monks watered the world, and the winter air turned the water to ice. Blue-silver ice, hard as marble. On Christmas morning the round rink was ready. Brother Simon was out there skating, his face even uglier, reddened by lack of oxygen, his carbuncles polished by the stinging wind. For a huge, monstrous man he sure could dance out there on the ice! He had some figure-skating moves, dips and twirls, his arms raised slightly, the hockey stick acting as a balancing pole. And as I watched him, Brother Simon the Ugly became airborne. It seemed he was up there for a whole minute, and during that time he pirouetted lazily. This stunt robbed me of my breath and made my knees quiver... I said to myself, Leary, if you could do that, no one could ever stop you. It took me some months to learn to skate like Brother Andrew the Fireplug. I call it Bulldogging. Miles Renders, who is currently coaching the Toronto Maple Leafs, calls it "achievement through perseverance and mental imaging," and I say that one of the reasons the Leafs are faring so poorly is that Renders would call Bulldogging something like that...

One night, I couldn't sleep. There was a full moon, and it filled the window across from my cot, and for some strange reason I could make out all the mountains and craters. The moon was a strange colour, too, a silver like a nickel had been flipped into the sky.

Then I heard the sounds, the soft windy sweeping of hockey sticks across ice. At first I thought I was dreaming, but then I recalled that I never did dream to speak of. I moved across to the window, soft on my feet so as not to wake the other delinquents. The moon was so bright that I do believe I squinted up my eyes. I have never seen it like that since.

I could see the rink, and I could see the shadows moving on it. The monks were playing a little midnight shinny. It quickened my heart. I threw on some clothes and flew outside.

There were five of them. I watched from a distance at first. I couldn't understand what sort of game they were playing. The action would move erratically within the circle, and sometimes the five would split so that three men would rush two, or four would rush one, and then sometimes the five of them would move in cahoots, the idea seeming to be to achieve a certain prettiness of passing. Then a man would break from the pack, and another man would chase him around the circle, and as quick as that happened they'd rejoin the three in the centre. There were no goal nets on the ice. Just five men, a puck, and a lot of moonlight. They played in silence. I moved closer.

Simon the Ugly was the easiest to pick out, because he was the biggest. He was dancing, jumping into the air, and sometimes I could see his monstrous frame silhouetted against the troutsilver moon. Theodore the Slender cut a shadow so fine that it was hard to pick out, but I could tell him from the quick, precise movements of his twiggy arms as he took a shot. And Andrew the Fireplug, it was he who was likeliest to make a break for the boards, to drift like gun smoke around them. I watched him scoot off with the puck, and then I watched a man slip up easily behind Andrew and relieve him of the rubber. That was Isaiah the Blind. I could scarcely credit it. Playing goaler is one thing – I mean, at least Isaiah was standing still between the pipes, and you could always convince yourself that he was simply the luckiest son of a bee ever – but here he was skating around like a madman, stealing pucks, passing and receiving, and the moonlight was sitting on his dead eyes like it does on the still surface of a lake...

I have never in my life seen such a good goaler as Brother Isaiah, and I have seen everyone from the Chicoutimi Cucumber to that tall slender fellow who looked like a schoolteacher and played so well for the Montreal Canadiens. Yet I am convinced to this day that Brother Isaiah was blind as a bat, though he denied it. Isaiah might occasionally admit to being "a tad shortsighted," but you'd have to catch him walking into a brick wall. The other monks couldn't get a shot by him. Isaiah would just reach out and grab them in his glove (and gloves back then didn't amount to much), or else he'd get the toe on them, or the chest in front of them, or bang them away with his stick. Brother Simon the Ugly tried to jimmy one by him, dancing right up to the goal crease, flipping the puck off his backhand as he made one of his ballerina twirlabouts. Brother Isaiah flicked it away with his wood. Then Andrew the Fireplug comes barrelling along the wing, taking out a couple of bystander brothers just for style, and he unleashes a slapshot even though the damn thing isn't even invented back then! Brother Isaiah the Blind raises his left shoulder maybe a quarter inch and the rubber is dancing harmlessly behind the net.

But there was Brother Theodore the Slender standing in the centre of the huge silver circle, and his eyes were popped open all the way and his mouth had ceased working. In front of him was a puck. Brother Theodore brought his stick back real slow, and then, with a motion that cut the air like a knife, Brother Theodore whacked the rubber... and it didn't even look like he was trying.

Theodore the Slender gave me the gam on shooting, which is this: shooting is more mental than physical. You just practice so much that you can feel the puck, like the blade of your lumber was the palm of your hand, and then you just inner-eye that puck into the back of the net. "See it there first," Brother Theodore was wont to say, "and then put it there." In other words, *wham, bingo.*

THE BLACK QUEEN

BARRY CALLAGHAN

Hughes and McCrae were fastidious men who took pride in their old colonial house, the clean simple lines and stucco walls and the painted pale blue picket fence. They were surrounded by houses converted into small warehouses, trucking yards where houses had been torn down, and along the street, a school filled with foreign children, but they didn't mind. It gave them an embattled sense of holding on to something important, a tattered remnant of good taste in an area of waste overrun by rootless olive-skinned children.

McCrae wore his hair a little too long now that he was going gray, and while Hughes with his clipped moustache seemed to be a serious man intent only on his work, which was costume design, McCrae wore Cuban heels and lacquered his nails. When they'd met ten years ago Hughes had said, "You keep walking around like that and you'll need a body to keep you from getting poked in the eye." McCrae did all the cooking and drove the car.

But they were not getting along these days. Hughes blamed his bursitis, but they were both silently unsettled by how old they had suddenly become, how loose in the thighs, and their feet, when they were showering in the morning, seemed bonier, the toes longer, the nails yellow and hard, and what they wanted was tenderness, to be able to yield almost tearfully, full of a pity for themselves that would not be belittled or laughed at, and when they stood alone in their separate bedrooms they wanted that tenderness from each other, but when they were having their bedtime tea in the kitchen, as they had done for years using lovely green and white Limoges cups, if one touched the other's hand then suddenly they both withdrew into an unspoken, smiling aloofness, as if some line of privacy had been crossed. Neither could bear their thinning wrists and the little pouches of darkening flesh under the chin. They spoke of being with younger people and even joked slyly about bringing a young man home, but that seemed such a betrayal of everything that they had believed had set them apart from others, everything they believed had kept them together, that they sulked and nettled away at each other, and though nothing had apparently changed in their lives, they were always on edge, Hughes more than McCrae.

One of their pleasures was collecting stamps, rare and mint-perfect, with no creases or smudges on the gum. Their collection, carefully mounted in a leather-bound blue book with seven little plastic windows per page, was worth several thousand dollars. They had passed many pleasant evenings together on the Directoire settee arranging the old ochre- and carmine-coloured stamps. They agreed there was something almost sensual about holding a perfectly preserved piece of the past, unsullied, as if everything didn't have to change, didn't have to end up swamped by decline and decay. They disapproved of the new stamps and dismissed them as crude and wouldn't have them in their book. The pages for the recent years remained empty and they liked that; the emptiness was their statement about themselves and their values, and Hughes, holding a stamp up into the light between his tweezers, would say, "None of that rough trade for us."

One afternoon they went down to the philatelic shops around Adelaide and Richmond Streets and saw a stamp they had been after for a long time, a large and elegant black stamp of Queen Victoria in her widow's weeds. It was rare and expensive, a dead-letter stamp from the turn of the century. They stood side by side over the glass countercase admiring it, their hands spread on the glass, but when McCrae, the overhead fluorescent light catching his lacquered nails, said, "Well, I certainly would like that little black sweetheart," the owner, who had sold stamps to them for several years, looked up and smirked, and Hughes suddenly snorted, "You old queen, I mean why don't you just quit wearing those goddamn Cuban heels, eh, I mean why not?" He walked out leaving McCrae embarrassed and hurt and when the owner said, "So what was wrong?" McCrae cried, "Screw you," and strutted out.

Through the rest of the week they were deferential around the house, offering each other every consideration, trying to avoid any squabble before Mother's Day at the end of the week when they were going to hold their annual supper for friends, three other male couples. Over the years it had always been an elegant, slightly mocking evening that often ended bitter-sweetly and left them feeling close, comforting each other.

McCrae, wearing a white, linen shirt, starch in the cuffs and mother-of-pearl cufflinks, worked all Sunday afternoon in the kitchen, and through the window he could see the crabapple tree in bloom and he thought how in previous years he would have begun planning to put down some jelly in the old pressed glass jars they kept in the cellar, but instead, head down, he went on stuffing and tying the pork loin roast. Then in the early evening he heard Hughes at the door, and there was laughter from the front room and someone cried out, "What do you do with an elephant who has three balls on him... you don't know silly, well you walk him and pitch to the giraffe," and there were howls of laughter and the clinking of glasses. It had been the same every year, eight men sitting down to a fine supper with expensive wines, the table set with their best silver under the antique carved wooden candelabra.

Having prepared all the raw vegetables, the cauliflower and carrots, the avocados and finger-sized miniature corns-on-the-cob, and placed porcelain bowls of homemade dip in the centre of a pewter tray, McCrae stared at his reflection for a moment in the window over the kitchen sink and then he took a plastic slipcase out of the knives-and-forks drawer. The case contained the dead-letter stamp.

He licked it all over and pasted it on his forehead and then slipped on the jacket of his charcoal brown crushed velvet suit, took hold of the tray, and stepped out into the front room.

The other men, sitting in a circle around the coffee table, looked up and one of them giggled. Hughes cried, "Oh my God." McCrae, as if nothing were the matter, said, "My dears, time for the *crudités*." He was in his silk stocking feet, and as he passed the tray he winked at Hughes who sat staring at the black queen.

AUGUST 7, 1921

Steven Hayward

After ten years of "Give-Away Days," the Yankees had managed to dole out a greater variety of baseball paraphernalia than any other team in the history of baseball. The first Give-Away Day was on June 3, 1918 (when 6,500 Yankee caps were given away), and the last was on September 17, 1927 (when over 80,000 pretzels shaped like Yankee logos were distributed). In between, there had been Cap Day, Bottle Opener Day, Pennant Day, Cigar Day, Pillow Day, Sock Day, Mug Day, Pretzel Day, Jersey Day, Sneaker Day, Baseball Card Day, Camera Day, Hot Dog Day, Tobacco Day, Chewing Tobacco Day, Cracker Jack Day, and Peanut Day, to name a few.

August 7, 1921, was Bat Day.

According to *The Completely Complete Book of Baseball Statistics* by Dr. Venue Guzman, there were 21,106 paying customers in Yankee Stadium that day, and 15,000 of them had been given complimentary baseball bats as they entered the stadium. This story is concerned with seven of those people. The first two are Mary and Lyman Labrow.

I know about the Labrows thanks to an article published on September 21, 1923 (roughly two years after Bat Day), that I found in the archives of a now-defunct newspaper called the *New York Reflector*. The article described the circumstances that led to both of the Labrows being in Yankee Stadium that day, and was accompanied by a photo of the couple; in it, Mary and Lyman are smiling and wearing clothes which were already out of fashion in 1921. The Grand Canyon is visible in the background. Lyman Labrow was an optometrist and Mary Labrow was a seamstress. They lived in Bergen County, New Jersey, and had no children.

On August 7, 1921, Mary Labrow was sitting one row ahead of me in Yankee Stadium. She was a small, birdlike woman and was wearing a nondescript brown dress that day. She did not look at the field once during the game. Instead, she was looking at two people sitting three rows ahead of her, at a man and a woman.

The man she was looking at was her husband, Lyman Labrow. Mary had come to the game specifically to spy on him, and she could see him perfectly from where she was sitting. Lyman, however, did not see her until it was too late; until after she had noticed the same thing I had noticed, that he was not alone.

Lyman Labrow had come to the game that day with his secretary, a twenty-three-year-old woman named Jackie Hubbs. She was wearing a bright yellow dress and carried a small white purse that had a medium-sized bulge in it. She was exactly the kind of girl you look at during baseball games when there is no one at bat.

For the first three innings, no one could have guessed that Lyman Labrow and Jackie Hubbs were romantically involved, despite the fact they were sitting next to one another. They watched the game and their hands did not even touch. Jackie Hubbs' white purse sat chastely on her lap and her white fingers were folded chastely on top of it. However, it became evident during the fourth inning, when Jackie Hubbs reached into her purse and removed the medium-sized bulge, that she and Lyman Labrow were having an affair.

I suppose that today, she and Lyman Labrow could have complicated sexual intercourse in the stands behind third base, and no one would think, or say, anything. But those were different times. On August 7, 1921, Jackie Hubbs caused a sensation in Yankee Stadium by eating a medium-sized Granny Smith apple.

She shined the apple by rubbing it extensively and energetically against her bright yellow dress. Instead of biting into it, she licked it three times, extraordinarily slowly, and handed it to Lyman Labrow. He looked at the apple, took a bite, and gave it back to her. Jackie Hubbs stroked the white part of the apple with her finger, and then she touched Lyman Labrow's lips, softly.

And Mary Labrow sat perfectly still, three rows behind them, watching.

Those are the first three people who matter in this story.

The fourth person who matters in this story is a drunken off-duty policeman from Evansville, Indiana, named John Seidl, and the fifth person who matters in this story is a sober Yiddish typewriter salesman from New York City named Norman Flax. John Seidl was sitting in the seat to my right and Norman Flax was sitting directly in front of me.

I know that Norman Flax was a Yiddish typewriter salesman from New York City because he stood up in the bottom of the second inning and introduced himself to a rabbi who was sitting behind me. Norman's mother was sitting beside him, and it was she who pointed out the rabbi to her son. Clearly, Norman Flax was the sort of salesman who was always on the lookout for rabbis.

"I'm Norman Flax," he said, reaching over my head to shake the rabbi's hand. "If you need a Yiddish typewriter, you know who to call."

"I've already got a typewriter," said the rabbi. "What should I need another one for?"

"Maybe you don't need one now," said Norman Flax. "But you never know. When you do need one, call this number and ask for Flax."

And I know that John Seidl was a drunken off-duty policeman from Evansville, Indiana, because he spent most of the game talking loudly to another drunken off-duty policeman from Evansville, Indiana, whose name I never found out.

"I gotta take a leak," announced John Seidl, in the bottom of the fourth inning (just as Jackie Hubbs was reaching for the medium-sized bulge in her purse). "And when John Seidl has to take a leak, John Seidl has to take a leak."

John Seidl was the sort of man who habitually refers to himself in the third person, and that is why I happen to know his name.

"Whattya want me to do?" asked the other off-duty policeman from Evansville, Indiana.

"Ahhh," replied John Seidl, as he was standing up. "You're hilarious."

Now, John Seidl was a big man, and when he stood up to make his way out into the aisle, he steadied himself by putting his hand on the shoulder of the person sitting next to him, and almost fell down. It was not a shoulder that provided much support, because it was the shoulder of a ten-year-old boy.

It was my shoulder. That was me. I was sitting beside the sixth person who matters in this story.

Unlike the majority of people in the stands behind third base that day, the sixth person who matters in this story was concentrating on the game. His real name was Giovanni Spadafina, but everyone – even my mother – called him Samson Spadafina. He was my father.

My father worked at the Heinzman Piano Factory where he was one of twenty-three men responsible for the manufacture of the tiny hammers that strike the strings inside Heinzman pianos. He had come to New York from Italy in 1911 with my mother. "The name of the ship," he used to tell me, "was the *Santa Maria*."

This was something that he said repeatedly. Like Christopher Columbus, my father was from Genoa, and the fact that he landed at Ellis Island in a ship called the Santa Maria was of great symbolic importance to him. It allowed him to claim, only half ironically, that he had arrived in the New World in the same vessel as Columbus. I am aware this is an extremely dubious, if not dangerous, claim to make in this age of political correctness, but it is one that my father – were he still alive today – would continue to make. To my father, Columbus represented everything a man should be: he was intelligent, resourceful, brave, industrious, physically strong, self-sufficient, and very, very rich.

"The Italians," my father used to say, "civilized the world."

When he was not working at the Heinzman Piano Factory he supplemented his income by gambling, and won almost every bet he ever placed. This was not because my father was particularly lucky, but because he always bet on the same thing; himself. He had developed a routine that would usually result in someone agreeing to bet against him. First, he would walk into a bar and order a drink. Then he would begin to talk. He always said the same thing.

"In the Old Country," he would say, "everyone was afraid of me."

Then he would tell the story of his impossible strength, about the earthquake that shook Italy in the spring of 1887, and how the roof of his parents' house landed on his father's leg. He was only a child then, and said he didn't give much thought to what he'd done until after he'd done it. He just lifted the roof off his father.

"And that," he would say, "was when they started calling me Samson."

The routine usually worked. After he finished telling the story of his impossible strength, the other men in the bar would begin to look at him, to size him up.

The truth is that my father was not a physically imposing man. He was less than five feet tall and did not look strong. There was almost always someone willing to wager he wasn't strong at all.

There were a number of stunts he could perform to demonstrate his impossible strength, and these stunts were usually the subject of the bets he would place. He could pick up tables with his teeth, perform one-arm chin-ups with another man clinging to his back, arm-wrestle three people at once, rip telephone books in half, and on one occasion, I saw him juggle a rusted cannonball, a butcher's knife, and a small St. Bernard.

But my father had to be careful never to go into the same bar too many times. Otherwise people would challenge him to do something that was impossible. This was what almost happened when he won the tickets to the Yankee game.

I was with him that day. My mother had sent us down to East 88th Street, to the Columbus Bakery, to buy a loaf of bread. On the way he stopped into a bar called O'Malley's and ordered a drink. Then he began to talk.

"In the Old Country," he said, "everybody was afraid of me..."

I suppose that if he had been paying closer attention, he would have seen the look on the bartender's face, how he whispered to another man behind the bar, and the way they both laughed. My father would have known it was a set-up.

"All right, Samson," said the bartender, "I've got a pair of Yankee tickets right here that say you can't lift the man sitting at the back of the bar."

"That's all?" he asked.

"That's all," said the bartender. "You just lift him up, and you walk out of here with the tickets, if not then you pay me for the tickets and I keep them."

"*Adesso,*" said my father, waving both his hands. In Genoese dialect this is an expression that can mean almost anything. It can be a confirmation, a contradiction, a compliment, a protest, a warning, a congratulation, a shout of dismay, or a way of asking someone to pass the pasta. In that particular context, it was the Genoese equivalent of my father announcing that he was ready to demonstrate his impossible strength.

Everyone followed the bartender to the back of the bar.

It was impossible not to recognize the man my father was required to lift. He was perhaps the most easily identifiable person in the whole of New York. He had been interviewed by every major newspaper, been photographed by the Guinness Book of World Records, and had shaken Charlie Chaplin's hand. People came from all over the world to catch a glimpse of him, or to have their photograph taken while sitting on his lap. However, many people declined such a photo opportunity because the man charged a nickel (which in those days was a lot of money) for the privilege. He had a concession at the foot of the Statue of Liberty and it was rumoured that he made a pretty fair living. His real name was Brian Flanagan, but everyone called him what the papers called him: The Fattest Man in New York City.

He was sitting at the back of the bar in a reinforced steel chair which had been specially constructed to bear his weight. He looked like he had been born in that chair.

When my father saw The Fattest Man in New York City he looked worried. He wiped his hands on his pants. This meant that his palms were sweating. I knew this was a bad sign. My father had palms that never sweated.

"I've made a bet," he whispered to me. "I have to try."

"Good luck," said The Fattest Man in New York City, as my father moved closer to him. "You'll need it."

The bar became completely silent. All I could hear was the sound of my father breathing and The Fattest Man in New York City's uneven wheeze.

"I'm very fat," said The Fattest Man in New York City. "No one has ever lifted me."

"Perhaps I will be the first," said my father, moving to the man.

Now, I knew exactly what my father was thinking. He was thinking about Columbus; about being first. I remember watching my father as he paced circles around The Fattest Man in New York City and – for the first time in my life – wondering if there was something he couldn't do.

I'm not sure exactly how it happened.

"*Adesso*," called out my father, and in a split second, with one perfectly fluid clean-and-jerk movement, it was over. He had somehow taken hold of a foot and a shoulder, and lifted the huge man over his head. The Fattest Man in New York City looked worriedly at the floor, and vomited.

My father quickly put him down, picked up the Yankee tickets, and walked out of the bar wiping off one of his coat sleeves. "Don't tell your mother about this," he said, when we were out on the street, "and I'll take you to the game tomorrow."

They were good seats, but they weren't great seats. My father didn't seem to mind. That was before television, and he had never seen a baseball game before. He had no idea what was going on.

"I understand the strikes," he said to me, "but what's a ball?"

I was about to explain when Babe Ruth came up to bat.

He is the seventh person who matters in this story.

Now, in the bottom of the ninth inning, only the core of Jackie Hubbs' Granny Smith apple remained. She held it between her lips and made a loud sucking noise that drew the attention of everyone sitting in the stands behind third base. I think even Lyman Labrow was embarrassed, although he didn't look like he was about to complain. Mary Labrow found that she could not contain herself any longer. She stood up and spoke to her husband.

This is what she said: "Lyman, you snake, I'm going to kill you."

Unlike myself, John Seidl and the other drunken off-duty policeman from Evansville, Indiana, were paying no attention to the domestic dispute occurring two rows ahead of them. They were deep in conversation. They had already discussed criminals, the criminal mind, specific criminals John Seidl had arrested, the difference between criminals in New York City and criminals in Evansville, the trouble with John Seidl's kids, the trouble with all kids, the trouble with John Seidl's wife, the trouble with having a wife at all, and then, finally, in the bottom of the ninth inning, they began to discuss the 1919 World Series, and who was responsible for fixing it.

"It's them Jews that done it," said John Seidl, loudly.

"I don't know," said the other drunken off-duty policeman from Evansville, Indiana.

"John Seidl is here to tell ya," said John Seidl. "It's them Jews."

"Ain't none of the players that were Jews," pointed out the other man.

Norman Flax turned around in his seat to see who was speaking, and then went back to watching the game.

John Seidl saw him turn around and kept talking.

"It don't matter that none of them was Jews," he said, sounding so ugly that even Norman Flax's mother turned to look at him.

"It was them Jews – they're the ones with the money."

That was when Norman Flax stood up.

"Which Jews exactly?" asked Norman Flax. "Just tell me which of them Jews it was, so that I can get them."

"Siddown boy," said John Seidl. "You don't want no trouble from John Seidl."

"I'll sit down," said Norman Flax, "when you shut up."

That was when John Seidl stood up.

Babe Ruth stepped into the batter's box. The pitcher threw the first pitch. Babe Ruth took a swing, and hit a high foul ball into the stands behind third base, right where we were sitting.

If it had been any other day at Yankee Stadium nothing would have happened. It would have been a foul ball and the game would have continued.

But it was August 7, 1921.

Bat Day.

Everyone swung at exactly the same time.

Mary Labrow reached across two rows of seats and attempted to hit Lyman Labrow with her complimentary bat. Lyman saw the complimentary bat coming at him and ducked out of the way. In fact, everyone sitting in that row ducked out of the way, with the conspicuous exception of Jackie Hubbs, who, with both of her eyes closed, was preoccupied with sucking an apple core.

The complimentary bat hit her in the face, and flattened her nose completely. There was a strangely silent moment just before Jackie Hubbs began to scream, when she reached up to her nose, and found it crushed.

And Norman Flax reached for his complimentary bat and took a swing at John Seidl.

And John Seidl reached for his complimentary bat and took a swing at Norman Flax.

And both men were knocked instantaneously unconscious. They fell forward and rolled out into the aisle, in each other's arms.

And my father moved with the same unreal fluidity with which he had lifted The Fattest Man in New York City over his head. The foul ball headed right toward us, and before I knew what was happening, he had reached for his complimentary bat and jumped onto his seat.

"*Adesso*," he told me, and bent his knees slightly, and took a swing at the foul ball, and hit it right back at Babe Ruth.

The last thing I remember seeing as we walked quickly out of Yankee Stadium was Babe Ruth lying over home plate. No one knew what had happened. One moment Babe Ruth was hitting his cleats with his bat, and the next, he had collapsed into the dust.

We walked straight home and my father did not say a word. It was not until we got to our house, until he had opened the front door, that he noticed the bat was still in his hands.

"Carmella," he told my mother, "I think I killed Babe Ruth."

What happened next happened very quickly.

My mother decided that we had to do something. So, we neither waited for the papers the next day (which said that Babe Ruth was still alive), nor went to the police station (which was already filling with the casualties of Bat Day). Instead: we panicked. We packed our things and got on a train the next morning. We came to Toronto.

After that, my father stopped doing impossible things. He became a quiet, ordinary carpenter who earned his living building porches and installing kitchen cabinets. People no longer called him Samson and he never told anyone about August 7, 1921. He died when he was sixty-two years old, of prostate cancer. They sent him home after the treatment had failed. His hair had fallen out and he was completely blind.

The last picture of him was taken just before he died, at my daughter's fifth birthday party. He had already been sent home by the hospital. In the picture he is singing "Happy Birthday," but looking the wrong way as my daughter blows out the candles on her cake. On the table in front of him there are some walnuts that he has cracked open. The nuts are still in them. My father never liked eating walnuts, but loved cracking them open. He would pick up a nut and squeeze it until the shell cracked. He was the only one I ever knew who could do that with only one hand. I've tried it more times than I can count. I suppose that this is the picture that would have to go at the end of his story. Or maybe just a close-up of the walnuts.

August 7 1921 was the first and last Bat Day in the history of baseball. One-hundred-eighty-seven people, including Babe Ruth, were injured that day. According to the article in the *New York Reflector*, the Labrows divorced and Jackie Hubbs had reconstructive surgery on her face. In the paper she was quoted as saying that she liked her new nose "better." I have no idea what happened to John Seidl and Norman Flax. The last time I saw them, they were lying with their eyes closed, in each other's arms at the end of our aisle. We stepped over them as we exited the stadium. Perhaps they lived happily ever after.

I still have the complimentary bat that my father got that day. Today it is a rotted piece of wood, and the Yankees logo on its side has faded during the years it was kept in the damp basement of my house. The truth is that if I could show it to you, you would be unimpressed. It does not look at all like a bat that might have changed the course of history.

But I still have it. I am an old man now, with grandchildren of my own, but there are days when I go into the basement just to touch it. The feel of the wood never fails to bring back that day, the day my father became afraid. I close my eyes and I can see myself standing beside him in Yankee Stadium. The game is about to begin and both of us are singing "Oh say can you see by the dawn's early light..." His real name was Giovanni, but everyone – even my mother – called him Samson. I smell the grass and hear the roar of the crowd, the final note dissolving into sunshine.

GALAXIE

AUSTIN CLARKE

After the twenty-nine years he born and living in Barbados, drunk as Calvin was, he saying, "Well, I won't be see you for a while, man, I going up." Canada now gone straight to his head long time and with a king o' power, so that when the airplane start up Calvin imagine that he own the whole blasted plane along with the white ladies who tell him, "Good morning, sir"; he feel that the plane is the big motorcar he intent to own one year after he land pon Canadian soil. The plane making time fast fast, and Calvin drink rum after rum till he went fast asleep and didn't even know he was in Toronto. The white lady come close to him, and tap him soft soft pon his new tropical suit and say, "Sir?" like she is asking some important question, when all she want is to wake up Calvin outta the white man plane. Well, Calvin wake up. He stretch like how he uses to stretch when he wake up in his mother bed. He yawn so hard that the white lady move back a step or two, after she see the pink inside his mouth and the black and blue gums running all round them white pearly teets. Calvin eyes red red as a cherry from lack o' sleep and too much rum drinking, and the body tired like how it uses to get tired and wrap up like a old motorcar fender. But is Canada, old man, and in a jiffy, before the white lady get to the front o' the place to put down the last glass, Calvin looking out through the window. "Toronto in your arse!" he went to say to himself, but it come out too loud, "Toronto in your arse, man!"

Before the first week come and gone, Calvin take up pen and paper:... *and I am going to tell you something, this place is the greatest place for a workingman to live. I hear some things about this place, but I isn't a man to complain, because while I know I am a man, and I won't take no shit from no Canadian, white, black, or red, I still have another piece of knowledge which says that I didn't born here. So I controls myself to suit, and make the white man money. The car only a couple of months off. I see one already that I got my eyes on. And if God willing, by the next two months I sitting down in the driver's seat. The car I got my eyes on is a red one with white tires. The steering wheel as you know on the left side, and we drives on the right-hand side of the road up here, not like back in Barbados where you drive on the left-hand. Next week, I taking out my licence. I not found a church I like yet, mainly because I see some strange things happening up here in church. You don't know, man, but black people can't or don't go in the same church as white people. God must be have two colours then. One for black people and one for white people. And a next thing. There is some fellas up here from the islands who talking a lot of shit about Black Power. I am here working for a living and a motorcar and if my mother herself come in my way and be an obstacle against me getting them two things, a living and a motorcar, I would kill her by Christ...* Calvin was going to write more; about the room he was renting for twenty dollars a week, which a white fellow tell him was pure robbery, because he was paying ten dollars for a more larger room on the ground floor in the same house; and he didn't write bout the car-wash job he got the next day down Spadina Avenue, working for a dollar a hour, and when the first three hours pass he felt he been working for three days, the work was so hard; he didn't tell that a certain kind of white people in Canada didn't sit too close to him on the streetcar, that they didn't speak to him on the street... lots o' things he didn't worry to tell... so Calvin work hard, man, Calvin work more harder than when he was washing off cars back in Barbados. The money was good too. Sal'ry and tips. From the two carwash jobs he uses to clear a hundred dollars a week, and that is two hundred back home, and not even Dipper does make that kind o' money, and he is the fucking prime minister! The third job, Calvin land like a dream: night watchman with a big big important company which put him in big big important uniform and thing, big leather belt like what he uses to envy the officers in the Volunteer Force back home wearing pon a Queen Birthday parade on the Garrison Savannah, shoes the company people even provide, and the only thing that was missing, according to what Calvin figure out some months afterwards, was that the holster at his side, join-on to the leather belt, didn't have in no blasted gun. He tell it to a next Barbadian he make friends with, and the Bajun just laugh and say, "They think you going rass-hole shoot yourself, boy!" But Calvin did already become Canadified enough to know that the only people he see in them uniforms with guns in the leather holster was certain white people, and he know he wasn't Canadified so much that he did turn white overnight. "Once it don't stop me from getting that Galaxie!"... he went down by the Tropics Club where they play calypsos and dance, one time, and he never went back cause the ugly Grenadian fellow at the door ask him for "three dollars to come in!" and he curse the fellow and leff. But the bank account was mounting and climbing like a woman belly when she in the family way. Quick quick so, Calvin have a thousand dollars pon the bank. Fellas who get to know Calvin and who Calvin won't 'sociate with because 'sociating does cost money, boy!" Them fellas so who here donkey years, still borrowing money to help pay their rent, fellas gambling like hell, throwing dice every Fridee night right into Mondee morning early, missing work and getting fired from work, fellas playing poker and betting, "Forty dollars more for these two fours, in your rass, sah! I *raise*!" – them brand o' Trinidadian, Bajun, Jamaican, Grenadian and thing, them so can't understand at all how Calvin just land and he get rich so fast. "I bet all-yuh Calvin selling pussy!" one fella say. A next bad-minded fella say, "He peddling his arse to white boys down Yonge Street," and a third fella who did just bet fifty dollars pon a pair o' deuces, and get broke at the poker game, say quick quick before the words fall out o' the other fella mouth, "I goint peddle mine too, then! Bread is bread."

Calvin start slacking up on the first car-wash work, and he humming as he shine the white people car, he skinning his teet in the shine and he smiling, and the white people thinking he smiling because he like the work and them, cause his hands never tarried whilst he was car-dreaming, they drop a little dollar bill pon Calvin as a tip, and a regular twenty-five-cent piece, and Calvin pinching pon the groceries, eating a lotta pigs feet and chicken necks and salt fish... all the time work work so that Calvin won't even spend thirty cents pon a beer with a sinner, an' the only time he even reading is when he clean out a car in the car wash and it happen to have a used paper inside it, or a throwaway paperback book. For Calvin decided long time that he didn't come here for eddication. He come for a living and a motorcar. And he intend to get both. And by the look o' things, be-Christ, both almost in his hand. Only now waiting to see the right model o' motorcar, with the right colour inside it, and the right mileage and thing. The motorcar must have the right colour o' tires, right colour o' gearshift and in the handle too. And it have to have-in radio; and he see a fella in the car wash with a thing inside his Cadillac, and Calvin gone crazy over Cadillacs until he walk down by Bay Street and price the price of a old one. He bawl for murder, "Better stick to the Galaxie, boy!" he tell himself; and he do that. But he really like the thing inside the white man Cadillac and he ask the man one morning what it was, and the man tell Calvin. Now Calvin must have red Galaxie, with not more than twenty-thousand miles on the register, black upholstery, red gearshift, radio, AM and FM and a tellyfone. Them last three things is what the man had inside his Cadillac. Calvin working even on a Syundee, bank holidays ain' touching Calvin, and the Old Queen back home who send a occasional letter asking Calvin to remember the house rent and the Poor Box in the Nazarene Church where he was a testifying brother, preaching and thing, and also to remember "who birthed him," well, Calvin tell the Old Queen, his own own mother, *Things hard up here, Mother. Don't let nobody fool you that because a man emigrade it mean that he elevate.*

Even so, a month and a half later, two days before Calvin decide he see the right automobile, a card drop through the door where Calvin living, address to Calvin: *What are you doing up there, then? Canadians buying out all the island. You standing for that? Send down a couple of dollars and let me invest it in a piece of beach land for you, Brother. Power to the people! Salaam and love. WILLY X.* Calvin get so blasted vex, so damn vex, cause he sure now that this Willy gone mad too, like everybody else he been reading bout in the States and in England; black people gone mad, Calvin say; and he get more vex when he think that it was the landlady, Mistress Silvermann, who take up the postcard from the linoleum and hand it to him, and he swear blind that she hand it to him after she done read the thing: and now she must be frighten like hell for Calvin, cause Calvin getting letters from these political extremists, and birds of a feather does flock together, she thinking now that Calvin perhaps is some kind o' political maniac, crying Black Power! All this damn foolishness bout Power to the People, and signing his name Willy X, when everybody in Barbados know that that damn fool's name is really

William Fortesque: Calvin get shame shame shame that the landlady thinking different bout him, because sometimes she does be in the house alone all night with Calvin, and she must be even thinking bout giving him notice, which would be a damn bad thing to happen right now, cause the motorcar just two days off, the room he renting now is a nice one, the rent come down like the temperature in May when he talk plain to Mistress Silvermann bout how he paying twice as much as other tenants, but what really get Calvin really vex vex vex as hell is that a little Canadian thing in the room over his head come downstairs one night in a mini-dress and thing, bubbies jumping bout inside her bosom, free and thing and looking juicy, and giggling all the time and calling sheself a women liberation, all her skin at the door, and the legs nice and fat just as Calvin like his meats, and Calvin already gone thinking that this thing is the right woman to drive bout in his new automobile with, this Canadian thing coming downstairs every night for the past month, and out of the blue asking him, "You'll like a coffee?" When she say so the first time, coffee was as far from Calvin mind as lending Willy twenty-five cents for the down payment for the house spot pon the beach back home. Now, be-Christ, Willy X, or whatever the hell that bastard calling himself nowadays, is going to stay right there down in Barbados and mash up Calvin life so! Just so? Simple so? Oh, God, no, man! But the landlady couldn't read English, she did only uses to pretend she is a genius; but the Canadian girl is who tell Calvin not to worry; one night when they was drinking the regular coffee in the communal kitchen, the Canadian girl say, "Missis Silvermann is only a D.P. She can't read English." Calvin take courage. The bankbook walking bout with him, inside his trousers all the time, he counting the digits going to work, coming from work, in the back seat alone, pon the streetcar, while waiting for the subway early on a morning at the Ossington Station, and then he make a plan. He plan it down to a T. Every penny organize for the proper thing, every nickel with its own work to do: the bottle of wine that the Canadian girl gave him the name to; the new suit from Eaton's that he see in the display window one night when he get hold of the girl and he get bold bold as hell and decide to take she for a lover's walk down Yonge Street; the new shoes, brown brown till they look red to match the car; and the shirt and tie – every blasted thing matching up like if he is a new bride stepping down the aisle to the wedding march. And he even have a surprise up his sleeve for the thing, too. He isn' longer a stingy man, cause he see his goal; and his goal is like gold. The car delivery arrange for three o'clock, Sardah; no work; the icebox in his room have in a beer or two, plus the wine; and he have a extra piece o' change in his pocket... "I going have to remember to change the money from this pocket," he tell himself, as if he was talking to somebody else in the room with him, "to the next pocket in the new suit"... and he have Chinese food now on his mind because the Canadian thing mention a nice Chinese restaurant down in Chinatown near Elizabeth Street. Calvin nervous as arse all Fridee night; all Fridee night the thing in Calvin room (here of late she behaving as if she live in Calvin room), and Calvin is a man with ambitions: one night she tantalize Calvin head so much that he start talking bout high-rise apartment; perhaps, if she behave sheself he might even put a little gold thing pon her pretty little pink finger... the girl start asking Calvin if he want some; not in them exact words, but that is what she did mean; and Calvin turn shame shame and nearly blush, only thing, as you know black people can't show really if they blushing or if they mad as shit with a white person, and Calvin turn like a virgin on the night before she getting hang in church and in marriage, and he saying all the time cause his mind pon the mileage in the motorcar, "Want some o' what?" And the girl laugh, and she throw back she head and show she gold fillings and she pink tongue and the little speck o' dirt under she neck; and she laugh and say to sheself, "This one is a real gentleman, not like what my girlfriend say to expect from West Indian men, at all..." And you know something? She start one big confessing: "...and do you know what, Calvin? Would you like to hear something that I been thinking..." Calvin thinking bout motorcar and this blasted white woman humbugging him bout sex! Calvin get vex, he play he get vex bout something different from the woman and she sex, and he send she flying back upstairs to she own room. He get in bed too, but he ain' sleeping, he wide awake in the dark like a thief, and he eyes open wide wide wide like a owl eyes, and in that darkness in that little little room that only have one small window way up by the ceiling and facing the clotheslines and the dingy sheets that the landlady does spend all week washing, Calvin see the whole o' Toronto standing up and watching him drive by in his new motorcar – with the Canadian thing beside o' him in the front seat! – dream turn into different dream that Fridee night, because he was free to dream as much as he like since Sardah wasn' no work. Sardah is car day. He have everything plan. Go for the motorcar, pick it up, drive it home, pick up the Canadian thing, go for a spin down Bloor as far as Yonge, swing back up by Harbord, turn left at Spadina, take in College Street, and every West Indian in Toronto bound to see him in new car, before he get back home. Park she in front o' the house, *let everybody see me getting outta she, come in, have a little bite, change, change into the new suit, given the Canadian thing the surprise, and whilst she dressing, I sit down in the car...* "And I hope she take a long time dressing so I would have to press the car horn, press the horn just a little, a soft little thing, and call she outside, to see me in the..." Morning break nice. It was a nice morning round the middle o' September, fall time in the air, everybody stretching and holding up their head cause the weather nice. Even the cops have a smile on their fissiogomy.

The salesman-man smile and shake Calvin hand strong, and give Calvin the history of the bird although Calvin did already hear the bird history before. The salesman-man come outta the office still smiling, holding the motorcar keys between the index finger and the big thumb, and he drop them in Calvin hand. Calvin make a shiver. A shiver o' pride and ownership. "Galaxie in your arse!" He say that in his mind, and he thinking o' Willy and the boys back in Marcus rum shop. He get in the car. He shuffle bout a bit in the leather seat. He straighten he trousers seams. He touch the leather. He start up the motor. Listen to the motor. It ticking over like a fucking charm. He put the thing in gear. And he bout to make a little thing through the car park, and he would have gone straight back up Danforth if the

Canadian thing didn't wave she pocketbook to remind Calvin that she come with he, cause Calvin did forget she standing up there looking at a white convertible Cadillac, which she say is the car for Calvin, that there is lots o' "Negro-men driving them, even in Nova Scotia where I come from," that Calvin should have buy one o' them. "You start spending my blasted money already, woman! This is *mine*!" He didn't tell she out loud in words what he was really thinking bout she, but he was thinking so, though.

The Canadian she get in the motorcar, cause driving in a Galaxie more better than walking behind a Cadillac, and she sit down so comfortable that it look like if she own the car and she was giving Calvin a chance to try she out, and that it wasn't Calvin own own money that pay-down pon the car. Calvin didn't like that at all: he want she to sit down in the front seat like if he own the motorcar. But Calvin gone up Danforth with new motorcar and white woman beside o' him, like if he going to a funeral; "Got to break she in gently, man"; though the horses under the bonnet roaring like hell. Well, they drive and drive like if they was two explorers exploring Toronto: through Rosedale where the Canadian thing say she would just love to own a house; and in his mind, Calvin promise she she going get one in Rosedale; through the Bridle Path where she say the cheapest house cost a million dollars; through Don Mills where they see the big tall Foresters' Building, all up there by IBM; "You should get a job at IBM, dear" ("Doing wha? Cleaning out the closets?"... this Canadian thing like she is the wrong kind o' woman for me. Calvin thinking: I hads better get a black woman!); all this she talk as they driving back on the Don Valley Parkway. The highway nice. The motorcar open a new whole life to Calvin, and he love Toronto even better. Damn good thing he leff Barbados! The Galaxie like a horse, prancing pon the white man road. Night fall long time as they travelling, and Calvin experimenting with the dip-lights and the high beam. It nice to play with. The FM radio thing ain't working good cause Calvin never play one o' them radios before, and he forget to practice pon it when he was visiting the car in the lot after he pay-down something pon it, so that the salesman would keep it for him. So he working the AM thing overtime. A nice tune come on. Before the time come on, he thinking again that the Canadian thing may be the right woman for him: she nice, she tidy, and she quiet. And he raise-up liking quiet women; his mother tell him never marry a woman who ain' quiet, and like church. The tune is a calypso, man. "It's a nice calypso," Calvin say. "Sparrow, in your arse!" he shout, and he beg pardon, he excited because it is the first time he hear a calypso on the radio. He start liking Canada bad bad again. "Look at me, though! New car! A Galaxie, and you beside me..." The Canadian thing start working up she behind beside o' Calvin; she start saying she been going down in the islands for years now, that she have more calypso records than any white woman in Toronto, and she wish she had the money to take them outta storage and play one or two for Calvin. She start singing the tune, and Calvin vex as hell, cause he don't like no woman who does sing calypso, his Old Queen didn't even let him sing calypso when he was a boy in Barbados. And he was a man! Besides, the calypso that the Canadian thing singing now is a thing bout "…*three white women travelling through Africa*!" and something about "*Uh never had a white meat, yet*!" and this nice woman, this simple-looking Canadian girl know all the words, and she enjoying sheself too, and Calvin thinking that Sparrow watching him from through the AM radio thing, and laughing at him, and he vex as shit, cause the calypso mean that certain white women like black men to lash them, and… "Don't sing that!" he order the thing, as if he talking to his wife; and the Canadian thing tell him, in a sharp voice, that she isn't his damn wife, so "Don't you be uppity with me, buster!" Well, who tell she she could talk back to a Bajan man like Calvin? Calvin slam on the brakes. The motorcar cry out *screeennnnchhhhhh*! The Canadian thing head hit the windshield, *bram*! And she neck like it break in truth. The motorcar halfway in the middle o' the highway. Traffics whizzing by, and the wind from them like it want to smash-up Calvin new Galaxie. Calvin vex as shit but he can't do nothing cause he trembling like hell: the woman in the front seat turning white white white like a piece o' paper, and the blood gone outta she face; Calvin ain' see no dimples in she face; and she ain' moving, she ain' talking, not a muscle ain' shiver. Traffics whizzing by and one come so damn close that Calvin close his eyes, and pray. "Look my blasted crosses! And my Galaxie ain' a fucking day old yet!" He try to start up the motor and the motor only coughing like it have consumption. The woman like she sleeping or dead or something. The calypso still blaring over the AM radio, and Calvin so jittery he can't find the right button to turn the blasted thing off. And sudden so, one of the traffics flying by is a police. Calvin hear, *weeeeeeeeeeeeeeeeeeeeeeennnnnnnnnnnnnnnnnnnn*! Sirens! A police car in the rear-view mirror. Calvin stop shaking sudden sudden. He start thinking. White woman deading in his new motorcar, the car new, and he is a stranger in Canada. He jump out and lift up the hood, and he back his new jacket, playing he is a mechanic. The police stop. He face red as a beet. "What's holding you up, boy!" Calvin hear the "boy," and he get vex, but he can't say nothing, cause they is two gainst his one, and he remember that he black. But he ain' no damn fool. He talk fast and sweet, and soft, and he impress the police:… "and Officer, I just now now give this lady a lift, she say she feeling bas, and I taking she to the hospital, cause as a West Indian I learn how to be a Good Samaritan, and…" The police ask for the licence, and when he see that the ownership papers say that Calvin only had the car this morning, the police, he smile, and say, "You are a Good Samaritan, wish our coloured people were more like you West Indians…" They lift the Canadian thing with she neck half-popped outta the Galaxie and into the cruiser, and Calvin even had a tear in his eye too. But the police take she away, and the siren start up again, *weeeeeennnnnnnn*… Calvin manage to get the Galaxie outta the middle o' the road, the traffics still flying by, but now the new motorcar safe at the side o' the road. He put back on his jacket, and he shrug the jacket in shape and it fit pon his shoulders, he turn off the AM radio thing with the calypso, another calypso it was playing now, and fix the seams in his trousers, look back on the highway in the rear-view mirror, and start up the Galaxie. He driving slow slow on the highway and the traffics blowing their horn to tell him get the fuck outta the road, nigger, but all the time he smiling and holding his hand outta the window and waving them on. He outta habit bout to say something to the Canadian thing beside him, forgetting that she ain' there no more, and he still say, "This Galaxie is car for so! And godblummuh, look what a close shave I had!" He see the Canadian thing handbag open on the seat beside o' him, and he run his hand through it searching. It had in it five single dollar bills. He snap the handbag shut, touch the automatic window-winder, and throw the blasted handbag out the Don Valley Parkway, pon the road.

LAST SPRING THEY CAME OVER

MORLEY CALLAGHAN

Alfred Bowles came to Canada from England and got a job on a Toronto paper. He was a young fellow with clear, blue eyes and heavy pimples on the lower part of his face, the son of a Baptist minister whose family was too large for his salary. He got thirty dollars a week on the paper and said it was surprisingly good screw to start. For five dollars a week he got an attic room in a brick house painted brown on Mutual Street. He ate his meals in a quick-lunch near the office. He bought a cane and a light grey fedora.

He wasn't a good reporter but was inoffensive and obliging. After he had been working two weeks the fellows took it for granted he would be fired in a little while and were nice to him, liking the way the most trifling occurrences surprised him. He was happy to carry his cane on his arm and wear the fedora at a jaunty angle, quite the reporter. He liked to explain that he was doing well. He wrote home about it.

When they put him doing night police he felt important, phoning the fire department, hospitals, and police stations, trying to be efficient. He was getting along all right. It was disappointing when after a week the assistant city editor, Mr. H.J. Brownson, warned him to phone his home if anything important happened, and he would have another man cover it. But Bowles got to like hearing the weary, irritable voice of the assistant city editor called from his bed at three o'clock in the morning. He liked to politely call Mr. Brownson as often and as late as possible, thinking it a bit of good fun.

Alfred wrote long letters to his brother and to his father, carefully tapping the keys, occasionally laughing to himself. In a month's time he had written six letters describing the long city room, the fat belly of the city editor, and the bad words the night editor used when speaking of the Orangemen.

The night editor took a fancy to him because of the astounding puerility of his political opinions. Alfred was always willing to talk pompously of the British Empire policing the world and about all Catholics being aliens, and the future of Ireland and Canada resting with the Orangemen. He flung his arms wide and talked in the hoarse voice of a bad actor, but no one would have thought of taking him seriously. He was merely having a dandy time. The night editor liked him because he was such a nice boy.

Then Alfred's brother came out from the Old Country, and got a job on the same paper. Some of the men started talking about cheap cockney labourers crowding the good guys out of the jobs, but Harry Bowles was frankly glad to get the thirty a week. It never occurred to him that he had a funny idea of good money. With his first pay he bought a derby hat, a pair of spats, and a cane, but even though his face was clear and had a good colour he never looked as nice as his younger brother because his heavy nose curved up at the end. The landlady on Mutual Street moved a double bed into Alfred's room and Harry slept with his brother.

The days passed with many good times together. At first it was awkward that Alfred should be working nights and his brother the days, but Harry was pleased to come to the office each night at eleven and they went down the street to the hotel that didn't bother about Prohibition. They drank a few glasses of good beer. It became a kind of rite that had to be performed carefully. Harry would put his left foot and Alfred his right foot on the rail and leaning an elbow on the bar they would slowly survey the zigzag line of frothing glasses the length of the long bar. Men jostled them for a place at the foot rail.

Alfred said: "Well, a bit of luck."

Harry, grinning and raising his glass, said: "Righto."

"It's the stuff that heals."

"Down she goes."

"It helps the night along."

"Fill them up again."

"Toodle-oo."

Then they would walk out of the crowded barroom, vaguely pleased with themselves. Walking slowly and erectly along the street they talked with assurance, a mutual respect for each other's opinion making it merely an exchange of information. They talked of the Englishman in Canada, comparing his lot with that of the Englishman in South Africa and India. They had never travelled but to ask what they knew of strange lands would have made one feel uncomfortable; it was better to take it for granted that the Bowles boys knew all about the ends of the earth and had judged them carefully, for in their eyes was the light of faraway places. Once in a while, after walking a block or two, one of the brothers would say he would damn well like to see India and the other would say it would be simply topping.

After work and on Sundays they took a look at the places they had heard about in the city. One Sunday they got up in good time and took the boat to Niagara. Their father had written asking if they had seen the Falls and would they send some souvenirs. That day they had as nice a time as a man would want to have. Standing near the pipe-rail a little way from the hotel that overlooks the Falls they watched the waterline just before the drop, smooth as a long strip of bevelled glass, and Harry compared it favourably with a cataract in the Himalayas and a giant waterfall in Africa, just above the Congo. They took a car along the gorge and getting off near the whirlpool, picked out a little hollow near a big rock at the top of the embankment where the grass was lush and green. They stretched themselves out with hats tilted over their eyes for sunshades. The river whirled below. They talked about the funny ways of Mr. Brownson and his short fat legs and about the crazy women who fainted at the lifted hand of the faith healer who was in the city for a week. They liked the distant rumble of the Falls. They agreed to try and save a lot of money and go west to the Pacific in a year's time. They never mentioned trying to get a raise in pay.

Afterwards they each wrote home about the trip, sending the souvenirs.

Neither one was doing well on the paper. Harry wasn't much good because he hated writing the plain copy and it was hard for him to be strictly accurate. He liked telling a good tale but it never occurred to him that he was deliberately lying. He imagined a thing and felt it to be true. But it never occurred to Alfred to depart from the truth. He was accurate but lazy, never knowing when he was really working. He was taken off night police and for two weeks helped a man do courts at the City Hall. He got to know the boys at the press gallery, who smiled at his naïve sincerity and thought him a decent chap, without making up their minds about him. Every noon hour Harry came to the press gallery and the brothers, sitting at typewriters, wrote long letters about the country and the people, anything interesting, and after exchanging letters, tilted back in their swivel chairs, laughing out loud. Neither, when in the press gallery, seemed to write anything for the paper.

Some of the men tried kidding Alfred, teasing him about women, asking if he found the girls in this country to his liking; but he seemed to enjoy it more than they did. Seriously he explained that he had never met a girl in this country, but they looked very nice. Once Alfred and Bun Brophy, a red-headed fellow with a sharp tongue who did City Hall for the paper, were alone in the gallery. Brophy had in his hands a big picture of five girls in masquerade costumes. Without explaining that he loved one of the girls Brophy asked Bowles which of the lot was the prettiest.

"You want me to settle that," said Alfred, grinning and waving his pipe. He very deliberately selected a demure little girl with a shy smile.

Brophy was disappointed. "Don't you think this one is pretty?" – a colourful, bold-looking girl.

"Well, she's all right in her way, but she's too vivacious. I'll take this one. I like them kittenish," Alfred said.

Brophy wanted to start an argument but Alfred said it was neither here nor there. He really didn't like women.

"You mean to say you never step out?" Brophy said.

"I've never seemed to mix with them," he said, adding that the whole business didn't matter because he liked men much better.

The men in the press room heard about it and some suggested nasty things to Alfred. It was hard to tease him when he wouldn't be serious. Sometimes they asked if he took Harry out walking in the evenings. Brophy called them the heavy lovers. The brothers didn't mind because they thought the fellows were having a little fun.

In the fall Harry was fired. The editor in a nice note said that he was satisfied Mr. H.W. Bowles could not adapt himself to their methods. But everybody wondered why he hadn't been fired sooner. He was no good on the paper.

The brothers smiled, shrugged their shoulders and went on living together. Alfred still had his job. Every noon hour in the City Hall press room they were together, writing letters.

Time passed and the weather got cold. Alfred's heavy coat came from the Old Country and he gave his vest and a thin sweater to Harry, who had only a light spring coat. As the weather got colder Harry buttoned his coat higher up on his throat and even though he looked cold he was neat as a pin with his derby and cane.

Then Alfred lost his job. The editor, disgusted, called him a fool. For the first time since coming over last spring he felt hurt, something inside him was hurt and he told his brother about it, wanting to know why people acted in such a way. He said he had been doing night police. On the way over to No. 1 station very late Thursday night he had met two men from other papers. They told him about a big fire earlier in the evening just about the time when Alfred was accustomed to going to the hotel to have a drink with his brother. They were willing to give all the details and Alfred thankfully shook hands with them and hurried back to the office to write the story. Next morning the assistant city editor phoned Alfred and asked how it was the morning papers missed the story. Alfred tried to explain but Mr. Brownson said he was a damn fool for not phoning the police and making sure instead of trying to make the paper look like a pack of fools printing a fake story. The fellows who had kidded him said that too. Alfred kept asking his brother why the fellows had to do it. He seemed to be losing a good feeling for people.

Still the brothers appeared at noontime in the press room. They didn't write so many letters. They were agreeable, cheerful, on good terms with everybody. Bun Brophy every day asked how they were doing and they felt at home there. Harry would stand for a while watching the checker game always in progress, knowing that if he stood staring intently at the black and red squares, watching every deliberate move, he would be asked to sit in when it was necessary that one of the players make the rounds in the hall. Once Brophy gave Harry his place and walked over to the window where Alfred stood watching the fleet of automobiles arranged in a square in the courtyard. The police wagon with a load of drunks was backing toward the cells.

"Alfie, I often wonder how you guys manage," he said.

"Oh, first-rate."

"Well, you ought to be in a bad way by now."

"Oh, no, we have solved the problem," said Alfie in a grand way, grinning. There was a store in their block, he said, where a package of tobacco could be got for five cents; they did their own cooking and were able to live on five dollars a week. "What about coming over and having tea with us sometimes?" Alfred said.

Brophy, abashed, suggested the three of them go over to the café and have a little toast. Harry talked volubly on the way over and while having coffee. He was really a better talker than his brother. They sat in an armchair lunch, gripped the handles of their thick mugs, and talked about religion. The brothers were sons of a Baptist minister but never thought of going to church. It seemed that Brophy had travelled a lot during wartime and afterward in Asia Minor and India. He was telling them about a great golden temple of the Sikhs at Amritsar and Harry listened carefully, asking many questions. Then they talked about newspapers until Harry started talking about the East, slowly feeling his way. All of a sudden he told about standing on a height of land near Amritsar, looking down at a temple. It couldn't have been so but he would have it that Brophy and he had seen the same temple and he described the country in the words Brophy had used. Alfred liked listening to his brother but he said: "Religion is a funny business. I tell you it's a funny business." Alfred had a casual way of making a cherished belief or opinion seem unimportant, a way of dismissing even the bright yarns of his brother.

After that afternoon in the café Brophy never saw Harry. Alfred came often to the City Hall but never mentioned his brother. Someone said maybe Harry had a job but Alfred laughed and said no such luck in this country, explaining casually that Harry had a bit of a cold and was resting up. In the passing days Alfred came only once in a while to the City Hall, writing his letter without enthusiasm.

The press men would have tried to help the brothers if they had heard Harry was sick. They were entirely ignorant of the matter. On a Friday afternoon at three-thirty Alfred came into the gallery and, smiling apologetically, told Brophy that his brother was dead; the funeral was to be in three-quarters of an hour; would he mind coming? It was pneumonia, he added. Brophy, looking hard at Alfred, put on his hat and coat and they went out.

It was a poor funeral. The hearse went on before along the way to the Anglican cemetery that overlooks the ravine. One old cab followed behind. There had been a heavy snow in the morning, and the slush on the pavement was thick. Alfred and Brophy sat in the old cab, silent. Alfred was leaning forward, his chin resting on his hands, the cane acting as a support, and the heavy pimples stood out on the lower part of his white face. Brophy was uncomfortable and chilly but he mopped his shining forehead with a big handkerchief. The window was open and the air was cold and damp.

Alfred politely asked how Mrs. Brophy was doing. Then he asked about Mr. Brownson.

"Oh, he's fine," Brophy said. He wanted to close the window but it would have been necessary to move Alfred so he sat huddled in the corner, shivering.

Alfred asked suddenly if funerals didn't leave a bad taste in the mouth and Brophy, surprised, started talking absently about that golden temple of the Sikhs in India. Alfred appeared interested until they got to the cemetery. He said suddenly he would have to take a look at the temple one fine day.

They buried Harry Bowles in a grave in the paupers' section on a slippery slope of the hill. The earth was hard and chunky and it thumped down on the coffin case. It snowed a little near the end.

On the way along the narrow, slippery footpath up the hill Alfred thanked Brophy for being thoughtful enough to come to the funeral. There was little to say. They shook hands and went different ways.

After a day or two Alfred again appeared in the press room. He watched the checker game, congratulated the winner and then wrote home. The men were sympathetic and said it was too bad about his brother. He smiled cheerfully and said they were good fellows. In a little while he seemed to have convinced them that nothing important had really happened.

His last cent must have gone to the undertaker, for he was particular about paying bills, but he seemed to get along all right. Occasionally he did a little work for the paper, a story from a night assignment when the editor thought the staff was being overworked.

One afternoon at two-thirty in the press gallery Brophy saw the last of Alfred, who was sucking his pipe, his feet up on a desk, wanting to be amused. Brophy asked if anything had turned up. In a playful, resigned tone, his eye on the big clock, Alfred said he had until three to join the Air Force. They wouldn't take him, he said, unless he let them know by three.

Brophy said, "How will you like that?"

"I don't fancy it."

"But you're going through."

"Well, I'm not sure. Something else may come along."

No one saw him after that, but he didn't join the Air Force. Someone in the gallery said that wherever he went he probably wrote home as soon as he got there.

THE STALLION AND THE SULTAN OF SWAT A TRUE STORY

BRUCE MEYER

Out on Centre Island in Toronto bay, a white stallion leapt from the high scaffolding of the diving tower and disappeared beneath the green waters of the lagoon. Men cheered. Women gaped and young girls held their breath as the equine head, hind hooves and tail vanished beneath the waves. When the white muzzle broke the surface there were rounds of applause that pealed across the bay.

The white stallion's name was Goliath. He was billed as Toronto's greatest thrill, the King of the Island and Emperor of Summer. Each day the powerful beast mounted his scaffold like a condemned prisoner, hesitated for a moment perhaps perusing the steeples and chimney tops of the city across the harbour, before he took his headlong plunge into the tepid waters of the bay. Such power. Such a beast. Goliath, next to the island's great merry-go-round and carousel, each equine figure hand-carved with care and detail in a Philadelphia factory, was the most beloved creature of the lagoons and channels in the city's sidereal territories. Not even the baseball stadium beyond the merry-go-round could compete.

His rule was supreme. In the dry and pleasant mornings of July, the wonder horse was often paraded up and down Yonge Street, the ghostly shape of the white stallion, almost the size of a Clydesdale, clearing a path among the cart ponies, the draught horses and their wagons, and even the sombre black boxes of horseless carriages.

He became so familiar that even preachers mentioned his name from the stern heights of their Presbyterian seriousness; his name echoed in the consecrated rafters of Gothic ceilings from one end of the city to the other, from the spire of Cook's to the east to the impregnable walls of Royce Victoria in the west. Parents were warned that too much of this giant's suicidal yet somehow chivalric dive was a bad thing for children; and the children, knowing it might be bad for them, loved him all the more.

To some children, in their dreams the great white horse grew wings. It rose above the treetops and roof-crests and cast his mighty shadow on the streets below. Even adults, who rarely lifted their imaginations above the daily consequence of bread and shelter, felt young again in that heart-stopping moment when the beast took flight against a power of gravity greater than himself.

On a signal day, as the side-wheeler Trillium paddled its way toward the lighthouse island, where the diving tower loomed above Hanlan's Point and cast an elongated shadow upon the ballpark's right field, some talked anxiously of what they had seen in the darkness of the night before. A bright comet had crossed the sky. "You could read by it for an instant," said one man. Another shook his head: "It bodes poorly..." but those who were headed to the island for a final summer Saturday of carefree daring paid no attention to the gloom-mongers who insisted on carrying the world of the city with them to the islands of forgetful bliss.

Today they were there to watch a baseball game, the team from Providence was in town, the Red Sox, who were taking a long look at a stout young fellow whose pitching exploits had already made him the stuff of rumoured greatness.

They bought their tickets for twenty-five cents and filed into the tidy little stadium. Those who arrived early had the best view of the field, high up in the infield bleachers they could look across the outfield to Goliath's tower. For the price of admission to the game, they could watch the Providential kid who was called Babe, and the Mighty King who was called Goliath.

"He's also got a woman's name," someone yelled at the Babe before the first pitch had been thrown out, "Ruth," and the crowd broke into laughter. The large boy-child ambled toward the mound, shuffling, his great rounded shoulders seemingly bent beneath the weight of what was to come under the afternoon sun.

Two-thirds of the way to a complete game, the Toronto pitcher began to tire, the Red Sox began to take charge. The crowd grew hush. Babe, the new man, the pitcher from Providence, was at bat, grinning.

The first pitch was a strike. The crowd cheered. The second, low and inside, was swung at. Laughter broke out again. The umpire called time.

The Babe leaned his weight on the knob-end of his bat. The umpire looked toward the right field fence and shadowed his eyes against the glaring afternoon sun. A proud silhouette cast its shadow on the outfield.

Goliath had been raised upon the scaffold. The crowd in the bleachers rose to its feet and cheered. The batter stood in the box. The pitcher turned to watch the spectacle. "Hey Babe," yelled a voice from the stands. "Hold up and make way for the King of the Lake." The batter fixed his gaze on the white beast on the edge of the scaffold.

"Now," roared the batter. "Now or never."

"Play ball," called the ump. The pitcher heard the call and turned to face his opponent. The white beast reared its head high in a gesture of proud and sublime command. A cloud passed over the sun and for an instant the field darkened and then lightened again.

The pitch. The ball spun and twisted through the air. Hind legs reared up toward the emerging light.

Hooves lost contact with the platform and kicked out wildly at the ghosts of old riders in the sky.

A crack like the sound of lightning close by followed a split second after the ball made contact with the ash. A small greyish sphere lifted into the heavens. Its stitches spun and twisted like a tiny world in agony, rising, out of control, headed for someplace beyond the imagination. It climbed and climbed as if it would never stop.

The white beast's legs pranced madly as down, down it fell, rearing its head with a snarling pride, its white comet tail trailing behind.

The ball sank from sight over the horizon of the wooden fence. And the Babe whose last name was the name of a woman raised his hands as the bases cleared before him. His cleat touched home base, he shouted, "I am the King of the Lake now. I am the Sultan of Swat," as the crowd watched in disbelieving awe and a little boy shook his head and whispered, "You're the Babe."

The man on the scoreboard's catwalk reached for his stack of numbers only to knock them fluttering like long-lost songbirds into the crowd below. The great white beast who had been the idol of a dying summer, plunged beneath the green and churning waters of the bay, and was never seen again.

THE MINNIES

Gwendolyn MacEwen

The past was a place of pools, a place called the Mineral Baths behind the old Roma apartments between Quebec and Gothic avenues. The Minnies, it was called, and it had two pools - one an ordinary pool into which astounding divers flung themselves, often backwards, from impossible heights, and another pool which for some reason was darker and colder, the water freezing and black, where hardly anyone swam. He'd float in this one on his back and gaze at the big Victorian house on the hill, and wonder what country he was in. He lay there burning with cold, orgasmic cold, in August, and later he would slowly walk away eating ice cream and shivering and blazing with a delicious lonely joy...

from THE WARS (WINTER-SPRING, 1915-1916)

TIMOTHY FINDLEY

...the Boys' Brigade with band. Backyard minstrels, got up in cork, bang their tambourines and strut across a lawn on Admiral Road. Every parlour has its piano: here are soldiers, arm in arm and singing: "Keep Your Head Down, Fritzie Boy!" Tea-dance partners do the Castlewalk to orchestras of brass cornets and silver saxophones. Violins have been retired.

1915. This is the age of motorized portation. Over one thousand makes of motorcar can be had. Backyard blacksmiths build them to custom. ASK THE MAN WHO OWNS ONE! Here are families, sitting overdressed in Packards – posed aloof in the backs of Chevrolets and Russell Knights. Everyone, it seems, is journeying around the block. Children vie to blow the horns.

Then something happens... Six thousand dead and wounded...

Here come the troops down Yonge Street! Women abandon all their former reticence and rush out into the roadway, throwing flowers and waving flags. Here come the 48th Highlanders! Kilts and drums and leopard skins. Boys race after them on bikes. Little girls, whose mouths hang open, hardly dare to follow. Older men remove their hats. There is Sir Sam Hughes standing on the dais, taking the farewell salute. "GOD SAVE THE KING!!!" (a banner). Everywhere you look, trains are pulling out of stations, ships are sailing out of ports. Music drowns the long hurrah...

1916 Ypres

The road is lost at either end in rain. Robert's perception is limited by fog and smoke. Behind him, there are forty horses – every fifth horse bearing a rider. Only one of these riders is visible. Far to the rear there are seven wagons drawn by mules and carrying ammunition. Robert is in charge of this convoy. It is February, 1916. He has been in France for a month and two days; since Monday, January 24th.

At the centre of the world is Ypres and all around the centre lie the flats of Flanders. To its rear – which is to say South West – is the only physical landmark worth mentioning: Kemmel Hill. This is three hundred and fifty feet high. Nothing in Belgium rises higher. To the east and to the north there is a ridge of land that anywhere else would not be the least exceptional. Here, the ridge was what you fought for. If you could gain its heights, you had the advantage. So far the Germans had maintained this advantage and almost two years of fighting had failed to dislodge them. The plain on which Ypres stands stretches like a broken arm through Europe from the Russian frontier to the border of Spain. This is the one way west into France that does not encounter mountains. (Once, in Napoleon's time, it had been the only way east.) Because of its flatness this alleyway has been the scene of battles since the time of Caesar. All the great armies of modern history have passed this way and through this mud.

The mud. There are no good similes. Mud must be a Flemish word. Mud was invented here. Mudland might have been its bane. The ground is the colour of steel. Over most of the plain there isn't a trace of topsoil: only sand and clay. The Belgians call them "clyttes," these fields, and the further you go towards the sea, the worse the clyttes become. In them, the water is reached by the plough at an average depth of eighteen inches. When it rains (which is almost constantly from early September through to March, except when it snows) the water rises at you out of the ground. It rises from your footprints – and an army marching over a field can cause a flood. In 1916, it was said that you "waded to the front." Men and horses sank from sight. They drowned in mud. Their graves, it seemed, just dug themselves and pulled them down.

All this mud and water was contaminated. Dung and debris and decaying bodies lay beneath its surface. When the rivers and canals could no longer be contained – over they spilled into clyttes already awash with rain.

Houses, trees and fields of flax once flourished here. Summers had been blue with flowers. Now it was a shallow sea of stinking grey from end to end. And this is where you fought the war.

The day that Mr. and Mrs. Ross received the news that Robert was "missing in action" Mrs. Ross refused to dress. She remained in her nightgown and wandered around the house on South Drive with a bottle in one hand, a glass in the other. Miss Davenport locked her door and sat in a chair with her back to the window. The sound of Mrs. Ross's cries to heaven rose up through her room and made her stop her ears.

Peggy and Mr. Ross sat in the drawing room where Mr. Ross had drawn the curtains. Out beyond the windows, the robins sang and the sun shone and the lilacs were still in bloom.

Stuart sat on the bottom step in the front hall with Bimbo at his feet. His mother's appearance alarmed him. Frightened him. But his brother's apparent death was strangely exhilarating news in itself. Not that Stuart wished Robert ill. But the thought of going to school and saying: "Robert is dead. He'll probably get the Victoria Cross" – this was marvellous to contemplate and it sent a shiver down his back.

The cable had arrived just after lunch. Now it was early in the evening. Mrs. Ross had wandered the length and breadth of the house. She was in her bare feet. Her hair, in a plait, hung down her back.

Stuart went to the drawing room and sat on his father's other side. A strange and terrible silence descended. Even Miss Davenport became alarmed enough to unlock and open her door.

Mrs. Ross stood on the landing of the stairs. The bottle fell from her hand. It was empty and it rolled to the bottom step. She gave a final agonizing cry.

Everyone froze. Even the neighbours, listening through the open windows.

Mrs. Ross put her hands out and started forward. She found the bannister and leaned against it all the way to the bottom. At the bottom, she just avoided stepping on the bottle. She sat down beside it where Stuart had sat through the earlier part of the afternoon.

"Help," she said.

Mr. Ross, in the drawing room, stood up.

He advanced towards the hallway.

"Help me," said Mrs. Ross.

Mr. Ross put out his hand.

"Where?" said Mrs. Ross. "Where? Where are you?"

Mr. Ross said: "I'm here."

Mrs. Ross said: "I'm sorry. Please. I cannot see you."

Mr. Ross went across the parquet floor and sat beside his wife. He put his arm around her shoulder and held her against his side. She was cold.

"I'm blind," said Mrs. Ross. "I've gone blind."

There was not a trace of emotion left in her voice. But she fumbled with her fingers and found her husband's hand.

"Never mind," said Mr. Ross. "Never mind. Here we are."

Peggy came and stood in the doorway. Mr. Ross signalled for her to get her mother's coat. Peggy brought it from the cupboard and Mr. Ross put it around his wife's shoulders. Then Mr. Ross sent Peggy and Stuart and Bimbo away. They all went off and sat in the garden.

Upstairs, Davenport looked from her window.

The ravine was full of mist.

The sun was descending. It was cool.

In the distance, the traffic on Yonge Street and Bloor Street rumbled and clattered. Everyone was going home. All the clocks were striking.

Mrs. Ross began to fall asleep. Mr. Ross held her and rocked her from side to side. The house began to darken. They sat there, silently singing. Finally, she slept.

In the drawing room, sitting in its silver frame, Robert's picture started to fade.

It got completely dark.

MATCHBOX FOR A MOTHER'S HAIR

MATT SHAW

Where do I start, my name is Gordon Ween.

I am seventeen and three-quarters. Three quarters is three fingers out of four fingers, or three fingers over four fingers. Seventeen means that I have seventeen wholes–which I learned is sixteen groups of four fingers out of four fingers.

Mother played cards. There was Mrs. Baker, Mrs. Gingrinch and Mrs. Lowell. In the afternoon, at a table in my house, they played Yuke Her. I do not know how to play Yuke Her but I watched them every afternoon. When they played they tried to yuke each other, Mother and Mrs. Baker would look at the numbers they held in their hands and add them up and sort the pairs, and Mrs. Lowell leaned over Mrs. Gingrinch and then leaned back and then someone would lay cards down and Mrs. Lowell mumbled a dirty word and Mother scolded her, not in front of Gordon, don't say those things in front of Gordon, she said. Then the cards were down and Mrs. Lowell and Mrs. Gingrinch would be happy. On the table were cards with coloured shapes and unhappy faces, the shapes of shovels and hearts.

The house? The house was my house. The table was round and pretty, there were red flowers with thick stems in a bowl. It was an eating bowl, not a flower bowl. It was low and wide, for soup, but Mother always cut the stems and sat the petals in the bowl so there were no stems. They were coloured little heads, especially when they were tulips, and they got darker and darker until they curled and new heads were on the table for Yuke Her. As the heads turned dark and sad, their smell eroded and the bowl dried out. There were four black chairs around the big table, but my chair was by the window looking at the four big chairs. The window drapes were the colour of hedges and there were no dishes in the sink.

There were always bottles on the table, green with purple labels and Mrs. Gingrinch always laughed when she said we almost don't need the flowers on the table, these bottles are flowers themselves and make us bloom when we drink she said, and she giggled as she looked at me sitting in my chair.

My chair. I sat on a chair beside the table. It was my chair, I always sat in it, and it was red. It fit my back and Mother liked it because it always makes you sit up straight, Gordon, you never sit straight enough. People will not like you if you don't sit straight, Gordon, what will Mrs. Lowell and Mrs. Gingrinch think of you if you slouch, Gordon.

Oh no, Mrs. Lowell said, don't listen to her. You know I like you, you know how much I like you, I've shown you how I like you, you know that. She never said that when Mother was there, when Mother was there she said nonsense, Rette, you'll hurt the poor boy's feelings. Gordon is absolutely wonderful, we all love Gordon.

Did you know the pretty parts of flowers are the reproductive organs? said Mrs. Baker.

They're certainly more used than yours, said Mrs. Gingrinch, you're ugly.

I am not, said Mrs. Baker, her best friend.

Gordon, said Mrs. Gingrinch, don't listen to your mother. She's turning red because all day she loses all she has to us. Terrible. She's terrible.

Mother glared at her.

See, said Mrs. Gingrinch, she doesn't laugh at it because it's true, Gordon. Mrs. Baker and your mother never win together.

I don't cheat, and we win sometimes, said Mrs. Baker. It's not true.

You know it is, said Mrs. Gingrinch, you take from Rette too. I never won when I played with you, either. But Rette never stops playing with you and she never understands our faces.

I understand there's nothing else to understand in your faces, said Mother.

If you understood any faces, you would understand Mrs. Baker's, said Mrs. Gingrinch. Her face is so plain she cannot lie. Even when she puts on her mascara and makeup you know she is trying to hide her thoughts. When she tries to hide her thoughts you know exactly what they are. But you can't see that, said Mrs. Gingrinch, and we can so we win.

My face is not plain, said Mrs. Baker.

It is so, said Mrs. Gingrinch.

I do not wear makeup to hide things. I wear it to look pretty, said Mrs. Baker.

Hum, said Mrs. Gingrinch.

Mrs. Gingrinch and Mrs. Baker were best friends. They fought all the time at Yuke Her, Mrs. Baker accusing Mrs. Gingrinch of cheating and Mrs. Gingrinch calling Mrs. Baker too plain, she said a face that ugly should be much better at hiding things. Mrs. Baker is ugly, she looks like a squirrel I saw a dog catch from a tree. I would never say she looked like a squirrel from my chair because I wasn't supposed to talk from the chair I was supposed to watch for cheating.

If I talked Mother always told me to stop talking. Everything was good until I talked so I didn't. That's why I never said that Mrs. Baker looked like a fly I hit with a newspaper that crawled on its broken legs or that Mrs. Gingrinch sometimes farted when she took me upstairs to show me every week. Even though I knew what she wanted to show me I wanted to see again and I wanted to tell everyone at the table that all of them, except Mother, showed me the same thing all the time but only Mrs. Gingrinch smelled when she showed me, and I thought that was funny. They looked funny when they climbed on me to show me what they called love. When I talked it was never bad until Mrs. Gingrinch, Mrs. Lowell and Mrs. Baker went home. Then Mother would drink more of the bottles with the purple labels and stand up.

Wait for me in your chair, Gordon. I mean it.

So I sat and didn't say no because it would make it worse.

There are reasons I ask you not to talk, Gordon, but you didn't listen. You remember what we do every time you do talk, when I tell you not to. I would never hurt you Gordon, but you have to understand this Gordon, even if it is the only thing you understand. You have problems, Gordon, but you're not a completely stupid boy.

For each thing I said while she yuked her friends she plucked one hair from my head and she tickled my face. Here's another one, she'd say. Her lighter was the colour of a fire engine like my chair. She held the hair up to my nose and flicked the lighter and held the lighter to the scared hair.

I do this for your good, Gordon. Other mothers will hit their kids, I only make you sit here and ask you not to talk. If you talk I make you smell your hair burning. This will teach you that I love you and will make you a smarter boy than you are. It could be worse, Gordon. Other mothers don't love their children but I love mine. We could be poor or we could die in a fire ourselves and smell like this, this is what you will smell like if you are on fire, said Mother. It could be worse. Fire would be worse.

What did it smell like? I do not like to remember. I like Mrs. Lowell, Mrs. Gingrinch, Mrs. Baker, but mostly Mrs. Lowell.

Mrs. Lowell, Mrs. Gingrinch, Mrs. Baker never burned my hair. Mother never talked about burning my hair at Yuke Her. They drank and laughed and they looked at me with eyes that made me smell smoke and matchbooks when they lit their cigarettes and drank from the bottles. They played every morning and they finished before I was supposed to eat.

Mother did this on purpose. Gordon, she said, today I want you to walk Mrs. Baker home. Then you can eat your lunch. I will make you mashed potatoes and a sandwich, a tuna sandwich, dress warm it's snowing outside, she said. I don't like tuna sandwiches because I'm not allowed to talk in my red chair, just watch for cheating. I walked Mrs. Baker or Mrs. Gingrinch or Mrs. Lowell home every day and we walked slowly so I would not have to eat the tuna sandwich until I got home and if it took longer then it would be longer before I ate the sandwich. Mrs. Baker went home on Monday and Wednesday and Mrs. Gingrinch went home on Tuesday. I always walked fast with Mrs. Baker because on Wednesday Mother would make me mashed potatoes. Mrs. Baker is ugly and I do not like to walk with her anyway so I walk fast. On Thursday and Friday and Saturday I walked Mrs. Lowell home and Mother and Mrs. Gingrinch and Mrs. Baker stayed at the Yuke Her table and drank from the bottles all day. I walked slow on these days because I did not want to go back to the house when they had the bottles empty.

Who was first? It was Mrs. Lowell who first showed me things. That day we walked fast because Mrs. Lowell was walking fast and looking at the watch on her hand. It was ten after twelve, which means that we had fifty minutes until one o'clock because there are sixty minutes in one hour and twenty-four hours in one day.

Why are we walking fast, I asked Mrs. Lowell.

Because, she said, I don't have too much time and there's something I need to show you. It's cold, Gordon. It's January. Aren't you cold?

It is wrong to be cold. Show me, I said.

I can't show you here but I will show you. It's a thank-you for walking me home.

We are walking too fast.

If we are not fast I will not be able to show you because someone will come home. Besides it is very cold and you're not dressed properly. Why doesn't Rette dress you better.

I did not know other people lived with Mrs. Lowell. I never heard about other people when they played Yuke Her. It was twelve-thirty when we got to her white house, which means we had thirty minutes to one o'clock. Inside she sat me at the kitchen table, I sat at a chair, a chair different from mine. It is not red but tall.

Can you show me what it is, I like surprises I said.

She bit the corner of my ear, her brown hair smelled like mangos and she wore purple rings on her fingers ice, and there isn't any time, face icicles that fell from the roof as she touched me and shattered into pieces glass prisms her rings grey purple with red amethysts she moaned I screamed she took me upstairs to the bed lie there and don't move, there isn't any time, don't move the bed shook I shook isn't any time I never felt it before it was powerful as the hairs lit in my face does my mother do this do this I screamed don't move she screamed mother doesn't do this to me and we both moved and then the hair split and the clock on the bedside table wasn't counting anymore and then there wasn't any time and she sped up and then I didn't move and it was finished and there wasn't any more time and I didn't move.

I didn't talk because I didn't want to make Mrs. Lowell angry. She was not angry she was glowing and her mouth didn't smell so dirty now, so much like the smoke when she was in Mother's house. She was on her back on the green sheet the colour of hedges. Her feet were sweating. She smelled like mangos and cigarettes.

Do you know what that was, she said.

I did not want to answer because I did not want to be wrong. I don't know anything.

Did you like what I showed you, she said.

She put her hand on me and rubbed her palm against me and said you are very good. I just wanted you to lie still and you did and it was wonderful. You made me feel so good.

Your feet are sweaty, I said.

Next time we walk home I will show you something else, she said. You can never tell your mother that I show you things. She wouldn't understand and then I couldn't show you anymore. You have to be quiet. You have to go because Mr. Lowell will be home and you can't be here when Mr. Lowell gets here.

Her feet were moving and rubbing me. The smell of mangos was flying out of the window and Mrs. Lowell made the clock move again.

We are lovely and beautiful but your mother has never understood lovely and beautiful. She understands nothing about faces.

I wanted to leave.

No, she was not the only one, the other women at the game too. Mother told me to walk Mrs. Gingrinch home. It was winter still. Mrs. Gingrinch never said she was going to show me anything and we walked slow so I did not know anything.

Mrs. Gingrinch lives in a small house with a garage. It is white with tiny windows. The curtains are the colour of toothpaste, red white green, you can see them through the window. The shutters are blue. It was so pretty I wanted to go inside.

Are we going inside, I said.

No, we are going to go in the garage.

I'm cold, I said, I'd like some hot chocolate inside.

No, sweetie, you can't go inside. Mr. Gingrinch is upstairs in bed, sick. You can't come inside, Gordon. But you can come warm up in the garage before you go home. We can sit in the car. The garage will be warm. You like cars, all boys like cars.

The garage was not pretty. There was nothing there I wanted to see and it was grey and the car was too small for my knees.

I said, I don't fit, my knees are too big. Why can't I have any hot chocolate and then she touched me, like Mrs. Lowell. This is different now it knows she pulled the seats back and climbed on top and it was noisy the sounds of saws and wood the sound of pain and work and effort and the vice clamps closed and it was noisy and she moaned and I screamed and it was nothing new but it was and she said move, why aren't you moving so I moved a little but the car was too small for me to move and she moved more than me it hurt like a saw might hurt like a nail like a chain like a lawnmower on my belly and me parts and I screamed and she screamed louder and all I wanted was a hot chocolate and it was the sound of work and effort it was all sounds and Mr. Gingrinch was in the house somewhere and then she started making farting and she said don't laugh don't stop and it was the sound of work and effort and a lawnmower on my me parts. When she was finished showing me she fell asleep in the back seat and I sat beside her watching the clock in the garage. It was ten after one, which meant there were fifty minutes until two o'clock.

Now when they played Yuke Her it was different to me. Mrs. Baker was still ugly, Mrs. Gingrinch still called Mrs. Baker ugly. Mother still drank and burned my hair under my nose when I came home. A horrible smell, like Mrs. Gingrinch smells but the same the same.

Rette, that's cheating, said Mrs. Lowell. She slammed the cards on the table. I am not cheating. I made my own son watch to show there is not cheating. If I was cheating Gordon would have said something, wouldn't you, Gordon.

I didn't say anything. If I did Mother would burn hair under my nose.

That doesn't matter, said Mrs. Gingrinch, you're taking advantage of us, you and Mrs. Baker.

That's because nothing is going on, said Mother.

That's because you're ugly, Mrs. Gingrinch said.

I'm not ugly, said Mrs. Baker.

Mother knocked the flower heads on the floor and the low wide bowl broke into pieces. Mrs. Gingrinch shook a bottle with a purple label shouting this is ridiculous, this is ridiculous while Mrs. Lowell bent over to pick up the shards of the vase.

Don't get up, Gordon, she said, you'll hurt your feet.

Get up, Gordon, and clean your mess, said Mother.

Gordon should do the work, said Mrs. Gingrinch to Mrs. Lowell. He never does anything, he just lies there.

Why should he do anything, said Mrs. Lowell, this is not his fault, he is not his fault. You leave him alone. It's not his fault who he is.

I walked Mrs. Lowell home. It was snowing it was sunny. We walked slow but when we got there we went upstairs and Mrs. Lowell told me that I was so good at lying still she liked it best when I lay still and she moved and I liked it that she liked it, I did not want to think about Mother burning my hair there is all the time in the world she screamed and I did not I know there is a pattern a nice pattern and I lie still there is all the time in the world but I still don't move the smell I notice most is Mrs. Lowell's feet and my sweat much more pleasant than Mrs. Gingrinch in the car and much better to look all the time in the world at than ugly Mrs. Baker and I screamed and that made her scream louder and louder and the more I lay still the more she moved and when she finished I was sure there was all the time in the world.

I liked that she liked it, I liked her better than Mrs. Baker. I don't want to tell you about Mrs. Baker, with Mrs. Baker it felt dirty it was not fun then, not fun or warm it was almost as bad as the fire and hair. Mrs. Baker never took me home, we just went to a park. It was so cold and I wanted hot chocolate but knew I wouldn't get any.

Why, I don't want to talk about it. It's not special.

She threw herself under a tree, take me now she said.

I didn't understand. She grabbed me and pulled me under. The snow was soft and cold under my knees. She had a green hood and that made it better but it was so hard the sun was on my back and the wind bit my face not warm with Mrs. Lowell not work with Mrs. Gingrinch just empty like the bottles on the Yuke Her table, empty like the numbers on the cards, empty like the lighter Mother owned it was too much work and she screamed a little bit but I never said anything I knew I was doing it now and it was just doing not like Mrs. Lowell Mrs. Baker was not anything she was like Mother said ugly people are empty inside it was hard I knew what I was doing but it was empty.

I did not like when Mrs. Baker did that with me, but not because she was ugly. She was ugly, but she was empty. Mrs. Gingrinch was empty too, Mother was empty, Mrs. Lowell was not empty. And when it happened again every day it never felt better with Mrs. Gingrinch or Mrs. Baker, it felt awful and wrong, like cheating at Yuke Her.

When they played Yuke Her now it was awful. They were always fighting. I sat and did not talk while Mother and Mrs. Lowell Mrs. Gingrinch Mrs. Baker threw the flowers and the bottles and screamed and it was horrible and when it was all over I didn't get tuna any more. They didn't talk about me but they looked at me when they fought and I sat with my hands on the knees of my pants in the red chair at the window. Mother kept shouting at me, speak, Gordon, you son of a bitch, tell them I am not cheating, I just want to win and win. I win, everyone gets angry with me you dumb shit, you retard, speak.

Rette, not in front of Gordon, said Mrs. Lowell. It's your own fault for cheating.

Mrs. Baker said, I'm not cheating, Rette, it's you, I'm sick of losing with you.

Mother hit Mrs. Baker and she had the same look on her ugly nose she had when I finished at the park. I said that's the same look you had at the park and Mrs. Baker looked at me with scared eyes but no one else heard me. Mother threw the bowl at Mrs. Lowell and hit her in the face. The flowers fell everywhere on the floor and Mrs. Lowell screamed a different scream. Blood came through the fingers on her face and ran down her and she put it in her hair when she tried to push the hair off her face. She left a trail of blood. Mother stopped and Mrs. Baker cried and Mrs. Gingrinch had her hair in a mess.

I walked with Mrs. Gingrinch. I did not want her I wanted Mrs. Lowell but now Mrs. Lowell would never come back again she would never have a face again. It was not mine but it was pretty and she was better than Mrs. Gingrinch or Mrs. Baker. Mrs. Lowell.

I was angry. At the house we went to the garage. I did not want hot chocolate. She pulled me into the car and turned the car on. There was the sound of the radio. Mr. Gingrinch is upstairs, sick, asleep she said. I told him someone was coming to fix the car today there could be as much noise as she wanted. She said she really needed it now. I was angry and I wanted to hurt her, she was so mean and empty as empty as Mother.

I touched her first. She moaned and touched me you are going to move she said to me that is wonderful and I moved I was so angry I was like nails a saw a car engine and she scratched my back and bit my ear and I moved I moved I moved I did not lie still and I thought about Mrs. Lowell I wanted to cry I wanted to make Mrs. Gingrinch cry and scream and scratch me harder because I was moving after she told me not to but Mrs. Gingrinch was screaming and holding me all the time in the world because Mrs. Lowell would never come back it was two-thirty which means that there is forever before Mrs. Lowell comes back and tells me to be still. Her head moves everywhere and I grab her hair it is three o'clock which means we have been in the garage for thirty minutes.

You were incredible, she said, you moved so much, oh my god.

She fell asleep on the back seat and I started to cry I felt so bad. I don't know what I felt it was worse than the burning hair or Mother throwing the vase at Mrs. Lowell. I was so cold and empty, Mrs. Gingrinch and Mrs. Baker were so awful and empty. I got out of the car and closed the door softly and closed the garage door when I left so Mrs. Gingrinch could have her nap in the garage and I went to the park. When I got home Mrs. Baker was gone. Mother made me tuna but no mashed potatoes and she burned a whole patch of my hair in front of my face and screamed.

You were so bad today, Gordon, shame on you, don't you understand what you're doing. I asked you to talk and you didn't.

Mother, I don't know what to do, I cried, you hit Mrs. Lowell I am just supposed to sit by the window and tell you if people are cheating.

You don't even understand what you're doing, you're a dumb boy, Gordon. A dumb boy and you don't even do well by me and if you don't do well by me then those women don't deserve your kindness, they're mean dumb bitches and we don't need them. You are a burden, Gordon, a mule. You are good for nothing more than watching your mother play cards and being stupid. Those women don't like you, Gordon, they wanted you to say I cheat all the time at Yuke Her.

I do not know what else to tell you. I do not know what else. I don't know why you keep asking me about Mrs. Gingrinch. Mrs. Gingrinch is empty. I don't understand you, why you ask me about what happened to Mrs. Gingrinch. This story is not Mrs. Gingrinch's story, it's Mrs. Lowell's. This is about Mrs. Lowell, where is she. I told you about mother and my chair. The car you put me in never takes me home. Where is Mrs. Lowell, I told you about my chair.

THE CURE

Mazo de la Roche

I

He was washed and combed and scented, and set up in his easy chair by the sunny window – just like an old doll, he thought. Ada, his wife, had been very much like a little girl, washing and dressing her doll, and propping it up in a chair, just under the canary's cage. Very much like a little girl, she had backed away from him to admire the effect, when all was done. She had made him a sprightly little bow, her hands clasped against her breast, her small grey eyes twinkling in that secretive way they had, as though she had just been plotting against him... And so she had, often and often, plotted to buy finery for her body; or extravagant gewgaws for the house, like that set of Japanese birds painted on silk; or to give fanciful entertainments, like that Spring fête, when all the old chestnut trees in the garden had been strung with innumerable Chinese lanterns, and the summer house suffocated in paper flowers, and a band rigged out like Hungarian gypsies. She had provided the costumes, and the whole affair, only one of many, had cost the devil a lot of money. Why, the old silver punch bowls had never been allowed to be emptied. Even the band had had punch. Good stuff, too. Not like the disgusting fruit punches they gave you nowadays... Well, people had talked a lot about that fête. Twenty-five years ago it took less to amuse people. They'd talk over any fun they'd had for days afterward. Now they'd have forgotten it by the next day. They'd be off after something else. He'd like to see the garden fête that would excite his nephews, Gordon and Fred!

The canary hopped down to the bottom perch and peered at him over the little brass fence that enclosed its cage. It cocked its blond head at him. He hoped it wasn't going to sing, for its noise hurt his head, but before he could stop himself, he had said "tweet! tweet!" to it, and that was all the encouragement it needed. It burst into a cascade of shrill notes; then it turned to a piercing chatter from which, he thought, it would never desist. He lay back in his chair staring at it. He longed to have the bit of yellow fluff between his fingers. He would tweak its neck for it, by God – squeeze the senseless chatter out of it. Each note seemed like a tiny hammer on his brain. His forehead broke out in a sweat. He raised his voice and called, huskily:

"Ada! Ada!"

At the sound of his voice the canary sang more loudly than ever, completely drowning him out. He sat up and shook his fist at it and cursed it. Convulsed with joy it threw its head back on its ruffled throat and strained every nerve to excel all previous outbursts.

He sank back once more, and shut his eyes. Two tears pressed between the lids and trickled down his cheeks.

He lay quietly now, letting the sharp notes beat upon his brain, beat down his angry thoughts. He felt broken... A heavy lorrie rumbled down the street. The noise of it shook the summer air and rattled the window pane. When it had passed, the canary had ceased singing.

He weakly opened his eyes and looked up at it. It was eating a seed. It dropped the shell to the bottom of the cage and wiped its beak sharply on the perch. Then it hopped to the bottom perch and began to drink. There fell a delicious silence everywhere. Not a sound in the house, on the street. The full rich perfume of chestnut blossoms came in at the open window. He rolled his head towards the sweetness of it, and through the brightness of his tears saw the great tree standing in glory, its white plumes upright like perfumed candles.

Quietness in the street and through the house. Quietness now in his own spirit. He would soon be himself again if only the damned bird would let him be. It was an awful thing for a man to have a wife – to have been tied up to her for thirty-five years – who always wanted a canary singing or a music box jigging in the house.

Then she was coming now, up the stairs. Always that same tripping, high-heeled walk. Walk the same if her back was breaking. Great old girl, Ada. Lively for her age. Showed her clothes off. A good looker.

He tried to look even weaker than he was as she came into the room. He let his chin sink into his breast, his hands lie feebly on the arms of the chair. She had been humming a little, in forced gaiety as she came into the room, but when she saw the sunlight playing over his bowed head, and the way the silky white hair that curled like a child's, was gently stirred by the breeze, she hesitated, a look of mingled anxiety and compassion softening her features.

"Was he sleeping, then?" she asked, in a cooing voice.

"Hm – might ha' been if the damn canary hadn't screeched 'is head off. Nice bird to leave a helplesh man alone with." It was hard for him to speak distinctly. His tongue was thick and his throat husky.

His wife gave a trill of metallic laughter and made a little dart towards the canary.

"Oh, naughty, naughty, naughty," she said. "Tweenty-weenty! Tweenty-weenty!" Did he hurt his dear master's head with him's 'ittle song?"

The canary, recognizing her, began to twitter petulantly. Her black, curled "transformation" made her look top-heavy. Her small grey eyes twinkled in her pale, powdered face.

Dick Boone regarded both her and the bird with equal disfavour.

"The matter with you both is," he said, "that you think too much about yourselvesh. Always prinking and twittering and hopping from one perch to another. That's what'sh the matter with you and the bird, Ada mine."

With a fluttering movement she came from the canary to him, and bent her face towards his, smiling into his eyes.

"And I pleased him once, didn't I?" she breathed. "There wasn't a girl could match Ada, for elegance, for style!"

"Get away," he said, crossly, turning his face away. "Suffocatin' me. I don' wan' to be bothered."

But she pressed closer, her thin lips folded in a smile. One of her long earrings was sharp against his cheek. The large sleeves of her pale blue silk tea-gown of the period enveloped him. The smell of her powder, and some scent that she always used on her "transformation," made him feel choky and helpless.

"Going to be good?" she whispered, looking commandingly into his eyes.

"Hm-hm," he grunted, playing with her beads.

"And take you eggnog?"

"Hm-hm."

"And nothing else – now look at me – nothing else, to make you naughty and sick?"

"No-o."

She kissed him briskly and went into the bathroom.

In some ways the bathroom was like the little room behind a small chemist's shop. Phials, measuring glasses, miscellaneous appliances for the sick room and the toilette were everywhere in hopeless disorder. Almost empty bottles, grey with dust, their sticky labels quite illegible, crowded the stained shelves. It was like a small, untidy kitchen, too, for there were a gas ring, several saucepans, several bottles of milk – from the full bottle of morning's milk through sour degrees to the one whose curdled contents was crowned by a miniature forest of fuzzy green mould. Boxes of biscuits, cartons of eggs, tins of "foods", glasses of jelly overflowed to the top of the wicker soiled clothes basket. No servant was ever allowed in here to tidy up. This was Ada Boone's own secret room, where, filled with apprehensions, often sick at heart, though humming gaily so that Dick might not guess it, she administered to his needs in his bad times. And when he was "himself," it was from this room that they emerged in turn, fresh, scented, combed, shaved, curled, a still dashing, still to-be-stared-after couple. A strange, pathetic, vain, wayward couple, the Boones. Childless, they quarrelled and made it up like children themselves. Though each disliked the other's ways, they were deeply attached, very dependent on each other.

Presently, after the prolonged swishing of an egg-beater, she emerged, carrying an eggnog.

"Nice 'ittle eggnog for 'ittle boy," she said.

"Not hungry," he said, turning his head towards the window. "Rather look at the chestnut tree."

"Ah, but he must eat and drink to get well again."

He looked at her now, with a malicious grin.

"Drink?" he repeated.

"Not naughty stuff. Just milk to make him strong."

He took the glass and sipped.

"Pf," he said. "Insipid stuff."

"More sugar? A wee dash of nutmeg?"

He raised his childlike blue eyes imploringly to her face.

"Just a drop of rum, old girl, to take away that sickly taste, give some body to it."

All her softness was gone now. Her eyes struck compellingly into his. She said, harshly:

"Listen. Not one drop. Not if you went on your knees. Don't I know what's good for you? Am I not going to follow the doctor's orders?"

"Very well." He set the glass on the table beside him. "Shan't drink it then, and that'sh flat."

She went into one of her sudden passions. "You dare defy me?" she screamed. "I, who have not had my proper sleep in a fortnight because of you! You dare defy me!"

"I guessh I'm master in my own house."

She gave a loud, bitter laugh. "A fine master, you are, aren't you? Drinking yourself to death as fast as you can? I'd like to know where we'd be if it weren't for the boys. As loyal to you as if they were your own sons."

"You never gave me a son to go into the business," he sneered.

Her face became crimson.

"No. And I'm thankful I didn't, for he'd certainly have inherited your tastes. A man can't be like you and not affect his children."

Her voice beat him down, but he reiterated sullenly – "Shan't drink the beastly stuff."

"Not drink it? You'll do as I command – I am the major-general. You are the private. I am the Sultana. You are a—a—"

"Eunuch," he suggested, with a feeble laugh.

The canary, inspired by the hubbub, joined his hysteria to hers, rocking on his perch, his throat vibrating with madness.

Beads of sweat stood on Dick Boone's forehead. He reached submissively for the glass. He was broken. It rattled pathetically against his teeth as he gulped the sweet mixture. Seeing him so, Ada's anger melted as a tropical tempest into sunshine.

She took the empty glass from him, patted him encouragingly on the shoulder, and brought him the morning paper. But the eggnog had not agreed with him. He hiccoughed, and was glad that he did so, since it showed that all was not well. But she only flitted about the room, smiling at him as she passed, touching the canary's cage into dizzy jigging on its spiral holder.

"Another day or two," she remarked, at last, "and he will be quite himself again. Go down to business like a nice little gentleman."

She was called to the telephone... As soon as her loud, animated voice came from below he rose slowly from his chair, steadying himself by its arms, and grunting weakly. He took the empty glass in one hand and shuffled in his leather slippers to the tall old wardrobe. He fumbled with the key, opened the door cautiously, and thrust one hand into the back corner behind the coats, waistcoats and trousers.

He fumbled, and even put his head in among the clothes and peered into the dusk, but the bottle of Scotch he always kept there to be handy was there no longer. He made certain that this was so, then, baffled and resentful, he turned away. Someone had taken the bottle away. Ada, or one of the boys. If Gordon or Fred had done it, they'd hear from him. He'd not stand any damned interference from them. He'd make them eat humble pie! His sister Lizzie's sons daring to interfere with him! Well, Lizzie had been an interfering piece in her day, and her sons took after her.

The canary had put its beak between the wires of its cage to watch his proceedings before the wardrobe. Now it burst into jeering song. He knew it was jeering at him by the way it cocked one beady eye in his direction.

"Stop it, you little devil," he growled. "Whole world's againsht me - even canary."

It ceased its singing but began to utter ear-splitting "tweets!"

"I'll tweet you," he said, savagely, and struck the cage with his hand.

He had only intended to jar it, to vent some of his impotent anger in frightening the bird, but the blow must have been sharper than he knew, for one corner of the bottom of the cage was loosened and, like a golden flash, the canary shot forth, alighting with a wild flutter on the tall head of the bed.

He was horrified, contrite. What had he done? What would Ada say? There was the open window - Oh, dear! oh, dear!

"Pretty - pretty—" he coaxed, shuffling towards it, all his fine white hair standing on end, his delicate, aquiline face, flushed by concern. "Come down to Daddy, then - little rascal." Ada often called them Mammy and Daddy to the bird, and he unconsciously did so now in his anxiety to propitiate and capture it.

But it sped past his groping hand like a comet, floated on outstretched wings a second before the window, then struck itself against the mirror of the dressing-table.

Ada was coming. Humming as she came. He could not bear another scene. He would get into bed.

With sudden agility he clambered on to the high bed, and drew the rose pink satin quilt over him. Only his crest of white hair showed above the edge. He breathed heavily.

Ada entered with a sharp tapping of high-heeled shoes. There was a moment's silence, then she, in turn, exclaimed, "Oh, dear - Oh, dear—" And ran to the window and closed it. Now there were stealthy movements about the room. Deep sighs of aggravation. Then a "ha!" of blessed relief. She had caught him. He was in the cage.

Deeply, serenely, Dick breathed against the satin quilt. Ada leaned over him and looked into the smooth mask of his face. She drew the quilt down a little so he would get more air, lowered the blind, covered the canary's cage, and tiptoed from the room.

II

When he awoke he felt much better. He got up without assistance, and, when the gaunt manservant brought him his lunch, he spoke to him in a clearer, steadier voice than he had been able to produce since the last drinking bout.

He enjoyed his lunch. He had the fellow open the window and went and sat by it, breathing deeply of the warm, ambient air, scented with chestnut blossoms. A hose was playing on the greensward below, and a pair of robins were running in and out of the spray as if they loved it. New life beat in his blood like music. His hand, with its thick veins, that rested on the sunny windowsill, was steady.

Ada came in, dressed to go somewhere in a flowered organdie, with enormous sleeves, and trailing skirt. She told him how the canary's cage had come apart, and what a time she had had to catch him without making a noise. She was going out but would not be gone long. She smelled like a flower bed.

He leaned out of the window as she sailed down the walk. She looked up and blew him a kiss. He threw kisses back.

"Romeo, ah, Romeo!" she called.

"Ha, ha, Juliet! Good old girl!"

She was a very emotional woman. Emotions, real or pretended, filled her life. And he had always had the good sense, or the weakness perhaps, to play up to them.

He watched her out of sight. He watched a watering cart lumber heavily by, drawn by two sweating black horses. He was willing to bet they had belonged to an undertaker once. He watched young Mrs. Cowan ride gaily by on her new red bicycle, a small sailor hat topping her golden pompadour. A pretty piece, plum as a partridge.

He began to think about his business. He would telephone the office at once and see how things were going on. He had telephoned several times every day since he had been under the weather, but the boys spoke so indistinctly, there was such a buzzing in the phone, that there was not much satisfaction in it.

He took down the receiver and asked for the office number, that number about which hung an unfailing charm, for he was deeply proud of the wholesale tobacco and cigar business, that had been carried on by the Boones under the same roof for three generations, founded by his grandfather, a well-connected Carolinian.

"Main 3344."

He waited with almost pathetic eagerness in the dim hallway, a tousled-haired little man in a maroon dressing-gown.

"Hello," came in Gordon's deep, even tones.

"Oh, hello, Gordon. How's things?"

"Everything's fine. That is, Fred and I are working hard. How are you today, Uncle?"

"Oh-h, so, so. Anything new?"

"A big order from Martin Brothers. We don't know whether to fill it or not. I hear they're kind of shaky."

"Don't fill it!" His voice shook with excitement. "D-don't fill it till I look into things. Hear me, Gordon? Don't fill it!"

"All right, Uncle. All right. Just as you say. Good-bye."

"Now mind, Gordon - wait - better send Fred to the phone - tell Fred—?"

But Gordon was gone.

He hung up the receiver and climbed the three steps from the landing, shuffling back to his room... The exhilaration of business stirred his blood. Why had that fool Gordon left the telephone so quickly? Those boys were getting above themselves and no mistake. Needed calling down. And they'd get it!

The man brought him a cup of tea.

He felt refreshed by it, and hastened weakly to the telephone again. He cleared his throat and demanded in a firm voice.

"Main 3344."

"Hello." This time it was the stenographer's thin voice.

"Miss Wayling. It's Mr. Boone speaking. Is Mr. Fred Mitchell there?"

"Just a minute, please, Mr. Boone. Mr. Mitchell's in the outer office."

He waited several minutes, then Fred's sharp, nasal voice enquired curtly, "That you, Uncle?"

"Oh, hello Fred? H-how'sh things?"

He had intended to be stern, the heavy uncle, but Fred's hard, crisp tones made him feel suddenly confused. He forgot what he had in mind when he came to the telephone.

"H-how'sh things?" he repeated.

"Good as can be expected in times like these. Don't you worry. The new cigar is fine. Got a swell box. Screaming beauty of a Spanish girl on the lid. I'll tell you what you can do. Think up a name for it. We've got to have a striking name. Goodbye."

Before Dick could reply he was gone.

However, he spent the rest of the afternoon quite cheerfully, between playing Patience, and thinking of a name for the new cigar. At last he hit on Adabella, a fine sonorous name, and a compliment to his wife, Adabella, Ada beautiful.

He could hardly wait for her to come home so he could tell her. And when she did come and he told her, she was really charmed. She was especially tender with him that evening, and when the boys came in after dinner, they were especially nice. All three stood about him, smiling down at him, and looking, somehow, rather anxious about him; Ada in her flowered dress with a dash of rouge on her lips; Gordon with his built out shoulders, and, already, the smug, aggressive look of the successful business man; Fred, sharp as a whip.

It was Fred who came in later, with a small glass in his hand, and approached his chair, smiling.

"I guess a little drink wouldn't do you any harm, tonight, Uncle," he remarked, casually.

Something steely in his voice, penetrating in his cold eyes, arrested Dick's attention.

"When I want a drink, I'll ask for it," he said, sulkily.

Fred showed astonishment, chagrin.

"Well, from what I have heard you wanted one pretty badly today," he observed.

Anger flamed into Dick's eyes. So they talked him over among them, did they?

"You can mind your own business," he retorted. "I'll not stand any interference from you."

Gordon came in from the hall. He must have been listening, for he said, with nervous cheerfulness.

"Well, if you won't have one with Fred, Uncle, have it with me. You've reached the stage where it'll do you good. Brace you up."

Dick turned on the two young men with sudden vehemence. "What's the matter with you two, anyway? What are you trying to do? Make me drink so you can have the run of things a bit longer?" Suspicion crept into his eyes. "Get out. Do you hear? Get out! I won't have it!"

His wife's voice came from the downstairs hall, sharp with anxiety.

"What's the matter, boys?"

He started toward the door to go to her, but Fred laid his hand on his arm, his steely eyes looked into his. He held the glass to his lips.

"Look here, Uncle, you've got to drink it. There's no use objecting."

Gordon was on his other side, gripping his other arm. Still both were smiling. He felt suddenly weak and confused. If they were set on his taking a drink, he'd better do it. He wasn't strong enough to resist those two smiling, staring, bright-eyed nephews. Shaking, he gulped the whiskey down... Well, it was good. Nothing wrong about it, but they shouldn't have persisted that way. It wasn't respectful.

The room seemed to float around them, as though they were all under water. Above, the great globes of the gasolier shone like distant moons, through leagues of shimmering, green sea. The two nephews were white faced and goggle-eyed, like strange fish. A booming, as of distant surf, made other sounds indistinct but he faintly heard Gordon say:

"Pretty dopey, what?"

He had his coat on. His silk hat was over one eye. Strange to wear a frock coat and silk hat at the bottom of the sea. Ada was there, too, a long-tailed mermaid. Adabella. She was kissing him. Shedding salt, salt tears. Adabella, Ada mine...

Lights flashed by. Wheels rumbled. He slept.

He had slept for several hours when he opened his eyes, refreshed, but with a sort of buzzing in his ears. There was a soft light in the room, shaded from the bed by a screen. It was several minutes before the shapes of the furniture in the room resolved themselves from unfamiliar shadows, and he perceived that all about him was strange. He turned to look for Ada's head, divested of its "transformation," on the other pillow but it bulged, smooth and white beside him... A tremor of fear shook him. He raised himself on his elbow and stared wildly about the room. It was uncomfortable, with plain cretonne coverings on the chairs, in perfect neatness, very different from the luxurious disorder that he and Ada loved. He had never seen the room before.

With an exclamation of dismay, he would have sprung from the bed, but at the sound of his movements, a short thick-set man appeared from behind the screen and laid a restraining hand on his arm.

"Just lie down, Mr. Boone," he said, soothingly, in a muffled, heavy voice. "You haven't been very well. Dr. Searle will soon be in to see you."

Dr. Searle! The name struck his brain like a blow, and yet he could not dislodge from the murk of his bewilderment the sinister significance attached to it. Searle - White - Tom White - his friend, dead now, old Tom had been in Searle's Institute twice. The first time came out "cured," the second, died - after months - or was it years? - of it. Searle's Institute! A cure! He knew what their methods were. Disgusting.

And Ada had let him in for this. The boys he had generously taken into his business - the business of Boone and Son - had done this filthy trick to him - had persuaded Ada it was for the best. A cure! Searle's cure! A month of it would kill him. Kill him! And they'd be glad. Have the business to themselves. The miserable, ungrateful cubs. Lizzie's cubs. She'd been an ungrateful sister and now - her cubs!

The attendant regarded him speculatively. Was the old fellow going to be troublesome?

"Is there anything I can do for you, sir?" he asked "Would you like a cup of cocoa?"

"No, no." His face was a pale mask. No sign in it of the turmoil of his thoughts. "Except my nightshirt. I'd like that. Why am I just in my underclothes?"

"Well, you see, sir, you wasn't very bright when they brought you in, and they thought the less fussing over you the better."

"Good boys," murmured Dick. "Kind, thoughtful boys. my nephews."

"Yes, sir. I'll help you on with your nightshirt now."

The man went to a clothes closet, and Dick had a glimpse of his clothes hanging there, limp and expressionless, like a dead man's clothes.

He was so weak, it appeared, that the attendant had to support him while the nightshirt was put on. He sank bank on the pillow with a deep sigh of contentment.

"Let me be now," he muttered. "Want to shleep. Must get lots o' sleep."

The attendant lowered the gas. "If you want me, I'm right in the next room," he said. The only answer was a snuffling snore.

Dick heard him moving about in the next room. He heard footsteps coming along the passage, and another man's voice from the doorway asking:

"What's he like?"

"Quiet as a lamb. Sound asleep. I'm going to have a snooze myself. Goodness knows I need it after the time I had with Mr. Gidding last night. I'm going to make a big kick against all this night duty, you'll see."

His heart was hammering against his ribs as it hadn't done since he was a boy up to mischief, as, an hour later, he stood, fully dressed, in the doorway of the next room. It was a small sitting-room with a door leading into the passage. It stood open but when he had tried the outer door of the bedroom he had found it locked. He must pass through this room.

Carrying his top hat in one hand and his shoes in the other, he glided past the sleeping form of the attendant, huddled uncomfortably on a narrow sofa. The passage was dark, save for the moonlight that fell through a grated window at the end, but he could make out the dark cavern stairway, and, as he cautiously descended, the thick carpet deadened all sound, and his light weight caused no creaking of the steps. From a room above came a steady, dismal groaning that made his blood freeze. If he hadn't been wide awake, alert, resourceful, he might have stayed there to add his groans to the night.

The hall below was lighted by a gas jet burning under a coloured globe. Through an open double doorway, he saw the dim shape of a dining-table, and the faint glimmer of silver on a sideboard. He entered and examined the three windows. They were large, and locked securely by some patent device he could not discover. A cold sweat of fear bathed his body. Despair was about to seize him when he felt a cool draught on his back, and found that it came from the opening into a serving pantry. He thought:

"If I can only squeeze my body through there, I'm a free man."

Carefully he put his shoes and top hat through first, then, mounting a chair, he placed one knee on the projecting shelf.

"What a blessing, I am small," he thought, "for this hole is not much bigger than a rabbit's burrow."

Strained, bruised, shaking in every limb, he stood, at last, in the serving pantry. A fresh breeze gushed in through the wide open window.

With a sob of joy, he threw his hat and shoes out on to the grass, and clambered after them.

He was safe from that nightmare house! He was free beneath the velvet sky where the warm moon hung like a gilded lamp and the little stars trembled in the treetops.

He sat down on the grass and put on his shoes, fumbling over the lacing of them; he had already put his hat on one side of his head. No one saw him, a dishevelled little man, creep through the side gate into the street.

He paused a moment to cast a look of mingled triumph and abhorrence at the dark shape of the house towering above him, then moved like a shadow down the quiet street towards a small park that surrounded an old church, where he remembered a bench on which he could rest a while and think.

The City Hall clock struck four as he turned into the park. Already there was a faint luminous light in the east. He sank to the bench feeling weak, but filled with an odd exhilaration. He removed his hat and let the sweet air run like caressing fingers through his thick white hair. He emitted a great "whew" of relief and satisfaction. It was years since he had been out on the street at this hour alone. He recalled some of the nocturnal adventures of his young manhood and grinned audaciously at the dawn. Why, it must have been through this very park, at this hour, forty years ago, that he and that girl in the pink domino had run, with the others in pursuit. What a lovely, long white neck she had had! He thought of Fred and Gordon and their pleasures, and the thought made him sick. Gordon, and his built out shoulders – Fred, with his tight, sallow face... He chuckled as he savoured the surprise he had in store for them.

He dozed, and when he opened his eyes it was daylight. Milk carts were rattling down the street, empty street-cars jolting past. He boarded one and rode to the station. In the station restaurant he had a chop and a cup of coffee. In the station barber shop he had a shave, a haircut, and his clothes brushed, remarking to the man that travelling all night made one look very seedy.

From the station, he took a cab to the warehouse. The gilt sign – John Boone and Son – glittered in the morning sunlight. Well, there was life in Son yet – he'd show them. As he passed through the office, there were looks of surprise at his early arrival – perhaps surprise that he should arrive at all – but there were smiles, real smiles of pleasure, and he glowed in return.

Old Parsons, the book-keeper, took his coat and hat, and he sat down behind his desk to await his nephews. While he waited he dozed a little but he was sitting upright when they came in together. Fred was saying:

"Well, I wonder how old 3344 feels this morning. He won't be calling us up anyway. Thank goodness."

"Old 3344 feels very well, thank you," answered Dick, leaning over the desk to glare at them. "Yes, he'll be calling up this office quite often but you won't be here to answer."

"Why, Uncle—" stammered the young men.

"Yes - 'Why, Uncle'" - growled their uncle. "You thought you'd put me in a 'Cure', didn't you? Well, it worked faster than you expected. Now, you may put your hats on your swelled heads and go. Never let me see your faces again."

"Oh, Uncle," pleaded Gordon, "I think that for Mother's sake—"

"Yes, I've borne with you for your mother's sake, and I bore with her for her mother's sake. Now, I'm through. Go."

He paid the cabman at his own door, opened the low wrought-iron gate, and walked up the gravelled path with an almost bridegroom feeling of nervousness and elation. What would Ada be doing? He attached no blame to her in this affair. It was all the nephews' doing.

The chestnut tree held its white plumes towards the sun, the lawn unrolled its dewy greenness, the tones of the largest music-box tinkled from within. It was playing "The Blue Danube".

It did seem a little callous of Ada to have set it going this morning. But, when, panting from the exertion, he reached the door of their bedroom, the sight that met his eyes would have melted any heart. Ada was lying face downward on the bed sobbing bitterly, her pink silk peignoir rumpled, her "transformation" askew.

"Oh, Dick," she was sobbing, and again - "Oh, Dick."

He hurried to her and raised her. "It's all right, Ada mine. I'm here. Safe and sound. I'm here - I'm here—"

As she turned towards him with amazement and relief, he added, with his face twisted like a child's that is about to cry—"I'm going to be good, Ada," and sank into her arms.

THE IMMACULATE CONCEPTION PHOTOGRAPHY GALLERY

KATHERINE GOVIER

Sandro named the little photography shop on St. Clair Avenue West, between Lord's Shoes and Bargain Jimmies, after the parish church in the village where he was born. He had hankered after wider horizons, the rippled brown prairies, the hard-edged mountains. But when he reached Toronto he met necessity in the form of a wife and babies, and, never having seen a western sunset, he settled down in Little Italy. He photographed the brides in their fat lacquered curls and imported lace, and their quick babies in christening gowns brought over from home. Blown up to near life size on cardboard cutouts, their pictures filled the windows of his little shop.

Sandro had been there ten years already when he first really saw his sign, and the window.

He stood still in front of it and looked. A particularly buxom bride with a lace bodice and cap sleeves cut in little scallops shimmered in a haze of concupiscence under the sign reading: Immaculate Conception Photography Gallery. Sandro was not like his neighbors any more, he was modern, a Canadian. He no longer went to church. As he stared, one of the street drunks shuffled into place beside him. Sandro knew them all, they came into the shop in winter. (No one ought to have to stay outside in that cold, Sandro believed.) But he especially knew Becker. Becker was a smart man; he used to be a philosopher at a university.

"Immaculate conception," said Sandro to Becker. "What do you think?"

Becker lifted his eyes to the window. He made a squeezing gesture at the breasts. "I never could buy that story," he said.

Sandro laughed, but he didn't change the sign that year or the next and he got to be forty-five and then fifty and it didn't seem worth it. The Immaculate Conception Photography Gallery had a reputation. Business came in from as far away as Rosedale and North Toronto, because Sandro was a magician with a camera. He also had skill with brushes and lights and paint, he reshot his negatives, he lined them with silver, he had tricks even new graduates of photography school couldn't (or wouldn't) copy.

Sandro was not proud of his tricks. They began in a gradual way, fixing stray hairs and taking wrinkles out of dresses. He did it once, then twice, then people came in asking for it. Perhaps he'd have gone on this way, with small lies, but he met with a situation that was larger than most; it would have started a feud in the old country.

During a very large and very expensive wedding party, Tony the bridegroom seduced Alicia the bridesmaid in the basketball storage room under the floor of the parish hall. Six months later Tony confessed, hoping perhaps to be released from his vows. But the parents judged it was too late to dissolve the union: Diora was used, she was no longer a virgin, there was a child coming. Tony was reprimanded, Diora consoled, the mothers became enemies, the newlyweds made up. Only Alicia remained to be dealt with. The offence became hers.

In Italy, community ostracism would have been the punishment of choice. But this was Toronto, and if no one acknowledged Alicia on the street, if no one visited her mother, who was heavy on her feet and forced to sit on the sofa protesting her daughter's innocence, if no one invited her father out behind to drink homemade wine, Alicia didn't care. She went off to her job behind the till in a drugstore with her chin thrust out much as before. The in-laws perceived that the young woman could not be subdued by the old methods. This being the case, it was better she not exist at all.

Which was why Diora's mother turned up at Sandro's counter with the wedding photos. The pain Alicia had caused! she began. Diora's mother's very own miserable wages, saved these eighteen years, had paid for these photographs! She wept. The money was spent, but the joy was spoiled. When she and Diora's father looked at the tow of faces flanking bride and groom there she was - Alicia, the whore! She wiped her tears and made her pitch.

"You can solve our problem, Sandro. I will get a new cake, we will all come to the parish hall. You will take the photographs again. Of course," she added, "we can't pay you again."

Sandro smiled, it was so preposterous. "Even if I could afford to do all that work for nothing, I hate to say it, but Diora's out to here."

"Don't argue with me."

"I wouldn't be so bold," said Sandro. "But I will not take the photographs over."

The woman slapped the photographs where they lay on the counter. "You will! I don't care how you do it!" And she left.

Sandro went to the back and put his negatives on the light box. He brought out his magic solution and his razor blades and his brushes. He circled Alicia's head and shoulders in the first row and went to work. He felt a little bad, watching the bright circle of her face fade and swim, darken down to nothing. But how easily she vanished! He filled in the white spot with a bit of velvet curtain trimmed from the side.

"I'm like a plastic surgeon," he told his wife. "Take that patch of skin from the inner thigh and put it over the scar on the face. Then sand the edges. Isn't that what they do? Only it isn't a face I'm fixing, it's a memory."

His wife stood on two flat feet beside the sink. She shook the carrot she was peeling. "I don't care about Alicia," she said, "but Diora's mother is making a mistake. She is starting them off with a lie in their marriage. And why is she doing it? For her pride! I don't like this, Sandro."

"You're missing the point," said Sandro.

The next day he had another look at his work. Alicia's shoulders and the bodice of her dress *were* still there, in front of the chest of the uncle of the bridge. He couldn't remove them; it would leave a hole in Uncle. Sandro had nothing to fill the hole, no spare male torsos in black tie. He considered putting a head on top, but whose head? There was no such thing as a free face. A stranger would be questioned, a friend would have an alibi. Perhaps Diora's mother would not notice the black velvet space, as where a tooth had been knocked out, between the smiling faces.

Indeed she didn't, but kissed his hand fervently and thanked him with tears in her eyes. "Twenty-five thousand that wedding cost me. Twenty-five thousand to get this photograph and you have rescued it."

"Surely you got dinner and a dance too?" said Sandro.

"The wedding was one day. This is forever," said Diora's mother.

"I won't do that again," said Sandro, putting the cloth over his head and looking into his camera lens to do a passport photo. In the community the doctored photograph had been examined and re-examined. Alicia's detractors enjoyed the headless shoulders as evidence of a violent punishment.

"No, I won't do that again at all," said Sandro to himself, turning aside compliments with a shake of his head. But there was another wedding. After the *provolone e melone*, the veal *piccata*, the many-tiered cake topped with swans, the father of the bride drew Sandro aside and asked for a set of prints with the groom's parents removed.

"My God, why?" said Sandro.

"He's a bastard. A bad man."

"Shouldn't have let her marry his son, then," said Sandro, pulling a cigarette out of the pack in his pocket. These conversations made him nervous.

The father's weathered face was dark, his dinner jacket did not button around his chest. He moaned and ground his lower teeth against his uppers. "You know how they are, these girls in Canada. I am ashamed to say it, but I couldn't stop her."

Sandro said nothing.

"Look, I sat here all night long, said nothing, did nothing. I don't wanna look at him for the next twenty years."

Sandro drew in a long tube of smoke.

"I paid a bundle for this night. I wanna member it nice-like."

The smoke made Sandro nauseous. He dropped his cigarette and ground it into the floor with his toe, damning his own weakness. "So what am I going to do with the table?"

The father put out a hand like a tool, narrowed his eyes, and began to saw, where the other man sat.

"And leave it dangling, no legs?"

"So make new legs."

"I'm a photographer, not a carpenter," said Sandro. "I don't make table legs."

"Where you get legs is your problem," said the father. "I'm doing well here. I've got ten guys working for me. You look like you could use some new equipment."

And what harm was it if after all, it was only a photograph, said Sandro to himself. Then too there was the technical challenge. Waiting until they all got up to get their *bonbonniere*, he took a shot of the head table empty. Working neatly with his scalpel, he cut the table from this second negative, removed the in-laws and their chairs from the first one, stuck the empty table-end onto the table in the first picture, blended over the join neatly, and printed it. Presto! Only one set of in-laws.

"I don't mind telling you, it gives me a sick feeling," said Sandro to his wife. "I was there. I saw them. We had a conversation. They smiled for me. Now..." he shrugged. "An empty table. Lucky I don't go to church anymore."

"Let the man who paid good money to have you do it confess, not you," she said. "A photograph is a photograph."

"That's what I thought too," said Sandro.

The next morning Sandro went to the Donut House, got himself a take-out coffee and stood on the street beside his window.

"Why do people care about photographs so much?" he asked Becker. Becker had newspaper stuffed in the soles of his shoes. He had on a pair of stained brown pants tied up at the waist with a paisley necktie. His bottle was clutched in a paper bag gathered around the neck.

"You can put them on your mantel," said Becker. "They don't talk back."

"Don't people prefer life?" said Sandro.

"People prefer things," said Becker.

"Don't they want their memories to be true?"

"No," said Becker.

"Another thing. Are we here just to get our photograph taken? Do we have a higher purpose?"

Becker pulled one of the newspapers out of his shoe. There were Brian and Mila Mulroney having a gloaty kiss. They were smeared by muddy water and depressed by the joint in the ball of Becker's foot.

"I mean real people," said Sandro. "Have we no loyalty to the natural?"

"These are existential questions, Sandro," said Becker. "Too many more of them and you'll be out here on the street with the rest of us."

Sandro drained the coffee from his cup, pitched it in the bin painted "Keep Toronto Clean" and went back into his gallery. The existential questions nagged. But he did go out and get the motor drive for the camera. In the next few months he eradicated a pregnancy from a wedding photo, added a daughter-in-law who complained of being left out of the Christmas shots, and made a groom taller. Working in the darkroom, he was hit by vertigo. He was on a slide, beginning a descent. He wanted to know what the bottom felt like. After a year of such operations a man from the Beaches came in with a tiny black-and-white photo of a long-lost brother. He wanted it coloured and fitted into a family shot around a picnic table on Centre Island.

"Is this some kind of joke?" said Sandro. It was the only discretion he practiced now: he wanted to talk about it before he did it. "No. I'm going to send it to Mother. She thinks Christopher wrote us all off."

"Did he?" said Sandro.

"Better she should not know."

Sandro neglected to ask if Christopher was fat or thin. He ended up taking a medium-sized pair of shoulders from his own cousin and propping them up behind a bush, with Christopher's head on top. Afterward, Sandro lay sleepless in his bed. Suppose that in the next few months Christopher should turn up dead, say murdered. Then Mother would produce the photograph stamped Immaculate Conception Photography Gallery, 1816 St. Clair Avenue West. Sandro would be implicated. The police might come.

"I believe adding people is worse than taking them away," he said to his wife.

"You say yes to do it, then you do it. You think it's wrong, you say no."

"Let me try this on you, Becker," said Sandro the next morning. "To take a person out is only half a lie. It proves nothing except that he was not in that shot. To add a person is a whole lie: it proves that he was there, when he was not."

"You haven't proven a thing, you're just fooling around with celluloid. Have you got a buck?" said Becker.

"It is better to be a murderer than a creator. I am playing God, outplaying God at His own game." He was smarter than Becker now. He knew it was the photographs that lasted, not the people.

In the end the proof was in the proof. Though he hadn't prayed in thirty years, Sandro began to pray. It was like riding a bicycle: he got the hang of it again instantly. "Make me strong," he prayed, "strong enough to resist the temptation to expand the gallery, to buy a house in the suburbs. Make me say no to people who want alterations."

But Sandro's prayers were not answered. When people offered him money to dissolve an errant relative, he said yes. He said yes out of curiosity. He said yes out of a desire to test his skills. He said yes out of greed. He said yes out of compassion. "What is the cost of a little happiness?" he said. "Perhaps God doesn't count photographs. After all, they're not one of a kind."

Sandro began to be haunted, in slow moments behind the counter in the Immaculate Conception, by the faces of those whose presence he had tampered with. He kept a file – Alicia the lusty bridesmaid, Antonia and Marco, the undesired in-laws. Their heads, their shoes and their hands, removed from the scene with surgical precision, he saved for the moment when, God willing, a forgiving relative would ask him to replace them. But the day did not come. Sandro was not happy.

"Becker," he said, for he had a habit now of buying Becker a coffee first thing in the morning and standing out if it was warm, or in if it was cold, for a chat. "Becker, let's say it's a good service I'm doing. It makes people happy, even if it tells lies."

"Sandro," said Becker, who enjoyed his coffee, "these photographs, doctored by request of the subjects, reflect back the lives they wish to have. The unpleasant bits are removed, the wishes are added. If you didn't do it, someone else would. Memory would. It's a service."

"Which part is that?" said Sandro, but Becker didn't answer. He was still standing there when Diora came in. She'd matured, she'd gained weight, and her twins, now six years old, were handsome and strong. Sandro's heart flew up in his breast. Perhaps she had made friends with Alicia – perhaps Diora had come to have her bridesmaid reinstated.

"The long nightmare is over," said Diora. "I've left him."

The boys were running from shelf to shelf lifting up the photographs with their glass frames and putting them down again. Sandro watched them with one eye. He knew what she was going to say.

"I want you to take him out of those pictures," she said.

"You'd look very foolish as a bride with no groom," he said severely.

"No, no, not those," she said. "I mean the kids' birthday shots."

They had been particularly fine, those shots, taken only two weeks ago, Tony tall and dark, Diora and the children radiant and blond.

"Be reasonable, Diora," he said. "I never liked him myself. But he balances the portrait. Besides, he was there."

"He was not there!" cried Diora. Her sons went on turning all the pictures to face the walls.

"He was never there. He was running around, in his heart he was not with me. I was alone with my children. I'll take another one." Said Sandro. "Of you and the boys. Whenever you like. This one stays like it is."

"We won't pay."

"But Diora," said Sandro, "everyone knows he's their father."

"They have no father," said Diora flatly.

"It's immaculate conception," said Becker gleefully.

But Diora did not hear. "It's our photograph, and we want him out. You do your job. The rest of it's none of your business." She put one hand on the back of the head of each of her twins and marched them out the door.

Sandro leaned on his counter idly flipping the pages of a wedding album. He had a vision of a great decorated room, with a cake on the table. Everyone had had his way, the husband had removed the wife, the wife the husband, the bridesmaid, her parents, and so forth. There was no one there.

"We make up our lives out of the people around us," he said to Becker. "When they don't live up to standard, we can't just wipe them out."

"Don't ask me," said Becker. "I just lit out for the streets. Couldn't live up to a damn thing." Then he too went out the door.

"Lucky bugger," said Sandro. Alone, he went to his darkroom. He opened his drawer of bits and pieces. His disappeared ones, the inconvenient people. His body parts, his halves of torsos, tips of shiny black shoes. Each face, each item of clothing punctured him a little. He looked at his negatives stored in drawers. They were scarred, pathetic things. I haven't the stomach for it, not any more, thought Sandro.

As he walked home, St. Clair Avenue seemed very fine. The best part was, he thought, there were no relationships. Neither this leaning drunk nor that window-shopper was so connected to any other as to endanger his, or her, existence. The tolerance of indifference, said Sandro to himself, trying to remember it so that he could tell Becker.

But Sandro felt ill at ease in his own home, by its very definition of a dangerous and unreliable setting. His wife was stirring something, with her lips tight together. His children, almost grown up now, bred secrets as they looked at television. He himself only posed in the doorway, looking for hidden seams and the faint hairlines of an airbrush.

That night he stood exhausted by his bed.

His wife lay on her side with one round shoulder above the sheet. Behind her on the wall was the photo he'd taken of their village before he left Italy. He ought to reshoot it, take out that gas station and clean up the square a little. His pillow had an indentation, as if a head had been erased. He slept in a chair.

In the morning he went down to the shop. He got his best camera and set up a tripod on the sidewalk directly across the street. He took several shots in the solid bright morning light. He locked the door and placed the CLOSED sign in the window. In the darkroom he developed the film, floating the negatives in the pungent fluid until the row of shop fronts came through clearly, the flat brick faces, the curving concrete trim, the two balls on the crowns. Deftly he dissolved each brick of his store, the window and the sign. Deftly he reattached each brick of the store on the west side to the bricks of the store to the east.

I have been many things in my life, thought Sandro, a presser of shutters, a confessor, a false prophet. Now I am a bricklayer, and a good one. He taped the negatives together and developed them. He touched up the join and then photographed it again. He developed this second negative and it was perfect. Number 1812, Lord's Shoes, joined directly to 1820, Bargain Jimmies: the Immaculate Conception Photography Gallery at 1816 no longer existed. Working quickly, because he wanted to finish before the day was over, he blew it up to two feet by three feet. He cleared out his window display of brides and babies and stood up this new photograph – one of the finest he'd ever taken, he thought. Then he took a couple of cameras and a bag with the tripod and some lenses. He turned out the light, pulling the door shut behind him, and began to walk west.

THE TOWER

GWENDOLYN MACEWEN

He kept walking. Nobody knew him; the high-heeled woman who strode back and forth across the city in purple suede boots, taking up the whole sidewalk, her whole being in pursuit of some lavish dream, didn't know him, the Greeks carrying around the unbearable burden of their own existence didn't know him, the woman known as the Swedish Queen who wore pink harem pants and outrageous jewellery and a gold ribbon that said SOCIALISM across her chest didn't know him; the Chinese and Jamaicans and Hungarians and Filipinos didn't know him; the bag ladies didn't know him; the troubled young woman who cut up playing cards and left the pieces on the pavement in front of churches and police stations in some sort of private ritual didn't know him. (One morning he picked up a part of the Three of Diamonds and spent an hour looking for the rest because perhaps she was trying to communicate with him by means of a secret code.)

He walked all over the city, talking to popcorn vendors from places like Lisbon and Gibraltar and Corinth, to newspaper boys and mailmen and street cleaners. He wore a light brown trench coat, and because he looked like such a gentleman and spoke so softly and politely when he asked people if they knew who he was, they often dismissed the idea that he might be mad and were almost sorry that, no, they didn't know him and never had. Finally it was clear to him that nobody knew him and why should they? The world was theirs - or was it? Were they also alone? Was this city somebody's rough diagram of reality, or was it pure mirage? He gazed at the Tower - tallest free-standing structure in the world - and it shimmered in the grey air, a monument to nothing, a space ship that would never have liftoff, a rocket without a launching pad.

They didn't know who they were, so they came and built these big cities in the wilderness. They still found it empty, so they stuck up this tower in the emptiness...

from ARIADNE

R. Murray Schafer

SCENE 4 (CANON CANCRIZANS)

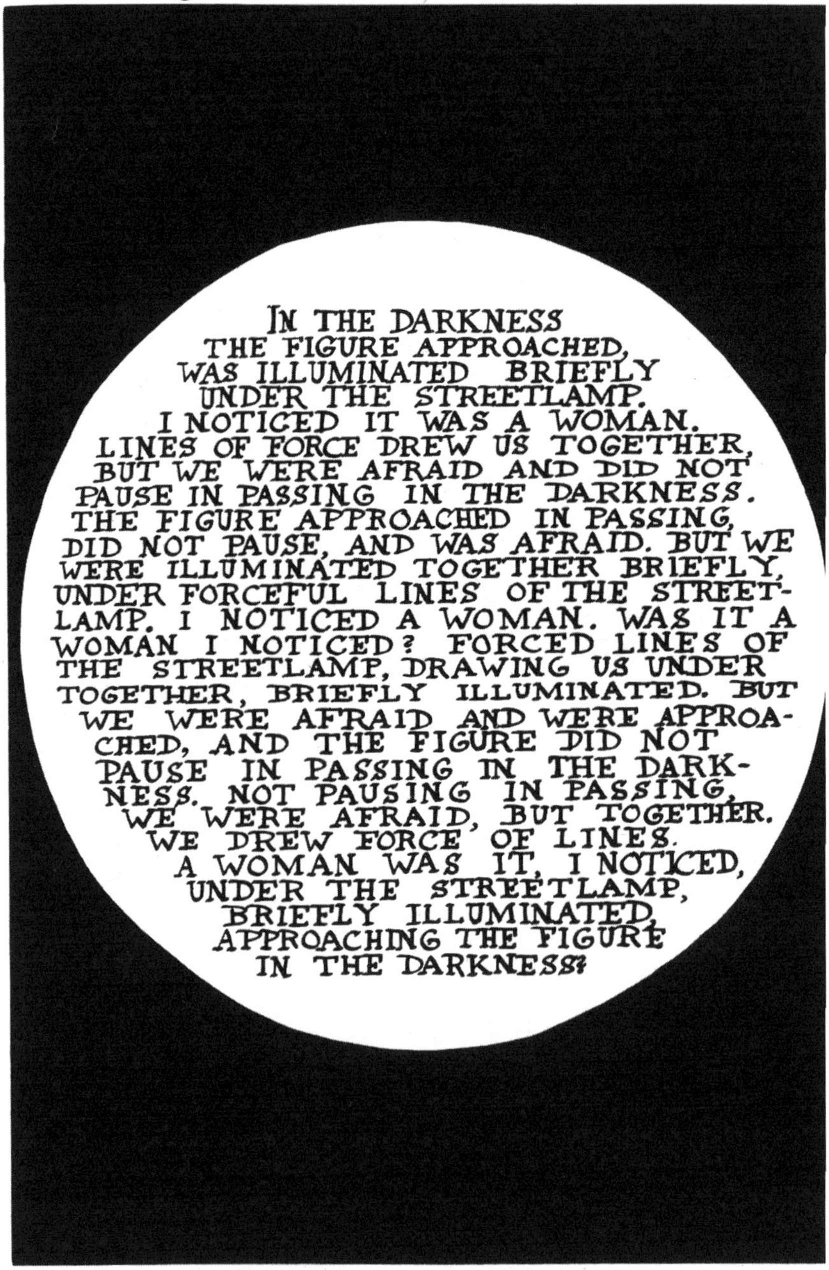

SCENE 6 (MEM)

SO WE SET OUT AND SAILED ACROSS THE OCEAN.

I ASKED HIM HIS NAME:

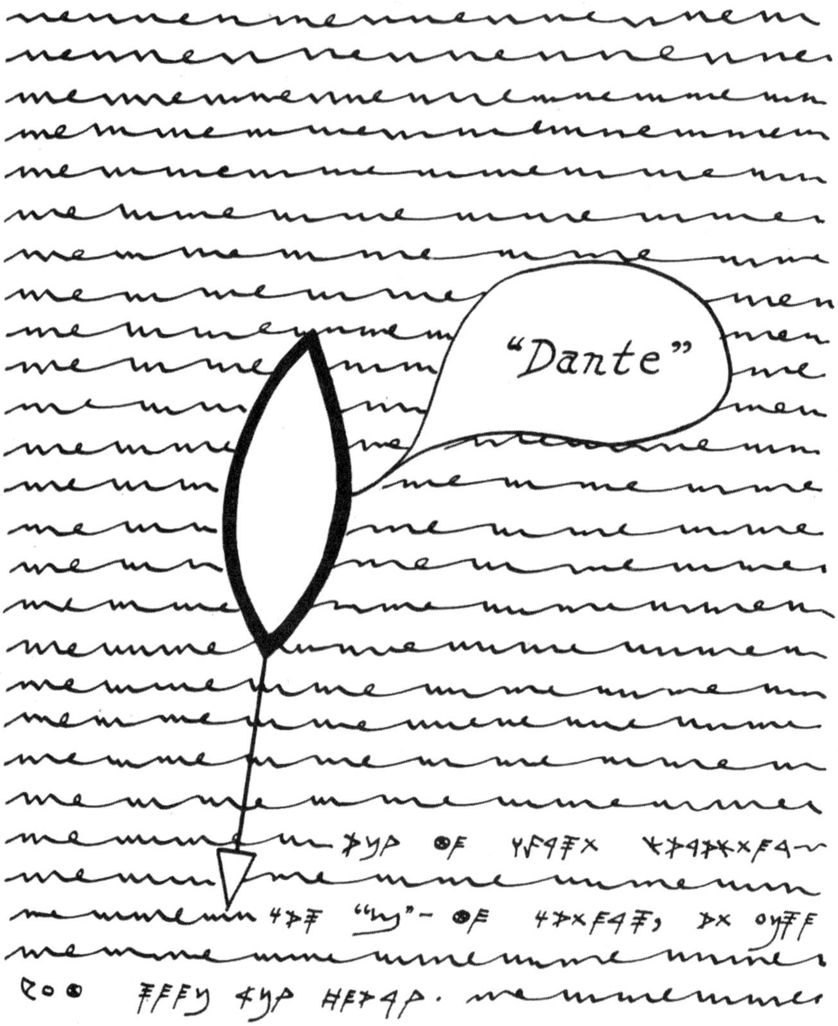

SCENE 9

AT ONCE I FOUND MYSELF IN ANOTHER WORLD, FOR I WAS IN WHAT APPEARED TO BE A CLUB OR DISCOTHEQUE. I STOOD IN THE FOYER.

TO MY RIGHT WAS A HAT-CHECK GIRL, WHO EVEN NOW WAS EXTENDING AN ARM TO TAKE MY CRUMPLED RAIN-COAT.

TO MY LEFT, THROUGH A WIDE ARCHWAY, I COULD SEE PEOPLE DANCING TO THE SOUNDS OF A JAZZ BAND. MANY OF THE DANCERS WERE MASKED.

I WAITED FOR A MOMENT UNTIL MY EYES GREW ACCUSTOMED TO THE LIGHT INSIDE THE CLUB, THEN I WENT IN AND TOOK A SEAT AT A TABLE NEAR THE DOORWAY.

HATS,
COATS,
UMBRELLAS,
VALISES.

Scene 10 (metathesis)

SCENE 12

SHE LAUGHED
AS WE PASSED OUT THE
DOOR INTO THE
COOL NIGHT AIR.

"DO YOU HAVE A NAME?"
I ASKED AFTER A WHILE.

JE T'AI DEMANDÉ TON NOM...
ᐱᐣᑊ/ ᑐᐯ ≡, SHE REPLIED.

T
S
T
H R
H
E
E A
D
I
E
T
T N
R
U
S
E
S
T
c
H I
o
N
T
E
N
E
M
H
S
E
T S
S
A
E
L E
V
V
T o
M
R
H
R
E
F
o

A E

N M

S T

H

E

T

E H

A

E

H

A

R

T I

V

S E

N

N

S

S THE U T S FORM

R I T E H

D E E

A N I

A L

S T V E N S T T

S V HER

E H O

N

H E

T R O E T

M

E C S NAME

U

S

T

F O R M

T

E E

I

D

L

T

O

T H E R

S

V

T

H

N

R

E

O E

M

S

E C N A M E

SHE WAS PURE MELODY:

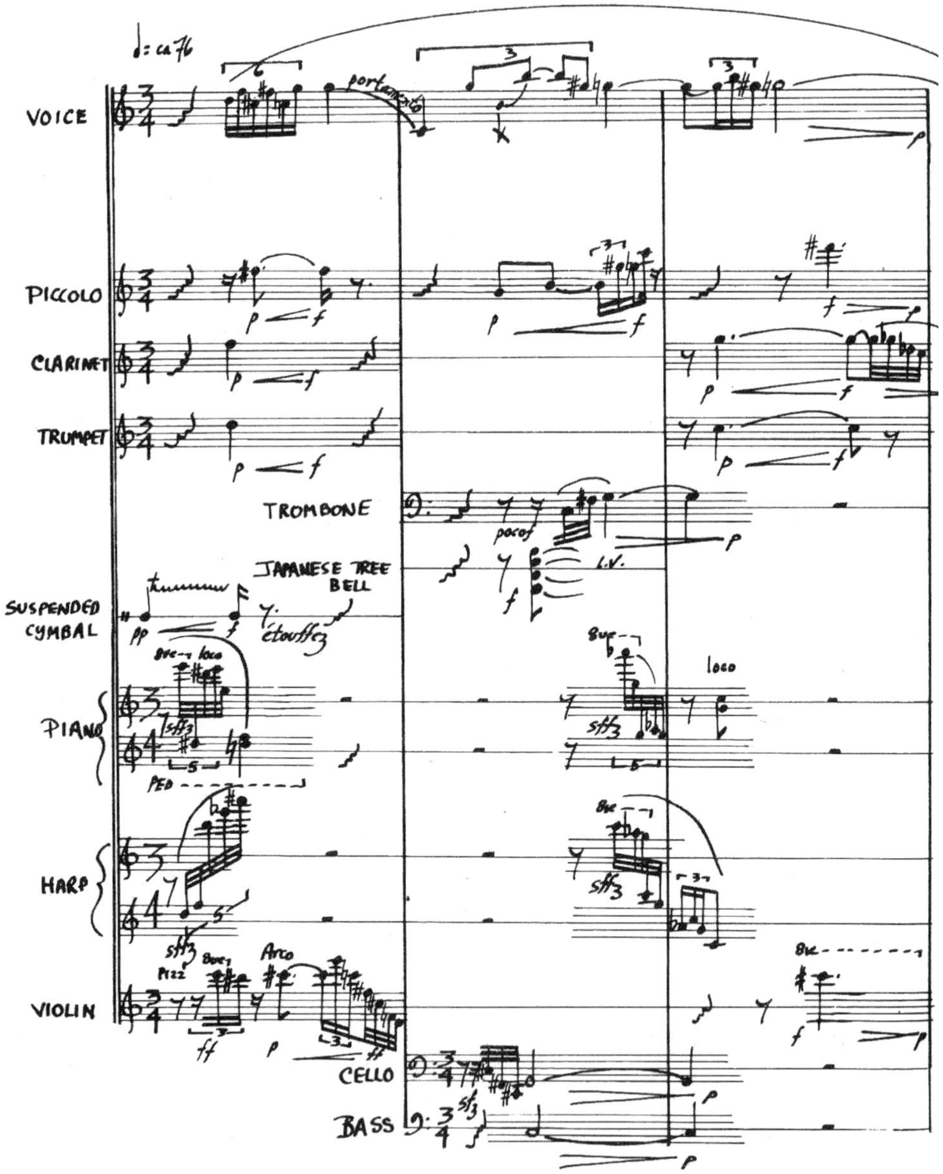

VOICE
PICCOLO
CLARINET
poco
GLOCKENSPIEL
8ve
PIANO
PED
loco
HARP
VIOLIN
poco
CELLO
BASS

One day we walked in a Persian Garden

THE GATE WAS ARCHED, AND OVER IT WERE VINES WITH CLUSTERS OF

GRAPES OF DIFFERENT COLOURS, THE RED LIKE RUBIES AND THE BLACK

SHE SMILED, AS IF TO SAY:

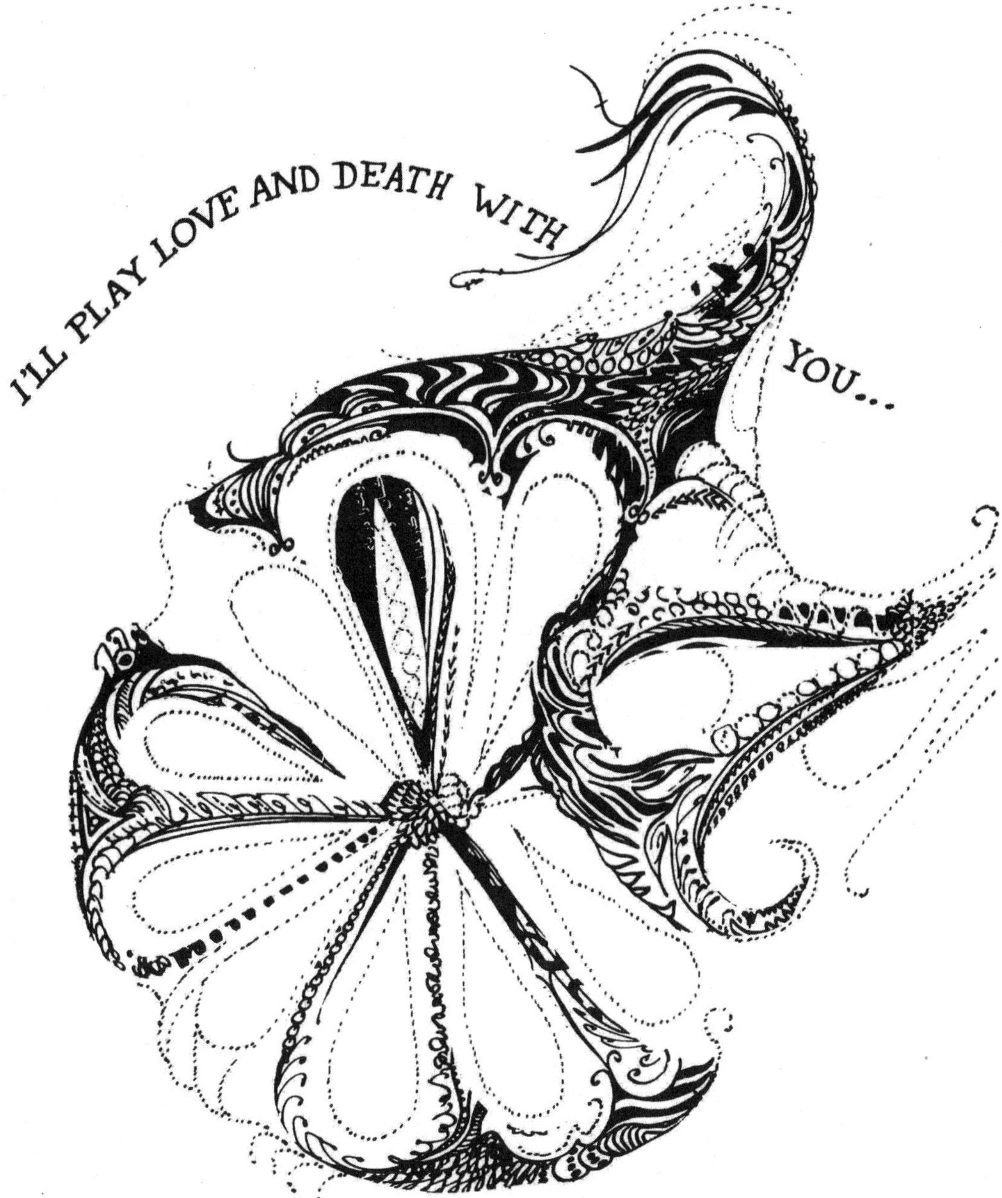
I'LL PLAY LOVE AND DEATH WITH
YOU...

SECOND LAST SCENE:

AUTUMN HAD COME. THE TREES WERE BARE, LIKE NEURONS: SCRAMBLED - STACHELDRAHT.

I RETURNED TO THE SHORE AND WAITED. THE WIND WAS COLD. THE SEA'S GREEN TOWERS HISSED ABOUT MY FEET.

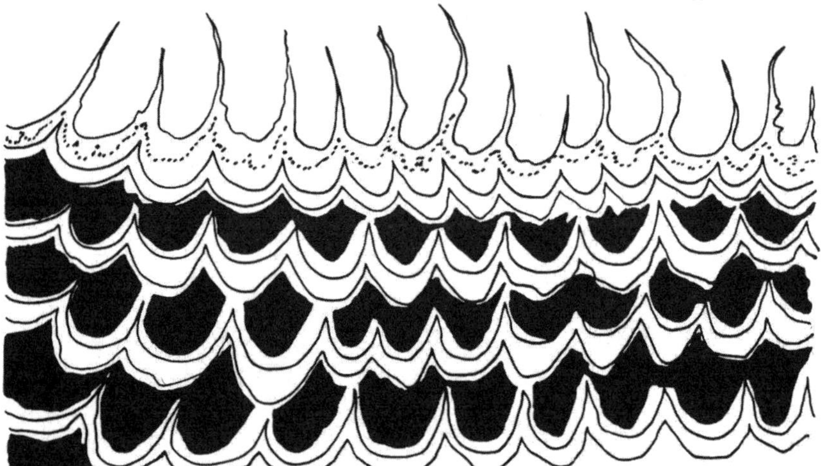

DANTE CAME FOR ME IN HIS BOAT.

LAST SCENE:

WHEN DANTE PUT ME ASHORE, I COULD SEE THE DARK OUTLINE OF THE CITY IN THE DISTANCE.

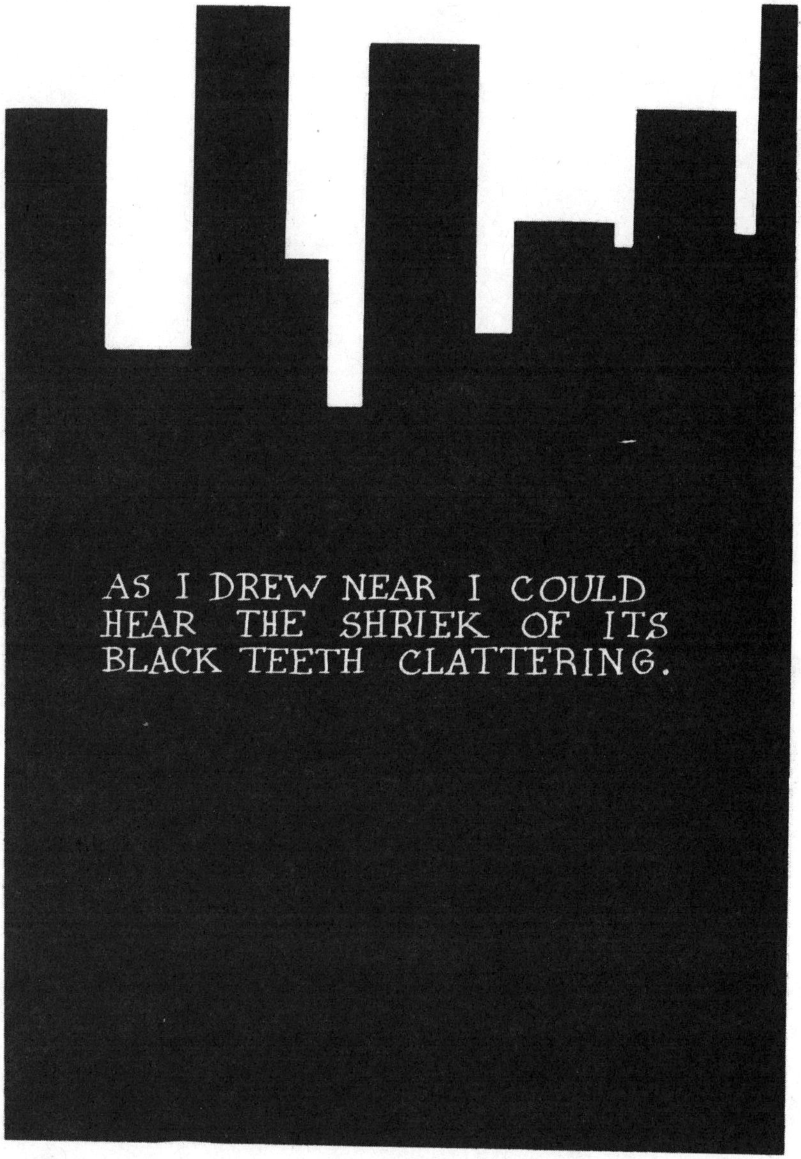
AS I DREW NEAR I COULD
HEAR THE SHRIEK OF ITS
BLACK TEETH CLATTERING.

GRADUALLY IT BLOTTED OUT
THE SKY

PAINTED TONGUE

JOSEPH BOYDEN

Painted Tongue cocked his ear to a loon calling from the lake, and it was like a dream, the sound dancing across the big water, the water pulling the sun into it. He laughed to himself.

I must not talk like Grandfather. Repeat one hundred times. I drink, therefore I am. Repeat. Write it one hundred times on the blackboard, then sit in the corner facing away from the class.

He laughed to himself again, then took a swig from his mickey of vodka. There was nothing left, so he sucked on the brown bag that held the bottle. He rocked on his boulder and sucked on the bag and hummed a song that his mother used to sing to him at Cedar Point.

Gnooshenyig go tobogganing. Your grandchildren go tobogganing. *Nooshenyig* go tobogganing. My grandchildren go tobogganing.

The words knotted around themselves before they left his tongue, so he flattened the letters with his damaged mouth and turned them into a hum that increased in tone until the sound echoed back across the water towards the loon. Painted Tongue hummed louder to remember his mother's song until the story in the song came back to him, the story of children sledding and falling through the weak ice of a river, the song of warning to children who acted foolishly with friends who didn't listen to the warnings of their mothers. He was drunk. He had a righteous buzz and wanted a drink. He wanted a drink so bad it made him shake, but the humming helped stop the shakes for a little while at least.

The boulder that he sat on was his boulder.

Let someone try to take it away, goddammit. I will cut your throat from ear to ear and count coup upon you, motherfucker.

This was his boulder on the lake, removed from the confusion of downtown, the rock heavy and squat and thick with a little natural chair cut into it at such an angle that he didn't have to see the ugliness of people, just the water and the sun dancing upon the water. This was Painted Tongue's rock, and he'd defended his turf against stinking hobo invaders. He'd counted many coups against them with rocks and broken bottles and his fists, and now this was his rock. Painted Tongue stopped his humming as a jogger in very white sneakers ran by behind him along the railroad tracks, the jogger turning his head away from this man who defended his rock, this man with long straight black hair and the crooked nose of a warrior.

You are a coward! Painted Tongue wanted to shout. The way you turn your eyes from me as you cross my rock. Don't run near here any more.

When the man had run away, Painted Tongue cocked his ear again, this time to the clang and chug of a train leaving the train yard far to his left. The 5:30 p.m. GO Train express to Oshawa. A warrior didn't need a clock to tell him what time it was. All he needed was to listen and watch the things around him.

When the sun was gone he would make his way back downtown to hustle change with his cup. His bottle was long empty and his lips were dry, and soon it would be time for dry lips to move downtown. Everything travelled in a circle. The sun, the moon, joggers, the world. Today already Painted Tongue had been hustling change at the corner of Dundas Street and Bay. He'd made enough by mid-afternoon to buy the mickey of vodka. He'd walked down Bay and underneath the moan and echo of the expressway, across the train tracks and to the crown of his boulder, far enough away from the electricity and noise of downtown, to where he could imagine for a time that he was back at home, back in the bush. And very soon he'd do his route again. Life hadn't always been this way, but memories of the rez dropped as fast as the sinking sun.

Oh, my brothers and sisters, Painted Tongue hummed to himself. The old ways die in the face of the new. They have taken our land, broken every promise, raised the price on a pint of booze and a case of beer, made it near impossible to afford a pack of smokes. Repeat one hundred times. Write it out on the blackboard five hundred times, then sit in the corner facing away from the class and throw up between your legs.

The lake had nearly swallowed the sun now. Maybe tonight Painted Tongue would finally find Kyle Root. Kyle was the only friend he had from Cedar Point who'd made it to the city and stayed. And besides, Kyle owed him money. Kyle was a painter, an artist who could afford anything he wanted now and who lived in a loft in the warehouse district with pretty white women and pine furniture and a kitchen made of steel. Kyle wore suit jackets with his jeans, his hair combed back and neat in a ponytail held by a silver Haida thunderbird. He'd first made it big with a series of portraits of Painted Tongue: Painted Tongue standing in a field with his bow raised to the sun, Painted Tongue leaping from a tall building and transforming into an eagle, Painted Tongue surfing a river with arms outstretched on the bow tip of a fancy canoe. Kyle was his best friend. He and Kyle used to run through summer back at the Point when they were five and six and seven, always with no shirts on, swinging lacrosse sticks and whipping pebbles at each other. They'd had a game. They'd sneak up on stray reservation dogs and smack the dogs' asses hard as they could with their lacrosse sticks. The winner was the one whose dog howled loudest. They'd always argued about which dog was uglier. Kyle used to read to Painted Tongue about their cousins, in the Sioux, how they counted coup on their enemies, how they got close enough to touch them in battle. To count coup on one's enemy made the warrior a great man. Painted Tongue's stomach suddenly cramped hard, making him shiver with a closed mouth. It was time to make the circle.

He stood up slowly on the dome of his rock, humming a song to the departing sun, and got bad headspins. He stumbled and fell head-first, imagining for a moment that he was flying until the bright pain of his nose crunching on smaller rocks made him think he was swimming deep, deep under water.

Painted Tongue awoke in the hospital, surrounded by bright lights and men in green doctor's pants and nurses in white. He tried to leave quietly, but they wouldn't let him. He grew angry and hummed his war song whenever a doctor or nurse approached his cot. I will count coup upon you, skinny brown doctor man, he hummed. I am not even afraid to wrestle your fat white nurse who calls me heathen. Painted Tongue still had a righteous buzz and the pills they gave him made it roar. He hummed louder and louder, increasing the burn of the new stitches on his nose that they had given him while he was unconscious.

You can do the paperwork if you want to call the mental ward, Painted Tongue heard one doctor say to the other as he hummed and rocked on his bed and stared them down. As he was about to leave again, a doctor who was older than the others appeared from the hall, asking, What's the problem in here?

He sat on the end of Painted Tongue's bed and spoke. He was the first man in a long time who didn't speak down to him, but spoke, without staring into Painted Tongue's eyes, directly to him. You're lucky a jogger found you and called the police, the doctor said. He was white but his nose looked very much like Painted Tongue's normally did. Have you considered leaving the city and going back to your home? Why don't you stay at the Harvest House on King Street if you don't want to go home? Painted Tongue listened politely. You get drunk and hurt yourself again, and I'll make sure you get institutionalized, the doctor said before letting Painted Tongue go. He knew the doctor meant it.

All last spring, summer and winter and again into this spring, Painted Tongue had held onto the chain-link fence and watched the construction workers swarming inside a big pit below him near the waterfront. He'd hum, There are four or five good workers among you. The rest are lazy shits who don't know how to work the foremen, and the foremen don't know how to work a crew. He hummed this until the hum had become a song that he'd moan every day as the construction in the pit reached street level then grew higher with the seasons. Now the building was almost finished.

He'd watched these men from the very beginning, these sunburnt, windburnt workies straying too close to his turf by the railway tracks, these men gouging a huge empty lot until it was a pit, then framing and pouring concrete all last summer, creating a foundation or something too big, it seemed, for the earth's back to bear. Almost every day for this whole last year, Painted Tongue had taken his walk around the site's perimeter, along the sidewalk that circled it like a huge track, stepping slowly so that a footfall was timed to hit the sidewalk every two seconds. I am a well-tuned clock, Painted Tongue hummed. Left foot, stop, one-two. Right foot, stop, one-two. He'd take a long and measured stride, stop and count, then stride again, stop and count. He walked slowly, exactly, to measure the distance around the site. He walked this way to try to slow down the people rushing all around him. Everybody always seemed in a hurry. Every day he walked the same route in his manner, the crowds on the sidewalk parting like a river around a boat's hull. He ignored the odd looks and laughing and catcalls of Whiskey Joe or crazy drunk or fruitcake. The people in this city were not capable of understanding.

It took Painted Tongue ninety minutes to walk the site's perimeter. He'd never witnessed so big a job, so huge a building being born from men and cement mixers and steel girders and cranes. Every day over the last few seasons the walls of the building had grown higher, as if they were being pulled by magic from the tired skin of the earth. Painted Tongue liked to stop after his walk and watch the men work; he recognized the good ones from the lazy at a distance. He was keeper of the secret of their daily progress. Now they were almost finished. The good and the lazy were almost finished.

Today Painted Tongue stood in his usual place at the site, the start and end of his daily walk around the construction, his hands above his head and holding onto the chain-link fence. His nose throbbed from last night's fall. He brought one hand down to his nose as he stared up at the workies scrambling around on the building, the workies straining and shouting and jackhammering the last of the domed roof into place. A large white bandage over Painted Tongue's nose concealed the zigzag of six stitches running the bridge. The pain pills had made him feel almost weightless, like a crow's wing, but now they were all gone. Last night's fall had been a good thing, he thought. It had loosened up some memories in his head.

That this huge building was round as a medicine wheel was no surprise to him. Nothing in the world existed without a reason. He stared up at the white dome roof, curved like an egg, curved like something he could still not quite figure. The big sign on the other side said in blue letters as tall as a person that this was a stadium, a dome for me to play in and for spectators to cheer. For the last two months Painted Tongue had felt an ugly fear, a wolf spider, creeping up his back. All fear made no sense, and this was no different. Painted Tongue was afraid of the day the men would finish construction, of the day they would pack up their tools and leave this new thing completed. Maybe it was the falling and the pills that were now helping him to recognize just what it was the men were building. His gut tightened in awe and fear.

Painted Tongue began his slow, long strides around the structure. His nose throbbed with each step. The pills were all gone. He glanced over to the site once in a while, then looked back quickly to the ground in front of him, trying to capture the essence of this stadium in the corner of his eye. His mother had once taught him a little trick. If you are trying to remember something, she said, and it is on the tip of your tongue, do not try to force the memory out, for very little good comes from force. Think of other things. Forget what you are trying to remember, and that memory will soon get lonely and come back to you.

Painted Tongue reached the first big curve and again peered quickly towards the dome. Nothing. He went back to the day he'd made a little boy, a small blond boy, cry. It was downtown near the entrance to First Canadian Place where Painted Tongue often sat on a piece of cardboard collecting change. He watched the boy walk along the crowded sidewalk towards him, clutching his pretty mother's hand. The boy stared at Painted Tongue, at his face and then at his paper cup containing a few coins. As they got nearer, the boy pulled on his mom's arm, trying to get her attention, trying to get her to look at the Indian crouching on the sidewalk surrounded by all the white men in business suits and the ladies who wore pretty dresses with sneakers. Painted Tongue spent his life watching. He knew from the boy's eyes all these thoughts he was thinking. The mother ignored the child's tugs.

As the two passed, the little boy held his nose. Painted Tongue screwed up his face and pursed his lips in an "O," then blew hard through his mouth. He made his face mimic the Iroquois mask, the Wind Spirit, he'd once seen at the Native Canadian Centre at Spadina and Bloor. The boy's eyes widened at the sight of the man with long black hair and a warrior's crooked nose and pockmarked skin. The boy wailed in fear and Painted Tongue felt the surge along his spine. The mix of sadness and victory made him want a gulp of vodka.

He saw his own eyes in the boy's. When Painted Tongue had been one year old he'd gotten thrush. He wouldn't stop crying. He remembered even now with his pill-fuzzy head as he walked his slow walk around the site, his mother holding him, whispering, *Gdaakwos na? Kaagiijtooge na?* Are you sick? Do you have an earache? And finally, quietly angry, *Aabiish ogaabinjibayin?* Where do you come from?

His mother told him stories later of bringing him to the reservation doctor who gave him a needle, then to the band's old medicine woman who told his mother to take him into the sweat lodge and hold him tight against her bare chest.

It wasn't until his tongue turned white that anyone figured out why he was sick. He got better and received his nickname.

Although the thrush had nothing to do with it, Painted Tongue remembered developing a lisp when he first learned to talk. The children teased him so much that he began talking less and less. By the time he left Cedar Point at eighteen, he didn't talk at all. His mother said he'd forgotten how. She was the only one who still called him by his birth name. Now, eight years later he still couldn't talk, and everyone who knew of him assumed he was dumb. Painted Tongue liked it that way.

As he neared the end of his slow walk, Painted Tongue began to grow angry that he had no booze and no money, and that whatever this goddamn building was would not show itself to him. I will blow you up, motherfucker stadium, with a thousand kilos of dynamite, he hummed. I will count coup on you, ugly concrete piece of shit. Why would anyone construct a building with a hotel and restaurants and stores and a baseball field in it? If a man desired, he could go inside and never have to come out again. It was crazy. This was a crazy fucking world.

At least the stadium was the same size. Painted Tongue walked up slowly to where he'd started his walk, staring down an ugly woman in tight shorts until she backed away from his place along the fence, the one that offered the best view of the stadium. Back off ugly woman from this warrior on pills, he hummed. I have no booze and I am not afraid to kick a woman's ass in such a state. At least the pills gave him an appetite. He couldn't remember the last time he'd eaten. A hot dog would be good about now. Cree Agnes from Penetanguishene would give him a hot dog. She was a good woman. And she knew Kyle. Kyle was a friend, and Kyle would have some money that he rightfully owed. But Painted Tongue needed to think of polite ways to ask him for it. Walking up Sherbourne, he thought of polite ways to ask for what was owed him. A hot dog would taste good about now, he hummed to himself.

It had been many weeks since he'd seen Kyle. Kyle had given up looking for Painted Tongue to take him out for a meal or coffee or drink a long time ago. Kyle had walked far from working construction with Painted Tongue, the first job the two had found years before when they'd driven together in the old Dodge war pony from Cedar Point to Toronto. Work was easy to find back then. Painted Tongue was as good as any goddamn man with a hammer and a level. He was never afraid to do roofing or construction way up high on a building, either. Balance and bravery were in his blood.

But Kyle had hated construction work from the beginning. It callused his fingers and left his hands too sore at night to hold a paintbrush. Most lunch breaks he'd go to whatever tavern was closest to drink beer and talk to Painted Tongue. Painted Tongue remembered those days with good feelings. Those afternoons when he first started drinking were warmer with a belly full of beer, his eyes focused only on the nails to be pounded or joists to be cut and fit or the shingles to be pulled and replaced. He and Kyle had been thrown off many jobs for being drunk, but there had always been more jobs waiting.

Then Kyle got a fancy job in a gallery selling others' art and, after a while, his own. Now he was a Big Chief in the city, and he'd given up the booze. Painted Tongue was left to find his own jobs, and the jobs got harder to find. Not many foremen wanted to hire a man who didn't talk. Kyle moved in with a pretty gallery woman, and Painted Tongue, after some decision-making, left walls and a roof on the first warm spring day two years ago to live more simply. He enjoyed living like the grandfathers, his days spent searching out food and drink, protecting himself from enemies and sitting quietly, listening to his few friends talk to him on park benches, or lying in the grass still left between the concrete buildings. He waited in winter until the heating grates of apartment buildings couldn't keep him warm any more to search out a bed in the hostels or, if he was lucky, a reinforced cardboard box and blankets in a quiet thicket of pine in High Park. A warrior walked the earth on strong legs or else he perished. Kyle knew that too. Although he'd taken a different path, Painted Tongue was sure Kyle respected him highly for his abilities as a warrior on the streets. Kyle knew what others couldn't see. Painted Tongue had found the circle to walk, and along the route of that circle he found everything he needed to live.

When Painted Tongue arrived at the Native Centre, Agnes was busy with customers, so he wandered the gallery and admired the paintings and wood carvings and jewellery. He stopped suddenly at a large painting of a turtle, each section of its curved shell coloured green or red or black. Its nose was hooked. Small squiggled people and pine trees grew from its back. The artist had titled the painting "Earth Mother Turtle." Painted Tongue recognized Kyle's signature, curved and sharp like a knife on the bottom right-hand side. Agnes stayed busy with the customers for a long time, so Painted Tongue went outside to hunt for food.

Four nights later, Painted Tongue sat by a small grove of trees and a pond in High Park. He stared up at the stars and the three-quarter, late-spring moon that shone through the city's lights. Ducks by the pond honked out warnings whenever a raccoon or cat, or some bigger, shadowed animal that he guessed was a dog or fox, prowled close to the small flocks huddled by the water's edge with their beaks buried in their wing feathers. As soon as the ducks settled down and grew quiet, the same or some other predator would make a leap from nearby bushes and send the flocks quacking and hissing, beating wings to the safety of the middle of the pond. It made Painted Tongue so nervous that he wrapped his arms around his chest and moaned out loud.

He heard the sudden, angry shouts of a small group of people through the trees by a hill to his left. He guessed they were about fifty metres away. He could see a good deal in the moon's light, but the men shouting were somewhere in the shadows of the trees. Their voices were sharp and mean, three of them, maybe four. Then some other man screamed, Leave me alone! In his fear he almost sounded like a woman. Painted Tongue got up on his haunches, rocking slowly and humming quietly, Where are the police? They sleep in their cruisers while men are beaten in High Park.

They were hitting the man with the high voice. Painted Tongue held himself tighter. The man was wailing now, and his pain filtered through the trees with the thud of boots and open hands on flesh followed by screams. Painted Tongue searched hard for his warrior song but it wouldn't come. This man needs help, he hummed. They are hurting him bad.

This was an empty part of the huge park. There was no one around but Painted Tongue and the men hidden in the trees. He could hear the honks of cars far off on Lakeshore Boulevard hundreds of metres over one hill and another. Finally it got quiet again. After a little silence, Painted Tongue stood in a crouch. He wanted to look in the trees. The voices erupted again.

Motherfuckers! The wounded man screamed.

He's running. Grab the bitch!

A naked man came dashing from the trees towards Painted Tongue with three men close behind him. He was streaked red in the moonlight and ran hard, but with a limp. Painted Tongue dropped quickly into the shadow of a bush without the man's seeing him and held himself rigid as the other men swooped by.

They quickly caught up to the wounded one and tackled him. They took turns kicking his head and groin and stomach with their boots. Two had shaved heads and the other wore his hair long like Painted Tongue. They chanted, Dirty faggot, cocksucking faggot, through their clenched teeth. Painted Tongue tried again, but his warrior song would not come. The long-haired one pulled out a knife.

Don't. Please don't, the man on the ground said, curled up and holding himself. He was close enough to Painted Tongue that Painted Tongue could taste the copper tang of fear in his own mouth. The long-haired one dropped down on his knees with both hands held above his head.

Do it, one of the standing men hissed.

Stick him. Fuck him, the other said.

Die, bitch, the long-hair said after a few seconds, then swung down hard. The bleeding man howled. Painted Tongue shivered as the three men ran into the darkness.

Painted Tongue stood up after a long while. He slowly walked up to the body on the ground, bent over him and peered down. The man blinked at Painted Tongue and Painted Tongue jumped back quickly. The man's chest was gurgling and his lips opened just a little. Then his chest stopped moving. Painted Tongue's legs told him to run away as fast as he could, but instead he hummed a death chant for the man slowly and quietly. Your last moments were spent in fear, he hummed, but now you are peaceful and sink into the waters of sleep. Your last moments were spent in fear and I could not help you, but now all is peaceful as you slip into sleep.

Painted Tongue thought he could see his own face for a second, reflected in the man's open eyes, but knew that wasn't possible. He realized as he ran back towards downtown that the man's last sight had been of an Indian standing over him and humming, looking down like a death angel, an Indian with a hook nose and black hair almost long enough that it tickled the man's face.

Two hours later, Painted Tongue made his way into a bar at Queen Street and Richmond and took a seat in one of the dark corners. He couldn't sit quietly, so he got up and went into the bathroom and washed his hands and face, then went back to his chair. He wanted a drink. He wanted to get fucked-up drunk. He'd seen two other men die in two years on the street, but both had been old rubbies whose bodies just gave up and quit on them. Those two had prayed every day for death to come and take them. This was different. There was no honour or peace in this man's death. Painted Tongue sat in his chair, rocking, and hummed, Bad trouble, there is bad trouble and I've seen it. He hummed it over and over again. Repeat one hundred times. Write it on the blackboard one thousand times. The old men and younger boys and girls who were crowded around the bar ignored Painted Tongue. They did not understand. When one of them got up to use the washroom, Painted Tongue weighed the odds of being able to grab her unattended drink. He went silent and watched until the people around him forgot he was there. He spotted a full bottle of Labatt's 50 on a table near him and, when nobody was looking, he grabbed it and drank it down in two gulps.

That's it, that's all, rubby, a big man said, grabbing Painted Tongue by the back of the neck and dragging him out the door. He heard people laughing as the big man gave him a final push, Painted Tongue's elbow whacking hard against the door frame. I will cut your throat a wide smile with a bottle neck, Painted Tongue moaned as he made his way down the sidewalk. I will count coup on you, smelly bouncer, and take your woman for my own. I will teach your children that you are worthless shit.

He walked to Kensington Market cradling his bruised elbow and found an alley that didn't stink so badly of fish. No one bothered you in the alleys here where crates of rotting meat and vegetables were left out for the garbagemen to pick up late at night. Painted tongue held his hurt elbow as he sat in the alley and thought hard. Other than the beer, he hadn't had a drink since morning. His body shook and shivered. He wanted a gulp of vodka to take the copper taste out of his mouth. To calm himself he thought about when he was a child and he would sit with his mother on the rock jetty facing Christian Island. She liked to tell him stories of his father and the Ojibwa.

He hummed himself the story of his father, and his mother's words came pouring back in the alley. His father had been hired with other men at the Cedar Point rez to build bridges in the bay, roads running up into the sky that linked the big islands to the mainland. The government thought that Indians had good balance high up in the air above the water, so building bridges was fine work for them. And the Indians were good at their job, Painted Tongue's mother told Painted Tongue as they sat on the jetty facing Christian Island and its lighthouse. The Indians scampered around on thin beams way up in the sky and the men didn't use safety lines because safety lines were for women. At Manitoulin Island Painted Tongue's father fell from a bridge and drowned when a big wind blew up off the bay. The Iroquois wind spirit – the blowing spirit – did it, Painted Tongue's mother told him, because the Iroquois and Ojibwa were old enemies. The Ojibwa made friends with the Jesuits long ago, and the Iroquois tortured and killed the black robes because they considered the black robes devils. But trouble between the two tribes had always been, from the time the earth was born.

That night he tried hard in the alley to remember his mother's story of how the earth came to be. He recalled her saying that before there was such a thing as land, a giant turtle rose up out of the water. Eventually, rocks and trees and animals and finally *Nmishoomsag*, the Grandfathers, sprouted from the turtle's back. Painted Tongue remembers the look in his mother's eyes, her stare out towards Christian Island. She believed the stories she told, and this made Painted Tongue want to believe them too.

It was the middle of the night now, and it would be impossible to find Kyle. But Kyle always knew what was going on. He always had the right answers. Even though he walked a different circle than Painted Tongue did, they'd both had the vision of the turtle. Kyle's was in paint and Painted Tongue's was in concrete. Although Painted Tongue hadn't talked in years, hadn't actually spoken in words for many years, he felt he wanted to talk again. He wanted to tell Kyle about the man getting killed in front of his eyes. He wanted to tell Kyle about the huge building growing out of the ground, the way it resembled a giant turtle with its roof nearly in lace. Strange things were happening all around Painted Tongue, and they were frightening. All of these events were omens warning him that something big and awful was coming. A new turtle had risen on the waterfront, a new world had been born in front of his own eyes over the last year, and Painted Tongue needed to know its significance. Big men were hurting smaller ones; three killed one and another had smashed Painted Tongue's elbow. He needed Kyle to sit down with him and talk it out. He needed a drink bad.

He felt calmer just before the morning broke. He walked from the alley and began the trek to the lake and his boulder, walking quickly and quietly underneath the expressway. There were men who lived in cardboard boxes and old refrigerators there, men who didn't want others like them in their territory. They stashed bricks and pipes and sharp shards from bottles. They'd chased Painted Tongue many times before, whooping and hollering, shouting, Cut up the wagon-burner.

Painted Tongue made it safely to the water and shimmied up his boulder, then turned east to watch the rising sun. Just as the sun's rays crawled then shot over the grain elevators and shipyards, dense, low clouds scuttled up on the horizon from the lake. It wouldn't be much of a sunrise today. He loved feeling the sun's warmth crawling across the water and rocks, the heat settling on his face. He lay back with his arms outstretched, let his hair fall down to the boulder's side, shivered in the dawn, then curled up to sleep for a few hours.

His stomach woke him. This day is the colour of a pigeon, he hummed, and the forecast calls for pigeon shit. His stomach was empty and burning and made him feel sick. He crawled from the boulder, dropped his pants and squatted. The evil poured from him in a stinking rush.

He was hungry and he needed food in his belly. Then he could hustle change and get a mickey in the afternoon. He walked slowly up to Spadina and Bloor, stopping occasionally to catch his breath. He'd considered walking his circle around the stadium. It would give him a chance to sort out the troubles of last night, maybe offer him a clear direction to take, but now saw that the construction workers had put up a large fence on the lake side of the stadium. They were already busy levelling the ground for parking spaces.

It wasn't a good thing to go without a drink for long. His luck had been bad lately. He wanted the man who'd been killed in front of him last night to have disappeared like a bad dream this morning. All of this was bad. No more walks around the construction. They'd broken his circle. No good could come from it.

When he walked into the hallway of the Native Centre, he saw Agnes sitting in a chair reading a newspaper. He recognized the man's face taking up most of the front page. Above the picture the words "Hate Crime" were written.

Aneen Anishnabe, she spoke, looking up to him. Hello, Indian. *Aanish ezhwebiziiyan*? What is the matter with you? You've hurt your nose. Painted Tongue leaned on the wall. You look sick, she continued. You need food. I'll get you a hot dog.

They walked to a cart on Bloor, then cut up a side street to a little park. Agnes spoke to Painted Tongue slowly between bites of her food. He kept trying to sneak glimpses at her newspaper, but she'd folded it and left it sitting on the bench beside her. Your old friend Kyle is doing good, she said. The McMichael gallery has been asking about him. He's got another girlfriend again, and they moved to the Beach together.

Painted Tongue noticed that Agnes didn't say anything about Kyle asking after him. The smell of the cooked meat made his stomach feel worse.

The government's starting some new work programs up north, Agnes continued. It isn't my business, but maybe you should go back to Cedar Point for a while. You can rest there, maybe find some work.

Painted Tongue nodded his head slowly to be polite. Agnes stopped talking for a long while. Finally, she said, You can come over to my place and clean yourself up. I'll do some laundry for you. You can have a hot shower. Painted Tongue nodded a thank you. Again she went silent and they listened to squirrels and the traffic on Bloor.

When it was time for Agnes to head back to work, she gave Painted Tongue ten dollars. He knew that she knew he'd buy booze with the money, and her eyes told him she didn't like it but was doing it anyway. He held onto her newspaper as she was leaving. Agnes looked down to him, then handed it over.

Painted Tongue sat by himself and read the words. The man was a jogger. He was a lawyer. He was a gay. The newspaper was calling it a hate crime, a crime against a minority. Painted tongue hated when people called him a minority. It made him feel small. The police were looking for leads and witnesses. He wanted to leave the bench now. He wanted to go find a field to lie in and watch the clouds. He wanted to find Kyle and take him to a field away from the noise and traffic and all the people living. He'd seen the minority murdered. His circle had been broken. Painted Tongue would find Kyle and surprise him by talking to him.

Painted Tongue walked to the liquor store with his back a little straighter. I will get a bottle and pray for the spirit in that bottle to release itself and talk to me, he hummed. The best spirits are in vodka because vodka is distilled from potatoes and potatoes are the fruit of the earth and live under the ground with other spirits of the earth, he hummed, walking into the liquor store. But the man at the counter wouldn't let him come inside, so Painted Tongue had to give him his money first and point to the row of shiny vodka bottles. The man handed him a bottle in a bag along with the change, and Painted Tongue left for the Beach in search of Kyle Root.

A small crowd had gathered on Queen Street near the Beach. Painted Tongue watched from a distance as a man on a box in a shabby black suit screamed at the people gathered around him. The Lord told me last night, the man shouted, looking at the crowd with fiery eyes, that there is no place in sweet heaven for those of you who sin. There is no room in the sky for those of you who gamble, who drink, who find false love in a married woman's arms. The Lord will purge the wicked from the earth. He will cast out the cheaters, the homosexuals, the unbelievers. He spoke to me in a dream last night, and told me to pass the word.

Painted Tongue left the crowd quickly. He'd heard those words before. Now the man in the black suit had forced him to remember.

A new world is coming, boys, Mr. Grainger, the white teacher, used to shout out the window of the rez school when he caught Painted Tongue and Kyle behaving badly during recess, chasing girls with garter snakes or taking the air out of their enemies' bicycle tires. A new world is coming, and this one will erupt in flames. There is no room for your heathen beliefs in God's heaven, boys! he'd shout louder from his window, his face red and shaking when Painted Tongue and Kyle laughed at him. The innocent will perish because of the wicked, and the wicked will gnash their teeth in hellfire. Hellfire will burn your heathen ways from your bodies and minds! Think about that next time you act heinously against Janine or Tom. The Lord is watching!

Kyle would talk to Painted Tongue about the cuckoo teacher after school. Even the students he gave "A's" to thought he was mad. Even though they agreed the teacher was a crazy old bastard while they sat out at the dock puffing cigarettes stolen from their parents, Crazy Old Grainger still scared Painted Tongue horribly, the way his face turned red and shook when he screamed about burning death, the spittle flying from his mouth. Kyle thought it was good that Grainger always separated him and Painted Tongue from the rest to scream at, but Painted Tongue, in some small way, started believing that he was worse than the rest. Sometimes even now he'd wake up sweating, the ghost of Grainger's face come to remind him of the Second Coming of the Lord.

Kyle was nowhere to be found. Painted Tongue walked west on Bloor with the setting sun, stopping in doorways of shops to take a swig of vodka. The nothing smell calmed his stomach, gave him courage enough to wander along Bloor. He could tell by the crowds that it was Friday night, the streets busy with students finished with school and people who liked nights late in the spring. Painted Tongue walked by the bars and stores with his mickey snug in his belt. There were a few good gulps left. He'd make it through midnight when people were everywhere and at ease with their spare change.

I will count coup on this man-made turtle, Painted Tongue hummed as he walked. I will count coup on the god with the white beard who wants me to burn in hell. I will find a thousand kilos of dynamite and blow you up, motherfucker. Kyle will help me and call it art. I will seek revenge for the gay who was stabbed in the park. Repeat two hundred times. Write it on the blackboard two thousand times and then you can drink the rest of your vodka.

When Kyle was found, Painted Tongue would get him to take him to the police and Kyle would draw a glorious picture of what Painted Tongue had seen in the park. The men would be caught, and Kyle would sell the picture for thousands of dollars and give the money to Painted Tongue so that he could buy enough explosives.

At Bloor and Clinton, Painted Tongue spotted a man from behind that he thought must be Kyle, a man walking with his arm around a woman with blonde hair. He ran towards them as they climbed into a car, the man holding the door for the woman, then shutting it and walking around to the driver's seat. Painted Tongue tried to shout his friend's name, but only a hot wind came out. The car pulled into traffic just as Painted Tongue reached the passenger side. He pounded on the window and the woman looked up at him through the glass and wailed. Painted Tongue strained to look in the window as he ran beside the car, trying to see Kyle's face. The car veered sharply away and sped up until Painted Tongue was left gasping by the curb.

It could not have been Kyle. If it was Kyle, he did not see his old friend Painted Tongue. He walked back along Bloor.

His nose was itchy, the stitches drying into his skin. He sneaked into a bar with a loud band and went into the washroom. He stared into the mirror and picked at the stitch knots, six of them in a crooked line that ran the bridge of his nose. One by one, he found a good enough hold to yank five of them out. I will not go back to do battle with that fat nurse, he repeated over and over again in his hum.

The threads burned as they exited. The skin on his nose mostly held together, but beads of blood popped up and ran in little lines to his mouth. The last stitch held stubbornly, so Painted Tongue took a gulp of vodka and walked outside.

He found an empty paper coffee cup. He squatted by the bar's entrance and held it out in front of him for coins. When the loud band took a break, the people poured outside and stood talking around him. A group of boys in baseball caps gathered near and talked loudly about Painted Tongue. The one with bright eyes looked down at him.

Are you a Mohawk? he asked. Painted Tongue looked away. Are you Cree? the boy continued. Painted Tongue pretended not to notice him. The boy's friends stopped talking and looked down at Painted Tongue.

Do you want a beer? another asked.

Of course he does, another said, and they all laughed.

Are you Iroquois? the one with bright eyes asked. Painted Tongue stood up angrily. His head was spinning, and now up off the sidewalk he felt unprotected. He pulled his bottle from his belt and drained the rest.

I will count coup on you, baseball cap motherfucker, Painted Tongue hummed. The tones of his war chant came to him. I will take a knife and cut your scalp from your skull for calling me Iroquois. I will rip your ears from your head and eat them in front of you. He let his hand drop, dangling the bottle. The boys backed away a little.

Lookit that! He's got attitude, one of them shouted as they formed a circle on the sidewalk around him.

Painted Tongue began to pace slowly around the inside of the circle. He felt a warrior's control suddenly, all eyes upon him, watching closely his every move. When Painted Tongue walked by one of the boys, he'd stare at the boy's eyes until he recognized the wolf spider of fear in them. He walked carefully, slowly by their feet, watching their faces pass his. The boys widened the ring. Painted Tongue concentrated on his own feet moving. He picked up the pace. He could hear the pound of the drum in his head. The boys began clapping in time. Check it out, one said. He's on the warpath.

Painted Tongue reached out and touched each boy as he passed. He counted coup upon every single one in the group and watched the look of shame and disgust on their faces as they shrank away from his outstretched hand. He was happy. He was a warrior. He moved faster, bent far forward, lifting his knees high. He closed his eyes and danced the circle. It was effortless, like a strong wind picking him up and carrying him. He saw red behind his eyelids, then yellow and blue. In his mind it was he and Kyle running fast, chasing their shadows on a bright day in the tall grass, their shadows stretching in front of them and trying to get away.

They ran across the field that turned into a hill that got steeper and steeper. Kyle caught his own shadow and Painted Tongue could see Kyle's body now, his thin brown back, his red shorts, his skinny legs pumping. Kyle was always the faster one. The circle of boys sped up their clapping in time with Painted Tongue. The hill grew steeper and the grass thinned out to smooth grey stone. Kyle was getting away. He was near the top where the hill curved round. Painted Tongue's chest heaved with the effort of catching up. He looked behind him for a second and could see the field far below. He was so high up it made his head spin. Painted Tongue reached the top and it was the stadium, a colourless turtle shell he was running upon. Kyle was gone.

Just when Painted Tongue knew he could dance no longer, he felt one of the boy's boots catch his foot. Painted Tongue was happy for it. His dance was over. He stumbled over the boot and the momentum carried him forward with arms outstretched, one hand still clutching the empty bottle. He really was flying into the air now, off the stadium roof, off the turtle's back. I am flying, he tried to hum. Oh shit, I am flying high.

His hands hit the pavement first and the bottle shattered. The long broken neck of it pointed up to him like a skinning knife. He wanted to keep flying but the earth was pulling him down, wanted to say that the circle had not been completed yet but there wasn't enough time.

GLOBAL VILLAGE

Sorel Etrog

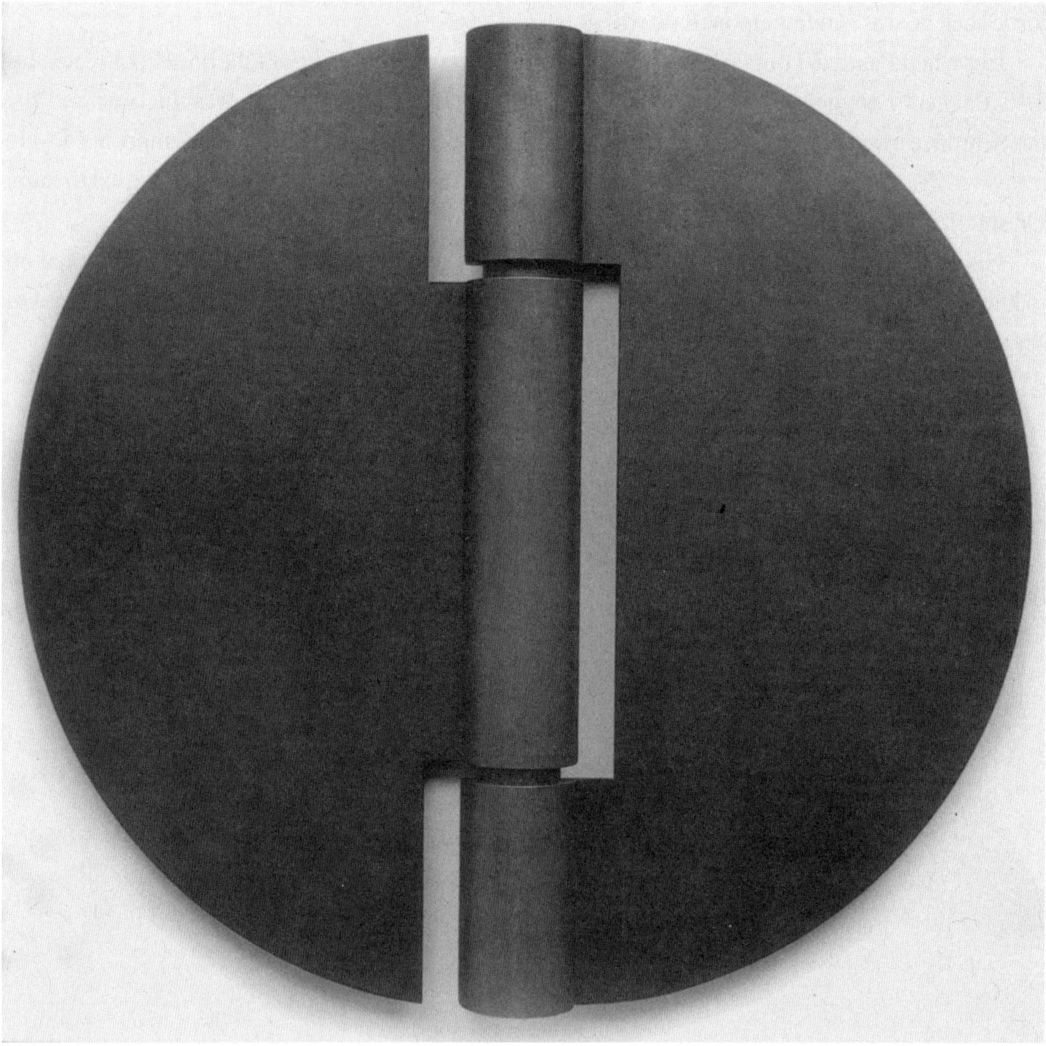

GO, GO, GO ON

JOE FIORITO

I walked along Queen Street, smiling idly, past the flower shops, past the flower shop that sells big underwear and lucky candles, past the stoners, past the solitary men who mutter to themselves, high-stepping as if they were walking up a flight of stairs and trying not to step on the butterflies. And then, in front of the drugstore, there was a flurry. Two men, struggling. I knew what was happening in an instant.

A security guard – compact and powerful, his face impassive and his head close-shaved – was holding what seemed to be a small white jar of beauty cream. With his other hand, he gripped the elbow of a small brown man. The small brown man was holding on to a backpack. They were linked together, a slow-motion frieze of misery.

I thought, if he hurts the small brown man...

Because I tend to be twitchy about cops, all cops, any cops, uniforms make me nervous. I am even twitchier about security guards. Their powers and my view of their powers do not ever coincide. And I don't ever want to test the limits of that lack of coincidence.

But if he hurts this little man...

The security guard held on firmly, and I heard him say, "Come with me." The small man said, "Please, sir, forgive!" They struggled some more, but the security guard was stronger and the smaller man slumped into submission, as if the heart for struggle had gone out of him as I passed by; he just gave up. A relief. No harm done. I didn't have to intervene.

The stronger man dragged the smaller one back into the store. A simple case of shoplifting. No big deal. I kept on walking. I took four more steps and... wait a minute.

Something was about to happen here which may have been routine for the security guard and which might have been no big deal for the druggist, but it was going to change the life of the little man in some big way.

I stopped. I turned. I went into the store. I interrupted the druggist in mid-prescription and gave him a short fast spiel: there is a lot of shoplifting in this town; we all pay the price in higher prices; everybody knows that, but nobody knows what happens when someone is caught because we never see the consequences; could I watch?

He pointed me downstairs and said if it was okay with the security guard... and so I did my song and dance again downstairs. The security guard weighed the request and took a chance.

I never know why anybody trusts me.

The small brown man sat on a folding chair. The security guard was writing a report. The jar of cosmetics had been placed on the table, along with the rest of the contents of the backpack, including a jar of pills, several empty plastic shopping bags, two Hindi videocassettes, and a new universal remote control, still in its package, with a legitimate receipt.

The room was claustrophobic; low ceiling, and the shelves overflowing with boxes of toiletries, a first-aid kit, old flyers with best price discounts, a microwave, packets of needles, junk.

The small brown man could not comprehend my presence. He had a particular expression on his face, as if he wouldn't have been surprised if I'd hit him. He looked so low, one more blow would not have mattered. I thought for a moment that he might have been relieved if I did hit him; at least then he'd have been on familiar ground.

I sat. I watched. I kept my mouth shut and took notes.

The security guard asked for the man's identification. No reply. He asked again and got the same answer. He asked a third time, and the small man said, "This will spoil my whole thing."

I supposed that it would. Too late for that now. The security guard said, "The police will get your name if you don't give it to me." The small man's thing was spoiling fast, the whole of it. He smiled wanly.

"Please, forgive."

"I want to see your ID. I'm allowed to grab it off you if I want. I'm being nice." The security guard looked hard and bored. There was a flicker of insight in the eyes of the small man, and a quick calculation from me: the security guard restraining himself because I was there. The small man glanced at me, and he took another stab.

"Please, forgive."

"The guard said, "There's nothing you can do. I caught you. If you're not charged, this goes nowhere. Give me your ID."

The small man sighed. He had no choice. He'd lost the battle, and it was just one in a long line of battles lost. He fished his wallet from his jeans and opened it, his gestures clumsy, as if he was unused to having a wallet, or jeans, or anything to put in them. His identification consisted of some bits of paper in a small plastic sleeve. He also gave the security guard his address and his phone number; these, he'd been carrying around with him, written on a piece of paper.

The serious questions started.

"You're not working?"

"No, sir."

"On welfare?"

"I am a refugee. I am waiting for a work permit."

"Do you have any money?"

A key question, a Jean Valjean thing: if you steal and you have no money, that's a certain kind of crime; if you steal and you have money to pay for what you stole, that's another kind of crime.

"I have this."

The small man reached into his pocket and knelt on the floor and showed his money – three Canadian five-dollar bills, nine American singles and a twenty-rupee note.

It was easy to see what he was thinking as he knelt with his hands out and the money held up like a gift: perhaps this man will take my money and let me walk away; I have done this before; this is what I know to do on occasions such as this.

The security guard took the money and counted it and put it on the table. He told the small man to sit down in his chair, hard pity in his voice. The small man sat back down with the same sad smile. The security guard completed his report.

He listed the stolen items: one jar of anti-cellulite pills, and one jar of Fade-Out, a kind of cream for bleaching liver spots. It seemed peculiar to me. Cellulite would have been a foreign notion for this skinny man. Not in his lifetime would he have seen cellulite, unless he had a big fat girl back home; nor would liver spots have shown on his skin. Did he have a girlfriend? Were these things for his mother?

Total value? Thirty-five dollars.

According to the security guard, the small man selected the products, walked around the store idly, removed the jars from the boxes, dropped the jars in his backpack and then put the empty boxes back on the shelves. And then he had tried to leave.

And he got nabbed on the sidewalk in front of the store, and I came along and saw what happened next. Now it was a matter of waiting for the police. I had a few questions of my own for the small man.

"Where are you from?"

"Tibet. Please forgive."

It was not my place to forgive, but the story suddenly got larger. A few months earlier, some two hundred Tibetans seeking refuge had been kicked out of the United States. They landed here in Toronto; was he one of them? I don't know much about the detention of refugees in the U.S.A. I know even less about jail in Tibet. But I know the little man was terrified.

"Are you a Buddhist?"

"Yes."

"Buddhists don't steal."

He smiled at my naïveté. "Not everyone is the same, sir."

"When did you come here?"

"Two months ago."

My hunch was right.

"Why did you come?"

"To escape the Chinese."

The security guard was listening, in spite of himself. These things were complications. What had happened was quite simple: the refugee had stolen, he'd been caught and the consequences were serious enough to spoil his whole thing. I pointed to the loot on the table.

"Do you know what cellulite is?"

No answer.

"Are you married?"

"No, sir."

"Please tell me, why did you take the cream?"

No answer.

"Why did you take the cream?"

"Please, forgive."

My forgiveness and a dollar would buy him a cup of bad coffee. I pressed him, even though I had no right.

"Yes, but why did you take the cream?"

He looked at me, pleadingly, as if he didn't want to say out loud what should have been obvious to all of us but was clear only to him. He touched his cheek with his hand.

"Because of this."

I didn't, I couldn't, I gaped, I gasped.

"What do you mean?"

"To make lighter."

Oh, Christ.

"Your skin?"

"It will be better for me here, sir."

He meant it would be better if he had lighter skin.

The police arrived then: a young constable, so tall he had to duck his head in the low room; he was corn-fed, butter-blond, hard as maple and highly amused. He took down the particulars. He went to the phone. He had questions for Immigration: was the little man here legally, were there outstanding charges, and so on. He hung up. We waited for some official to call back. The phone rang. The cop whispered and conferred. And then he had a private chat with the security guard.

The young cop looked down at the little man with a bright smile. "You understand you could go to jail for this?"

"Yes, sir."

"The store is going to be nice to you today. They're going to let you go." The small brown man opened his eyes wide for an instant. He couldn't believe what he had just heard.

"No jail?"

"Not this time."

He didn't move. They told him to stand. He wasn't sure. They led him up the stairs and through the store, and they led him out the door. They stood together on the sidewalk.

The security guard told the little Tibetan once again that he was banned from the store. "Don't come in here ever again." The small brown man heard. But he did not understand. He didn't move. He looked at the big blond cop. The cop said he was free to go. The small brown man hesitated.

"Go, go, go on, get out of here."

The small brown free man took three or four steps. He looked back. He was expecting a cruel trick: let's just pretend to let him go so we can say he was trying to escape, and then we can catch him and beat the snot out of him. Instead, they smiled and shooed him away. "Go, go."

He looked over his shoulder one more time, and then he disappeared. He hadn't known. He couldn't know.

from *IN THE SKIN OF A LION*
THE BRIDGE

MICHAEL ONDAATJE

A truck carries fire at 5 a.m. through central Toronto, along Dundas Street and up Parliament Street, moving north. Aboard the flatbed three men stare into passing darkness – their muscles relaxed in this last half-hour before work – as if they don't own the legs or the arms jostling against their bodies and the backboard of the Ford.

Written in yellow over the green door is DOMINION BRIDGE COMPANY. But for now all that is visible is the fire on the flatbed burning over the three-foot by three-foot metal dish, cooking the tar in a cauldron, leaving this odour on the streets for anyone who would step out into the early morning and swallow the air.

The truck rolls burly under the arching trees, pauses at certain intersections where more workers jump onto the flatbed, and soon there are eight men, the fire crackling, hot tar now and then spitting onto the back of a neck or an ear. Soon there are twenty, crowded and silent.

The light begins to come out of the earth. They see their hands, the textures on a coat, the trees they had known were there. At the top of Parliament Street the truck turns east, passes the Rosedale fill, and moves towards the half-built viaduct.

The men jump off. The unfinished road is full of ruts and the fire and the lights of the truck bounce, the suspension wheezing. The truck travels so slowly the men are walking faster, in the cold dawn air, even though it is summer.

Later they will remove coats and sweaters, then by eleven their shirts, bending over the black rivers of tar in just their trousers, boots, and caps. But now the thin layer of frost is everywhere, coating the machines and cables, brittle on the rain puddles they step through. The fast evaporation of darkness. As light emerges they see their breath, the clarity of the air being breathed out of them. The truck finally stops at the edge of the viaduct, and its lights are turned off.

The bridge goes up in a dream. It will link the east end with the centre of the city. It will carry traffic, water, and electricity across the Don Valley. It will carry trains that have not even been invented yet.

Night and day. Fall light. Snow light. They are always working – horses and wagons and men arriving for work on the Danforth side at the far end of the valley.

There are over 4,000 photographs from various angles of the bridge in its time-lapse evolution. The piers sink into bedrock fifty feet below the surface through clay and shale and quicksand – 45,000 cubic yards of earth are excavated. The network of scaffolding stretches up.

Men in a maze of wooden planks climb deep into the shattered light of blond wood. A man is an extension of hammer, drill, flame. Drill smoke in his hair. A cap falls into the valley, gloves are buried in stone dust.

Then the new men arrive, the "electricals," laying grids of wire across the five arches, carrying the exotic three-bowl lights, and on October 18, 1918 it is completed. Lounging in mid-air.

The bridge. The bridge. Christened "Prince Edward." The Bloor Street Viaduct.

During the political ceremonies a figure escaped by bicycle through the police barriers. The first member of the public. Not the expected sow car containing officials, but this one anonymous and cycling like hell to the east end of the city. In the photographs he is a blue of intent. He wants the virginity of it, the luxury of such space. He circles twice, the string of onions that he carries on his shoulder splaying out, and continues.

But he was not the first. The previous midnight the workers had arrived and brushed away officials who guarded the bridge in preparation for the ceremonies the next day, moved with their own flickering lights – their candles for the bridge dead – like a wave of civilization, a net of summer insects over the valley.

And the cyclist too on his flight claimed the bridge in that blurred movement, alone and illegal. Thunderous applause greeted him at the far end.

On the west side of the bridge is Bloor Street, on the east side is Danforth Avenue. Originally cart roads, mud roads, planked in 1910, they are now being tarred. Bricks are banged into the earth and narrow creeks of sand are poured in between them. The tar is spread. *Bitumiers, bitumatori*, tarrers, get onto their knees and lean their weight over the wooden block irons, which arc and sweep. The smell of tar seeps through the porous body of their clothes. The black of it is permanent under the nails. They can feel the bricks under their kneecaps as they crawl backwards towards the bridge, their bodies almost horizontal over the viscous black river, their heads drunk within the fumes.

Hey Caravaggio!

The young man gets up off his knees and looks back into the sun. He walks to the foreman, lets go of the two wooden blocks he is holding so they hang by the leather thongs from his belt, bouncing against his knees as he walks. Each man carries the necessities of his trade with him. When Caravaggio quits a year later he will cut the thongs with a fish knife and fling the blocks into the half-dry tar. Now he walks back in a temper and gets down on his knees again. Another fight with the foreman.

All day they lean over tar, over the twenty yards of black river that has been spread since morning. It glistens and eases in sunlight. Schoolgirls grab bits of tar and chew them, first cooling the pieces in their hands then popping them into their mouths. It concentrates the saliva for spitting contests. The men plunk cans of beans into the blackness to heat them up for their lunch.

In winter, snow removes the scent of tar, the scent of pitched cut wood. The Don River floods below the unfinished bridge, ice banging at the feet of the recently built piers. On winter mornings men fan out nervous over the whiteness. Where does the earth end? There are flares along the edge of the bridge on winter nights – worst shift of all – where they hammer the nails in through snow. The bridge builders balance on a strut, the flares wavering behind them, aiming their hammers towards the noise of a nail they cannot see.

The last thing Rowland Harris, Commissioner of Public Works, would do in the evenings during its construction was have himself driven to the edge of the viaduct, to sit for a while. At midnight the half-built bridge over the valley seemed deserted – just lanterns tracing its outlines. But there was always a night shift of thirty or forty men. After a while Harris removed himself from the car, lit a cigar, and walked onto the bridge. He loved this viaduct. It was his first child as head of Public Works, much of it planned before he took over but he had bullied it through. It was Harris who envisioned that it could carry not just cars but trains on a lower trestle. It could also transport water from the east-end plants to the centre of the city. Water was Harris' great passion. He wanted giant water mains travelling across the valley as part of the viaduct.

He slipped past the barrier and walked towards the working men. Few of them spoke English but they knew who he was. Sometimes he was accompanied by Pomphrey, an architect, the strange one from England who was later to design for Commissioner Harris one of the city's grandest buildings – the water filtration plant in the east end.

For Harris the night allowed scope. Night removed the limitations of detail and concentrated on form. Harris would bring Pomphrey with him, past the barrier, onto the first stage of the bridge that ended sixty yards out in the air. The wind moved like something ancient against them. All men on the bridge had to buckle on halter ropes. Harris spoke of his plans to this five-foot-tall Englishman, struggling his way into Pomphrey's brain. Before the real city could be seen it had to be imagined, the way rumours and tall tales were a kind of charting.

One night they had driven there at eleven o'clock, crossed the barrier, and attached themselves once again to the rope harnesses. This allowed them to stand near the edge to study the progress of the piers and the steel arches. There was a fire on the bridge where the night workers congregated, flinging logs and other remnants onto it every so often, warning themselves before they walked back and climbed over the edge of the bridge into the night.

They were working on a wood-facing for the next pier so that concrete could be poured in. As they sawed and hammered, wind shook the light from the flares attached to the side of the abutment. Above them, on the deck of the bridge, builders were carrying huge Ingersoll-Rand air compressors and cables.

An April night in 1917. Harris and Pomphrey were on the bridge, in the dark wind. Pomphrey had turned west and was suddenly stilled. His had reached out to touch Harris on the shoulder, a gesture he had never made before.

Look!

Walking on the bridge were five nuns.

Past the Dominion Steel castings wind attacked the body directly. The nuns were walking past the first group of workers at the fire. The bus, Harris thought, must have dropped them off near Castle Frank and the nuns had, with some confusion at that hour, walked the wrong way in the darkness.

They had passed the black car under the trees and talking cheerfully stepped past the barrier into a landscape they did not know existed – onto a tentative carpet over the piers, among the night labourers. They saw the fire and the men. A few tried to wave them back. There was a mule attached to a wagon. The hiss and jump of machines made the ground under them lurch. A smell of creosote. One man was washing his face in a barrel of water.

The nuns were moving towards a thirty-yard point on the bridge when the wind began to scatter them. They were thrown against the cement mixers and steam shovels, careering from side to side, in danger of going over the edge.

Some of the men grabbed and enclosed them, pulling leather straps over their shoulders, but two were still loose. Harris and Pomphrey at the far end looked on helplessly as one nun was lifted up and flung against the compressors. She stood up shakily and then the wind jerked her sideways, scraping her along the concrete and right off the edge of the bridge. She disappeared into the night by the third abutment, into the long depth of air which held nothing, only sometimes a rivet or a dropped hammer during the day.

Then there was no longer any fear on the bridge. The worst, the incredible had happened. A nun had fallen off the Prince Edward Viaduct before it was even finished. The men covered in wood shavings or granite dust held the women against them. And Commissioner Harris at the far end stared along the mad pathway. This was his first child and it had already become a murderer.

The man in mid-air under the central arch saw the shape fall towards him, in that second knowing his rope would not hold them both. He reached to catch the figure while his other hand grabbed the metal pipe edge above him to lessen the sudden jerk on the rope. The new weight ripped the arm that held the pipe out of its socket and he screamed, so whoever might have heard him up there would have thought the scream was from the falling figure. The halter thulked, jerking his chest up to his throat. The right arm was all agony now – but his hand's timing had been immaculate, the grace of the habit, and he found himself a moment later holding the figure against him dearly.

He saw it was a black-garbed bird, a girl's white face. He saw this in the light that sprayed down inconstantly from a flare fifteen yards above them. They hung in the halter, pivoting over the valley, his broken arm loose on one side of him, holding the woman with the other. Her body was in shock, her huge eyes staring into the face of Nicholas Temelcoff.

Scream, please, Lady, he whispered, the pain terrible. He asked her to hold him by the shoulders, to take the weight off his one good arm. A sway in the wind. She could not speak though her eyes glared at him bright, just staring at him. *Scream, please.* But she could not.

During the night, the long chutes through which wet concrete slid were unused and hung loose so the open spouts wavered a few feet from the valley floor. The tops of these were about ten feet from him now. He knew this without seeing them, even though they fell outside the scope of light. If they attempted to slide the chute their weight would make it vertical and dangerous. They would have to go further – to reach the lower-deck level of the bridge where there were structures built for possible water mains.

We have to swing. She had her hands around his shoulders now, the wind assaulting them. The two strangers were in each other's arms, beginning to swing wilder, once more, past the lip of the chute which had tempted them, till they were almost at the lower level of the rafters. He had his one good arm free. Saving her now would be her responsibility.

She was in shock, her face bright when they reached the lower level, like a woman with a fever. She was in no shape to be witnessed, her veil loose, her cropped hair open to the long wind down the valley. Once they reached the catwalk she saved him from falling back into space. He was exhausted. She held him and walked with him like a lover along the unlit lower parapet towards the west end of the bridge.

Above them the others stood around the one fire, talking agitatedly. The women were still tethered to the men and not looking towards the stone edge where she had gone over, falling in darkness. The one with that small scar against her nose... she was always falling into windows, against chairs. She was always unlucky.

The Commissioner's chauffeur slept in his car as Temelcoff and the nun walked past, back on real earth away from the bridge. Before they reached Parliament Street they cut south through the cemetery. He seemed about to faint and she held him against a gravestone. She forced him to hold his arm rigid, his fist clenched. She put her hands underneath it like a stirrup and jerked upwards so he screamed out again, her whole body pushing up with all of her strength, groaning as if about to lift him and then holding him, clutching him tight. She had seen the sweat jump out of his face. *Get me a shot. Get me...* She removed her veil and wrapped the arm tight against his side. *Parliament and Dundas... few more blocks.* So she went down Parliament Street with him. Where she was going she didn't know. On Eastern Avenue she knocked at the door he pointed to. All these abrupt requests – scream, swing, knock, get me. Then a man opened the door and let them into the Ohrida Lake Restaurant. *Thank you, Kosta. Go back to bed, I'll lock it.* And the man, the friend, walked back upstairs.

She stood in the middle of the restaurant in darkness. The chairs and tables were pushed back to the edge of the room. Temelcoff brought out a bottle of brandy from under the counter and picked up two small glasses in the fingers of the same hand. He guided her to a small table, then walked back and, with a switch behind the zinc counter, turned on a light near her table. There were crests on the wall.

She still hadn't said a word. He remembered she had not even screamed when she fell. That had been him.

Nicholas Temelcoff is famous on the bridge, a daredevil. He is given all the difficult jobs and he takes them. He descends into the air with no fear. He is a solitary. He assembles ropes, brushes the tackle and pulley at his waist, and falls off the bridge like a diver over the edge of a boat. The rope roars alongside him, slowing with the pressure of his half-glove hands. He is burly on the ground and then falls with terrific speed, grace, using the wind to push himself into corners of abutments so he can check driven rivets, sheering valves, the drying of the concrete under bearing plates and padstones. He stands in the air banging the crown pin into the upper cord and then shepherds the lower cord's slip-joint into position. Even in archive photographs it is difficult to find him. Again and again you see vista before you and the eye must search along the wall of sky to the speck of burned paper across the valley that is him, an exclamation mark, somewhere in the distance between bridge and river. He floats at the three hinges of the crescent-shaped steel arches. These knit the bridge together. The moment of cubism.

He is happiest at daily chores – ferrying tools from pier down to trestle, or lumber that he pushes in the air before him as if swimming in a river. He is a spinner. He links everyone. He meets them as they cling – braced by wind against the metal they are riveting or the wood sheeting they hammer into – but he has none of their fear. Always he carries his own tackle, hunched under his ropes and dragging the shining pitons behind him. He sits on a coiled seat of rope while he eats his lunch on the bridge. If he finishes early he cycles down Parliament Street to the Ohrida Lake Restaurant and sits in the darkness of the room as if he has had enough of light. Enough of space.

His work is so exceptional and time-saving he earns one dollar an hour while the other bridge workers receive 40 cents. There is no jealousy towards him. No one dreams of doing half the things he does. For night work he is paid at $1.25, swinging up into the rafters of a trestle holding a flare, free-falling like a dead star. He does not really need to see things, he has charted all that space, knows the pier footings, the width of the cross-walks in terms of seconds of movement – 281 feet and 6 inches make up the central span of the bridge. Two flanking spans of 240 feet, two end spans of 158 feet. He slips into openings on the lower deck, tackles himself up to bridge level. He knows the precise height he is over the river, how long his ropes are, how many seconds he can free-fall to the pulley. It does not matter if it is day or night, he could be blindfolded. Black space is time. After swinging for three seconds he puts his feet up to link with the concrete edge of the next pier. He knows his position in the air as if he is mercury slipping across a map.

EARLY MORNING

ALICE BOISSONNEAU

Sunlight Soap the sign says, and every day is washing-day.

The little Rice girl. Oh Annie Rice. Little Annie, with a ring-worm circle under her eye from ring-worm, waving palely and delicately at the trains, impressing the pale delicate signature of her wave on the air. Annie stands at the corner of Bathurst and Front Streets and she is a member of the Rice family, one of the thirteen Rices so casually brought into the world.

"How do you like school, Annie?" you ask her.

"Mm?" she replies vaguely and happily.

"Do you think you had better go home now?"

"Mm?" she asks...

Annie's front yard is the train-track, her backyard the street, where you walk along to the coal sheds in the winter and see the ad on the fence, where a man made of coal carries a pail.

BUY BURNS COAL, it says.

STORMED BY SUNLIGHT

Joe Rosenblatt

My parents settled in Kensington Lane in Kensington Market a year before I was born, the rented cold-water flat had only one water tap and a sink in the bathroom. They paid twelve dollars a month for the slum and often when I go past that laneway, I wonder where it was, exactly. Father earned two dollars a day when he worked. Like millions of people my parents suffered deprivation during the Depression and yet, because I was over-protected, I have no memory of hardships. Staring into a family photo, circa 1936, I see a fat child in short pants, dour between my smiling parents. I am seated on a family table which is as polished and bright as I am melancholic, peeping out at a world making faces at me...

I remember the old peddlers who led their old and sway-backed stallions, loyal nags who loved a fresh carrot with black soil on its tapered carotene body, pulling a junk wagon or a cart heaped with voluptuous vegetables down our street. During the heat of a summer's day, kids offered the nag a sugar cube or an apple, and the long yellow nicotine-colored teeth chomped on our tidbits, our offerings. Then, the peddler shooed us away, complaining we had molested his precious and boon companion. The peddlers have disappeared; chrome-plated horseless machines have taken over, but I remember when an old bearded peddler lifted me up on his nag's back and I cried when I stared down at the ground and kicked the creature in the flanks with my baby shoes. I'm sure the old horse smiled. They always seemed to smile in their garage-style barns, the dirt floors strewn with hay. How they survived the winters I'll never know. I don't recall wood-burning stoves, although there were plenty of horse blankets and an old man's affection. A deep bond existed between horse and peddler, a miserable pair broken by a deadening vocation, existing on the small change of life, making the street rounds searching for broken shoes, a soiled jacket, a tie, an ironing board, a frayed lamp shade. It was a cycle: the poor feeding on the poor. Horse and master, a visible minority verbally abused by street toughs. Shunned, both horse and peddler were considered – by those riding the wheels of social mobility – fossilized ghetto figures.

There was a happier time when a horse had his or her favourite watering hole. I remember a coppery fountain on the southwest corner of Spadina and College, the fountain's green skin of floral patterns fringing its surface. The artisan who designed the fountain had a sense of humour: there was a cherubic figure who greeted the snouts of horses with a jet of cold water and a small nude comedian peed in an arc and many a kid leaped under it, frolicking in the maw of the fountain during a July heat wave. Until nudged by a horse, and then the kid retreated, the peddler shouting that the sanctity of the fountain had been profaned by a pint-sized hooligan. To make his point, the man waved his horse whip above his head.

So, horse and wagon have disappeared, along with trails of steaming golden apples glittering in the afternoon sun, apples scooped up for fertilizer by street folk to increase the voltage of plants in a front garden so that in the summer I stared at the supernatural glow in the faces of sunflowers and marvelled at the brashness of such pagan beauty, marvelled at how that magical dung had jiggered and sustained those wild blooms...

My parents moved out of Kensington Lane and settled on Markham Street, not far from the market. It is the house I recall during the Hitler war years: sirens wailing in the city...practice drills...people hurrying home although no bombs rained down...but there was fear itself, and it invaded the psyche of a ten-year-old who would soon learn the dreadful truth about the Final Solution on that dancing beam of light in the La Salle Theatre. It happened at a regular Saturday matinee. That devastating feature changed my life in a matter of twenty minutes. The regular movie had ended, some inane flick titled the *Curse of the Mummy*, which had scared the juices out of me, and I was dry, or so I thought. The sights and sounds of snapping linen as the stiffs broke free from their bondage and bandages had had me leaping from my seat, and then had left me limp.

When this regular silver screen delight ended, the ushers told the kids that they had to leave. They waved droves of kids towards the exits. What was next on the bill was for a mature audience only, and ushers flashed their flashlights, bellowed out orders, looked under seats and moved us all in single files down the aisles. Teachers, ushers, single files. I ducked into the washroom to hide. I had no intention of missing Mickey Mouse with teeth or Minnie with tits.

The silence in the half-empty theatre gave it another dimension: the other side of the grave. A booming voice described the death camp survivors just liberated by the advancing British forces. Cadaveric sights flashed across the screen. I felt an icy presence, a chill: those hills of shoes scattered about immediately grabbed my lights...I spotted a child's shoe, and then many children's shoes...tons of sorrowful shoes...stark black and white...hills of corpses suddenly appeared to be moving...a harvest of naked death...skeletal dunes, twisted...their bones falling apart...skulls...spare legs that had no flesh...mounds of dead...starved beyond death itself...their eyes bulging in disbelief...their mouths open...screaming...at whom?...at the young Tommies, their young faces pallid, soldiers covering their faces...the acid sweet smell of rotting hands, hearts...sprawled...flung...a child...a rhythmic flow of death...the dead screaming in flecks of silver before my eyes...as though static electricity had become the larvae of death...but still, there were those among the dead who were reaching out at the living...

The Tommies delicately carried a few skeletal children, their dangling chalky limbs moving...and the flesh on their limbs...what flesh?...there didn't seem to be any...flesh...white loose skin...a skein of terror...the gritty quality of the film gave the elements a life form of their own...a rain had fallen, giving the film a feeling there was dew clinging to it...a wash to the permanent stain...and now the whole mongrelized feeling was present...a montage of super death...the machinery, fresh...no time to move the evidence, the technology that went into this industry of death...fillings become bars of gold...hair becomes mattress stuffing...the doors of the ovens...swung open...white mounds...the crematoriums for turning corpses into potash...half-baked, hair still on the skulls in the narrow ovens...Tommy groomed to a T, held a delicate handkerchief to his nose and explored the dead. A frightened gleam appeared in his eyes, his face without emotion, his pistol drawn, leading a rigid SS officer dressed smartly in leather into the building. In the next shot, the officer had the glazed look of a marble.

I left the theatre before the newsreel ended. There wasn't anybody in the lobby. I had moved ahead of the crowd. In the street I felt suddenly strange, like a moth stormed by sunlight I drifted, as a ghost would drift, away from the surface of the planet.

from ONCE NEAR WATER

VERA FRENKEL

AFTER DINNER BUTTERFLIES

MATT COHEN

They were sitting in the library, drinking coffee. She noticed that he had a hand in one of his pockets, he seemed to be fiddling with something.

George?

What?

What have you got there?

Nothing, he said.

Show it to me immediately.

It's nothing, he said. He took his hand out of his pocket and puffed elaborately on his cigar. Good cigar, he said.

No cigar, she said. Take that thing out of your pocket.

George stood up and leaned against the mantel, still puffing on his cigar. He pulled a rabbit out of a vase. Look at the nice rabbit, he said.

Put it away.

He stuck the rabbit out the window and returned to his chair. He picked up an old newspaper and started reading it. When he was sure she wasn't looking he put his hand back into his pocket.

George!

What.

Let me see it.

There's nothing here.

Oh yes there is. I saw you fiddling with it. Now let me see it.

All right, he said. He reached into his pocket. Then he changed his mind. No, you have to guess.

I'm not playing one of your stupid games.

Okay, George said. Let's forget it then. He relit his cigar and stuck his hand back into his pocket. Time passed. His cigar went out. Mary got another cup of coffee. The fire was going. George kept his hand in his pocket. He got tired of the newspaper. He went over to the library table and sat down to work on the jigsaw puzzle. He was so absorbed in a little bit of orange and green that he didn't hear Mary sneak up on him.

There, she exclaimed. I've got it. Her hand was in his pocket. Then she withdrew it, puzzled. There's nothing there, she said.

They sat back down. A few moments later she noticed that George was working his hand in his pocket. When he looked up he saw her watching him. Do you want to see what's in my pocket?

You don't have anything in your pocket.

Yes I do.

Prove it.

Okay, George said. He reached into his pocket and pulled out a shiny bit of metal. It appeared to be some sort of complicated miniature. He brought it over to her, holding it cupped in the palm of his hand. But when she reached for it, he drew back. Don't touch, he said. You'll break it. He held it out to her again so she could look at it. It was a metal sphere with little red things sticking out of its silver surface.

What is it? she asked.

It's a spaceship.

That's nice.

Watch this. He walked to the side of the room farthest from the fire. Come here, he said. She stood beside him. He threw his metal gizmo into the fire. There was a clicking sound, metal against brick-work.

Well, she said, you could have done that with a firecracker.

Right, George said. They sat back down. After a while Mary noticed that she had, in a very faint way, the same sort of feeling in her stomach that she sometimes got in an elevator.

George, she said.

Yes?

I feel funny. I feel like we're in an elevator.

Or in a spaceship, George said. He walked over to the sideboard and poured himself a glass of sherry. Cheers, he said.

Don't think you can upset me with your silly games.

Oh no, George said.

I was once married to a Hungarian count.

Were there bagpipes at your wedding? Yes there were. I was there. I remember them clearly: they were off key.

Mary crossed her legs and tried to pull her skirt down over her knees. They felt strange, as if something was about to land on them. George, she said, prove to me that we are on a spaceship.

All right, George said. He snapped his fingers. Nothing happened. Then a delicate golden butterfly landed on Mary's right knee. Isn't that beautiful?

Isn't what beautiful? Mary said. She could have sworn that a golden butterfly had landed on her knee.

The music, George said. He turned up the radio so that the library was filled with sounds. A second golden butterfly landed on Mary's knee.

I don't like it, she said. She got up and turned the radio off. The butterflies followed her, circling her head like a halo. Go on, she said when she sat down, flicking at her shoulders, go sit on someone else. But they just came back.

You'd better leave them alone, George said.

Why? I don't like them.

But they like you.

I don't like the feeling of them sitting on my shoulders, watching me.

They're very pretty.

I can't even see them without straining my neck.

I'll get you a mirror, George said.

I don't want a mirror. Let's just forget them and see if they go away.

All right, George said. He lit a new cigar and sipped at his sherry. After a while Mary noticed that he had a hand in his pocket again and seemed to be fiddling with something.

George.

What?

What are you doing now?

Nothing, George said. He took his hand out of his pocket. I'm just trying to get this damned thing turned around.

What thing?

The spaceship.

The butterflies were still perched on Mary's shoulders, waiting patiently. George snapped his fingers again. A white wolf appeared in the middle of the room. Its eyes were as golden as butterflies. It walked over to George's chair, climbed up into it, and licked its paws. Go on, George said. Sit on the floor. The wolf looked up at him and then returned to its paws.

You see? You don't know how to do anything right.

I'm sorry, George said.

What a lovely wolf. Look at its eyes.

I wish it would get off my chair.

It likes you, Mary said. That's why it wants to sit on your chair.

If it really liked me it would get off of my chair and fetch a stick or something. He took a cigar from the mantel and waved it in the air. Fetch, doggie, he said. He threw the cigar across the room. The wolf looked at him, looked over at the cigar, raised its eyebrows, and went back to sleep.

That reminds me, Mary said. Did I ever tell you that I was once married to a Hungarian count?

Yes, George said. You just told me five minutes ago. Do you mind if I sit on the arm of your chair? The butterflies were still perched on her shoulders, waiting patiently.

Yes, she said. I do mind. Why don't you stand at the mantel and try to look unconcerned?

There was a knock at the door. Come in, George shouted. A man wearing gray coveralls and carrying a toolbox entered the room.

Is this the place with the television?

Yes, George said, it's there in the corner. I don't know what's wrong with it.

Probably blew a tube, the repairman said. It often happens. Nice dog.

Yes.

The repairman pushed the television out from the wall and began poking at its innards.

Do you want a glass of sherry?

No thanks, the man said. He reached into the television and pulled out three stuffed camels. Here's your problem, he said. There were three stuffed camels in the back of your television set.

Oh, George said. I was hiding them there for my wife's birthday.

You should've told me. He turned on the set. Works fine now. He pushed the television back against the wall and packed up his tools. I'll send you a bill, he said, and left the room.

The repairman made two more house calls and then went home. His wife was sitting up, waiting for him. He changed out of his coveralls, washed up, and then got his dinner out of the oven and a beer from the refrigerator.

How did it go tonight?

The usual. Is Jimmy asleep?

Yes, he went to bed hours ago.

What else did you do?

Nothing much, she said. She crossed her legs and tried to pull her skirt down over her knees. I watched TV for a while and read Jimmy a story.

Is there anything for dessert?

There's some pie. He went into the kitchen and found a coconut cream pie in the refrigerator. He brought it back into the living room.

Have you ever wanted to throw a pie in my face?

Once, she said. Remember that dance we went to just after we started going out? You put an ice cube down my dress? Well, when you took me home my parents were still up and we had strawberry pie with whipped cream. You were all sitting at the table and I was getting the pie. I could feel the ice water trickling down my skin, and the inside of my dress was wet. I almost dumped the pie right on your head.

He leaned back and lit a cigarette, God, he said, that must have been ten years ago.

Eleven, she said. Eleven years and two months. I remember standing there. I was just about to turn the pie onto your head when I decided to marry you. She crossed the room and sat down beside him on the couch. I don't know why I never told you, she said. I always meant to.

What else didn't you ever tell me?

Did I ever tell you that I was once married to a Hungarian count?

No, he said. And I wouldn't believe you if you did. He was leaning back with his eyes closed. She dipped her hand into the pie and spread it gently over his face. She formed little ridges at the eyebrows, being careful not to get any into his eyes. She spread it on his cheeks with the palms of her hands and then swirled it with her index finger so that his cheeks stood out in spiral puffs. She gave him a moustache and a beard – a nice pointed Vandyke beard that reminded her of a picture. When the beard started to drip she pushed it back up onto his chin and drew a picture of a rose in it. All the whipped cream was gone. She took a fork and fed him some of the coconut filling.

How does it taste?

Good, he said.

I should have saved you some of the whipped cream.

That's all right. He stuck out his tongue and licked a path along his right cheek. Tonight I saw a woman with two golden butterflies perched on her shoulders.

That's nice, dear.

AT THE LISBON PLATE

DIONNE BRAND

The sky in the autumn is full of telephone and telegraph wires; it is not like sitting in the Portuguese bar on Kensington in the summer, outside – the beer smell, the forgetful waiter. I wonder what happened to Rosa. She was about forty and wore a tight black dress, her face appliquéd with something I could barely identify as life. Her false mole, the one she wore beside her mouth, shifted every day and faded by evening. She had a look that was familiar to me. Possibly she had lived in Angola or Mozambique and was accustomed to Black women, so she looked to me kindly, colonially.

"Do you have fish, Rosa?" I would ask.

"Oh yes, good Portuguese fish."

"From the lake or from the sea?"

"Ah the sea, of course."

This would be our conversation every time I would come to the bar, her "of course" informing me of her status in our relationship.

My life was on the upswing, and whenever that happened I went to the bar on Kensington. That was usually in the summertime. After twenty years and half my life in this city I still have to wait for the summertime to get into a good mood. My body refuses to appreciate dull, grey days. Truthfully, let me not fool you, my life was neither up nor down, which for me is an upswing and I don't take chances, I celebrate what little there is. Which is why I come to this bar. This is my refuge, as it is. I believe in contradictions.

So Rosa ran from Angola and Mozambique. Well, well! By the looks of it she'd come down a peg or two. At the Lisbon Plate, Rosa seems quite ordinary, quite different from the woman who entertained in the European drawing rooms in Luanda and Lorenções Marques. Then, she gave orders to Black women, whom she called *as pretinhas*. Then, she minced over to the little consul from Lisbon and the general, whose family was from Oporto and whom she made promise to give her a little gun for her protection when the trouble started.

I figured anyone who left Angola was on the other side, on the run. Rosa did have a kind enough look, personally. The wholesale merchant she was married to or his general manager, whom she slept with from time to time, had to leave. So, Rosa left too. This does not absolve Rosa however. I'm sure that she acquired her plumpness like a bed bug, sucking a little blood here, a little there.

As I've said, my life was on the upswing. Most other times it was a bitch. But I had spent two successive days with no major setbacks. Nobody called me about money, nobody hurt my feelings, and I didn't wake up feeling shaky in the stomach about how this world was going. And, I had twenty clear bucks to come to the bar. This is my refuge. It is where I can be invisible or, if not invisible drunk. Drinking makes me introspective, if not suicidal. In these moments I have often looked at myself from the third floor of the furniture store across from the bar. Rheumy-eyed, I have seen a woman sitting there whom I recognize as myself. A Black woman, legs apart, chin resting in the palm of her hand, amusement and revulsion travelling across her face in uneasy companionship; the years have taken a bit of the tightness out of my skin but the expression has not changed, searching and uneasy, haunted like a plantation house. Surrounded by the likes of Rosa and her *compadres.* A woman in enemy territory.

It has struck me more than once that a little more than a century ago I may have been Rosa's slave and not more than twenty-five years ago, her maid, whom she maimed, playing with the little gun that she got from the general from Oporto. My present existence is mere chance, luck, syzygy.

Rosa's brother, Joao the priest, was now living in New Jersey. He used to live in Toronto, but before that he lived in Angola. One day, in a village there, during the liberation war, two whites were kidnapped and the others, including Rosa's brother, the priest, went into the village and gunned down a lot of people – women, children, to death, everything. He told this story to Maria de Conseçao, my friend, and she told me. Women and children, everything. People think that saying women and children were killed makes the crime more disgusting. I was sorry that Maria de Conseçao told me, because whenever I think about it I see Joao the priest confiding this crime as if he relished it, rather than repented it. I think Maria de Conseçao told me the story just to get rid of it. I've kept it.

I am not a cynical woman under ordinary circumstances, but if you sit here long enough anyone can see how what appears to be ordinary, isn't.

For, on the other hand, I look like a woman I met many years ago. As old as dirt, she sat at a roadside waiting her time, an ivory pipe stuck in her withered lips and naked as she was born. That woman had stories, more lucid than mine and more frightening for that.

The day I met her, her bones were black powder and her fingers crept along my arm causing me to shiver. She was a dangerous woman. I knew it the moment I saw her and I should have left her sitting there, the old gravedigger. But no. Me, I had to go and look. I had to follow that sack of dust into places I had no right being. Me, I had to look where she pointed. She wanted to show me her condiments and her books. I thought nothing of it. Why not humour an old woman, I said in my mind. They were old as ashes. All tied up and knotted in a piece of cloth and, when she opened it up, you would not believe the rattling and the odour, all musty and sweet. A bone here and a fingernail there. They looked like they'd been sitting in mud for centuries, like her. When it came to the books, it was before they had pages and the writing was with stones, which the old thing threw on the ground and read to me. I never laughed so much as I laughed at her jokes, not to mention her stories which made me cry so much I swore I'd turn to saltwater myself. It was one of her stories which led me here, in search of something I will recognize, once I see it.

But back to things that we can understand, because I want to forget that harridan in the road and her unpleasantness.

Today I am waiting for Elaine, as usual. She likes to make entrances of the type that white girls make in movies. The truth is she's always getting away from something or someone. She is always promising too much and escaping, which is why we get along. I never believe a promise and I, myself, am in constant flight.

Elaine is a mysterious one. Two days ago she told me to meet her here at one o'clock. I've been sitting here ever since. I know that she'll turn up a new woman. She'll say that she's moving to Tanzania to find her roots. She'll have her head tied in a wrap and she'll have gold bracelets running up her arms. She'll be learning Swahili, she'll show me new words like *jambo* and she'll be annoyed if I don't agree to go with her. Elaine wants to be a queen in ancient Mali or Songhai. A rich woman with gold and land.

The bar has a limited view of Kensington Market. Across the street from it there's a parkette, in the centre of which there is a statue of Cristobal Colon. Columbus, the carpetbagger. It's most appropriate that they should put his stoney arse right where I can see it. I know bitterness doesn't become me, but that son of a bitch will get his soon enough too. The smell from the market doesn't bother me. I've been here before, me and the old lady. We know the price of things. Which is why I feel safe in telling stories here. They will be sure to find me. For fish you must have bait; for some people you must have blood. Spread the truth around enough, and you must dig up a few liars.

In the summertime, I come to the bar practically every day. After my first beer I'm willing to talk to anyone. I'm willing to reveal myself entirely. Which is a dirty habit, since it has made me quite a few enemies. Try not to acquire it. The knots in my head loosen up and I may start telling stories about my family.

I keep getting mixed up with old ladies; for instance, I have an old aunt, she used to be beautiful. Not in the real sense, but in that sense that you had to be, some years ago. Hair slicked back to bring out the Spanish and hide the African. You could not resemble your mother or your father. This would only prove your guilt. This aunt went mad in later years. I think that it must have been from so much self-denial, or given the way that it turned out...

Anyway, when I was a child we used to go to their house. It was made of stone and there was a garden around it. A thick green black garden. A forest. My aunt worked in the garden every day, pruning and digging. There was deep red hibiscus to the far right wall. The soil was black and loose and damp and piled around the roots of roses and ixoras and anthuriums and orchids. In the daylight, the lack and bright; in the night, it was shadowy and dark. Only my aunt was allowed to step into the garden. At the edges, shading the forest-garden were great calabash mango trees. Their massive trunks and roots gave refuge from my aunt when she climbed into a rage after merely looking at us all day. She would run after us screaming, "Beasts! Worthless beasts!" Her rage having not subsided, she would grab us and scrub us, as if to take the black out of our skins. Her results would never please her. Out we would come five still bright-black little girls, blackness intent on our skins. She would punish us by having us stand utterly still, dressed in stiffly starched dresses.

Elaine never reveals herself and she is the most frustrating storyteller. She handles a story as if stories were scarce. "Well," she says, as she sits down at the table. Then she pauses, far too long a pause, through which I say, in my mind, "I'm going to last out this pause." Then quickly getting upset, I say, "For God's sake, tell me." Then I have to drag it out of her, in the middle of which I say, "Forget it I don't want to hear," then she stops what she thinks is the sinker and I nonchalantly say, "Is that it?" to which she swears that never again would she tell me a story. The truth is that Elaine picks up on great stories, but the way she tells them makes people suffer. I, on the other hand, am quite plain. Particularly when I'm in my waters. Drink, I mean. I've noticed I'm prepared to risk anything. But truthfully, what makes a good story if not for the indiscretions we reveal, the admissions of being human. In this way, I will tell you some of my life; though I must admit that some of it is fiction, not much mind you, but what is lie, I do not live through with any less tragedy. Anyway, these are not state secrets, people live the way that they have to and handle what they can. But don't expect any of the old woman's tales. There are things that you know and things that you tell. Well, soon and very soon, as they say.

Listen, I can drink half a bottle of whisky and refuse to fall down. It's from looking at Rosa that I get drunk and it's from looking at Rosa that I refuse to fall down. I was a woman with a face like a baby before I met Rosa, a face waiting to hold impressions.

I saw the little minx toddle over to the statue of Columbus, the piss-face in the parkette, and kiss his feet. Everyone has their rituals, I see. And then, before her mirror, deciding which side to put the mole on. Her face as dry as a powder. Perfuming herself in her bedroom in Lourenços Marques, licking the oil off that greasy merchant of hers. Even though the weather must have been bad for her, she stuck it out until they were driven away. It's that face that Rosa used cursing those "sons of bitches in the bush," when the trouble started. "When the trouble started," indeed. These European sons of bitches always say "when the trouble started" when *their* life in the colonies begins to get miserable.

I never think of murder. I find it too intimate and there's a smell in the autumn that I do not like. I can always tell. The first breath of the fall. It distracts me from everyone. I will turn down the most lucrative dinner invitation to go around like a bloodhound smelling the fall. Making sure and making excuses, suggesting and insinuating that the summer is not over. But of course, as soon as I get a whiff of that smell I know. It's the autumn. Then the winter comes in, as green and fresh as spring and I know that I have to wait another ten months for the old woman's prophecy to come true. That hag by the road doesn't know what she gave me and what an effort I must make to see it through. On top of that, I have to carry around her juju belt full of perfidious mixtures and insolent smells and her secrets. Her secrets. My god, you don't know what a soft pain in the chest they give me. I grow as withered as the old hag with their moaning. She's ground them up like seasoning and she's told me to wear them close to my skin, like a poultice. I thought nothing of it at first. A little perfume, I said, a little luxury. I now cannot take the juju off. I lift up my camisole and have a look. It's hardly me there anymore. There's a hole like a cave with an echo.

At this bar, I have my first beer and wait for the African princess Elaine, I discover substantive philosophical arguments concerning murder. The beauty is, I have a lot of time. I have watched myself here, waiting. A woman so old her skin turned to water, her eyes blazing like a dead candle. I'm starting to resemble that bag of dust, the longer I live.

Now they have a man waiting on tables at the bar. I suppose the pay must be better. Elaine says he resembles Rosa except for her beauty mole and her breasts. It doesn't matter how Rosa looks in her disguises, I am doomed to follow her like a bloodhound after a thief. He is quite forgetful. Twenty minutes ago I asked him for another beer and up to now he hasn't brought it. Elaine's the one who got me into beer drinking anyway. In the old days – before the great mother old soul in the road and before I sussed out Rosa and her paramour, Elaine and I used to roam the streets together, looking. The old bone digger must have spotted my vacant look then. Elaine, on the other hand, had very definite ideas. Even then Elaine was looking for a rich African to help her make her triumphal return to the motherland.

Still, a rumour went around that Elaine and I were lovers. It wouldn't have bothered either of us if it were true at the time or if it wasn't said in such a malicious way. But it was because of how we acted. Simply, we didn't defer to the men around and we didn't sleep with them, or else when we did we weren't their slaves forever or even for a while. So both factions, those we slept with and those we didn't, started the rumour that we were lovers. Actually, Elaine and I laughed at the rumours. We liked to think of ourselves as free spirits and realists. We never attempted to dispel the rumours; it would have taken far too much of a commitment to do that. It would be a full-time job of subjecting yourself to any prick on two legs. And anyway if the nastiest thing that they could say about you is that you loved another woman, well.

Elaine and I would take the last bus home, bags full of unopened beer, or pay a taxi, after I had persuaded her that the man she was looking at was too disgusting to sleep with, just for a ride home. Elaine takes the practical to the absurd sometimes.

We've been to other bars. Elaine looked for the bars, she scouted all the hangouts. She determined the ambience, the crowd, and then she asked me to meet her there. There's no accounting for her taste. I'd get to the appointed bar and it would be the grungiest, with the most oily food, the most vulgar horrible men and a jukebox with music selected especially to insult women. This was during Elaine's nationalist phase. Everything was culture, rootsy. The truth is, I only followed Elaine to see if I could shake the old woman's stories or, alternately, if I could find the something for her and get her off my back. It's not that I don't like the old schemer. At first I didn't mind her, but then she started to invade me like a spirit. So I started to drink. You get drunk enough and you think you can forget, but you get even greater visions. At the beginning of any evening the old woman's stories are a blip on the horizon; thirteen ounçes into a bottle of scotch or four pints of beer later the stories are as lurid as a butcher's block.

I had the fever for two days and dreamt that the stove had caught afire. My big sister was just standing there as I tried furiously to douse the fire, which kept getting bigger and bigger. Finally, my sister dragged the stove from the wall and, with a knowledgeable air, put the fire out. When I woke up, I heard that the stock exchange in Santiago had been blown up by a bomb in a suitcase and that some group called the communist fighting cell had declared war on NATO by destroying troop supply lines in Belgium. Just as I was thinking of Patrice Lumumba. For you Patrice! From this I surmised that my dreams have effects. Though, they seem somewhat unruly. They escape me. They have fires in them and they destine at an unknown and precipitous pace.

I followed Elaine through her phases, though there were some that she hid from me. Now we come to this bar, where we cannot understand the language most of the time. Here Elaine plans the possibilities of living grandly and, if not, famously. As for me, I tolerate her dreams because when Elaine found this bar I knew it was my greatest opportunity. All of the signs were there. The expatriates from the colonial wars, the money changers and the skin dealers, the whip handlers, the coffle makers and the boatswains. Their faces leathery from the African sun and the tropical winter. They were swilling beer like day had no end. Rosa was in her glory, being pawed and pinched. Of course, they didn't notice me in my new shape. Heavens, I didn't notice me. It scared the hell out of me when the juju surged to my head and I was a thin smoke over the Lisbon Plate. What a night! They said things that shocked even me, things worse than Joao, the priest. The old-timers boasted about how many *piezas de indias* they could pack into a ship for a bauble or a gun. The young soldiers talked about the joys of filling a Black with bullets and stuffing a black cunt with dynamite. Then they gathered around Columbus, the whoremaster, and sang a few old songs. The old woman and I watched the night's revelry with sadness, the caves in our chest rattling the echo of unkindness, but I noticed the old woman smiling as she counted them, pointing and circling with her hand, over and over again, mumbling "jingay, jingay, jingay, where you dey." We stayed with them all night, counting and mumbling. Now, all I have to do is choose the day and the spot and it's done. The old woman loves fanfare and flourish, so it will have to be spectacular. If Elaine knew what a find this bar was, she'd charge me money.

Elaine never cared for Rosa one way or the other, which is where Elaine and I are different. Some people would have no effect on her whatsoever. This way she remained friends with everyone. Me, I hate you or I love you. Always getting into fights, always adding enemies to my lists. Which is why I'll never get any place, as they say. But Elaine will. Elaine, sadly, is a drunk without vision. I unfortunately, am a drunk with ideas. Which is probably why the old woman chose me to be her steed.

I pride myself with keeping my ear to the ground. I read the news and I listen to the radio every day, even if it is the same news. I look for nuances, changes in the patter. It came to me the other night, when listening to the news. One Polish priest had been killed and the press was going wild. At the same time, I don't know how many African labourers got killed and, besides that, fell to their deaths from third-floor police detention rooms in Johannesburg; and all that the scribes talked about was how moderate the Broderbond is. We should be grateful I suppose.

It occurred to me that death, its frequency, causes, sequence and application to written history, favours, even anticipates, certain latitudes. The number of mourners, their enthusiasms, their entertainments, their widows' weeds, all mapped by a cartographer well-schooled in pre-Galileo geography. I'm waxing. Don't stop me. I couldn't tell you the things I know.

Meanwhile back at the bar, still waiting for Elaine to surface, there have been several interesting developments. Speaking of politics first, I hear that the entire bourgeoisie of Bolivia is dead. It was on the radio not more than half an hour ago. The deaths are not significant in and of themselves. What is interesting is that only a few days ago, when I heard that President Zuazo was kidnapped in La Paz and that there was possibly a coup, I said in my mind, that the entire bourgeoisie should perish. It was the Bolivian army who killed Ernesto Che Guevara, you see. They put his body in the newspapers with their smiles. Now, I hear the news that the entire bourgeoisie of Bolivia is dead. Of course from this I learned that as I become more and more of a spirit, I have more and more possibilities. First Santiago and Belgium and now Bolivia.

Second, and most, most important, the big white boy has arrived here. He's ordered a beer from Rosa's brother. The last time I saw them, I was lying in the hold of a great ship leaving Conakry for the new world. It was just a glimpse, but I remember as if it were yesterday. I am a woman with a lot of time and I have waited, like shrimp wait for tide. I have waited, like dirt waits for worms. That hell-hole stank of my own flesh before I left it, its walls mottled with my spittle and waste. For days I lived with my body rotting and the glare of those eyes keeping me alive, as I begged to die and follow my carcass. This is the story the old road woman told me. Days and days and nights and nights, dreaming death like a loved one; but those hellish eyes kept me alive and dreadfully human until reaching a port in the new world. His pitiless hands place me on a block of wood like a yoke, when my carcass could not stand any more for the worms had eaten my soul. Running, running a long journey over hot bush, I found a cliff one day at the top of an island and jumped – jumped into the jagged blue water of an ocean, swimming, swimming to Conakry.

Elaine has also arrived and disappeared again, she's always disappearing into the bar to make phone calls. I never get an explanation of these phone calls mainly because I simply continue with my story. But I have the feeling, as the afternoon progresses into evening, and as different moods cross Elaine's face after every phone call, that some crisis is being made, fought and resolved. I have a feeling that Elaine needs my stories as a curtain for her equally spyish dramas.

The big white boy was sitting with his dog. I did not see his face at first, but I recognized him as you would recognize your hands. His hair was cut with one patch down the middle. He was wearing black and moaning as he sat there smoking weed. Like Rosa, he had fallen on his luck. I heard him say this.

"I don't have nobody, no friends, I ain't got no love, no nothing, just my dog."

He was blond. At least, that was the colour of his hair presently. I felt for him the compassion of a warship, the maudlin sentiment of a boot stepping on a face. He said this to Rosa, who gave him an unsympathetic look as she picked her teeth. I'm not fooled by their lack of affection for each other. They are like an alligator and a parasite. I felt like rushing to his throat, but something held me back. The old woman's burning hand. I've seen him and Rosa whispering behind my back. What would a punk ku klux klansman and a washed-up ex-colonial siren have in common. Except me and the old lady. I suppose they're wondering who I am. Wonder away you carrion! I wonder if they recognize me as quickly as I, them. I saw them do their ablutions on the foot of the statue in the parkette. How lovingly they fondled his bloody hands. They have their rituals, but I've lived longer than they.

Listen, I neglected to say that my old aunt of the forest has gone mad. She told my sister, and indeed the whole town of Monas Bay, that on Easter Sunday of 1979, this year, Jesus Christ had descended from the heavens and entered her bedroom and had been there ever since. She had had a vision. After days of fasting and kneeling on the mourning ground, she had entered a desert where nothing grew. No water and inedible shrubs. The sun's heat gave the air a glassiness upon looking into the distance. Then she saw Christ. He was withered and young as a boy of twenty. Christ and my aunt conversed for many days and planned to marry three years from the time of their meeting. They would have a son who would grow to be the new Christ. My aunt related this incident to any one who would listen and cursed into hell and damnation anyone who did not believe. Few, needless to say, didn't. Anyone with a vision was helpful in bad times and people said that at least she had the guts to have a vision, which was not like the politicians in those parts.

Even my aunt's garden had descended into sand and touch shrub. It had become like the desert of her vision. She no longer made any attempt to grow plants, she said that Armageddon was at hand anyway. Her bedroom, she turned into a shrine on the very day of her meeting with Christ. On the wall hung bits of cardboard with glossy photographs of her fiancé cut out of the *Plain Truth*, and candles burnt endlessly in the four corners of the shrine. Sundry chaplets of jumbie beads, plastic and ivory manoeuvered themselves on the windows and bedposts. My aunt knows that some people think that she is mad; so, in the style of her affianced, she prays for their salvation. If she is mad... Which is a debate that I will never personally enter, having seen far too much in my short life and knowing that if you live in places with temporary electricity and plenty of hard work, Jesus Christ (if not god) is extant. Not to mention that, the last time that I saw her, she stood at what was once the gate to the forest garden and was now dead wire, wearing a washed-out flowered dress and showing her last remaining tooth, even though she was only a woman of fifty, and told me that the land taxes for the forest and the stone house was paid up or would be as soon as she went to town. This, to me, attested to her sanity. Come hell or high water, as they say, though these might be the obvious cause of her madness, if she were mad, they were certainly legal. Anyway, if she is mad, her vision is clearly not the cause of it. Rather it has made her quite sane. At any rate she no longer uses face powder.

This trick that I learned in Bolivia and the dream in Santiago has set me to thinking. She, the old *poui* stick, is not the only one who can have plans. The dear old lady only gave me seven red hot peppers and told me to write their names seven times on seven scraps of paper. Then put the seven pieces of paper into the seven red hot peppers and throw them into seven latrines. This, she said, would do for them. This and sprinkling guinea pepper in front of their door every morning. Then, she said, I should wait for the rest. The old hag is smart, but she never anticipated the times or perhaps that's what she means.

Elaine thinks I'm taking things too far, of course. But, I cannot stand this endless waiting. I've practically turned into a spirit with all this dreadfulness around the Lisbon Plate. I want to get back to my life and forget this old woman and her glamorous ideas. So, what must be done, must be done. Elaine's on her way to Zaire, at any moment anyway. I think she's landed Mobutu Sese Seko.

For now I've taken to hiding things from her. She doesn't care about anything. Each time I mention it she says, "Oh for god's sake, forget them." As if it's that easy. You tell me! When there's a quaily skinned battle-axe riding on your shoulder and whispering in your ear. Well fine, if Elaine can have her secret telephone calls, and I don't think that I mentioned her disappearances, I can have my secret fires too. She can't say that I didn't try to warn her.

Wait! Well, I'll be damned! They're coming in like flies, old one. I eavesdrop on conversations here. I listen for plots, hints. You never know what these people are up for. This way, I amuse myself and scout for my opportunity. Listen.

"Camus' *Outsider* can be interpreted as the ultimate alienation!"

Ha! Did you hear that? Now, literature! Jesus. That's the one who looks like a professor, all scruffy and sensitive. If the truth be known several hundred years ago he made up the phrase "Dark Ages," then he attached himself to an expedition around the Bight of Benin from which, as the cruder of his sea company packed human cargo into the hold of their ship, he rifled the gold statues and masks and he then created a "museum of primitive art" to store them. Since his true love was phrase-making he made up "museum of primitive art," elaborating his former success, "Dark Ages." Never trust white men who look sensitive. They're the worst kind of phonies. They want the best of both worlds. Compared to him, the big white boy looks like a saint.

Anyway, alienation, my ass! Camus! Camus wrote a novel about a European, *un pied noir*, killing an Arab on a beach outside Algiers. He works it so that the sun gets into the European's eyes (they have their rituals) and the heat and his emotionlessness to his mother's dying and all this. But killing an Arab, pumping successive bullets into an Arab, is not and never has been an alienating experience for a European. It was not unusual. It need not symbolize any alienation from one's being or anything like that. It was customary in Algeria, so how come all this high shit about Camus. Didn't it ever strike you that Meursault was a European and the Arab on the beach was an Arab? And the Arab was an Arab, but this European was Meursault.

You want to hear a story? Let me tell you a real story. I have no art for phraseology. I'll warn you.

Ahmed. Ahmed. Ahmed. Ahmed came to the beach with Ousmane to get away. The town, stiffly hot, drove him from the bicycle factory, making an excuse to his boss. Headache, my little brother has a headache three days now. He needs the salt air. The grimy hands of the boss closed around a dry cigar in the tin can ashtray. "Ahmed, if you leave I don't pay for the week. That's it. That's it you hear." Ahmed retreating, feeling free already, seat trickling and drying under his chin. He would go to the beach. Ousmane was waiting for him, the sand would be damp. Ousmane was at the corner, he held his flute anxiously looking up and down the narrow street. His face lit up as he saw Ahmed. "You got away, good Ahmed," running beside Ahmed's bicycle. Ousmane climbed onto the handle bars. Ahmed pedalled in the hot silence toward the beach. Nearing the sea, their legs and arms eased from the tension of the town. Ousmane's bare feet leapt from the makeshift seat at the same time that Ahmed braked. They headed for their favourite rock wheeling and lifting the bicycle through the sand, hot and stinging. Already he felt tranquil as the thin wind shaking the flowers. He dropped the bicycle, raced

Ousmane to the water, crushing softly underfoot the vine and silky mangrove. Ahmed and Ousmane fell into the sea fully clothed, he washing away the sticky oil of the bicycle shop, Ousmane drowning his headache. Then they lay beside the rock, talking and falling asleep.

Ousmane awakening, felt hungry; his dungarees, still damp, felt steamy on his legs. Shading his eyes from the sun which had narrowed the shadow of the rock, his headache came back. He stood up, lifted his flute and played a tune he'd made over and over again as if to tame the ache in his head. After a while he wandered down the beach, looking for a foodseller.

Ahmed. Ahmed. Ahmed awoke, feeling Ousmane's absence at the same moment that he heard an explosion close to his ear. Ahmed felt his eyes taking an eternity to open into the glassy haze of the afternoon. A blurred white form wobbling in the heat's haze. Sound exploded on the other side of Ahmed. He barely raised his body, shielding his eyes as he made out the white form of a European. Far out in the ocean a steamer was passing. The sand around Ahmed pulsated with the heat and the loud ringing in his ears. Ousmane! Run!

Ahmed's vision pinpointed the white's face, the toothpick between the white's teeth and lip moving. The gun transfixed his arms. Beneath a veil of brine and tears, his eyes were blinded; they watched the steamer's latitude longingly. "Born slackers!" Ahmed's chest sprang back, tendrilled. "Born liars!" A pump of blood exploded in his left side. "Born criminals!" Sheets of flame poured down his ribs. "Born...!" Ahmed!

That is what happened! And as for Camus. Murderer.

This is it baby. The old woman has given the go-ahead. Now that they're all gathered – Rosa, the big white boy, the professor, the money-changers and the skin dealers, the whip handlers, the coffle makers and the boatswains, the old timers and the young soldiers. I'm going to kill them. I'll tell them I have something to sell. That'll get them going; it always has. Then we'll strangle them. It'll be a night for the old woman to remember. That'll make up for it. Then that'll be the end of it.

We chained them around the statue of Cristobal Colon, the prick head. The old woman and I slashed his face to ribbons then we chewed on the stones and spit them into the eyes of the gathering. When that was over and they were all jumping and screaming, the old woman drew out her most potent juju and sprayed them all with oceans of blood which, she said, she had carried for centuries.

"En't is blood all you like?!" she whispered in their ears maliciously.

Then we sang "jingay..." and made them call out everything that they had done over and over again, as they choked on the oceans of blood from the old hag's juju. Then we marinated them in hot peppers, like the old woman wanted. What an everlasting sweet night we had. The old woman was so happy, she laughed until her belly burst.

When Elaine returned from her continuous phone call, I convinced her to stuff the bodies in her trunk to Zaire. It wasn't easy, as she almost could not see me and kept saying how much my face had changed. I promised her the Queendom and riches of Songhai. She bought it. The old lady has promised me her big big juju, so this is where the African princess and I must part. I'm off to see my new love and companion, the old hag of a banyan tree.

Endnote: "Ahmed's death" is intended to echo and counterpoint the corresponding scene in *L'Étranger* and therefore echoes the language of the Penguin edition, English language translation.

OUR THIRTEENTH SUMMER

BARRY CALLAGHAN

I was a child during the war and we lived on the upper floor of a duplex in what was then called a railroad apartment, which was a living-room at the front end and a sunroom at the back end and a long hall with rooms running off the hall in between. The apartment below was the same. "The same," my father said, "but not exactly the same." A chemist and his family lived there. He was an expert in explosives, working with the war department. He was not old but his hair was white. He told my mother that he was working on "a bomb so big that when it hit, when it blew, the war would end up on Mars."

He was called George Reed. He was a chain-smoker and his teeth were yellow and irregular. He had a port wine stain on the back of his left hand. He often kept his left hand in his suit coat pocket. He didn't talk much. He seemed to be shy and reticent but I always felt that he disapproved of me, disapproved of all of us, but he didn't want to be forced to say so, and so he hid how he felt behind his shyness. Sometimes his left hand fluttered in his pocket, and sometimes he couldn't stop it fluttering, not once it got going. "It's like he's got a trapped bird in there," my mother said. As for his wife, I heard my mother tell my father once that "she looks like someone who's been swept over by sadness and has gone strange."

She was from Vienna. That's what she had told my mother and father. I didn't know where Vienna was. "That's where it all began," my father told me, "Hitler's town, except she's Jewish." She was short and had thick black hair. When she talked she got excited. She leaned down and breathed into my face, she peered into my eyes, like she was looking for something that was way beyond me, beyond my mother and father, like she didn't know what she was looking for and yet she was sure it was out there, whatever it was, long gone and lost. And one day, she breathed in my face and said, "I'm not Jewish," and her son Bobbie told me the same thing. "My father's English and nobody's Jewish." Bobbie and I played together on the front lawn. He had his father's wine stain on his neck, just below his left ear. We played war games with soldiers and tin tanks in the rockery. There were no flowers in the rockery, only mud and stones because the landlord refused to spend money on flowers. He said money was too scarce because of the war. But Bobbie and I didn't want any flowers. We wanted the mud and the stones. We could spend a whole afternoon shifting our soldiers from ledge to ledge, country to country. We took turns being the enemy. Whenever he had to be the Germans, even though they always lost, he always said, "Don't tell my mother, don't let my grandfather hear us."

Every day at 10:30 in the morning and at 4:00 in the afternoon his grandfather came out of their sunroom, which was below my bedroom. Bobbie said he slept there and studied his books there with the shades down and then he would come out and take one of his walks, shuffling in his slippers from our house to the end of the street and back. He never spoke to Bobbie. He never spoke to me. He was dressed all in black, in a black suit. He had a long pale face and a long blade nose. He sometimes wore a black broad-brimmed hat and sometimes a shiny black skullcap, and he had long curls of hair that hung down beside his ears. He didn't wear shoes, he wore his black leather slippers.

"If he isn't Jewish, I don't know who is," my mother said.

"We're not Jewish," Bobbie told me.

"Sure you are, you gotta be," I said.

He punched me as hard as he could in the chest. When I got my breath, when I wiped away the tears that had come to my eyes from the punch, I told Bobbie to put up his dukes. My father had taught me how to box. He had bought me boxing gloves, and kneeling down in front of me, he had sparred with me, teaching me how to jab and hook, and how to block punches and take a punch. He'd hit me really hard two or three times. "That's so he'll understand that getting hit never hurts as much as he thinks it's going to hurt," he told my mother. "Once you know that, then you won't worry about getting hurt and you can learn how to hit and hit real good."

Bobbie put up his fists. I flicked a left jab in his face. He didn't know what I was doing. He didn't look scared. He looked bewildered, helpless, as he tried to duck his head. I hit him with a left hook. His nose began to bleed. He tasted his blood, he looked astonished, and then when he saw blood all over his shirt, he was terrified. "My mother will kill me." He began to bawl, but he was afraid to run into the house. His mother came running out. Her black hair was loose and long and flying all about her head. She screamed and pulled Bobbie behind her, to protect him, but I didn't want to hit him again. I felt sorry. I wished he hadn't hit me and I hadn't hit him.

"Why?" she screamed.

"Because he said I was Jewish," Bobbie said.

"Because he's Jewish... He's not Jewish," and she swung and hit me in the head, knocking me down. She hauled Bobbie into the house. I looked up from where I was, lying flat on my back, and the old grandfather, who was wearing his skullcap, was standing by their open front window, staring at me, twisting one of his long curls in his fingers.

Later, when I told my father what had happened he said to my mother, "I know they're terrified, I know they're from Vienna, but that's not the point," and he went downstairs and stood very close to

Mr. Reed and said through his teeth, "If either one of you ever hits my boy again, I don't care how big your bomb is, I'll knock your block off."

There was a Jewish family up the street, just north of us. Mrs. Asch was plump, almost fat. She wasn't too fat because she didn't waddle, but she had a huge bosom and she would hold my head to her chest. Mr. Asch worked with furriers. He was, my father said, "a cutter." It sounded dangerous, like he should be on *Inner Sanctum Mystery* radio. But he didn't look dangerous. He was small, had pasty-coloured skin, a round closely cropped head, and always wore his skullcap, even under his hat. He came home every evening at 6:30, sat down looking sullen, ate cold chicken that was shiny and pimpled in its boiled white skin, and drank Coca-Cola. We never drank Coca-Cola in our house. "Rot-gut," my mother called it, so I drank Hires Root Beer, telling my friend, my pal, Nathan Asch, that it was a kind of real beer. He didn't believe me but sometimes we put aspirins in it to give it a boost and he drank it with me and usually he said, "This is living," and we got a headache that we called a hangover.

Nathan, who was plump like his mother, had one leg shorter than the other. He wore an ox-blood boot with a double-thick sole and heel. He couldn't run very fast and he could hardly skate at all, and so, because I wanted to be a baseball pitcher, he was my catcher. His sister, who was a lot older and very pretty and worked in a fur salon modelling coats, had bought him a big round catcher's glove. It was the best glove anybody on the street had and Nathan knew it and he was proud to be a catcher and I was proud that he was my catcher be-cause he was good at blocking any curve balls I threw into the dirt.

On the weekends when Bobbie Reed's mother and grandfather walked up the street together to the grocery store on Dupont Street, they would pass the Asch house, and most of the time in the summer the Asches would be sitting out on the front porch listening to Mel Allen broadcast the Yankee games on WBEN Buffalo, or Ruth the daughter would have her portable record player set up by the porch stairs, playing Frankie Laine singing:

My heart goes where the wild goose goes,
wild goose, mother goose,
which is best,
a wandering fool or a heart at rest...

and the old man dressed in black would sometimes get a hitch in his step and hesitate and glance up the walk to the porch. He always wore some kind of white tasselled cloth under his suit coat that looked like a piece of torn sail. If Mr. Asch was sitting on the porch, he'd glower at the old man and if Mrs. Reed looked at him, then Nathan's father would get up, still small no matter how tall he tried to stand, and he'd push his chin out and down and spit. This seemed awful to me, particularly because Mr. Asch was no good at spitting and whatever he hocked out of his mouth it always went splat and sat there on his own porch stairs. I didn't understand why he was so angry and why he was spitting at a woman and I didn't understand spitting on your own stairs. I didn't understand any of this at all. The second time it happened, I asked Nathan and he said, "It's because Bobbie and the whole bunch of them tell everybody they're not Jewish. My father hates them for that."

"I never heard the old man say he wasn't Jewish," I said.

"He don't say nothing," and Nathan shouted, "You don't say nothing," hoping the old man would hear him. "You might as well be from Mars."

I watched Mrs. Reed thrust out her chin and quicken her stride as the old man unbuttoned and then buttoned his suit coat, shuffling away from us, and he looked bonier and sharper in the shoulder blades than I'd thought he was, but then, I'd always thought of him as slumped through the shoulders and he wasn't slumped. His shoulders were very straight, though he did push his feet along the sidewalk like he was tired when he walked.

"Just look at him like he's not there," my mother said. "That's best."

"But he is there," I said.

"So you say," she said and laughed.

About two months after Nathan shouted at the old man it was time for Nathan's birthday. August was always a big month for the kids on the street. August was the last month of the summer holidays and Nathan's birthday was at the beginning of the month and Bobbie's birthday was at the end and all of us were always invited to wear paper hats and blow whistles and bob for apples and eat cake and play hide-and-seek down the alleys between the houses after dark, before we went to bed. I didn't like my birthday because it was in February and it was too cold to play outside. But this year, Nathan's party was different. It was smaller. There were kids there that I didn't know and the kids I knew and expected to see weren't there. Nathan told me that this wasn't going to be his real birthday party, his real birthday party was going to be his *bar mitzvah* because he was turning thirteen and he was going to be a man. After we ate the cake and his mother's cookies, when I said goodbye to him at the door and he thanked me for my gift, a Yankee baseball cap my father had brought from New York, he said, "I can't see you so much anymore."

"What?"

"My father says I can't see you so much, not now that I'm a man."

"Why?"

"'Cause you're a *goy*."

"What's that?"

"One of the *goyim*, you eat unclean food so you got unclean hearts."

When I came home early, surprising my mother, she was standing alone out on the sidewalk under a street lamp that had just come on. I was crying quietly, not quite sure why because I had done nothing wrong, or maybe it was because Mrs. Asch was never going to hold my head against her big bosom again. The Reed front windows were open and there was loud music coming from the windows as I told my mother what had happened with Nathan and she folded me into her arms and said, "There, there, there's nothing you can do with some people." She sounded very sad but I could tell she was also very angry. As we walked up to our door into the duplex I could hear the music and see the Reeds spinning and twirling, Mrs. Reed with her head thrown back, laughing, and I asked my mother, "What's that they're doing?"

"Waltzing," she said. "That's the way they dance in Vienna, they waltz."

"Like that?"

"It can be very beautiful," she said.

At the end of August, Bobbie turned thirteen, too. I was playing more and more by myself. Once or twice I lay on my bedroom floor with my ear to the floor to see if I could hear Bobbie in the old man's bedroom below me but I never did hear him. Sometimes I heard the old man complaining and singing a kind of moan and once, as he was going out walking, he paused beside the rockery and looked down at me as I lined up two Lancasters at the bottom of the stones. I looked up and he looked down. "Bombers," I said, and another time I had my baseball and my glove beside me and I asked, "Hey, you wanta play catch?" He looked startled and then he laughed. Not a loud laugh, but quiet, like a chuckle. "You speak English?" I asked. He took two steps away and then stopped, turned around, and said in a voice that seemed to be as much heavy breathing as it was a voice, "Of course," and then he kept on walking without looking back.

I asked Bobbie if he was going to have a *bar mitzvah*, too. He sneered at me and said, "Of course not. What d'you think I am?" Then I realized that every night, just before supper, Bobbie and his father were putting on boxing gloves in their living room and Mr. Reed, who probably didn't know anything about boxing, was trying to teach Bobbie how to box. One late afternoon as I stood out on the lawn watching their heads and shoulders duck and weave, I realized that the old man was standing near me and he was watching, too.

"Hi," I said.

He just looked at me, a strange look, like for a minute he thought I was someone else that he was surprised to see, but he didn't say anything. He sighed and went into their house.

Two days before his birthday, Bobbie's mother stopped my mother and me. Usually they said something nice to each other without meaning it, but this time his mother didn't bother. She said, "From now on, nobody calls Bobbie 'Bobbie' anymore. His name is Robin. A man's name. Robin Reed." Bobbie looked kind of mopey, so I said, "Well Robin, I don't hardly see you anymore, not even on the weekend."

"I go with my father on Saturdays now."

"Where?"

"To his lab. He takes me to his lab."

"What for?"

"To teach me chemistry, to teach me what he does."

"Terrific," I said. "He makes bombs."

"He doesn't let me make bombs," he said. "Not yet."

On the afternoon of his birthday, I was all alone. My father was away again and my mother was out shopping. Mr. Reed came home early, his head down, his left hand in his suitcoat pocket, fluttering. I thought he was home to get ready for the party, but not long after, Robin came out on to the front lawn wearing boxing gloves and carrying another pair for me. I thought it was really strange, the gloves were the exact same colour as the wine stain on his neck. He said his father had told him that he had to box me before there could be any party. "He says I'm turning thirteen, you know."

For the first time in my life I just suddenly felt all tired, like my whole body was tired. And sad. I tried to laugh while the two of us stood there with great big gloves hanging off the ends of our arms, but I felt so sad I was almost sick, and though I could tell right away, as soon as Robin put up his gloves, that he was still the same old Bobbie, that he didn't know how to box at all, I only remembered the last time I'd hit him, the blood, and how sorry I felt, and I was half leaning toward him while I was thinking about that and he swung a wild looping left that caught me behind the ear and knocked me down. I wasn't hurt, and he didn't know that I knew he couldn't hurt me no matter how hard he hit me because my father had taught me how to take a really hard punch and not to be afraid. So I got up and pawed the air around Robin, trying not to let him hit me, not really punching him because I felt too tired even if I had wanted to punch him, and then he cuffed me a couple of times, but he didn't know how to punch off the weight of his back leg, so I staggered a little and I saw that Mr. Reed was standing in their front window, his hands flat on the glass, a great big glad smile on his face, but the old grandfather had come out on to the cement stoop beside the rockery. He had on his broad-brimmed black hat and he stood with his arms folded across his chest, the torn sail hanging out from under his arms. He was silent and intent. I let Robin take a bang at my body. I was glad my father wasn't home. He'd have been ashamed and angry and I would have had to fight, had to really beat up Robin or Bobbie or whoever he was. Instead, I wanted to cry. Not because I was hurt. I just wanted it all to be over so that I could cry and so I sat down on the lawn and stayed there because no one I loved could see me, no one I loved was there to make me do anything I didn't want to do, and at last, Robin, totally astonished, turned and ran into the house, ran into his father's arms.

I got up and went down the lawn to the sidewalk and sat on the curb and slowly undid the laces to the boxing gloves with my teeth and pulled the gloves off. I wasn't really sniffling. The Reeds were crazy if they thought I was going to get up and go to Robin's birthday party, but I didn't know why they were actually crazy. Then I heard shuffling leather slippers behind me. I thought he'd gone into the house, too, to be with them, but he was standing close behind me, and when I turned and looked up I was almost angry at him but he was smiling, looking down from under the wide brim of his hat and shaking his head with a kind of bent sorrowful smile.

"It's not so easy to hurt you," he said.

"Nope," I said.

"You would make a good Jew," he said.

"How would you know," I said, real sharp, "you're not Jewish."

"No, that's right," he said, smiling a little more, and then he leaned down and whispered, "I'm the man from Mars."

THE RINGER

Max Haines

During the racing season of 1923, gangster Frankie Yale, best known as a prime supplier of booze to the Al Capone organization and owner of the notorious Harvard Inn in New York, arrived in Toronto to take in the races at Woodbine. Frankie, complete with buxom blonde and bodyguards, stayed at the posh King Edward Hotel.

Late at night he frequented Hennessey's Drug Store for a bite at the counter. That's where Frankie made the acquaintance of Russ, the personable young man who worked the soda fountain. Through Russ, Frankie got to know his brother Jack, behind the counter. The big-time gangster took a shine to Russ and Jack. Eventually, he asked Jack if he wanted to move to New York, where he could give him a job at the Harvard Inn. Both boys jumped at the chance to move and work in the Big Apple.

As promised, Frankie placed Jack at the Harvard. Russ caught on at another restaurant, but it was Jack who was constantly in the company of Frankie Yale. All that winter, the counterman from Canada and the Brooklyn-born gangster saw each other every other day that Frankie wasn't tied up with his precarious business interests or following the ponies all over the continent.

Early that spring, Frankie was at Woodbine surveying the stable area when, quite by chance, he spotted a nag called Maternal Pride. He was sure he had seen the same horse at Saratoga Race Track. Being a keen punter looking for an edge, he checked out the horse. Maternal Pride had never been at Saratoga. Frankie, accompanied by an ex-jockey named Billy travelled to Saratoga to check out the horse, whom he was sure was the exact image of Maternal Pride.

Billy, who was well connected at Saratoga, contacted a friend, a track employee called Ted. He showed Ted a photograph of Maternal Pride. Ted blinked and wondered when they had taken a picture of a horse stabled at Saratoga. Frankie was shown the horse. The similarities between Maternal Pride and the horse stabled at Saratoga were astounding. Coloration, markings and posture were identical. Ted let Frankie and Billy know they were looking at a horse which had won several stakes races.

Then and there, Frankie figured there had to be a way to switch horses. He talked it over with Billy and Ted. All agreed that Ted could handle the Saratoga end. He could see to it that the "ringer," who was often put out to pasture for a few days, would not be missed. This could be big. Frankie required the organizational ability and the money to pull it off. He contacted Jack "Legs" Diamond, one of the most notorious hoodlums of the Roaring '20s. Legs wanted more details, but fell in love with the idea. Returning to Toronto, Billy learned that Maternal Pride was running in the King's Plate. The horse had only been in one previous race and had come in last. The results would be astronomical. Legs decided to finance the scheme. The big money would not be wagered at Woodbine because the odds would be adversely affected. Legs arranged for three conspirators to place bets in two establishments in Detroit and one each in Chicago and Philadelphia.

Using false names, they would travel to the three cities, where they would stay in the best hotels for a few weeks prior to the King's Plate. In general, they would establish themselves as free spenders, with lots of cash. In addition, they were to place long-shot bets of $100 or $200 with local bookies. The three men were performing as instructed but at no time were they in on the scheme.

The King's Plate was scheduled to run on May 17, 1924, at Woodbine. The plan was in motion. Ten days before the race, Billy commenced hanging around the stable area at Woodbine. As a former jockey, he was well known and told anyone who asked that he just liked to be around horses. He was particularly attentive to Maternal Pride. Within a few days, he was a fixture, helping out around the stable.

Jack, the transplanted counterman from Toronto, would be responsible for the Toronto end of the operation. A car and a horse trailer were purchased. On the Wednesday morning before the big race, Jack drove from Toronto to Saratoga with the horse trailer in tow. He met Ted and together they stocked the trailer with straw, hay, oats and water. At 3 a.m. Ted had no trouble loading the ringer into the trailer. Twelve hours later, they were in Toronto. Jack had made previous arrangements to have the horse bedded down for Thursday night in the barn off Logan Ave.

The boys checked the early line on Maternal Pride. The odds were 80 to 1. So that everything looked kosher, that Thursday night the men in the American cities were instructed to bet $1,000 and were given the names of long shots, as usual. Just as usual, they lost.

Now the switch. Jack and Ted loaded the ringer onto the trailer. Jack knew the night watchmen at Woodbine waved in any vehicle lugging a horse trailer. No problem there. They drove up behind Maternal Pride's stall. Jack got out. To divert attention from the stall, he chatted up the night watchman. At that precise moment, Billy took Maternal Pride out of his stall for a walk. Ted took the ringer out of the trailer. Billy and Ted met and switched horses. Maternal Pride was put in the trailer and the ringer was put into Maternal Pride's stall. Billy stayed with Maternal Pride all that night.

That same night, the men in the American cities were each given their instructions – bet $1,000 on a horse called Maternal Pride in the King's Plate at Woodbine in Toronto. The bookies didn't find it unusual. These well-heeled idiots had each bet $1,000 on a long shot the night before.

They're at the post. Maternal Pride took off like a shot and led all the way. As the *Toronto Telegram* reported, "There was no fluke about it, for the Oakville gelding was always best, he went out by himself to set all the pace."

Maternal Pride paid a whopping $193.35 for a $2-winning ticket.

Both H.S. Wilson, the owner of the winner, and the jockey, P. Walls, had no idea of the switch. On Monday, Wilson's picture accepting 50 guineas and the trophy emblematic of the win was featured in newspapers across the country.

After the race, the real Maternal Pride was taken out of the trailer and hosed down by Ted to make it look as if it had just run a race. The regular stable hand was thrilled when Billy told him he was wanted at the winner's circle. Billy said he would walk the horse back to its stall. In under a minute the ringer was in the trailer and the real Maternal Pride was back in its stall. The reverse switch had been completed.

The boys stopped along the way to Saratoga to call Frankie Yale in New York and inform him that everything had gone according to plan. The ringer was taken back to Saratoga without incident. Some were suspicious about the race. Many suspected doping. Others talked of a ringer but a search of Woodbine uncovered no such horse. The rumours of foul play died down. Owner Wilson had not even placed a bet on his own horse.

The men in the three American cities were paid off by the bookies. Following instructions, hundreds of thousands of dollars found its way into the gangsters' hands in New York. Everyone involved was paid off to their satisfaction.

On July 1, 1927, three years after the King's Plate, Frankie Yale was wheeling his roadster down New York City's 44th Street when he was suddenly overtaken by a large touring car loaded with gunmen. A fusillade of bullets tore Frankie apart. At his funeral, 28 cars of flowers followed him to his final resting place.

On December 17, 1939, "Legs" Diamond was acquitted of kidnapping one James Duncan. After celebrating his acquittal into the wee hours, he was shot to death while he slept.

EPONA AT HER MIRROR

LUDWIG ZELLER

from STRANGE FUGITIVE

MORLEY CALLAGHAN

They took a Carlton car and transferred to Bay and got off at Queen. They walked over to Elizabeth, the street of Chinese merchants, chop-houses and dilapidated roughcast houses used for stores. Some cafés were of new tan brick, with electric signs. Chinese men sat on steps or stood in groups under street lights. No women were to be seen. They crossed over from Elizabeth Street by the registry office, the new white stone building oddly out of place in the neighbourhood, and walked up Chestnut Street to Angelina's, a brick house with a storefront and big white letters on the plate glass, "Italian Restaurant." It was dark and no lights were in the windows.

They went to the side door. Harry knocked gently. A square panel opened. A woman peered out.

"How's Angelina?" Harry asked.

"Jimmie Nash and Harry Trotter," Jimmie said.

The door opened and Angelina stood there smiling at them, a plump Italian woman with good features, not too fat. She had nice plump legs. Harry tried in an offhand, friendly way to put his arm around her waist, and she grinned, removing the arm seriously. In the front room there was no light. Along the hall they heard voices.

"Many people upstairs?" Jimmie asked.

"You boys don't want to eat?"

"No, just a drink."

"How are tricks?" she said playfully.

"Fine, how are they going with you, you still love me?"

"Sure, Mr. Trotter. Be nice boys now."

They passed Angelina's father sitting at the cash register. A dining room was on the right along the hall. Many people eating noisily, but laughing quietly, glanced at them as they passed the dining-room door. They stood opposite the kitchen, while Angelina spoke to one of the chefs. She was proud of the chefs and the kitchen. The cooking was done publicly, only a rail between the hall and the kitchen. Two chefs, whiskered, plump, were roasting ducks, turkeys, chickens, legs of pork veal, or fried steaks. A chef wiped a pan with a piece of garlic, and the steak on the hot pan sizzled. One chef smiled, acknowledging the rich odours.

Angelina led the way upstairs to the front room.

"Who's upstairs, Angelina?" Jimmie said.

"Nobody you know, Mr. Nash."

The front room was well lighted, the blinds drawn down, heavy curtains over the blinds. It was early, not many customers were at the round tables with white tablecloths. More people would come in after the shows. They sat down in a corner. Harry's elbow brushed against a curtain, shifting from its position the blind that fitted snugly into the window frame.

"Be careful please," Angelina said, adjusting the blind so no light could be seen from the street.

"A single Scotch," Jimmie said.

"A double Scotch," Harry ordered.

Harry heard girls laughing in the front room Angelina used for nice people who wanted to drink in a bootlegger's. "After all, Vera likes nice people," he thought. He drank the double Scotch quickly. He thought vaguely of Chinamen standing on Elizabeth Street, wondering if it were true they had a peculiar way of making love to white girls. He thought of it nearly every time he walked up Elizabeth Street.

He discussed the matter with Jimmie, and they got interested, and when they had exhausted the subject, they exchanged interesting opinions about lesbians. Then Jimmie told of an aunt who had greatly impressed him when he was very young, and whom he would like to know now that he was older. She had gone away, to Mexico, people thought, and no one had heard from her since.

There was a disturbance at the door, Angelina preventing two Italian girls, bold strapping wenches, from entering the room. One of the girls pointed angrily at two girls sitting with two fellows at a table. Angelina was shaking her head resentfully and whispering to the girls, backing them away from the door. The girls stood at the door, watching sullenly.

"They been cut out I guess," Harry said, measuring each word.

More noise at the door. Angelina had taken the Italian girls by the arms and was attempting to push them downstairs. Angelina's face was flushed. One of the Italian girls had caught the eye of a young fellow sitting with the girls and, smiling, was exhibiting her bust, her hand on the curve of her hip. Angelina was angry.

"The wops are getting snotty," Jimmie said.

"Are they?"

"How about the way Cosantino carried on!"

The night Harry had met Al Cosantino in Angelina's, they had shaken hands and Cosantino had mildly asked how was business. He had grinned at Cosantino, shaking hands vigorously, but had felt that he was bigger than he, and could never be touched by him, a small man with a wife and two children, a fruit store, many relatives, barrels of fruit, a fat father – all of it making him grin at Cosantino.

They had talked a good deal about Cosantino, who was not as strong as O'Reilly but more important than Asche or Weinreb and making big deliveries all over the city. He had held Cosantino's hand and grinned at him, feeling he would have no trouble with him, a little Italian, nearly bald, rubbing the bald spot gently with the palm of his hand, a worried expression on his face.

Angelina was walking over to the fellows at the table. It was getting late. Everybody was going. "You'll have to go someplace else with the girls," Angelina said. "It's all right to meet them here but you'll have to go someplace else."

For two weeks Jimmie and Sam Martin watched Cosantino. They found out how many trucks he had on the road, and where he made his biggest deliveries, and how many men were usually on a truck. Cosantino had good trucks in four garages in different sections of the city. He was called a fruit importer and had a fruit store in the city run by his father and mother. In the daytime these trucks made deliveries all over the city to regular customers mainly on streets in the centre of town.

Once a week in the evening three trucks went along the highroad to Hamilton.

In three days Harry had rented eight houses in downtown sections because respectable people and university fellows liked to do their drinking away from home. For the houses he got good men who knew they would be well paid, if forced to do a stretch in jail. He picked out men with wives and children so they would be more reliable, and promised to pay at the end of every week. It took three hundred dollars to pay a month's rent on eight houses. The salary list was increasing.

They had to make money quickly. Their own truck was making small but regular deliveries, and some customers were behind in payment. They had just enough money to pay store rent and wages for two weeks. Thinking of money worried Harry and he was restless because the houses weren't ready to be used for storing liquor.

At half-past eleven it was cold out. The slush on the street had frozen. Snow was falling lightly. Harry, Sam Martin, Eddie Thomas and Joe Atkins drove out to the highway and across the river, where there were hardly any houses, back a little from the road. Lights from a suburb were a few miles ahead across fields in the big curve of the highway and, looking back, they could see a line of city lights curving around the margin of the lake.

It was hard driving in the icy ruts. They drove the last mile without talking. Harry, sitting in the back seat, looked straight ahead, following the glare of the headlights, avoiding thoughts of anything but a suitable place for parking the car. The highway curved by a clump of trees, and they drove the car at the snowbank and into the shadow of the trees. They got out of the car and Joe Atkins switched off the lights. Sam, Eddie and Joe got the sawed-off shotguns from under the back seat, and Joe went back to the road and stood there looking toward the city. But there were no lights on the highway and the snow was falling heavily.

Joe waved his arm when he saw lights coming along the highway, and the others got into the car again and Joe went further down the road. They knew it was a truck because it sounded heavy on the road and the engine was powerful. Joe came back and said: "I'm sure it's them, all right."

"Are we all set?" Harry said, and the truck came around the bend.

The truck stopped when three men stepped out with the sawed-off shotguns. Harry stood a few feet back from the road. The boys didn't have to use the guns. Three men got out of the truck and stood in the middle of the road. They were Italians and stood there without speaking.

"Tie the wops up, Eddie," Harry said, "over there by the tree."

Eddie went back to the car and got some rope. He tied them up quickly, their hands and feet. Eddie and Sam dragged them over to the tree and gagged them. Atkins got in the truck and had a hard time turning it around in the snow. Harry talked to him and then watched the tail light of the truck going toward the city.

They waited for Cosantino's second truck. The air got colder and a sharp wind from the lake blew across the field. They sat in the car, huddled together, talking quietly. Harry talked casually and good-naturedly to the boys. They were close together in the car.

An hour later they had more trouble with the second truck. Sam and Eddie stood in the road, but the truck didn't stop and they exchanged gunfire. Harry fired from the side of the road. The truck stopped twenty paces further along. A man jumped from the passenger's seat and ran across the field, twisting and dodging. They ran up to the truck. The driver had been hit in the arm. They had no trouble tying him up. Harry was glad the man had been hit because Sam had also been hit in the hand, not a bad wound, but Sam was swearing softly. They carried the man who had driven the truck over to the tree and backed him against the trunk with the other two.

Then Eddie got the truck's engine going and, turning around, drove toward the city. Disappointed, Harry watched the truck until it was out of sight. No use waiting for another truck. He tied a handkerchief on Sam's hand and they went over to the car near the trees. They finally got the engine going, but the wheels spun in the snow and wouldn't grip till Harry got out and pushed. He got into the car again.

They drove back to the city. Once off the highway and on the lighted streets Harry was more contented. The two trucks were heavily loaded. It was over and he let himself think about it. Things could move forward. He drove faster, turning north near Exhibition Park and along Queen, heading for University Avenue. He was sure a truck would be parked near the corner of Winslow Street. No one could interfere. It had been hard getting police protection. In a week's time they had only four policemen from the beats. These policemen had been useful in getting others who were easier because not many of them wanted to miss anything.

The car was going along residential streets, with old houses, in the district above the Arcadia dance hall. Then they passed Cosantino's store, an old-fashioned fruit store on a corner, fruit on stands on the sidewalk. Across the road was a three-storied vacant house, the windows boarded and nailed. On the other corner was a grocery store and to the left a garage and a lane. Two drunks were pretending to play catch in the lane, as if it were summer. Eddie turned the car around the corner for three blocks to the Catholic church and then came back slowly. A woman with a black shawl over her head came out of the store. They passed the corner again going a few blocks west before turning. Harry moved uneasily, rubbing his back against the seat. Cosantino might not come out of the store, he thought. He glanced angrily at Eddie, but they were at the corner and three men were coming out of the side door of the fruit store. Harry leaned forward, the breath whistling in his nostrils; he rubbed his left arm gently, then touched his head, and pulled down the peak of the cap he had put on. The car turned at the corner. One of the men coming out the side door was Cosantino, short and dark. The two men with him were taller and wore caps. Cosantino's overcoat was open, the white scarf flapping loosely over the blue coat. They were on the sidewalk. They were crossing the road. The car passed, moving slowly. Harry fired three times at Cosantino. Eddie fired twice. The car was moving very slowly. Cosantino and one of the men fell on the road. The other man with the cap stumbled, lurched to one side, and staggered across the road toward the lane. The car jerked forward, gaining speed. They didn't speak to each other. At the first corner Eddie spun the wheel, the car swung round, coming back along the street, the woman who had come out of the store screamed and ran, the car passed within a few feet of Cosantino who was sprawled in the middle of the road, his face down, one knee hunched up. The white scarf had got tangled around his neck. His hat had fallen off. The car passed over the hat, close to Cosantino, and Harry fired two more shots into the body, and the car leaped forward, swinging around the corner. People running along the streets were yelling. A cop on a bicycle came along but they sped by him and he blew his whistle.

They turned north. "We got the wop," Harry said, "we got the wop." The blood seemed to be surging into his head. He heard the whistle again and laughed out loud. The car turned east, north, west, north, south, zigzagging down to the lakefront. In Exhibition Park Eddie got out of the car and changed the licence plate. Then they took off their caps and put on felt hats. Harry grinned at Eddie when they were driving along the lakefront.

"That was a good job," he said.

"The best in the world," Eddie said.

They drove downtown. There seemed to be no noise in the city, everything quiet, and Harry couldn't hear car wheels moving on the road. He listened intently, waiting to hear wheels, and heard a purring sound and felt better. Suddenly he thought of Cosantino standing bewildered on the road, then swaying drunkenly and spinning a little on his heel before going down. Cosantino on the road, his face against the pavement. He closed his eyes, opened them quickly, looking at Eddie. Eddie's fat face had a pleasant expression. Harry wiped his lips with his tongue, deliberately avoiding bad thoughts. He thought of something else, anything that had happened the night before.

The car stopped outside the bookstore. Jimmie came out on the sidewalk and grinned, waving his hand. Harry was suddenly glad to see Jimmie. He put his hand on his shoulder as though he hadn't seen him for a long time. He looked at him as if he hadn't really expected to see him, and had experienced all the disappointment, and then, accidentally, had encountered him again.

Eddie stayed in the car to drive it over to the garage. Jimmie and Harry went through the store to the office and sat down, and Harry told him about it. He didn't use many words.

"It was going to be me or Cosantino," he said.

THE MAN FROM MARS

MARGARET ATWOOD

A long time ago Christine was walking through the park. She was still wearing her tennis dress; she hadn't had time to shower and change, and her hair was held back with an elastic band. Her chunky reddish face, exposed with no softening fringe, looked like a Russian peasant's, but without the elastic band the hair got in her eyes. The afternoon was too hot for April; the indoor courts had been steaming, her skin felt poached.

The sun had brought the old men out from wherever they spent the winter: she had read a story recently about one who lived for three years in a manhole. They sat weedishly on the benches or lay on the grass with their heads on squares of used newspaper. As she passed, their wrinkled toadstool faces drifted towards her, drawn by the movement of her body, then floated away again, uninterested.

The squirrels were out, too, foraging; two or three of them moved towards her in darts and pauses, eyes fixed on her expectantly, mouths with the ratlike receding chins open to show the yellowed front teeth. Christine walked faster; she had nothing to give them. People shouldn't feed them, she thought; it makes them anxious and they get mangy.

Halfway across the park she stopped to take off her cardigan. As she bent over to pick up her tennis racquet again someone touched her on her freshly bared arm. Christine seldom screamed; she straightened up suddenly, gripping the handle of her racquet. It was not one of the old men, however: it was a dark-haired boy of twelve or so.

"Excuse me," he said, "I search for economics building. Is it there?" He motioned toward the west.

Christine looked at him more closely. She had been mistaken: he was not young, just short. He came a little above her shoulder, but then, she was above the average height; "statuesque," her mother called it when she was straining. He was also what was referred to in their family as "a person from another culture": oriental without a doubt, though perhaps not Chinese. Christine judged he must be a foreign student and gave him her official welcoming smile. In high school she had been president of the United Nations Club; that year her school had been picked to represent the Egyptian delegation at the Mock Assembly. It had been an unpopular assignment – nobody wanted to be the

Arabs – but she had seen it through. She had made rather a good speech about the Palestinian refugees.

"Yes," she said, "that's it over there. The one with the flat roof. See it?"

The man had been smiling nervously at her the whole time. He was wearing glasses with transparent plastic rims, through which his eyes bulged up at her as though through a goldfish bowl. He had not followed where she was pointing. Instead he thrust towards her a small pad of green paper and a ballpoint pen.

"You make map," he said.

Christine set down her tennis racquet and drew a careful map. "We are here," she said, pronouncing distinctly. "You go this way. The building is here." She indicated the route with a dotted line and an "X." The man leaned close to her, watching the progress of the map attentively; he smelled of cooked cauliflower and an unfamiliar brand of hair grease. When she had finished Christine handed the paper and pen back to him with a terminal smile.

"Wait," the man said. He tore the piece of paper with the map off the pad, folded it carefully and put it in his jacket pocket; the jacket sleeves came down over his wrists and had threads at the edges. He began to write something; she noticed with a slight feeling of revulsion that his nails and the ends of his fingers were so badly bitten they seemed almost deformed. Several of his fingers were blue from the leaky ballpoint.

"Here is my name," he said, holding the pad out to her.

Christine read an odd assemblage of "G"s, "Y"s and "N"s, neatly printed in block letters. "Thank you," she said.

"You now write your name," he said, extending the pen.

Christine hesitated. If this had been a person from her own culture she would have thought he was trying to pick her up. But then, people from her own culture never tried to pick her up; she was too big. The only one who had made the attempt was the Moroccan waiter at the beer parlour where they sometimes went after meetings, and he had been direct. He had just intercepted her on the way to the ladies' room and asked and she said no; that had been that. This man was not a waiter though, but a student; she didn't want to offend him. In his culture, whatever it was, this exchange of names on pieces of paper was probably a formal politeness, like saying thank you. She took the pen from him.

"That is a very pleasant name," he said. He folded the paper and placed it in his jacket pocket with the map.

Christine felt she had done her duty. "Well, goodbye," she said. "It was nice to have met you." She bent for her tennis racquet but he had already stooped and retrieved it and was holding it with both hands in front of him, like a captured banner.

"I carry this for you."

"Oh no, please. Don't bother, I am in a hurry," she said, articulating clearly. Deprived of her tennis racquet she felt weaponless. He started to saunter along the path; he was not nervous at all now, he seemed completely at ease.

"*Vous parlez français?*" he asked conversationally.

"*Oui, un petit peu,*" she said. "Not very well." How am I going to get my racquet away from him without being rude? she was wondering.

"*Mais vous avez un bel accent.*" His eyes goggled at her through the glasses: was he being flirtatious? She was well aware that her accent was wretched.

"Look," she said, for the first time letting her impatience show. "I really have to go. Give me my racquet, please."

He quickened his pace but gave no sign of returning the racquet. "Where are you going?"

"Home," she said. "My house."

"I go with you now," he said hopefully.

"*No,*" she said: she would have to be firm with him. She made a lunge and got a grip on her racquet; after a brief tug of war it came free.

"Goodbye," she said, turning away from his puzzled face and setting off at what she hoped was a discouraging jog-trot. It was like walking away from a growling dog: you shouldn't let on you were frightened. Why should she be frightened anyway? He was only half her size and she had the tennis racquet, there was nothing he could do to her.

Although she did not look back she could tell he was still following. Let there be a streetcar, she thought, and there was one, but it was far down the line, stuck behind a red light. He appeared at her side, breathing audibly, a moment after she reached the stop. She gazed ahead, rigid.

"You are my friend," he said tentatively.

Christine relented: he hadn't been trying to pick her up after all, he was a stranger, he just wanted to meet some of the local people; in his place she would have wanted the same thing.

"Yes," she said, doling him out a smile.

"That is good," he said. "My country is very far."

Christine couldn't think of an apt reply. "That's interesting," she said. "*Très intéressant.*" The streetcar was coming at last; she opened her purse and got out a ticket.

"I go with you now," he said. His hand clamped on her arm above the elbow.

"You... stay... here," Christine said, resisting the impulse to shout but pausing between each word as though for a deaf person. She detached his hand – his hold was quite feeble and could not compete with her tennis biceps – and leapt off the curb and up the streetcar steps, hearing with relief the doors grind shut behind her. Inside the car and a block away she permitted herself a glance out a side window. He was standing where she had left him; he seemed to be writing something on his little pad of paper.

When she reached home she had only time for a snack, and even then she was almost late for the Debating Society. The topic was, "Resolved: That War Is Obsolete." Her team took the affirmative and won.

Christine came out of her last examination feeling depressed. It was not the exam that depressed her but the fact that it was the last one: it meant the end of the school year. She dropped into the coffee shop as usual, then went home early because there didn't seem to be anything else to do.

"Is that you, dear?" her mother called from the living room. She must have heard the front door close. Christine went in and flopped on the sofa, disturbing the neat pattern of cushions.

"How was your exam, dear?" her mother asked.

"Fine," said Christine flatly. It had been fine; she had passed. She was not a brilliant student, she knew that, but she was conscientious. Her professors always wrote things like "A serious attempt" and "Well thought out but perhaps lacking in *élan*" on her term papers; they gave her Bs, the occasional B+. She was taking political science and economics, and hoped for a job with the government after she graduated; with her father's connections she had a good chance.

"That's nice."

Christine felt, resentfully, that her mother had only a hazy idea of what an exam was. She was arranging gladioli in a vase; she had rubber gloves on to protect her hands as she always did when engaged in what she called "housework." As far as Christine could tell her housework consisted of arranging flowers in vases: daffodils and tulips and hyacinths through gladioli, irises and roses, all the way to asters and mums. Sometimes she cooked, elegantly and with chafing dishes, but she thought of it as a hobby. The girl did everything else. Christine thought it faintly sinful to have a girl. The only ones available now were either foreign or pregnant; their expressions usually suggested they were being taken advantage of somehow. But her mother asked what they would do otherwise; they'd either have to go into a home or stay in their own countries, and Christine had to agree this was probably true. It was hard, anyway, to argue with her mother. She was so delicate, so preserved-looking, a harsh breath would scratch the finish.

"An interesting young man phoned today," her mother said. She had finished the gladioli and was taking off her rubber gloves. "He asked to speak with you and when I said you weren't in we had quite a little chat. You didn't tell me about him, dear." She put on the glasses which she wore on a decorative chain around her neck, a signal that she was in her modern, intelligent mood rather than her old-fashioned whimsical one.

"Did he leave his name?" Christine asked. She knew a lot of young men but they didn't often call her; they conducted their business with her in the coffee shop or after meetings.

"He's a person from another culture. He said he would call back later."

Christine had to think a moment. She was vaguely acquainted with several people from other cultures, Britain mostly; they belonged to the Debating Society.

"He's studying philosophy in Montreal," her mother prompted. "He sounded French."

Christine began to remember the man in the park. "I don't think he's French, exactly," she said.

Her mother had taken off her glasses again and was poking absent-mindedly at a bent gladiolus. "Well, he sounded French." She meditated, flowery sceptre in hand. "I think it would be nice if you had him to tea."

Christine's mother did her best. She had two other daughters, both of whom took after her. They were beautiful; one was well married already and the other would clearly have no trouble. Her friends consoled her about Christine by saying, "She's not fat, she'd just big-boned, it's the father's side," and "Christine is so healthy." Her other daughters had never gotten involved in activities when they were at school, but since Christine could not possibly ever be beautiful even if she took off weight, it was just as well she was so athletic and political, it was a good thing she had interests. Christine's mother tried to encourage her interests whenever possible. Christine could tell when she was making an extra effort, there was a reproachful edge to her voice.

She knew her mother expected enthusiasm but she could not supply it. "I don't know, I'll have to see," she said dubiously.

"You look tired, darling," said her mother. "Perhaps you'd like a glass of milk."

Christine was in the bathtub when the phone rang. She was not prone to fantasy but when she was in the bathtub she often pretended she was a dolphin, a game left over from one of the girls who used to bathe her when she was small. Her mother was being bell-voiced and gracious in the hall; then there was a tap at the door.

"It's that nice young French student, Christine," her mother said.

"Tell him I'm in the bathtub," Christine said, louder than necessary. "He isn't French."

She could hear her mother frowning. "That wouldn't be very polite, Christine. I don't think he'd understand."

"Oh, all right," Christine said. She heaved herself out of the bathtub, swathed her pink bulk in a towel and splattered to the phone.

"Hello," she said gruffly. At a distance he was not pathetic, he was a nuisance. She could not imagine how he had tracked her down: most likely he went through the phonebook, calling all the numbers with her last name until he hit on the right one.

"It is your friend."

"I know," she said. "How are you?"

"I am very fine."

There was a long pause, during which Christine had a vicious urge to say, "Well, goodbye then," and hang up; but she was aware of her mother poised figurine-like in her bedroom doorway. Then he said, "I hope you also are very fine."

"Yes," said Christine. She wasn't going to participate.

"I come to tea," he said.

This took Christine by surprise. "You do?"

"Your pleasant mother ask me. I come Thursday, four o'clock."

"Oh," Christine said, ungraciously.

"See you then," he said, with the conscious pride of one who has mastered a difficult idiom.

Christine set down the phone and went along the hall. Her mother was in her study, sitting innocently at her writing desk.

"Did you ask him to tea on Thursday?"

"Not exactly, dear," her mother said. "I did mention he might come round to tea *some*time, though."

"Well, he's coming Thursday. Four o'clock."

"What's wrong with that?" her mother said serenely. "I think it's a very nice gesture for us to make. I do think you might try to be a little more cooperative." She was pleased with herself.

"Since you invited him," said Christine, "you can bloody well stick around and help me entertain him. I don't want to be left making nice gestures all by myself."

"Christine, *dear*," her mother said, above being shocked. "You ought to put on your dressing gown, you'll catch a chill."

After sulking for an hour Christine tried to think of the tea as a cross between an examination and an executive meeting: not enjoyable, certainly, but to be got through as tactfully as possible. And it *was* a nice gesture. When the cakes her mother had ordered arrived from the *patisserie* on Thursday morning she began to feel slightly festive; she even resolved to put on a dress, a good one, instead of a skirt and blouse. After all, she had nothing against him, except the memory of the way he had grabbed her tennis racquet and then her arm. She suppressed a quick impossible vision of herself pursued around the living room, fending him off with thrown sofa cushions and vases of gladioli; nevertheless she told the girl they would have tea in the garden. It would be a treat for him, and there was more space outdoors.

She had suspected her mother would dodge the tea, would contrive to be going out just as he was arriving: that way she could size him up and then leave them alone together. She had done things like that to Christine before; the excuse this time was the Symphony Committee. Sure enough, her mother carefully mislaid her gloves and located them with a faked murmur of joy when the doorbell rang. Christine relished for weeks afterwards the image of her mother's dropped jaw and flawless recovery when he was introduced: he wasn't quite the foreign potentate her optimistic, veil-fragile mind had concocted.

He was prepared for celebration. He had slicked on so much hair cream that his head seemed to be covered with a tight black patent-leather cap, and he had cut the threads off his jacket sleeves. His orange tie was overpoweringly splendid. Christine noticed, however, as he shook her mother's suddenly braced white glove that the ballpoint ink on his fingers was indelible. His face had broken out, possibly in anticipation of the delights in store for him; he had a tiny camera slung over his shoulder and was smoking an exotic-smelling cigarette.

Christine led him through the cool flowery softly padded living room and out by the French doors into the garden. "You sit here," she said. "I will have the girl bring tea."

This girl was from the West Indies. Christine's parents had been enraptured with her when they were down at Christmas and had brought her back with them. Since that time she had become pregnant, but Christine's mother had not dismissed her. She said she was slightly disappointed but what could you expect, and she didn't see any real difference between a girl who was pregnant before you hired her and one who got that way afterwards. She prided herself on her tolerance; also there was a scarcity of girls. Strangely enough, the girl became progressively less easy to get along with. Either she did not share Christine's mother's view of her own generosity or she felt she had gotten away with something and was therefore free to indulge in contempt. At first Christine had tried to treat her as an equal. "Don't call me 'Miss Christine,'" she had said with an imitation of light, comradely laughter. "What you want me to call you then?" the girl had said, scowling. They had begun to have brief, surly arguments in the kitchen, which Christine decided were like the arguments between one servant and another. Her mother's attitude towards each of them was similar; they were not altogether satisfactory but they would have to do.

The cakes, glossy with icing, were set out on a plate and the teapot was standing ready; on the counter the electric kettle boiled. Christine headed for it, but the girl, till then sitting with her elbows on the kitchen table and watching her expressionlessly, made a dash and intercepted her. Christine waited until she had poured the water into the pot. Then, "I'll carry it out, Elvira," she said. She had just decided she didn't want the girl to see her visitor's orange tie; already, she knew, her position in the girl's eyes had suffered because no one had yet attempted to get *her* pregnant.

"What you think they pay me for, Miss Christine?" the girl said insolently. She swung towards the garden with the tray; Christine trailed her, feeling lumpish and awkward. The girl was at least as big as she was but in a different way.

"Thank you, Elvira," Christine said when the tray was in place. The girl departed without a word, casting a disdainful backward glance at the frayed jacket sleeves, the stained fingers. Christine was now determined to be especially kind to him.

"You are very rich," he said.

"No," Christine protested, shaking her head, "we're not." She had never thought of her family as rich; it was one of her father's sayings that nobody made any money with the government.

"Yes," he repeated, "you are very rich." He sat back in his lawn chair, gazing about him as though dazed.

Christine set up his cup of tea in front of him. She wasn't in the habit of paying much attention to the house or the garden; they were nothing special, far from being the largest on the street; other people took care of them. But now she looked where he was looking, seeing it all as though from a different height: the long expanses, the border flowers blazing in the early-summer sunlight, the flagged patio and walks, the high walls and the silence.

He came back to her face, sighing a little. "My English is not good," he said, "but I improve."

"You do," Christine said, nodding encouragement.

He took sips of his tea, quickly and tenderly as though afraid of injuring the cup. "I like to stay here."

Christine passed him the cakes. He took only one, making a slight face as he ate it; but he had several more cups of tea while she finished the cakes. She managed to find out from him that he had come over on a church fellowship - she could not decode the denomination - and was studying philosophy or theology, or possibly both. She was feeling well disposed towards him: he had behaved himself, he had caused her no inconvenience.

The teapot was at last empty. He sat up straight in his chair, as though alerted by a soundless gong. "You look this way, please," he said. Christine saw that he had placed his miniature camera on the stone sundial her mother had shipped back from England two years before. He wanted to take her picture. She was flattered, and settled herself to pose, smiling evenly.

He took off his glasses and laid them beside his plate. For a moment she saw his myopic, unprotected eyes turned towards her, with something tremulous and confiding in them she wanted to close herself off from knowing about. Then he went over and did something to the camera, his back to her. The next instant he was crouched beside her, his arm around her waist as far as it could reach, his other hand covering her own hands which she had folded in her lap, his cheek jammed up against hers. She was too startled to move. The camera clicked.

He stood up at once and replaced his glasses, which glittered now with a sad triumph. "Thank you, Miss," he said to her. "I go now." He slung the camera back over his shoulder, keeping his hand on it as though to hold the lid on and prevent escape. "I send to my family; they will like."

He was out the gate and gone before Christine had recovered; then she laughed. She had been afraid he would attack her, she could admit it now, and he had; but not in the usual way. He had raped, *rapeo, raper, rapui*, to seize and carry off, not herself but her celluloid image, and incidentally that of the silver tea service, which glinted mockingly at her as the girl bore it away, carrying it regally, the insignia, the official jewels. Christine spent the summer as she had for the past three years: she was the sailing instructor at an expensive all-girls camp near Algonquin Park. She had been a camper there, everything was familiar to her; she sailed almost better than she played tennis.

The second week she got a letter from him, postmarked Montreal and forwarded from her home address. It was printed in block letters on a piece of the green paper, two or three sentences. It began, "I hope you are well," then described the weather in monosyllables and ended, "I am fine." It was signed, "Your friend." Each week she got another of these letters, more or less identical. In one of them a colour print was enclosed: himself, slightly cross-eyed and grinning hilariously, even more spindly than she remembered him against her billowing draperies, flowers exploding around them like firecrackers, one of his hands an equivocal blur in her lap, the other out of sight; on her own face, astonishment and outrage, as though he was sticking her in the behind with his hidden thumb.

She answered the first letter, but after that the seniors were in training for the races. At the end of the summer, packing to go home, she threw all the letters away.

When she had been back for several weeks she received another of the green letters. This time there was a return address printed at the top which Christine noted with foreboding was in her own city. Every day she waited for the phone to ring; she was so certain his first attempt at contact would be a disembodied voice that when he came upon her abruptly in mid-campus she was unprepared.

"How are you?"

His smile was the same, but everything else about him had deteriorated. He was, if possible, thinner; his jacket sleeves had sprouted a lush new crop of threads, as though to conceal hands now so badly bitten they appeared to have been gnawed by rodents. His hair fell over his eyes, uncut, ungreased; his eyes in the hollowed face, a delicate triangle of skin stretched on bone, jumped behind his glasses like hooked fish. He had the end of a cigarette in the corner of his mouth, and as they walked he lit a new one from it.

"I'm fine," Christine said. She was thinking, I'm not going to get involved again, enough is enough, I've done my bit for internationalism. "How are you?"

"I live here now," he said. "Maybe I study economics."

"That's nice." He didn't sound as though he was enrolled anywhere.

"I come to see you."

Christine didn't know whether he meant he had left Montreal in order to be near her or just wanted to visit her at her house as he had done in the spring; either way she refused to be implicated. They were outside the political science building. "I have a class here," she said. "Goodbye." She was being callous, she realized that, but a quick chop was more merciful in the long run, that was what her beautiful sisters used to say.

Afterwards she decided it had been stupid of her to let him find out where her class was. Though a timetable was posted in each of the colleges: all he had to do was look her up and record her every probable movement in block letters on his green notepad. After that day he never left her alone.

Initially he waited outside the lecture rooms for her to come out. She said hello to him curtly at first and kept on going, but this didn't work; he followed her at a distance, smiling his changeless smile. Then she stopped speaking altogether and pretended to ignore him, but it made no difference, he followed her anyway. The fact that she was in some way afraid of him – or was it just embarrassment? – seemed only to encourage him. Her friends started to notice, asking her who he was and why he was tagging along behind her; she could hardly answer because she hardly knew.

As the weekdays passed and he showed no signs of letting up she began to jog-trot between classes, finally to run. He was tireless, and had an amazing wind for one who smoked so heavily: he would speed along behind her, keeping the distance between them the same, as though he were a pull-toy attached to her by a string. She was aware of the ridiculous spectacle they must make, galloping across campus, something out of a cartoon short, a lumbering elephant stampeded by a smiling, emaciated mouse, both of them locked in the classic pattern of comic pursuit and flight; but she found that to race made her less nervous than to walk sedately, the skin on the back of her neck crawling with the feel of his eyes on it. At least she could use her muscles. She worked out routines, escapes: she would dash in the front door of the ladies' room in the coffee shop and out the back door, and he would lose the trail, until he discovered the other entrance. She would try to shake him by detours through baffling archways and corridors, but he seemed as familiar with the architectural mazes as she was herself. As a last refuge she could head for the women's dormitory and watch from safety as he was skidded to a halt by the receptionist's austere voice: men were not allowed past the entrance.

Lunch became difficult. She would be sitting, usually with other members of the Debating Society, just digging nicely into a sandwich, when he would appear suddenly as though he'd come up through an unseen manhole. She then had the choice of barging out through the crowded cafeteria, sandwich half-eaten, or finishing her lunch with him standing behind her chair, everyone at the table acutely aware of him, the conversation stilting and dwindling. Her friends learned to spot him from a distance; they posted lookouts. "Here he comes," they would whisper, helping her collect her belongings for the sprint they knew would follow.

Several times she got tired of running and turned to confront him. "What do you want?" she would ask, glowering belligerently down at him, almost clenching her fists; she felt like shaking him, hitting him.

"I wish to talk with you."

"Well, here I am," she would say. "What do you want to talk about?"

But he would say nothing; he would stand in front of her, shifting his feet, smiling perhaps apologetically (though she could never pinpoint the exact tone of that smile, chewed lips stretched apart over the nicotine-yellowed teeth, rising at the corners, flesh held stiffly in place for an invisible photographer), his eyes jerking from one part of her face to another as though he saw her in fragments.

Annoying and tedious though it was, his pursuit of her had an odd result: mysterious in itself, it rendered her equally mysterious. No one had ever found Christine mysterious before. To her parents she was a beefy heavyweight, a plodder, lacking in flair, ordinary as bread. To her sisters she was the plain one, treated with an indulgence they did not give to each other: they did not fear her as a rival. To her male friends she was the one who could be relied on. She was helpful and a hard worker, always good for a game of tennis with the athletes among them. They invited her along to drink beer with them so they could get into the cleaner, more desirable ladies' and escorts' side of the beer parlour, taking it for granted she would buy her share of the rounds. In moments of stress they confided to her their problems with women. There was nothing devious about her and nothing interesting.

Christine had always agreed with these estimates of herself. In childhood she had identified with the false bride or the ugly sister; whenever a story had begun, "Once there was a maiden as beautiful as she was good," she had known it wasn't her. That was just how it was, but it wasn't so bad. Her parents never expected her to be a brilliant social success and weren't overly disappointed when she wasn't. She was spared the manoeuvring and anxiety she witnessed among others her age, and she even had a kind of special position among men: she was an exception, she fitted none of the categories they commonly used when talking about girls; she wasn't a cock-teaser, a cold fish, an easy lay or a snarky bitch; she was an honourable person. She had grown to share their contempt for most women.

Now, however, there was something about her that could not be explained. A man was chasing her, a peculiar sort of man, granted, but still a man, and he was without doubt attracted to her, he couldn't leave her alone. Other men examined her more closely than they ever had, appraising her, trying to find out what it was those twitching bespectacled eyes saw in her. They started to ask her out, though they returned from these excursions with their curiosity unsatisfied, the secret of her charm still intact. Her opaque dumpling face, her solid bear-shaped body became for them parts of a riddle no one could solve. Christine sensed this. In the bathtub she no longer imagined she was a dolphin; instead she imagined she was an elusive water-pixie, or sometimes, in moments of audacity, Marilyn Monroe. The daily chase was becoming a habit; she even looked forward to it. In addition to its other benefits she was losing weight.

All those weeks he had never phoned her or turned up at the house. He must have decided however that his tactics were not having the desired result, or perhaps he sensed she was becoming bored. The phone began to ring in the early morning or late at night when he could be sure she would be there. Sometimes he would simply breathe (she could recognize, or thought she could, the quality of his breathing), in which case she would hang up. Occasionally he would say again that he wanted to talk to her, but even when she gave him lots of time nothing else would follow. Then he extended his range: she would see him on her streetcar, smiling at her silently from a seat never closer than three away; she could feel him tracking her down her own street, though when she would break her resolve to pay no attention and would glance back he would be invisible or in the act of hiding behind a tree or hedge.

Among crowds of people and in daylight she had not really been afraid of him; she was stronger than he was and he had made no recent attempt to touch her. But the days were growing shorter and colder, it was almost November, often she was arriving home in twilight or a darkness broken only by the feeble orange streetlamps. She brooded over the possibility of razors, knives, guns; by acquiring a weapon he could quickly turn the odds against her. She avoided wearing scarves, remembering the newspaper stories about girls who had been strangled by them. Putting on her nylons in the morning gave her a funny feeling. Her body seemed to have diminished, to have become smaller than his.

Was he deranged, was he a sex maniac? He seemed so harmless, yet it was that kind who often went berserk in the end. She pictured those ragged fingers at her throat, tearing at her clothes, though she could not think of herself as screaming. Parked cars, the shrubberies near her house, the driveways on either side of it, changed as she passed them from unnoticed background to sinister shadowed foreground, every detail distinct and harsh: they were places a man might crouch, leap out from. Yet every time she saw him in the clear light of morning or afternoon (for he still continued his old methods of pursuit), his aging jacket and jittery eyes convinced her that it was she herself who was the tormentor, the persecutor. She was in some sense responsible; from the folds and crevices of the body she had treated for so long as a reliable machine was emanating, against her will, some potent invisible odour, like a dog's in heat or a female moth's, that made him unable to stop following her.

Her mother, who had been too preoccupied with the unavoidable fall entertaining to pay much attention to the number of phone calls Christine was getting or to the hired girl's complaints of a man who hung up without speaking, announced that she was flying down to New York for the weekend; her father decided to go too. Christine panicked: she saw herself in the bathtub with her throat slit, the blood drooling out of her neck and running in a little spiral down the drain (for by this time she believed he could walk through walls, could be everywhere at once). The girl would do nothing to help; she might even stand in the bathroom door with her arms folded, watching. Christine arranged to spend the weekend at her married sister's.

When she arrived back Sunday evening she found the girl close to hysterical. She said that on Saturday she had gone to pull the curtains across the French doors at dusk and had found a strangely contorted face, a man's face, pressed against the glass, staring in at her from the garden. She claimed she had fainted and had almost had her baby a month too early right there on the living-room carpet. Then she had called the police. He was gone by the time they got there but she had recognized him from the afternoon of the tea; she had informed them he was a friend of Christine's.

They called Monday evening to investigate, two of them. They were very polite, they knew who Christine's father was. Her father greeted them heartily; her mother hovered in the background, fidgeting with her porcelain hands, letting them see how frail and worried she was. She didn't like having them in the living room but they were necessary.

Christine had to admit he'd been following her around. She was relieved he'd been discovered, relieved also that she hadn't been the one to tell, though if he'd been a citizen of the country she would have called the police a long time ago. She insisted he was not dangerous, he had never hurt her.

"That kind don't hurt you," one of the policemen said. "They just kill you. You're lucky you aren't dead."

"Nut cases," the other one said.

Her mother volunteered that the thing about people from another culture was that you could never tell whether they were insane or not because their ways were so different. The policeman agreed with her, deferential but also condescending, as though she was a royal halfwit who had to be humoured.

"You know where he lives?" the first policeman asked. Christine had long ago torn up the letter with his address on it; she shook her head.

"We'll have to pick him up tomorrow then," he said. "Think you can keep him talking outside your class if he's waiting for you?"

After questioning her they held a murmured conversation with her father in the front hall. The girl, clearing away the coffee cups, said if they didn't lock him up she was leaving, she wasn't going to be scared half out of her skin like that again.

Next day when Christine came out of her modern history lecture he was there, right on schedule. He seemed puzzled when she did not begin to run. She approached him, her heart thumping with treachery and the prospect of freedom. Her body was back to its usual size; she felt herself a giantess, self-controlled, invulnerable.

"How are you?" she asked, smiling brightly.

He looked at her with distrust.

"How have you been?" she ventured again. His own perennial smile faded; he took a step back from her.

"This the one?" said the policeman, popping out from behind a notice board like a Keystone Cop and laying a competent hand on the worn jacket shoulder. The other policeman lounged in the background; force would not be required.

"Don't *do* anything to him," she pleaded as they took him away. They nodded and grinned, respectful, scornful. He seemed to know perfectly well who they were and what they wanted.

The first policeman phoned that evening to make his report. Her father talked with him, jovial and managing. She herself was now out of the picture; she had been protected, her function was over.

"What did they *do* to him?" she asked anxiously as he came back into the living room. She was not sure what went on in police stations.

"They didn't do anything to him," he said, amused by her concern. "They could have booked him for 'watching and besetting,' they wanted to know if I'd like to press charges. But it's not worth a court case: he's got a visa that says he's only allowed in the country as long as he studies in Montreal, so I told them to just ship him down there. If he turns up here again they'll deport him. They went around to his rooming house, his rent's two weeks overdue; the landlady said she was on the point of kicking him out. He seems happy enough to be getting his back rent paid and a free train ticket to Montreal." He paused. "They couldn't get anything out of him though."

"*Out* of him?" Christine asked.

"They tried to find out why he was doing it; following you I mean." Her father's eyes swept her as though it was a riddle to him also. "They said when they asked him about that he just clammed up. Pretended he didn't understand English. He understood well enough, but he wasn't answering."

Christine thought this would be the end, but somehow between his arrest and the departure of the train he managed to elude his escort long enough for one more phone call.

"I see you again," he said. He didn't wait for her to hang up.

Now that he was no longer an embarrassing present reality, he could be talked about, he could become an amusing story. In fact, he was the only amusing story Christine had to tell, and telling it preserved both for herself and for others the aura of her strange allure. Her friends and the men who continued to ask her out speculated about his motives. One suggested he had wanted to marry her so he could remain in the country; another said that oriental men were fond of well-built women: "It's your Rubens quality."

Christine thought about him a lot. She had not been attracted to him, rather the reverse, but as an idea only he was a romantic figure, the one man who had found her irresistible; though she often wondered, inspecting her unchanged pink face and hefty body in her full-length mirror, just what it was about her that had done it. She avoided whenever it was proposed the theory of his insanity: it was only that there was more than one way of being sane.

But a new acquaintance, hearing the story for the first time, had a different explanation. "So he got you, too," he said, laughing. "That has to be the same guy who was hanging around our day camp a year ago this summer. He followed all the girls like that. A short guy, Japanese or something, glasses, smiling all the time."

"Maybe it was another one," Christine said.

"There couldn't be two of them, everything fits. This was a pretty weird guy."

"What... *kind* of girls did he follow?" Christine asked.

"Oh, just anyone who happened to be around, but if they paid any attention to him at first, if they were nice to him or anything, he was unshakeable. He was a bit of a pest, but harmless."

Christine ceased to tell her amusing story. She had been one among many, then. She went back to playing tennis, she had been neglecting her game.

A few months later the policeman who had been in charge of the case telephoned her again.

"Like you to know, miss, that fellow you were having the trouble with was sent back to his own country. Deported."

"What for?" Christine asked. "Did he try to come back here?" Maybe she had been special after all, maybe he had dared everything for her.

"Nothing like it," the policeman said. "He was up to the same tricks in Montreal but he really picked the wrong woman this time – a Mother Superior of a convent. They don't stand for things like that in Quebec – had him out of here before he knew what happened. I guess he'll be better off in his own place."

"How old was she?" Christine asked, after a silence.

"Oh, around sixty, I guess."

"Thank you very much for letting me know," Christine said in her best official manner. "It's such a relief." She wondered if the policeman had called to make fun of her.

She was almost crying when she put down the phone. What *had* he wanted from her then? A Mother Superior. Did she really look sixty, did she look like a mother? What did convents mean? Comfort, charity? Refuge? Was it that something bad happened to him, some intolerable strain just from being in this country; her tennis dress and exposed legs too much for him, flesh and money seemingly available everywhere but withheld from him wherever he turned, the nun the symbol of some final distortion, the robe and veil reminiscent to his nearsighted eyes of the women of his homeland, the ones he was able to understand? But he was back in his own country, remote from her as another planet; she would never know.

He hadn't forgotten her though. In the spring she got a postcard with a foreign stamp and the familiar block-letter writing. On the front was a picture of a temple. He was fine, he hoped she was fine also, he was her friend. A month later another print of the picture he had taken in the garden arrived, in a sealed manila envelope otherwise empty.

Christine's aura of mystery soon faded; anyway, she herself no longer believed in it. Life became again what she had always expected. She graduated with mediocre grades and went into the Department of Health and Welfare; she did a good job, and was seldom discriminated against for being a woman because nobody thought of her as one. She could afford a pleasant-sized apartment, though she did not put much energy into decorating it. She played less and less tennis; what had been muscle with a light coating of fat turned gradually into fat with a thin substratum of muscle. She began to get headaches.

As the years were used up and the war began to fill the newspapers and magazines, she realized which eastern country he had actually been from. She had known the name but it hadn't registered at the time, it was such a minor place; she could never keep them separate in her mind.

But though she tried, she couldn't remember the name of the city and the postcard was long gone – had he been from the north or the south, was he near the battle zone or safely far from it? Obsessively she bought magazines and pored over the available photographs, dead villagers, soldiers on the march, colour blow-ups of frightened or angry faces, spies being executed; she studied maps, she watched the late-night newscasts, the distant country and terrain becoming almost more familiar to her than her own. Once or twice she thought she could recognize him but it was no use, they all looked like him.

Finally she had to stop looking at the pictures. It bothered her too much, it was bad for her; she was beginning to have nightmares in which he was coming through the French doors of her mother's house in his shabby jacket, carrying a packsack and a rifle and a huge bouquet of richly coloured flowers. He was smiling in the same way but with blood streaked over his face, partly blotting out the features. She gave her television set away and took to reading nineteenth-century novels instead; Trollope and Galsworthy were her favourites. When, despite herself, she would think about him, she would tell herself that he had been crafty and agile-minded enough to survive, more or less, in her country, so surely he would be able to do it in his own, where he knew the language. She could not see him in the army, on either side; he wasn't the type, and to her knowledge he had not believed in any particular ideology. He would be something nondescript, something in the background, like herself. Perhaps he had become an interpreter.

from CABBAGETOWN

HUGH GARNER

Toronto's Cabbagetown, the largest Anglo-Saxon slum in North America —H.G.

In 1929 most Cabbagetowners rented their houses, believed in God, the Royal Family, the Conservative Party and private enterprise. They were suspicious and a little condescending towards all heathen religions, higher education, "foreigners" and social reformers. They were generally unskilled working people, among whom were scattered, like raisins in a ten-cent cake, representatives of the state - such as postmen, civic employees, streetcar conductors and even a policeman or two.

As Ken hurried south towards his own street he became conscious of children shouting and crying, more traffic on the narrow streets, more raucous pedlars, and above all this the constant noise of the factories, the whir of machinery, the clang of metal on metal, the increased noise of streetcars on their older roadbeds.

The smells were also different. Coal smoke, chemicals, horse manure, wet mattresses, old wallpaper and dirty snow. As he passed the open windows of a mill he caught the smell of hot metal curling from the lathes. But the prevailing smell was one of decay, of old wet plaster and rotting wooden steps, the smell of a landlord's carelessness and neglect.

He turned off Sumach Street into a narrow alley whose broken street sign read TIMOTHY PLACE. Beyond the sign was a short strip of broken pavement on each side of which stood facing blocks of narrow undivided red brick houses, their only signs of separateness being their vari-painted wooden doors and individual "parlour" windows...

Ken crossed the street to the south side and walked along the broken sidewalk to the third wooden door. A lopsided figure 5 which he had cut out in tinsmithing class hung on the door.

The house was cold, and he shivered as he took off his windbreaker and hung it on a nail behind the front door. From the dirty linoleum of the hallway he picked up a letter. On the envelope was the name of a credit clothing firm and it was addressed to his mother, Mrs. Mabel Tilling. He carried it into the small middle room.

He called out, "Ma!" but there was no answer, so he shoved his way past the big old sideboard into the kitchen. After he shook the fire he moved a dry half-loaf of bread and an empty milk bottle to the back of the table and with a damp cloth wiped off the crumbs, tea spots and ketchup stains. Then he rinsed out a cup under the sink's one tap and dried it on a dishtowel made from an old sugar sack. When the fire was red he poured some coke onto it from a pail beneath the stove.

Returning to the middle room he looked into the sideboard cupboard for something to eat. A plate held four sausages congealed in their grease, and he carried them along with the butter dish into the kitchen. When the kettle boiled he made his tea. Placing a slice of buttered bread on a plate, he poured the sausages and grease over it and sat down hungrily to eat his dinner.

1929

One evening in October the newspapers printed extra editions reporting a stock market crash. Of all the city's neighbourhoods Cabbagetown probably took the news most quietly. In the wealthier districts, and even in the middle-class neighbourhoods, the citizens were either shocked or sloughed off the news as merely a temporary halt to the inevitable spiralling of the economy. In the Bay Street financial district crowds filled the evening streets, clustering in front of the newspaper offices waiting for the latest bulletins. In residential neighbourhoods families sat down in their living rooms and laughed at Amos 'n' Andy or listened with mounting impatience as the bulletins from New York and other financial centres cried havoc and interrupted the A & P Gypsies...

Ken was out of work except for two days at Christmas selling trees. He had stood half frozen in front of Joe Pergoli's Fruit and Vegetable Market on Parliament Street trying to interest the hurrying crowds of Christmas shoppers in the scruffy-looking Christmas trees. He managed to sell ten of them, and for this he received a dollar bill from Joe.

When Mabel (his mother) was sober she watched Ken moving listlessly around the house, usually staying slovenly and unwashed until after supper. At times she felt a rush of maternal pity for her son as she watched him falling apart under his forced idleness and its attendant hopelessness.

One day as she watched him roll one cigarette after another while sitting before the stove reading a book she said to him, "You know, Ken, you're smoking too much."

Without looking up from his book he barked, "What of it!"

"I don't like to watch you killing yourself like that," she said.

"Never mind me killing myself. Holy Jees, as though that's anything!"...

The worst part of their poverty, to Ken, was his weekly visits to the House of Industry, an old grey stone downtown building used as a food-distributing agency by the city's Welfare Department. The building had long been used by the city to house elderly indigents. At the House of Industry long lines of men and women first had their employment cards stamped and then shuffled along beside a series of bare wooden counters where the week's groceries were placed in individual bags by other reliefees who were working their weekly stint. Some of the men were refused their groceries until they completed a few hours' work, chopping logs or sluicing down the floor. Public assistance was still looked upon as charity, and those who asked for it had to atone for their mendicancy by honest toil.

One afternoon as Ken slowly shuffled towards the counter a fidgety little man just ahead of him turned and said, "Look at some of these people carryin' club-bags and paper to wrap their stuff up in. They don't fool nobody. I seen a man last week walk back two car stops along Dundas before he got in a streetcar goin' the other way, just so's people wouldn't know he'd been here. He had his rations in a suitcase too."

The little man laughed...

A woman farther down the queue turned around and asked, "What do you do with the rolled oats?" This caused more laughter. A man answered, "Burn 'em in your stove, lady. They burn good." "No, don't," warned the little man in front of Ken. "I tried that but they plugged up the stovepipes." Several people in the queue, and in the one next to it, began to laugh. The men who were filling the bags looked up and a policeman walked over to see what was causing the unfamiliar laughter.

Ken was handed his family's weekly ration of bread and milk tickets, and an order for coke. Then he was given his rationed packages of beans, rolled oats, potatoes and other staples of the relief diet and finally, as an unlooked-for treat, a small cardboard container of apple butter...

As he ambled slowly along Dundas Street Ken eyed the houses he passed with their signs in the windows proclaiming their faith, fad or fatuity: Sunday Seances, Toronto Anabaptist Society, BRITISH ISRAEL, Ontario Heart & Lungs Foundation, Salon De Dance, 126th Battalion Club, Lupino's School of the Hawaiian Guitar, Milady's Hair Bobbing, Astrology, Ont. Theosophical Society, and ROOMS FOR MEN - 25 cents.

SHADOWS

Alice Boissonneau

Along Queen. The look of towers, cruet-shaped in the distance, turned into Polish or Ukrainian halls. Huge complicated structures, windows fashioned with the grandeur of another day, like cream-painted picture frames. An assortment of dusty stores, housed bleak in the base of the old brick section, maroon-coloured, with black cornices of grillwork. The quaint gable windows catching a delicate sad glitter of sun in late afternoon.

With some, the old number appears still, marked out black on a doorstep of white bathroom tile. Stately ceilinged showcases offer a florid mingling of second-hand magazines, spread in an orderly way over a brown striped surface of bare linoleum, at eye level. Doors have decorated wood. A store sells china trinkets, artificial flowers or plaster stags, small plaques. Also aprons and slips.

Further west where Queen tilts over, down toward the C.N.R. Station, beyond the black shafts of the underpass and the lumberyard, Fred says: "*The farmers got off there to go to the Parkdale Hotel.*"

The Ontario Lunatic Hospital was thought to cast a shadow. "*Like a spell on the row of stores opposite.*"

"*It held business back a lot.*" Stores opened, did not prosper, people failed to buy. They found it bad luck to transact business on the one side only. Were forced to close, to their sorrow.

FAMILY, 1970

CHARLES PACHTER

from *WHAT'S BRED IN THE BONE*

Robertson Davies

The O'Gormans moved to Toronto, and at once made themselves known at St. James' Anglican Cathedral.

"It's no use trying to get a trust company on its feet unless you're seen and known where money is," said Gerald Vincent to his wife. She agreed, because he knew Toronto better than she; had he not been making visits to it for the last eighteen months? But she wondered aloud if in a city sometimes called "the Rome of Methodism" it might not be better to ally themselves with one of the Methodist churches where affluence and the godliness of John Wesley were mingled in a peculiarly Torontonian brew. When she discovered that the Methodist ladies appeared in the evening in a characteristic sort of gown in which the bosom was hidden as high as to the chin, and no jewellery was worn except a few discreet, chunky diamonds (good investments), she plumped for the more easy-going Anglicans. In their first three months of Toronto residence, before the Trust opened its doors to the public, the O'Gormans had caused themselves to be noticed in Toronto society. Noticed - and favourably noticed.

The question that was asked, of course, was whether they were Old Money, or New Money? The difference, though subtle to the vast population which was No Money, was important. Old Money usually reached back to colonial days, and some of it was Empire Loyalist; Old Money was Tory of an indigo that put to shame the weaknesses and follies of such wobblers as the first Duke of Wellington; Old Money sought to conserve and strengthen whatever was best in the body politic and knew precisely where this refined essence was to be found; it was in themselves and all that pertained to them. Even in the early twenties of this century, Old Money clung to its carriages, at least for ladies making calls, and had other tribal customs that spoke of assured distinction. The high priests of Old Money frequently wore top hats on weekdays, if they were going to do something priestly with money. They fought furiously against short coats for dinner dress, and white waistcoats with tailcoats. They kept mistresses, if at all, of such dowdiness they might almost have been mistaken for wives. For them the nineteenth century had not quite ended.

New Money, on the other hand, had taken its cue from Edward VII, who had a high regard for wealth however it was come by, and liked people with some "go" in them. New Money aspired to be

Big Money, and did not greatly care if the drawing rooms of Old Money were not easily opened. New Money wore dinner suits, which it called tuxedos, and smoked big cigars from which it removed the band before lighting up – an unthinkable solecism, for what if you should get a tobacco stain on your white glove? The O'Gormans knew they were New Money, but were aware that a trust company which was not on good terms with Old Money could run into quite unnecessary obstructions. The Senator, too, presented a problem. His gallant manners and handsome person recommended him anywhere, but it could not be concealed from the never-sleeping vigilance of Old Money that he was a Roman Catholic and a Liberal in politics. A difficult situation was avoided by the Cornish family, just as the Senator had foreseen.

Everything fell into place on June 3, when the Birthday Honours were announced, and Major Francis Cornish, resident of the soon-to-be-opened Cornish Trust, became Sir Francis Cornish, K.B.E. How did he get it? The whisper was that he had done extraordinary work in Intelligence during the War, and not simple Canadian Intelligence, which was rather small potatoes. Non-military people, and even a lot of military people, have a notion that Military Intelligence implies uncommon brilliance of intellect, extraordinary resource and daring, ability to solve codes over which the enemy has toiled for years, and iron control over beautiful and alluring female spies. Of course, this may be quite true, but nobody knows, and everybody speculates. The passing of time had given the Wooden Soldier an air of distinction, of the grizzle-headed, frozen-faced, uncommunicative variety. His monocle gleamed with suppressed secrets; his moustache spoke of Nature subdued, tamed, domineered over. Just the man to trust your money to: just the man to ask to dinner...

Sir Francis also decided on Colborne for his son...

Much may be learned about any society by studying the behaviour and accepted ideas of its children, for children – and sometimes adults – are shadows of their parents, and what they believe and what they do are often what their parents believe in their hearts and would do if society would put up with it. The dominant group, though by no means the majority of the boys at Colborne College, were the sons of Old Money, and in their behaviour the spirit of Old Money was clear. They were the conservers of tradition, and they imposed tradition without discrimination and without mercy. The tradition best calculated to reduce a New Boy to his lowest common denominator was fagging.

On the first day of the autumn term, each senior boy was assigned, by decision of the prefects, a New Boy who was to be his fag for the year that followed, and it was clearly understood that the fag was the slave and creature of his fag-master, to do his bidding without question at any hour. There was an understanding that if a fag were seriously ill-used he could complain to the prefects, but to do so was squealing, and incurred contempt. Like all such systems it was conditioned by the people who practised it, and some fags had an easy time; it was even known for a fag-master to help a junior boy with his work. A few fag-masters were brutes, and a few fags lived in hell; the majority, like all slave classes, were genially derisive of their masters when they could get away with it, respectful when they had to be, and cleaned boots and put away laundry as badly as they could without incurring punishment. If the system taught them anything at all it was that all authority is capricious, but may be appeased by a show of zeal, unaccompanied by any real work...

The religion of the school: it was a kind of middle-brow Anglicanism, not too heavily stressed because the school contained boys of all denominations, including several Jews, and some richly coloured boys from South America who were probably Papists. The hymns were loud, chiefly unexceptionable admonitions to live decently and honourably, and the music to which they were sung was superior stuff from the public school hymnal – Holst, Vaughan Williams, and unsentimental tunes that would not have been strange to Luther. The headmaster preached a short extempore sermon every Sunday night, and because he was a man whose enthusiasms sometimes outran his judgement, he was likely to say things which a more discreet man would have left unsaid. Musing on the theme of sin and perhaps forgetting where he was, he once quoted Nietzsche, declaring: "Sins are necessary to every society organized on an ecclesiastical basis; they are the only reliable weapons of power; the priest lives upon sins; it is necessary to him that there be sinning"... It was a religion well suited to Old Money and to the toadies of Old Money. It was a religion that Never Went Too Far.

from *HOW SHOULD A PERSON BE?* WHAT IS DESTINY?

SHEILA HETI

I continue to write *soul* as *sould.* It is my only consistent typo. My unease about it goes so deep that I try never to speak about it to anyone. Every time I write that word, I quickly erase the *d* and try not to think about it anymore. It's like when you hit a bird on an empty street at night – you just fix your eyes straight ahead and keep driving. No one saw you; it's between you and the bird. There's nothing to be done about it now – it happened.

Like *sould.* It happened. Nothing to be done about it now. Move on. Life is so short, and of all the questions I ask myself in this life, none should involve this typographical error, or whether in fact I have sold my soul, or had no soul to begin with to sell. I shouldn't dwell on it. Who gives a fuck in this fucked-up world. There are problems so vast and so deep that a young woman sitting alone in her room should slit her throat and die sooner than bother about the state of her soul, when so many great artists before her spent decades recalibrating a single blank canvas in their studio, fifteen, sixteen hours a day, as their marriages crumbled into the soil.

I know better than to let my life crumble around me just because somewhere inside me I am without a soul. For I sold it. And I don't remember to whom. Or why. Or when.

When I strip away my dreams, what I imagine to be my potential, all the things I haven't said, what I imagine I feel for other people in the absence of my expressing it, all the rules I've made for myself that I don't follow – I see that I've done as little as anyone else in this world to deserve the grand moniker *I.* In fact, apart from being the only person living in this apartment, I'm not sure what distinguishes me.

There are people whose learning is so great, they seem to inhabit a different realm of species-hood entirely. Somehow, they appear untroubled by the nullness. They are filled up with history and legends and beautiful poetry and all the gestures of all the great people down through time. When they talk, they are carried on a sea of their own belonging. It is like they were born to be fathers to us all. I should like one day to impale them all on a long stick. But I know I won't. It will never be one of the gestures by which I am known, so I might as well forget about it. Thinking about it does little to help me inhabit the realm of living.

Yet there is one character in history who is reassuring me these days: Moses. I hadn't realized until last week that in his youth he killed a man, an Egyptian, and buried him under some sand. The next day he saw two men fighting. When he tried to stop them, they said to Moses, "What? And if we don't – are you going to kill us too?" He became afraid. He thought. *Everyone knows what I have done.*

Then he fled town.

And he is king of the Jews – *my* king. If that is what my king is like, what can I expect for myself? If the king of my people had to be told by God to take off his shoes for he was standing on holy ground when God addressed him for the first time, I should not worry that I – who have never been addressed by God – am all the time standing on holy ground with running shoes on. I used to worry that I wasn't enough like Jesus, but yesterday I remembered who was my king: a man who, when God told him to lead the people out of Egypt, said, "But I'm not a good talker! Couldn't you ask my brother instead?" So it should not be so hard to come at this life with a little bit of honesty. I don't need to be great like the leader of the Christian people. I can be a bumbling murderous coward like the king of the Jews.

WE SO SELDOM LOOK ON LOVE

BARBARA GOWDY

When you die, and your earthly self begins turning into your disintegrated self, you radiate an intense current of energy. There is always energy given off when a thing turns into its opposite, when love, for instance, turns into hate. There are always sparks at those extreme points. But life turning into death is the most extreme of extreme points. So just after you die, the sparks are really stupendous. Really magical and explosive.

I've seen cadavers shining like stars. I'm the only person I've ever heard of who has. Almost everyone senses something, though, some vitality. That's why you get resistance to the idea of cremation or organ donation. "I want to be in one piece," people say. Even Matt, who claimed there was no soul and no afterlife, wrote a P.S. in his suicide note that he be buried intact.

As if it would have made any difference to his energy emission. No matter what you do – slice open the flesh, dissect everything, burn everything – you're in the path of a power way beyond your little interferences.

I grew up in a nice, normal, happy family. My parents and my brother are still living. My dad owned a flower store. Now my brother owns it. My brother is three years older than I am, a serious, remote man. But loyal. When I made the headlines he phoned to say that if I needed money for a lawyer, he would give it to me. I was really touched. Especially as he was standing up to Carol, his wife. She got on the extension and screamed, "You're sick! You should be put away!"

She'd been wanting to tell me that since we were thirteen years old.

I had an animal cemetery back then. Our house was beside a woods beside a city golf course and we had three outdoor cats, great hunters who tended to leave their kills in one piece. Whenever I found a body, usually a mouse or a bird, I took it into my bedroom and hid it until midnight. I didn't know anything about the ritual significance of the midnight hour. My burials took place then because that's when I woke up. It no longer happens, but I was such a sensitive child that I think I must have been aroused by the energy given off as day clicked over into the dead of night and, simultaneously, as the dead of night clicked over into the next day.

In any case, I'd be wide awake. I'd get up and go to the bathroom to wrap the body in toilet paper. I felt compelled to be so careful, so respectful. I whispered a chant. At each step of the burial I chanted. "I shroud the body shroud the body, shroud little sparrow with broken wing." Or "I lower the body, lower the body..." And so on.

Climbing out the bathroom window was accompanied by: "I enter the night, enter the night..." At my cemetery I set the body down on a special flat rock and took my pajamas off. I was behaving out of pure inclination. I dug up four or five graves and unwrapped the animals from their shrouds. The rotting smell was crucial. So was the cool air. Normally I'd be so keyed up at this point that I'd burst into a dance.

I used to dance for dead men, too. Before I climbed on top of them, I'd dance all around the prep room. When I told Matt about this he said that I was shaking my personality out of my body so that the sensation of participating in the cadaver's energy eruption would be intensified. "You're trying to imitate the disintegration process," he said.

Maybe – on an unconscious level. But what I was aware of was the heat, the heat of my danced-out body, which I cooled by lying on top of the cadaver. As a child I'd gently wipe my skin with two of the animals I'd just unwrapped. When I was covered all over with their scent, I put them aside, unwrapped the new corpse and did the same with it. I called this the Anointment. I can't describe how it felt. The high, high rapture. The electricity that shot through me.

The rest, wrapping the bodies back up and burying them, was pretty much what you'd expect.

It astonishes me now to think how naïve I was. I thought I had discovered something that certain other people, if they weren't afraid to give it a try, would find just as fantastic as I did. It was a dark and forbidden thing, yes, but so was sex. I really had no idea that I was jumping across a vast behavioural gulf. In fact, I couldn't see that I was doing anything wrong. I still can't, and I'm including what happened with Matt. Carol said I should have been put away, but I'm not bad-looking, so if offering my body to dead men is a crime, I'd like to know who the victim is.

Carol has always been jealous of me. She's fat and has a wandering eye. Her eye gives her a dreamy, distracted quality that I fell for (as I suppose my brother would eventually do) one day at a friend's thirteenth birthday party. It was the beginning of the summer holidays, and I was yearning for a kindred spirit, someone to share my secret life with. I saw Carol standing alone, looking everywhere at once, and I chose her.

I knew to take it easy, though. I knew not to push anything. We'd search for dead animals and birds, we'd chant and swaddle the bodies, dig graves, make Popsicle-stick crosses. All by daylight. At midnight I'd go out and dig up the grave and conduct a proper burial.

There must have been some chipmunk sickness that summer. Carol and I found an incredible number of chipmunks, and a lot of them had no blood on them, no sign of cat. One day we found a chipmunk that evacuated a string of foetuses when I picked it up. The foetuses were still alive, but there was no saving them, so I took them into the house and flushed them down the toilet.

A mighty force was coming from the mother chipmunk. It was as if, along with her own energy, she was discharging all the energy of her dead brood. When Carol and I began to dance for her, we both went a little crazy. We stripped down to our underwear, screamed, spun in circles, threw dirt up into the air. Carol has always denied it, but she took off her bra and began whipping trees with it. I'm sure the sight of her doing this is what inspired me to take off my undershirt and underpants and to perform the Anointment.

Carol stopped dancing. I looked at her, and the expression on her face stopped me dancing, too. I looked down at the chipmunk in my hand. It was bloody. There were streaks of blood all over my body. I was horrified. I thought I'd squeezed the chipmunk too hard.

But what had happened was, I'd begun my period. I figured this out a few minutes after Carol ran off. I wrapped the chipmunk in its shroud and buried it. Then I got dressed and lay down on the grass. A little while later my mother appeared over me.

"Carol's mother phoned," she said. "Carol is very upset. She says you made her perform some disgusting witchcraft dance. You made her take her clothes off, and you attacked her with a bloody chipmunk."

"That's a lie," I said. "I'm menstruating."

After my mother had fixed me up with a sanitary napkin, she told me she didn't think I should play with Carol anymore. "There's a screw loose in there somewhere," she said.

I had no intention of playing with Carol anymore, but I cried at what seemed like a cruel loss. I think I knew that it was all loneliness from that moment on. Even though I was only thirteen, I was cutting any lines that still drifted out toward normal eroticism. Bosom friends, crushes, pajama-party intimacy, I was cutting all those lines off.

A month or so after becoming a woman I developed a craving to perform autopsies. I resisted doing it for almost a year, though. I was frightened. Violating the intactness of the animal seemed sacrilegious and dangerous. Also unimaginable – I couldn't imagine what would happen.

Nothing. Nothing would happen, as I found out. I've read that necrophiles are frightened of getting hurt by normal sexual relationships, and maybe there's some truth in that (although my heart's been broken plenty of times by cadavers, and not once by a live man), but I think that my attraction to cadavers isn't driven by fear, it's driven by excitement, and that one of the most exciting things about a cadaver is how dedicated it is to dying. Its will is all directed to a single intention, like a huge wave heading for shore, and you can ride along on the wave if you want to, because no matter what you do, because with you or without you, that wave is going to hit the beach.

I felt this impetus the first time I worked up enough nerve to cut open a mouse. Like anyone else, I balked a little at slicing into the flesh, and I was repelled for a few seconds when I saw the insides. But something drove me to go through these compunctions. It was as if I were acting solely on instinct and curiosity, and anything I did was all right, provided it didn't kill me.

After the first few times, I started sticking my tongue into the incision. I don't know why. I thought about it, I did it, and I kept on doing it. One day I removed the organs and cleaned them with water, then put them back in, and I kept on doing that, too. Again, I couldn't tell you why except to say that any provocative thought, if you act upon it, seems to set you on a trajectory.

By the time I was sixteen I wanted human corpses. Men. (That way I'm straight.) I got my chauffeur's licence, but I had to wait until I was finished high school before Mr. Wallis would hire me as a hearse driver at the funeral home.

Mr. Wallis knew me because he bought bereavement flowers at my father's store. Now there was a weird man. He would take a trocar, which is the big needle you use to draw out a cadaver's fluids, and he would push it up the penises of dead men to make them look semi-erect, and then he'd sodomize them. I caught him at it once, and he tried to tell me that he'd been urinating in the hopper. I pretended to believe him. I was upset though, because I knew that dead men were just dead flesh to him. One minute he'd be locked up with a young male corpse, having his way with him, and the next minute he'd be embalming him as if nothing had happened, and making sick jokes about him, pretending to find evidence of rampant homosexuality – colons stalagmite with dried semen, and so on.

None of this joking ever happened in front of me. I heard about it from the crazy old man who did the mopping up. He was also a necrophile, I'm almost certain, but no longer active. He called dead women Madonnas. He rhapsodized about the beautiful Madonnas he'd had the privilege of seeing in the 1940s, about how much more womanly and feminine the Madonnas were twenty years before.

I just listened. I never let on what I was feeling, and I don't think anyone suspected. Necrophiles aren't supposed to be blond and pretty, let alone female. When I'd been working at the funeral home for about a year, a committee from the town council tried to get me to enter the Milk Marketer's Beauty Pageant. They knew about my job, and they knew I was studying embalming at night, but I had told people I was preparing myself for medical school, and I guess the council believed me.

For fifteen years, ever since Matt died, people have been asking me how a woman makes love to a corpse.

Matt was the only person who figured it out. He was a medical student, so he knew that if you apply pressure to the chest of certain fresh corpses, they purge blood out of their mouths.

Matt was smart. I wish I could have loved him with more than sisterly love. He was tall and thin. My type. We met at the donut shop across from the medical library, got to talking, and liked each other immediately, an unusual experience for both of us. After about an hour I knew that he loved me and that his love was unconditional. When I told him where I worked and what I was studying, he asked why.

"Because I'm a necrophile," I said.

He lifted his head and stared at me. He had eyes like high-resolution monitors. Almost too vivid. Normally I don't like looking people in the eye, but I found myself staring back. I could see that he believed me.

"I've never told anyone else," I said.

"With men or women?" he asked.

"Men. Young men."

"How?"

"Cunnilingus."

"Fresh corpses?"

"If I can get them."

"What do you do, climb on top of them?"

"Yes."

"You're turned on by blood."

"It's a lubricant," I said. "It's colourful. Stimulating. It's the ultimate bodily fluid."

"Yes," he said, nodding. "When you think about it. Sperm propagates life. But blood sustains it. Blood is primary."

He kept asking questions, and I answered them as truthfully as I could. Having confessed what I was, I felt myself driven to testing his intellectual rigour and the strength of his love at first sight.

Throwing rocks at him without any expectation that he'd stay standing. He did, though. He caught the whole arsenal and asked for more. It began to excite me.

We went back to his place. He had a basement apartment in an old run-down building. There were books in orange-crate shelves, in piles on the floor, all over the bed. On the wall above his desk was a poster of Doris Day in the movie *Tea for Two*. Matt said she looked like me.

"Do you want to dance first?" he asked, heading for his record player. I'd told him about how I danced before climbing on corpses.

"No."

He swept the books off the bed. Then he undressed me. He had an erection until I told him I was a virgin. "Don't worry," he said, sliding his head down my stomach. "Lie still."

The next morning he phoned me at work. I was hungover and blue from the night before. After leaving his place I'd gone straight to the funeral home and made love to an autopsy case. Then I'd got drunk in a seedy country-and-western bar and debated going back to the funeral home and suctioning out my own blood until I lost consciousness.

It had finally hit me that I was incapable of falling in love with a man who wasn't dead. I kept thinking, "I'm not normal." I'd never faced this before. Obviously, making love to corpses isn't normal, but while I was still a virgin I must have been assuming that I could give it up any time I liked. Get married, have babies. I must have been banking on a future that I didn't even want, let alone have access to.

Matt was phoning to get me to come around again after work. "I don't know," I said.

"You had a good time. Didn't you?"

"Sure, I guess."

"I think you're fascinating," he said.

I sighed.

"Please," he said. "Please."

A few nights later I went to his apartment. From then on we started to meet every Tuesday and Thursday evening after my embalming class, and as soon as I left his place, if I knew there was a corpse at the mortuary – any male corpse, young or old – I went straight there and climbed in a basement window.

Entering the prep room, especially at night when there was nobody else around, was like diving into a lake. Sudden cold and silence, and the sensation of penetrating a new element where the rules of other elements don't apply. Being with Matt was like lying on the beach of the lake. Matt had warm, dry skin. His apartment was overheated and noisy. I lay on Matt's bed and soaked him up, but only to make the moment when I entered the prep room even more overpowering.

If the cadaver was freshly embalmed, I could usually smell him from the basement. The smell is like a hospital and old cheese. For me, it's the smell of danger and permission, it used to key me up like amphetamine, so that by the time I reached the prep room, tremors were running up and down my legs. I locked the door behind me and broke into a wild dance, tearing my clothes off, spinning around, pulling at my hair. I'm not sure what this was all about, whether or not I was trying to take part in the chaos of the corpse's disintegration, as Matt suggested. Maybe I was prostrating myself, I don't know.

Once the dancing was over I was always very calm, almost entranced. I drew back the sheet. This was the most exquisite moment. I felt as if I were being blasted by white light. Almost blinded, I climbed onto the table and straddled the corpse. I ran my hands over his skin. My hands and the insides of my thighs burned as if I were touching dry ice. After a few minutes I lay down and pulled the sheet up over my head. I began to kiss his mouth. By now he might be drooling blood. A corpse's blood is thick, cool and sweet. My head roared.

I was no longer depressed. Far from it, I felt better, more confident, than I had ever felt in my life. I had discovered myself to be irredeemably abnormal. I could either slit my throat or surrender – wholeheartedly now – to my obsession. I surrendered. And what happened was that obsession began to storm through me, as if I were a tunnel. I became the medium of obsession as well as both ends of it. With Matt, when we made love, I was the receiving end, I was the cadaver. When I left him and went to the funeral home, I was the lover. Through me Matt's love poured into the cadavers at the funeral home, and through me the cadavers filled Matt with explosive energy.

He quickly got addicted to this energy. The minute I arrived at his apartment, he had to hear every detail about the last corpse I'd been with. For a month or so I had him pegged as a latent homosexual necrophile voyeur, but then I began to see that it wasn't the corpses themselves that excited him, it was my passion for them. It was the power that went into that passion and that came back, doubled, for his pleasure. He kept asking, "How did you feel? Why do you think you felt that way?" And then, because the source of all this power disturbed him, he'd try to prove that my feelings were delusory.

"A corpse shows simultaneous extremes of character," I told him. "Wisdom and innocence, happiness and grief, and so on."

"Therefore all corpses are alike," he said. "Once you've had one you've had them all."

"No, no. They're all different. Each corpse contains his own extremes. Each corpse is only as wise and as innocent as the living person could have been."

He said, "You're drafting personalities onto corpses in order to have power over them."

"In that case," I said, "I'm pretty imaginative, since I've never met two corpses who were alike."

"You could be that imaginative," he argued. "Schizophrenics are capable of manufacturing dozens of complex personalities."

I didn't mind these attacks. There was no malice in them, and there was no way they could touch me, either. It was as if I were luxuriously pouring my heart out to a very clever, very concerned, very tormented analyst. I felt sorry for him. I understood his twisted desire to turn me into somebody else (somebody who might love him). I used to fall madly in love with cadavers and then cry because they were dead. The difference between Matt and me was that I had become philosophical. I was all right.

I thought that he was, too. He was in pain, yes, but he seemed confident that what he was going through was temporary and not unnatural. "I am excessively curious," he said. "My fascination is any curious man's fascination with the unusual." He said that by feeding his lust through mine, he would eventually saturate it, then turn it to disgust.

I told him to go ahead, give it a try. So he began to scour the newspapers for my cadavers' obituaries and to go to their funerals and memorial services. He made charts of my preferences and the frequency of my morgue encounters. He followed me to the morgue at night and waited outside so that he could get a replay while I was still in an erotic haze. He sniffed my skin. He pulled me over to the streetlights and examined the blood on my face and hands.

I suppose I shouldn't have encouraged him. I can't really say why I did, except that in the beginning I saw his obsession as the outer edge of my own obsession, a place I didn't have to visit as long as he was there. And then later, and despite his increasingly erratic behaviour, I started to have doubts about an obsession that could come on so suddenly and that could come through me.

One night he announced that he might as well face it, he was going to have to make love to corpses, male corpses. The idea nauseated him, he said, but he said that secretly, deep down, unknown even to himself, making love to male corpses was clearly the target of his desire. I blew up. I told him that necrophilia wasn't something you forced yourself to do. You longed to do it, you needed to do it. You were born to do it.

He wasn't listening. He was glued to the dresser mirror. In the last weeks of his life he stared at himself in the mirror without the least self-consciousness. He focused on his face, even though what was going on from the neck down was the arresting part. He had begun to wear incredibly weird outfits. Velvet capes, pantaloons, high-heeled red boots. When we made love, he kept these outfits on. He stared into my eyes, riveted (it later occurred to me) by his own reflection.

Matt committed suicide, there was never any doubt about that. As for the necrophilia, it wasn't a crime, not fifteen years ago. So even though I was caught in the act, naked and straddling an unmistakably dead body, even though the newspapers found out about it and made it front-page news, there was nothing the police could charge me with.

In spite of which I made a full confession. It was crucial to me that the official report contain more than the detective's bleak observations. I wanted two things on record: one, that Matt was ravished by a reverential expert; two, that his cadaver blasted the energy of a star.

"Did this energy blast happen before or after he died?" the detective asked.

"After," I said, adding quickly that I couldn't have foreseen such a blast. The one tricky area was why I hadn't stopped the suicide. Why I hadn't talked, or cut, Matt down.

I lied. I said that as soon as I entered Matt's room, he kicked away the ladder. Nobody could prove otherwise. But I've often wondered how much time actually passed between when I opened the door and when his neck broke. In crises, a minute isn't a minute. There's the same chaos you get at the instant of death with time and form breaking free, and everything magnifying and coming apart.

Matt must have been in a state of crisis for days, maybe weeks, before he died. All that staring in mirrors, thinking, "Is this my face?" Watching as his face separated into its infinitesimal particles and reassembled into a strange new face. The night before he died, he had a mask on. A Dracula mask, but he wasn't joking. He wanted to wear the mask while I made love to him as if he were a cadaver. No way, I said. The whole point, I reminded him, was that I played the cadaver. He begged me, and I laughed because of the mask and with relief. If he wanted to turn the game around, then it was over between us, and I was suddenly aware of how much I liked that idea.

The next night he phoned me at my parents' and said, "I love you," then hung up.

I don't know how I knew, but I did. A gun, I thought. Men always use guns. And then I thought, no, poison, cyanide. He was a medical student and had access to drugs. When I arrived at his apartment, the door was open. Across from the door, taped to the wall, was a note: "DEAD PERSON IN BEDROOM."

But he wasn't dead. He was standing on a stepladder. He was naked. An impressively knotted noose, attached to a pipe that ran across the ceiling, was looped around his neck.

He smiled tenderly. "I knew you'd come," he said.

"So why the note?" I demanded.

"Pull away the ladder," he crooned. "My beloved."

"Come on. This is stupid. Get down." I went up to him and punched his leg.

"All you have to do," he said, "is pull away the ladder."

His eyes were even darker and more expressive than usual. His cheekbones appeared to be highlighted. (I discovered minutes later he had makeup on.) I glanced around the room for a chair or a table that I could bring over and stand on. I was going to take the noose off him myself.

"If you leave," he said, "if you take a step back, if you do anything other than pull away the ladder, I'll kick it away."

"I love you," I said. "Okay?"

"No, you don't," he said.

"I do!" To sound like I meant it I stared at his legs and imagined them lifeless. "I do!"

"No, you don't," he said softly. "But," he said, "you will."

I was gripping the ladder. I remember thinking that if I held tight to the ladder, he wouldn't be able to kick it away. I was gripping the ladder, and then it was by the wall, tipped over. I have no memory of transition between these two events. There was a loud crack, and gushing water. Matt dropped gracefully, like a girl fainting. Water poured on him from the broken pipe. There was a smell of excrement. I dragged him by the noose.

In the living room I pulled him onto the green shag carpet, took my clothes off. I knelt over him. I kissed the blood at the corner of his mouth.

True obsession depends on the object's absolute unresponsiveness. When I used to fall for a particular cadaver, I would feel as if I were a hollow instrument, a bell or a flute. I'd empty out. I would clear out (it was involuntary) until I was an instrument for the cadaver to swell into and be amplified. As the object of Matt's obsession how could I be other than impassive, while he was alive?

He was playing with fire, playing with me. Not just because I couldn't love him, but because I was irradiated. The whole time that I was involved with Matt, I was making love to corpses, absorbing their energy, blazing it back out. Since that energy came from the act of life alchemizing into death, there's a possibility that it was alchemical itself. Even if it wasn't, I'm sure it gave Matt the impression that I had the power to change him in some huge and dangerous way.

I now believe that his addition to my energy was really a craving for such a transformation. In fact, I think that all desire is desire for transformation, and that all transformation – all movement, all process – happens because life turns into death.

I am still a necrophile, occasionally, and recklessly. I have found no replacement for the torrid serenity of a cadaver.

A SICK CALL

Morley Callaghan

Sometimes Father Macdowell mumbled out loud and took a deep wheezy breath as he walked up and down and read in his office. He was a bulky priest, white-headed except for a shiny baby-pink bald spot on the top of his head, and he was a bit deaf in one ear. His florid face had many red interlacing veins. For hours he had been hearing confessions and he was tired, for he always had to hear more confessions than any other priest at the cathedral; young girls who were in trouble, and wild but at times repentant young men, always wanted to tell their confessions to Father Macdowell, because nothing seemed to shock or excite him, or make him really angry, and he was even tender with those who thought they were most guilty.

While he was mumbling and reading and trying to keep his glasses on his nose, the house girl knocked on the door and said, "There's a young lady here to see you, Father. I think it's about a sick call."

"Did she ask for me especially?" he said in a deep but slightly cracked voice.

"Indeed she did, Father. She wanted Father Macdowell and nobody else."

So he went out to the waiting room, where a girl about thirty years of age, with fine brown eyes, fine cheekbones, and rather square shoulders, was sitting daubing her eyes with a handkerchief. She was wearing a dark coat with a grey wolf collar. "Good evening, Father," she said. "My sister is sick. I wanted you to come and see her. We think she's dying."

"Be easy, child; what's the matter with her? Speak louder. I can hardly hear you."

"My sister's had pneumonia. The doctor's coming back to see her in an hour. I wanted you to anoint her, Father."

"I see, I see. But she's not lost yet. I'll not give her extreme unction now. That may not be necessary. I'll go with you and hear her confession."

"Father, I ought to let you know, maybe. Her husband won't want to let you see her. He's not a Catholic, and my sister hasn't been to church in a long time."

"Oh, don't mind that. He'll let me see her," Father Macdowell said, and he left the room to put on his hat and coat.

When he returned, the girl explained that her name was Jane Stanhope, and her sister lived only a few blocks away. "We'll walk and you tell me about your sister," he said. He put his black hat square on his head, and pieces of white hair stuck out at the sides. They went to the avenue together.

The night was mild and clear. Miss Stanhope began to walk slowly, because Father Macdowell's rolling gait didn't get him along the street very quickly. He walked as if his feet hurt him, though he wore a pair of large, soft, specially constructed shapeless shoes. "Now, my child, you go ahead and tell me about your sister," he said, breathing with difficulty, yet giving the impression that nothing could have happened to the sister which would make him feel indignant.

There wasn't much to say, Miss Stanhope replied. Her sister had married John Williams two years ago, and he was a good, hard-working fellow, only he was very bigoted and hated all church people. "My family wouldn't have anything to do with Elsa after she married him, though I kept going to see her," she said. She was talking in a loud voice to Father Macdowell so that he could hear her.

"Is she happy with her husband?"

"She's been very happy, Father. I must say that."

"Where is he now?"

"He was sitting beside her bed. I ran out because I thought he was going to cry. He said if I brought a priest near the place he'd break the priest's head."

"My goodness. Never mind, though. Does your sister want to see me?"

"She asked me to go and get a priest, but she doesn't want John to know she did it."

Turning into a side street, they stopped at the first apartment house, and the old priest followed Miss Stanhope up the stairs. His breath came with great difficulty. "Oh dear, I'm not getting any younger, not one day younger. It's a caution how a man's legs go back on him," he said. As Miss Stanhope rapped on the door, she looked pleadingly at the old priest, trying to ask him not to be offended at anything that might happen, but he was smiling and looking huge in the narrow hallway. He wiped his head with his handkerchief.

The door was opened by a young man in a white shirt with no collar, with a head of thick, black, wavy hair. At first he looked dazed, then his eyes got bright with excitement when he saw the priest, as though he were glad to see someone he could destroy with pent-up energy. "What do you mean, Jane?" he said. "I told you not to bring a priest around here. My wife doesn't want to see a priest."

"What's that you're saying, young man?"

"No one wants you here."

"Speak up. Don't be afraid. I'm a bit hard of hearing," Father Macdowell smiled rosily. John Williams was confused by the unexpected deafness in the priest, but he stood blocking the door with sullen resolution as if waiting for the priest to try to launch a curse at him.

"Speak to him, Father," Miss Stanhope said, but the priest didn't seem to hear her; he was still smiling as he pushed past the young man, saying, "I'll go in and sit down, if you don't mind, son. I'm here on God's errand, but I don't mind saying I'm all out of breath from climbing those stairs."

John was dreadfully uneasy to see he had been brushed aside, and he followed the priest into the apartment and said loudly, "I don't want you here."

Father Macdowell said, "Eh, eh?" Then he smiled sadly, "Don't be angry with me, son. I'm too old to try and be fierce and threatening." Looking around, he said, "Where's your wife?" and he started to walk along the hall, looking for the bedroom.

John followed him and took hold of his arm. "There's no sense in your wasting your time talking to my wife, do you hear?" he said angrily.

Miss Stanhope called out suddenly, "Don't be rude, John."

"It's he that's being rude. You mind your business," John said.

"For the love of God, let me sit down a moment with her, anyway. I'm tired," the priest said.

"What do you want to say to her? Say it to me, why don't you?"

Then they both heard someone moan softly in the adjoining room, as if the sick woman had heard them. Father Macdowell, forgetting that the young man had a hold of his arm, said, "I'll go in and see her for a moment, if you don't mind," and he began to open the door.

"You're not going to be alone with her, that's all," John said, following him into the bedroom.

Lying on the bed was a white-faced, fair girl, whose skin was so delicate that her cheekbones stood out sharply. She was feverish, but her eyes rolled toward the door, and she watched them coming in. Father Macdowell took off his coat, and as he mumbled to himself he looked around the room, at the mauve silk bed-light and the wallpaper with the tiny birds in flight. It looked like a little girl's room. "Good evening, Father," Mrs. Williams whispered. She looked scared. She didn't glance at her husband. The notion of dying had made her afraid. She loved her husband and wanted to die loving him, but she was afraid, and she looked up at the priest.

"You're going to get well, child," Father Macdowell said, smiling and patting her hand gently.

John, who was standing stiffly at the door, suddenly moved around the big priest, and then bent down over the bed and took his wife's hand and began to caress her forehead.

"Now, if you don't mind, my son, I'll hear your wife's confession," the priest said.

"No, you won't," John said abruptly. "Her people didn't want her, and they left us together, and they're not going to separate us now. She's satisfied with me." He kept looking down at her face as if he could not bear to turn away.

Father Macdowell nodded his head up and down and sighed. "Poor boy," he said. "God bless you." Then he looked at Mrs. Williams, who had closed her eyes, and he saw a faint tear on her cheek. "Be sensible my boy," he said. "You'll have to let me hear your wife's confession. Leave us alone for a while."

"I'm going to stay right here," John said, and he sat down on the end of the bed. He was working himself up and staring savagely at the priest. All of a sudden he noticed the tears on his wife's cheeks, and he muttered as though bewildered, "What's the matter, Elsa? What's the matter, darling? Are we bothering you? Just open your eyes and we'll go out of the room and leave you alone till the doctor comes." Then he turned and said to the priest, "I'm not going to leave you here with her, can't you see that? Why don't you go?"

"I could revile you, my son. I could threaten you; but I ask you, for the peace of your wife's soul, leave us alone." Father Macdowell spoke with patient tenderness. He looked big and solid and immovable as he stood by the bed. "I liked your face as soon as I saw you," he said to John. "You're a good fellow."

John still held his wife's wrist, but he rubbed his other hand through his thick hair and said angrily, "You don't get the point, sir. My wife and I were always left alone, and we merely want to be left alone now. Nothing is going to separate us. She's been content with me. I'm sorry sir; you'll have to speak to her with me here, or you'll have to go."

"No; you'll have to go for a while," the priest said patiently.

Then Mrs. Williams moved her head on the pillow and said, "Pray for me, Father."

The old priest knelt down by the bed, and with a sweet unruffled expression on his florid face he began to pray. At times his breath came with a whistling noise as though a rumbling were inside him, and at other times he sighed and was full of sorrow. He was praying that young Mrs. Williams might get better, and while he prayed he knew that her husband was more afraid of losing her to the Church than losing her to death.

All the time Father Macdowell was on his knees, with his heavy prayer book in his two hands, John kept staring at him. John couldn't understand the old priest's patience and tolerance. He wanted to quarrel with him, but he kept on watching the light from overhead shining on the one baby-pink bald spot on the smooth, white head, and at last he burst out, "You don't understand, sir! We've been very happy together. Neither you nor her people came near her when she was in good health, so why should you bother her now? I don't want anything to separate us now; neither does she. She came with me. You see you'd be separating us, don't you?" He was trying to talk like a reasonable man who had no prejudices.

Father Macdowell got up clumsily. His knees hurt him, for the floor was hard. He said to Mrs. Williams in quite a loud voice, "Did you really intend to give up everything for this young fellow?" and he bent down close to her so he could hear.

"Yes, Father," she whispered.

"In Heaven's name, child, you couldn't have known what you were doing."

"We loved each other, Father. We've been very happy."

"All right. Supposing you were. What now? What about all eternity, child?"

"Oh, Father, I'm very sick and I'm afraid." She looked up to try to show him how scared she was, and how much she wanted him to give her peace.

He sighed and seemed distressed, and at last he said to John, "Were you married in the church?"

"No, we weren't. Look here, we're talking pretty loud and it upsets her."

"Ah, it's a crime that I'm hard of hearing, I know. Never mind. I'll go." Picking up his coat, he put it over his arm; then he sighed as if he were tired, and he said, "I wonder if you'd fetch me a glass of water. I'd thank you for it."

John hesitated, glancing at the tired old priest, who looked so pink and white and almost cherubic in his utter lack of guile.

"What's the matter?" Father Macdowell said.

John was ashamed of himself at appearing so sullen, so he said hastily, "Nothing's the matter. Just a moment. I won't be a moment." He hurried out of the room.

The old priest looked down at the floor and shook his head; and then, sighing and feeling uneasy, he bent over Mrs. Williams, with his good ear down to her, and he said, "I'll just ask you a few questions in a hurry, my child. You answer them quickly and I'll give you absolution." He made the sign of the cross over her and asked if she repented for having strayed from the Church, and if she had often been angry, and whether she had always been faithful, and if she had ever lied or stolen – all so casually and quickly as if it had not occurred to him that such a young woman could have serious sins. In the same breath he muttered, "Say a good act of contrition to yourself and that will be all, my dear." He had hardly taken a minute.

When John returned to the room with the glass of water in his hand, he saw the old priest making the sign of the cross. Father Macdowell went on praying without looking up at John. When he had finished, he turned and said, "Oh, there you are. Thanks for the water. I needed it. Well, my boy, I'm sorry if I worried you."

John looked at his wife, who had closed her eyes, and he sat down on the end of the bed. He was too disappointed to speak.

Father Macdowell, who was expecting trouble, said, "Don't be harsh, lad."

"I'm not harsh," he said mildly, looking up at the priest. "But you weren't quite fair. And it's as though she turned away from me at the last moment. I didn't think she needed you."

"God bless you, bless the both of you. She'll get better," Father Macdowell said. But he felt ill at ease as he put on his coat, and he couldn't look directly at John.

Going along the hall, he spoke to Miss Stanhope, who wanted to apologize for her brother-in-law's attitude. "I'm sorry if it was unpleasant for you, Father," she said.

"It wasn't unpleasant," he said. "I was glad to meet John. He's a fine fellow. It's a great pity he isn't Catholic. I don't know as I played fair with him."

As he went down the stairs, puffing and sighing, he pondered the question of whether he had played fair with the young man. But by the time he reached the street he was rejoicing amiably to think he had so successfully ministered to one who had strayed from the faith and had called out to him at the last moment. Walking along with the rolling motion as if his feet hurt him, he muttered, "Of course they were happy as they were... in a worldly way. I wonder if I did come between them?"

He shuffled along, feeling very tired, and couldn't help thinking, "What beauty there was to his staunch love for her!" Then he added quickly, "But it was just a pagan beauty, of course."

As he began to wonder about the nature of this beauty, for some reason he felt inexpressibly sad.

DANCING

GWENDOLYN MACEWEN

We approached a big skyway that was under construction. It was very late and there were only a few cars passing by. He told me to park beneath one of the huge concrete legs that were to support the overpass. For a long way the legs stretch out on either side of us. It was a kind of Stonehenge, an incomplete temple.

And then—

He stepped quickly out of the car and threw off his coat, his shirt, his socks, his shoes, and laid them in a heap at the bottom of the cold pillar. It was a full moon, a November night. Then he began to dance. Around and around, in and out between the pillars, the cranes, the small trucks and pieces of machinery that had been left standing for the night. It was as if everything had been arranged for him, for his dance...

All his bones were wings; his body was like one of those beautifully designed but deadly planes they made a hundred years ago. His back, from the shoulder blades to the bottom of his spine, was the tightly stretched, triangular frame of a kite. I imagined that the organs in his body floated in a kind of fluid tension, a suspended flight. And as he danced and flew, his body broke into alphabets!

A police car pulled up beside me then and a mouth leaned in the window of my car. "And what, may I ask, is *he* doing?" said the mouth.

"Dancing," I said. "He's a dancer."

The mouth let out a long low whistle. "It takes all kinds," it said. "I'll have to ask you both to move on. People don't dance half-naked in the streets of Trawnah."

"We're from out of town," I said.

"No reason to dance half-naked in the streets of Trawnah. What is he anyway, some kind of forriner?"

"Yes," I said. "Speaks a language unknown to man. A combination of Cree, Italian, Eskimo and Cabbagetown slang."

"I wouldn't know about that," said the mouth. "One born every day. Dancing half-naked under the overpass, beats everything. And what are *you* doing here?"

"*Watching* him dance half-naked under the overpass," I said.
"Move on, lady, unless you want to tell it to the judge."
We finally left, laughing and laughing all the way home.

WALKING WOMAN

MICHAEL SNOW

THE VICTORY BURLESK

MARGARET ATWOOD

I went to the Victory Burlesk twice, or maybe it was only once and one of my friends went the other time and told me about it. I enjoyed it both times. It was considered quite daring for young women to go to such a place, and we thought it was funny; it was almost as funny as church.

You got a stand-up comic, a movie and a man who sang or juggled plates, as well as the striptease act. They used a lot of coloured lighting, red and blue and purple. Each girl had a fake name: Miss Take, Miss Behave, Flame LeRew. I liked the names and the costumes, for their ingenuity, and I liked the more skillful girls, the ones who could twirl tassels or make their bellies or buttocks rotate in a circle. That was before they had to take it all off, there was an art to it, it was almost like the plate juggling. I liked the way they floated in the pools of coloured light, moving as if they were swimming, mermaids behind glass.

One woman began with her back to the audience, the spotlight on her. She was wearing long white gloves and a black evening gown with gauzy black sleeves that looked like membranous wings as she stretched out her arms. She did a lot with her arms and back, but when she finally turned around, she was old. Her face was powdered dead white, her mouth was a bright reddish purple, but she was old. I could feel shame washing through me, it was no longer funny, I didn't want this woman to take off her clothes, I didn't want to look. I felt that I, not the woman on the stage, was being exposed and humiliated. Surely they would jeer and yell things at her, surely they would feel they had been tricked.

The woman unzipped her black evening gown, slipped it down, and began to move her hips. She smiled with her white mask of a face and her purple mouth, inside her lips her teeth glinted, dull white pebbles, it was a mockery, she didn't intend it, she knew it, it was a trick of another kind but we didn't know who was playing it. The trick was that suddenly there was no trick: the body up there was actual, it was aging, it was not floating in the spotlight somewhere apart from us, like us it was caught in time.

The Victory Burlesk went dead. Nobody made a sound.

SKIN, JUST

CHRISTINE MISCIONE

Gum on the sidewalk, and all she can see are moles misshaped, moles deadly. Layers of tar covering potholes are moles too, tar on every street, melanoma in every city. And polka-dot bathing suits. And specks on shower tiles. Knots on floorboards, bruises on banana skins, rot in apples, soy sauce drips left over on tables and the arms of strangers, their tank-topped backs, their miniskirted legs where skin shines through: moleless, moleful, abnormal, normal, happy.

Happy Moles is the name of a band she imagined starting with her next-door neighbour Petey and his younger sister Tessa. The three of them could take photos of their moles and magnify them on T-shirts. Wear them to every gig. Sell some after the show with their signatures underneath: *Wear our moles with pride.* Except Tessa didn't have any moles. She was clear as a cup of water. She was so see-through you could see through to her veins, her bones, joints oiled and colon cancer screening made easy.

Patient demands assistance immediately, wants biopsy of mole. Mole approximately five millimetres, but hard to discern. Sample covered in blood.

It was growing down there for a long time. She saw it day after day, and the colour became angry. At first it was only a little baby speck, full of exuberance, ready for life. These were the happy days, when Happy Moles, the band, was a possibility. But then: slowly, itty-bitty slowly, itty-bitty baby mole began to get greedy. Wanted fame. Wanted to rock the calf right out of an auditorium with hundreds of screaming fans—

But it wasn't to be.

And then ANGER. Crawling anger. Anger slowly turning to multifarious shades of dark. Mole becoming monochrome. Sullen. Mole brooding in its epidermal throne, sinking lower and lower into layers of flesh, lower into dermis, then hypodermis where it grew manic and uncontrollable.

The growing wouldn't stop.

Wild aberrations, crazed mounds of melanocytes in skin's pigmental, skin overfloweth, her cup overflowing with showers of melanoma sparkles. All dangerous hues. All mutations in sacs of jelly mounds of mole on her calf and chest and down to the base of her spine where moles congregated to praise our Lord Jesus Christ, save her. Save her.

But sadly nothing could be saved. Not an inch or a centimetre. Not the skin protecting, skin holding in. Not the layers of billowy cauliflower florets bulbous in her brain, where thoughts began, where meat was turned to neuronal passages long ago during Neanderthal times. This is evolution: blue eyes. Fair skin. Deranged cells. Abysmal passages in neuroland. This is evolution: Skin cells replicating infinity. Skin cells never stopping. Skin cells' immortal magic.

Until one day she couldn't take it anymore. Squatting in her bedroom. Staring at her calf, at her mole growing crazy – SHE COULD NOT TAKE IT ANYMORE. How much can be encapsulated in that phrase? She, a pronoun. Could, separated from Not. Could, Not. Could, a verb of possibility. Not, the destroyer. Not destroys Could's possibility, as though errant pigment destroys She. Or Her. Take, a verb. It, a pronoun. Anymore, a state of being. Wrapped together: a phrase leading to action, leads to slicing open skin and digging out the darkness.

Because she just couldn't take it anymore. On her calf. She could not take it anymore on her calf, so she knifed it out of there. Dug like an excavation. Messy like a construction site. Blood everywhere like menstruation, and she just couldn't take it anymore, so she rushed to the doctor's. Demanded care. Demanded more action. "Doctor, Doctor, here's my mole. Look at my mole. Examine my mole, NOW! I have cancer. I have cancer in my mole and I need treatment immediately."

Patient presents with calf mole. Mole is cut out and in her hand.

It was the gasoline spill on the pavement outside her house. It was the way gasoline turns normal tar dark and irregular. It was how Tessa's molelessness destroyed Happy Moles, made her own skin seem speckled and malignant, made everything cancerous, cancer-filled, moles full of cancer. It was the way the ROM sprouted its own side growth, its jagged tumour, darkly pigmented zigzag malignancy sticking right out the fucking top and down the side while she was walking Bloor Street and couldn't take it anymore.

Patient slips in and out of consciousness. Post-traumatic stress and blood loss from "biopsy." Patient refuses treatment and sedatives. Patient wants mole tested.

And then mole from calf in hand, mole in hand in front of doctor. Doctor takes mole into hands, puts mole in bag. Doctor packages mole for laboratorial assessment.

Patient's mole sent to laboratory. Advised patient to seek emergency counselling and take sedatives. Patient refused. Will return when results are received.

And then waiting. Long stretch of waiting. Days and weeks of waiting. Heaving in her upstairs bedroom, hyperventilating. Reaching internet limits of skin cancer research. Scouring website after website, and then back to the beginning, first website first, then return to the second. Every day the same cyber circuit, the same heaving in her upstairs bedroom. And she doesn't eat. She doesn't sleep. Fungus grows on food: pancake tumours, floret moulds. Fungus grows on her mole-hole, infection everywhere, and she can't bear to look at it. She refuses. And now a big open sore fringed with pus.

And now a hole where a mole used to be. And she's waiting, moulding and waiting, moulding and waiting—

Until one day it comes.

A twinkling ring. A call from a receptionist. A soft-spoken charm through the phone earpiece: "Come in immediately, Dr. Urbanstein wants to see you. Your test results are in."

And then such *hurry hurry.* Dirty clothes thrown over dirty body, thrown into a taxicab speeding down College St., "Hurry, please, HURRY... Can't you go a little faster? I really have to get there NOW" – And jeans rub against calf-hole, rubbing dirty bacteria into calf-hole while taxicab swerves around cars, flies forward, quick left, left again, hands gripping seat cushion near calf-hole, hole leaky, bacterial, hole thrown left and right, cab turns, turns again and comes to a stop. Then: a money exchange. A door slam. The *tap tap tap* of feet hurrying across concrete, feet into a doorway.

"Clara Williamson...Yes, here to see Dr. Urbanstein. Yes, I received a call this morning... OK, thank you."

Feet tapping in a waiting room is not so unusual. Every patient taps something, fiddles something else, picks at other things while anxiously awaiting his or her turn. Flipping through sticky magazines isn't so unusual either – pick off crumbs on page seventeen, look at celebrity photos on page twenty-two, skim facts about silk-lined pillowcases and titillating meatloaf. But leaking holes on carpeted ground in a waiting room is irregular. Taxicab excitement tore it open again, blood dripping into jean fabric, and now it trickle-trickles on the floor.

OK, OK, so she's got an open wound. OK, so it's leaking everywhere, staining, stinking, but at least her results are in. At least she can be told what she could not know about her own body. At least the doctor can put it all on the table and tell her how much longer she has to live.

Patient looks skeletal, infection in her right calf where seven-millimetre mutilation occurred. Antibiotics prescribed. Patient self-describes as anxious and psychotic. Confirms she has not eaten in at least six days.

Cut to the chase, Doctor. She's not here to talk about her health. She doesn't care about infection. She doesn't want your antibacterials, your food suggestions, your sedation medications to relieve the stress of sitting here waiting for you to tell her the fucking results. Just give them to her. Tell her what her skin cells said. Tell her how much longer. Tell her what her mole was!

Negative.

Test results are negative; skin pigments are negating cancerous undertones, negating intra-body travel to different regions for fun in the sun and relaxation. But that can't be possible! – Can that be possible? Is it possible for skin cells, angry and black, to be jolly jubilee? Did she cut her mole, defile her calf, let infection seep for eight days all for NOTHING?

Patient seems upset at results. Patient bangs hand on forehead continuously. Eventually forced hand onto her lap. Appears patient has violence and anger management issues. Prescribed several medications listed below and six days of antibiotics to clear infection. Patient is discharged from clinic.

Tight grip on her antibacterial prescription. Fingers clasping antipsychotics, anti-anxieties, sedatives, sleeping pills. Five slips of prescriptions in her hand, she marches out of the doctor's office, out onto the concrete, into the sun, sun burning her eyelids, and there's a wrenching pain in her gut, fingers twisting her spleen and stomach into happy organ animals, insides burning like eyelids. All for nothing. All for nothing! Body RUINED all for nothing.

Then: five days of antibiotics, pus slurps back to origin, blood crusts into a convex dome, blackens, misshapes. Every day her mantra: ALL FOR NOTHING. Five days of nausea, puke in the bathroom, the kitchen, lethargy on her bed. She can barely get up. Antibiotics suck the life force out of people. But she wouldn't move anyway, even if she felt perfectly fine, even if the doctor assured her she'd live for another forty years. Because she can't bear to look in the mirror and face herself, what she did, how she self-mutilated for no particular reason. Wasn't cancer. Not melanoma. Not basilique or squirmish.

And, sure, the mole-hole starts to heal. No more infection or open wound. Instead: a concave dip, right where the dig happened. An irreversible hole where her mole used to be. And, sure, she's healthy, cancer-free, should be rejoicing, should be out dancing in the streets, living life again...

But all she can do is sit on her bed. Her calf-dip killing her. She can't take it, just can't bear to look at it, and everywhere – EVERYWHERE – holes dip, acne pits, the dip in the sidewalk outside her house, the blemishes of Christie Pits. She throws herself onto her bed and imagines the multitudes of dips and pits that surround her, doesn't want to face the world. Moves inward, into the centre, begins to fetal curl, but her bed dips. And her pillow dips. And she slams her fist onto the mattress making an itty-bitty pit. She just can't escape the pits and dips, the highs and lows. She just can't hide from holes and concavity. Moles and convexity. Skin is everywhere, surfaces everywhere, surfaces and skins ready to dip and valley, pit and dale, normal, abnormal, happy. And so it goes. She sighs, curls inward, fetal curl until she's nothing but a ball. A mole. A small growth of otherwise benign skin.

from *DEAD RINGERS*

DAVID CRONENBERG & NORMAN SNIDER

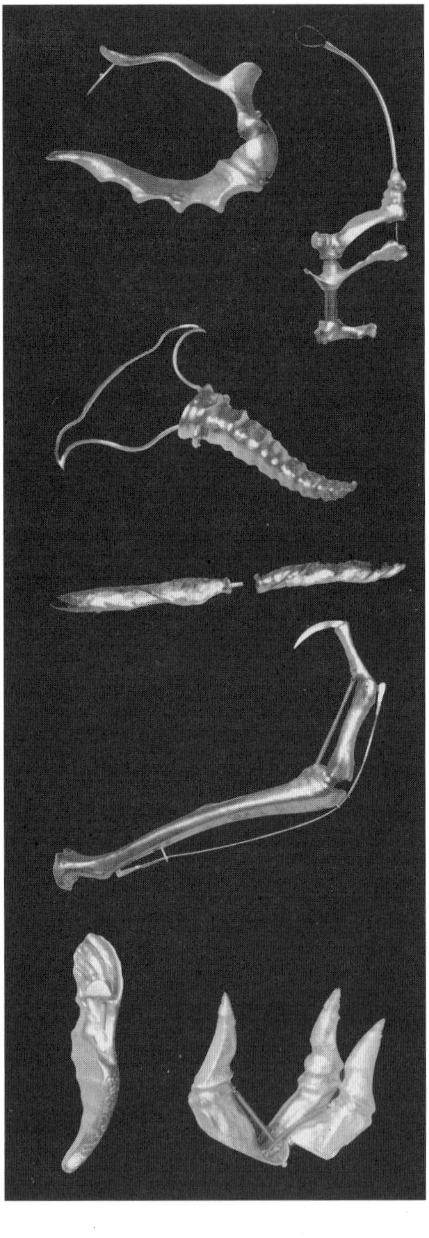

surgical instruments

EXT. IMMIGRANT STREET. DOWNTOWN TORONTO. 1954 – DAY § Scene One

A pair of 7-year-old twin boys, ELLIOT *and* BEVERLY *Mantle, sit on a porch step, talking.*

ELLIOT
You've heard about sex?

BEVERLY
Sure I have.

ELLIOT
I've discovered why sex is.

BEVERLY
You have? Fantastic!

ELLIOT
Yes. It's because human beings don't live under water.

BEVERLY
I don't get it.

ELLIOT
Fish don't need sex because they just lay eggs and fertilize them right in the water. Humans can't do that because they don't live in the water. They have to *internalize* the water. Therefore, we have sex.

BEVERLY
So humans wouldn't have sex if they lived under water?

ELLIOT
They'd have a kind of sex, but the kind where you don't have to *touch* each other.

BEVERLY

I like that idea.

(PAUSE)

Have you heard of SCUBA diving? It's just new.

ELLIOT

Self-Contained Underwater Breathing Apparatus.

BEVERLY

Exactly.

The twins notice a little girl - 9-years-old, precocious, dark complexion, Southern Italian - walking towards them along the street. They look at each other.

ELLIOT

Are you thinking what I'm thinking?

BEVERLY

Yes. You ask her.

ELLIOT *gets up and intercepts the little girl.*

ELLIOT

Luciana, would you like to have sex with us in our bathtub? It's an experiment.

LUCIANA

Fuck off, you freaks! I'm telling my father you talk dirty!

LUCIANA *runs off down the street, then stops to deliver one parting shot.*

LUCIANA

(YELLS)

Besides, I know for a fact you don't even know what fuck *is.*

She turns and disappears around a corner.

BEVERLY
(PAUSE)
They're so different from us
(BEAT)
And all because we don't live under water.

ELLIOT
(DETERMINED)
We're going to have to figure them out.

BEVERLY
How do we do it?

ELLIOT
(PAUSE)
Dissection.

BEVERLY
Dissection? You mean we find a girl and cut her apart?

ELLIOT
It works with frogs.

BEVERLY
(PAUSE)
Mom?

ELLIOT
I guess so. We don't know any other girls.

BEVERLY
Will she let us?

ELLIOT

Well, she says she loves us.

BEVERLY

It would probably hurt. And could we get her back together again?

ELLIOT

I think we could take her apart. I don't think we could get her back together again.

They think about this.

ELLIOT

Maybe not Mommy.

BEVERLY

Maybe not Mommy.

ELLIOT

We could practice first.

INT. TWINS' BEDROOM. TORONTO. 1956 – DAY § Scene Two

The twins are now 9-years-old and they are taking apart a transparent medical doll girl, the teaching kind. They are using strange little tools which they have made themselves to hold the doll down and take it apart.

ELLIOT
The morculum is working superbly.

BEVERLY
Shall I insert the menticulator?

ELLIOT
Please.

They are working away inside the doll's pelvis with their odd teeny tools.

BEVERLY
What's the diagnosis?

ELLIOT
Intra-ovular surgery.

INT. COLLEGE ANATOMY CLASS. 1967 – DAY § Scene Three

The twins, now 20, are at medical school. They share the same corpse – a woman's. There are five or six other teams of students working in the same room. The anatomy class SUPERVISOR *approaches the twins' table. He notices one of the tools with which they are working.*

SUPERVISOR
Where did you get that instrument?

ELLIOT
We had it made for us.

SUPERVISOR
Really?

He holds out his hand for it. ELLIOT *gives it to him. It is a beautiful, complex piece of surgical casting.*

SUPERVISOR
And how is it used?

BEVERLY
Like this.

BEVERLY *demonstrates.*

ELLIOT
It applies leverage to the pelvis while this inverse clamp dilates the...

SUPERVISOR
Yes, yes I see.
(DRIPPING SARCASM)
Well, it might be fine for a corpse, but it won't work on a living patient, I can tell you that.

INT. COLLEGE CONVOCATION HALL. 1969 – NIGHT § Scene Four

CU of a golden version of the instrument supported by an oak base. It is an award being presented at a huge medical awards banquet to the twins.

PRESENTER

To our fabulous twins who have as mere undergraduates already brought us glory and here it is – in solid gold... solid gold plate, that is...

(POLITE LAUGHTER)

...the Mantle Morticulator which is now the standard of the industry and financing our boys' further education at the Brill Medical Centre in Toronto. Here's to a brilliant future.

Wild applause as twin ELLIOT *takes the stage. There is no sign of* BEVERLY *in the hall.*

ELLIOTT

(ULTRA SMOOTH AND AT EASE)

Thank you... thank you all so much. I know I also speak for my brother Beverly when I say... "preguto." Let me interpret that for you. That was our secret childhood word for... thank you.

More wild applause: the twins are obviously very popular.

INT. COLLEGE DORMITORY - NIGHT § Scene Five

BEVERLY *is sitting at his desk in the twins' student pad, poring over various books and papers.* ELLIOT *comes in with the trophy.*

ELLIOT
Here it is.

BEVERLY
That's wonderful.
(EXAMINES THE TROPHY)
They got the pivot pin backwards.

ELLIOT
Bev, you should have been there.

BEVERLY
(A GENUINE SMILE)
I was.

They embrace, a manly, brotherly embrace.

INT. MANTLE CLINIC. EXAMINATION ROOM – NIGHT § Scene Six

It is the present in Toronto, and the twins have an ultra-slick and well-equipped private gynaecological clinic.

We are close on a woman in stirrups – CLAIRE NIVEAU. *She is gorgeous, in her early thirties.* BEVERLY *is inside her with his gloved fingers.*

CLAIRE
Well? Are all the necessary parts there, Doc?

BEVERLY
Yes, they are. But there are a few other ones I've never seen before.

CLAIRE
Not funny.

BEVERLY
Not a joke. Excuse me a moment. I'll be right back.

ELLIOT'S OFFICE - NIGHT § Scene Seven

ELLIOT *and* BEVERLY *have separate offices which open into the single central examination room.* ELLIOT *stands in front of the full-length mirror, checking out his tuxedo. He is dressed to kill.*

BEVERLY *walks in and closes the door behind him.*

BEVERLY
I want you to take a look at this woman before you go. She's a trifurcate. I've never seen anything like it before.

ELLIOT
I can't. I've got to wow the Chairman's wife so we can get our grant.

BEVERLY
It's Claire Niveau.

ELLIOT *stops in his tracks.*

ELLIOT
You're kidding me.

BEVERLY
No. She flew in from London to do a mini-series here. She's got three agents and a bodyguard in the waiting room.

ELLIOT
(DISBELIEVING)
The Claire Niveau?

BEVERLY

She says she was told that the Mantle Clinic was the best in the world, and...

ELLIOT

And she wants to get pregnant.

BEVERLY

How did you know?

ELLIOT

National Enquirer: "Star's Life Empty Without Children."

BEVERLY

Well, I hope the *National Enquirer* also explained how we're going to make her fertile. I don't think *I* can.

ELLIOT

(CHECKING HIS WATCH)

I guess *la bella Contessa* can wait.

ELLIOT *starts to remove his tux jacket.*

INT. EXAMINATION ROOM – NIGHT § Scene Eight

ELLIOT *enters and closes the door behind him.*

ELLIOT
OK, let's have another look.

CLAIRE
(NOTICING HIS TUX PANTS)
Hm. You've dressed for dinner. What is it exactly you're trying to tell me?

ELLIOT
(CHUCKLES AS HE HAS A LOOK)
Maybe just – that I'd like to take you out for dinner.
(TO HIMSELF)
Yes. Fantastic.

CLAIRE
I've never had anybody say that about the *inside* of my body before.

ELLIOT
(COMING UP FOR AIR)
You've heard of inner beauty, haven't you? I've often thought there should be beauty contests for the insides of bodies. You know, best spleen, most perfectly developed kidney. I mean, why is it that a beautiful woman would induce revulsion in a man if he saw the inside of her thoracic cavity? Why don't we have standards of beauty for the *entire* human body, inside and out?

CLAIRE
I have a feeling that you do.

ELLIOT
I do. You have the most exquisite uterus.

INT. RESTAURANT QUATRE SAISONS - NIGHT § Scene Nine

They are at dinner. He is still in his tux. With them is CLAIRE*'s agent, and old British gent named* LEO.

LEO
So I'll tell him to fuck off. Pardon my French.

CLAIRE
Don't tell him to fuck off. I need the work.
This mini-series is paying absolute peanuts.

LEO
You don't need to be humiliated.

CLAIRE
I've decided I *want* to be humiliated.
(TURNS TO ELLIOT)
Tell me about my uterus.

LEO *almost chokes on his veal piccata.*

ELLIOT
It has three doorways. Haven't any of your
lovers told you that?

CLAIRE
No. My lovers only tell me what I want to hear.
I've never wanted to hear that. Until now.

ELLIOT
You have three cervixes leading to three separate
compartments in your uterus. That's fabulously rare.
Do you have trouble with your periods?

LEO *gets up.*

LEO

Listen, I'm gonna be late for the Axelrod meeting...
(HE TILTS HIS HEAD DISAPPROVINGLY TOWARDS ELLIOT)
You'll be OK?

CLAIRE

Goodbye, Leo. Remember... I need the humiliation – as well as the money.

LEO *leaves.* CLAIRE *turns back to* ELLIOT, *picking up their conversation without missing a beat.*

CLAIRE

I almost never have periods. Twice a year, maybe. Not very enthusiastic ones.
(PAUSE)
Could I have triplets, do you think? One in each... compartment?

ELLIOT

No, it doesn't work that way.

CLAIRE

Really?
(INTENSELY, SEDUCTIVELY)
How does it work?

BLAZING FIGURES

ROBERT MARKLE

On stage Sexy Sadie is on a red plush settee doing astonishing things with her legs and one of her shoes. She moves to the floor, finding an imaginary lover, but only for a moment. Like all good strippers, she has learned to live her performance in a constant state of daring. She brings to her surface all that she's got to flash. She articulates her body with the special emphasis of wired bras, sequins and tassels. Sexy Sadie is very much involved in the art of self-fascination. Strippers – the good ones – reach out through the eyes of their audience to get a better look at themselves. Beside me, and it seems inevitable, an Oriental man is silently watching, *reading* her. Why are the Orientals so curious about sex shows? Maybe it's because they're often Buddhists and Buddhism is all about conquering desire. Maybe watching is a way of conquering. I watch with the hope that desire will grow into romance.

Sexy Sadie is waving her G-string and brushing the air with the curls of her public hair. Blurring, trembling, naked flesh. Solid, dark nipples reminiscent of those I've painted. She's now a fire in a black space that surrounds me. At this moment, like the rarest seduction, she's capable of fulfilling any promise. The Oriental gentleman beside me is inside himself, watching his own version of her. She finishes in a flurry; a glistening patch of sweat on the small of her back becomes a mirror that catches the fading spotlight.

She started out on Yonge Street as a model: "I remember as a very young girl being aware of my legs. I would compare their shape with those of the grown-up girls in magazines. I wanted them to be like those girls, their legs. It was too early for the rest of my body, only my legs seemed to have any real shape. I have been told that my legs were never those of a child, they were shapely, long, I was always moving, they were strong. I always thought of them as *dramatic*, so soon I was in black hose, the line of the back seam drawing the true shape of my legs. I was a little girl. I lived in an artistic community and soon I was posing for drawings and photographs. I remember catching glimpses of myself in shop windows, mirrors, and thinking that I was someone else, not me, someone to admire. The drawings helped me see myself better, I soon knew that what I wanted was to be continually on display. Of course by this time the rest of my body caught up with my legs, though not as well as I would have liked, but people wanted to see what I looked like, and I wanted them to see. I learned to use their light around me, I would roll through space..."

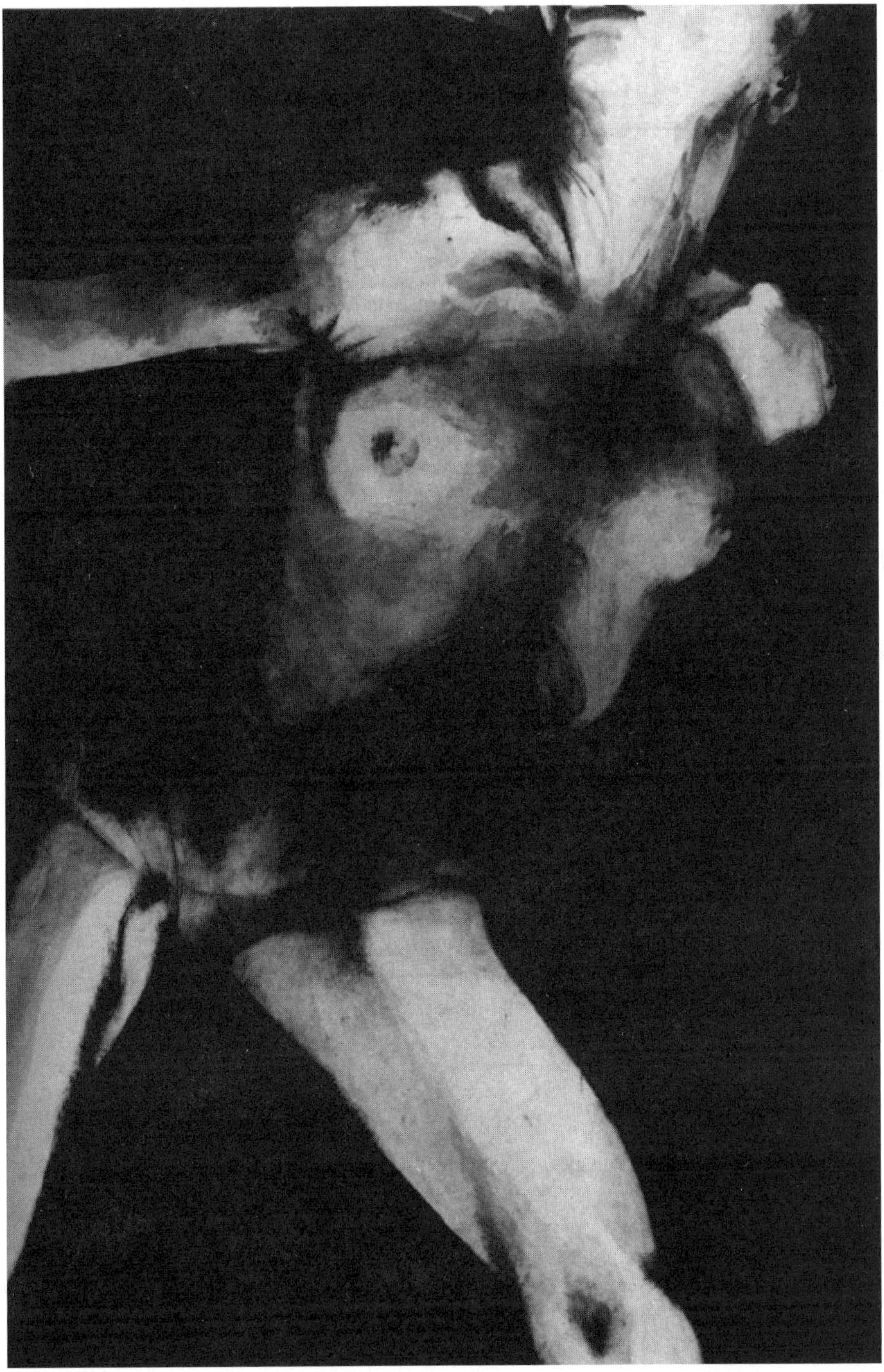

Like all religious experiences, the essential transforms. The high heel does just that. The Egyptians invented the high heel, can you imagine the startled glee when women, Nile beauties, walked into a room, their pelvises thrust forward, their backs straight, immediately transformed into treasures, the high heel became an ikon.

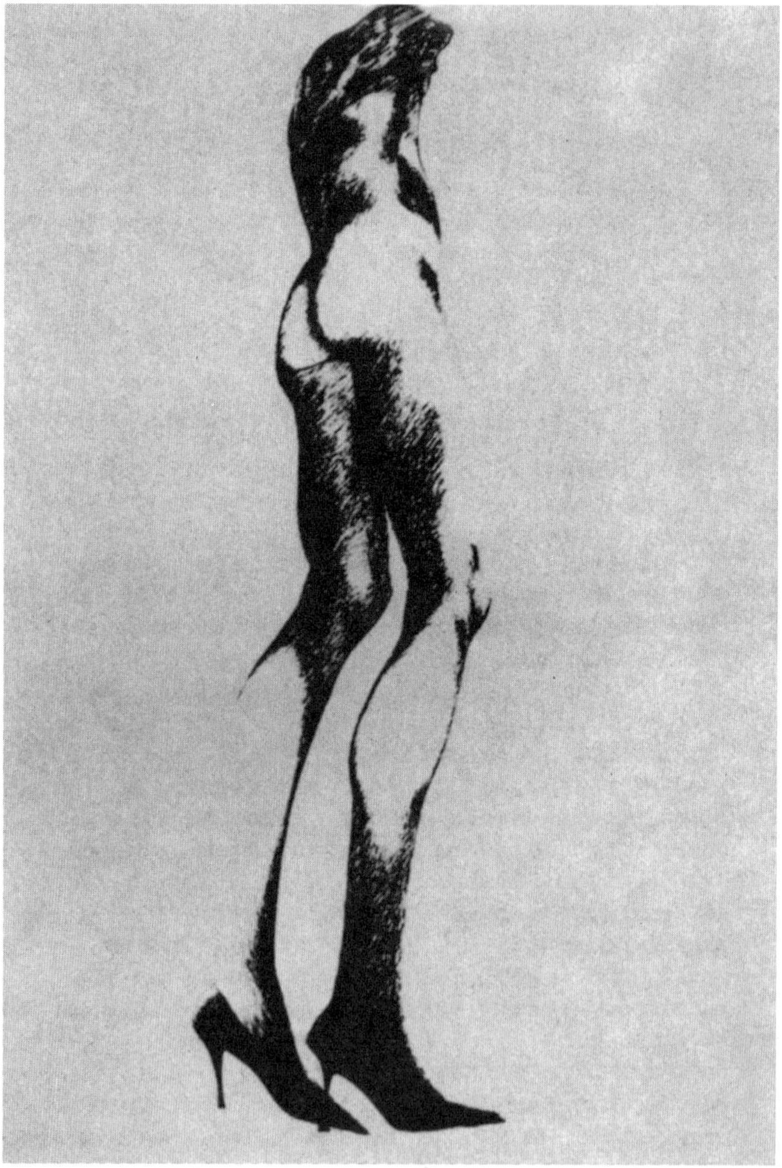

She is best when she's on the stage, held in space, *in potentia* – waiting to be recreated by the imagination. Not a young girl, but a heroine of sorts. "You have to understand that, like the men watching me, I fantasize, too. The G-string gives me mystery. I can look into their faces and I can tell if they're interested. I am for men. Sometimes the women say nasty things. They're jealous because their man is getting turned on by me. They try to destroy me because they're not satisfied with their own lives. They can't be loose. I'm loose. I'm enjoying myself. I'm doing something that they can only fantasize about. Their laughter isn't the laughter of people enjoying themselves. Their laughter is like knife wounds..."

Besides the politics of equal opportunity, there is a space, a distance, between men and women that has no culture, only a mysterious emotional life. Within this space compassion lies side by side with violence. It's a strange and devastatingly lonely landscape, the only topography I find worthwhile mining. It's my obsession with this space, this distance, that makes me hold on to the figure.

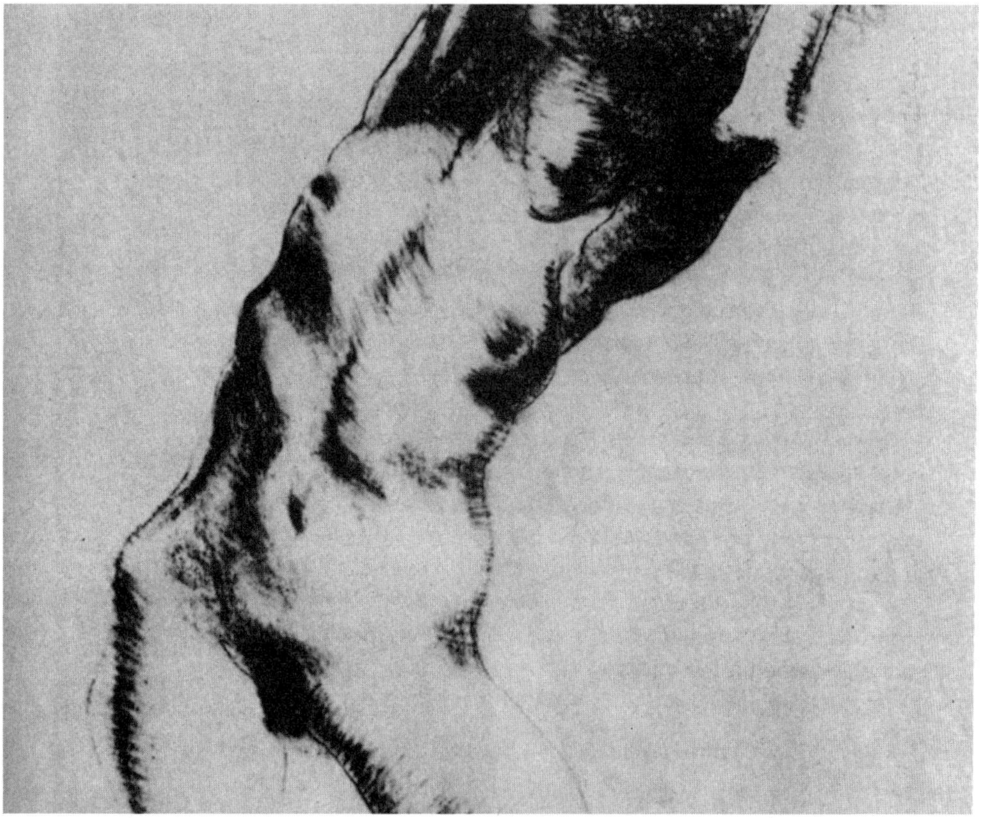

Morley Callaghan says the artist keeps looking at the appearance of things. De Kooning says that content is just a glimpse no more. When I was very young I saw a woman get a tattoo on that fleshy plane a woman has on her back just before it turns into a shoulder. *Woman adorned. Fascination with self. Beyond embellishment.* In order to fully understand the thighs of Sheena of the Jungle, you had to see the violence explicit in the ragged edge of her leopardskin loincloth: points on which to build a vision. And the wonderwomen of the strip are good company for glimpse and appearance. So I stay with it. The figure endures.

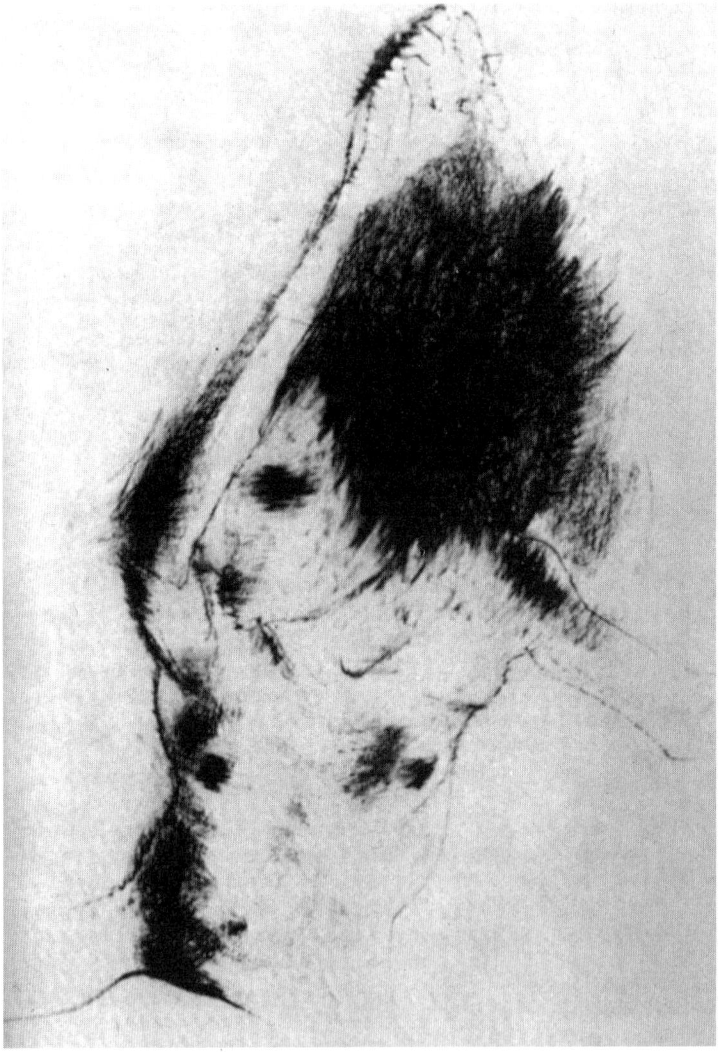

I saw a woman get a tattoo, a small rose etched into the nape of her neck, only to be seen by lovers, and at the edge of her pubic hair, blood butterflies. Woman adorned. Fascination with self. Beyond embellishment. Sheena of the Jungle. Wonderwomen everywhere. Their offerings of nipples like pencil erasers, innocent physical sharings on the streets of summer. Up alleyways, the real women had to compete.

Upstairs, the second-storey Yonge Street strip parlour built all wrong, the audience is in the dancer's lap. That close, the dancer becomes just another girl, a woman with no clothes, sweat and stretch marks, tiny webs of veins, everyday life bruises. Perfect distance is needed to measure a vision. I hesitate to place beauty: its hopelessness is the only reality. She risked that distance, making male masturbation motions, huge hard pumping, hissing through a red slashed mouth. As the lights died and she stooped to pick up her things the man in the front row reached through the unfair distance, touched her ankle, and she leapt back, stumbling, escaping. The man left, furious, humiliated, ice-cold in the fingertips.

CHESTNUTS

JOE FIORITO

In Parkdale, if you do not look too closely, you might think you were in some other Poland, unsacked, unburned, not hardened by all those centuries of war. I don't mean that the architecture is lovely. I mean that the shops are full of smoked fish, rye bread, ham hocks, sour pickles, strings of cured sausages, loaves of soft bread and bland, sweet jam-filled buns; a more practical loveliness.

It is of such a richness that when the Poles came here from the old country during the years of collective farms and Soviet domination, they saw in the windows of the shops on this street the kind of food they had only heard about from their grandparents.

At Christmas there are live fish flopping helplessly in blue plastic barrels, and frozen fish on cardboard trays, and salted fish as white as pocket handkerchiefs laid out in small wooden boxes stacked on the sidewalks outside the delis; this, too, is a loveliness.

One day, as I was walking home from work, I noticed an old Polish lady rooting around on a neighbour's lawn. She was hobbled by age and arthritis. She was bent over, picking up horse chestnuts from under a tree and stuffing them into a plastic sack. I stopped and asked her what she was going to do with all those nuts.

She said she was going to take them home and put them in a pot and boil them up, and then she was going to mash them. She moved her hands as she talked, miming a pot in one hand and a potato masher in the other, the gestures familiar to us both.

I asked her if she was going to eat the chestnut mash. She said no, it was not for eating; she was going to put the hot mash on her ankles like a poultice. She said she had arthritis very bad, it was hard for her to walk, the doctors gave her pills but the pills didn't help, and she hurt all the time; hurt in her ankles, hurt in her knees. I could see how badly her legs were swollen. She said there was no use sitting around doing nothing.

I picked up a chestnut, still slick from having just popped out of its casing, and put it in her sack. I asked if the hot-mashed horse-chestnut poultice was an old Polish remedy. She said no, it was Russian.

I wanted to know more, but I was in some vague hurry. I wished her well and went on my way, hoping I'd run into her a little later so I could find out if the poultice had worked. I had a proprietary curiosity. My knees, my shoulder. But I never saw her again that fall. The snow fell.

A year went by.

Déjà vu.

This time she was wearing a head scarf, a zippered sweater, a heavy skirt, and a pair of sturdy shoes with orthopedic stockings. She was bent over another lawn, stuffing more nuts in a sack. She looked a little older, a little slower, a little more tired.

I introduced myself and reminded her that we'd talked a year or so ago about the poultice, the hot horse-chestnut mash. She straightened stiffly, narrowed her eyes and sized me up. I took a nut from the lawn and put it in her bag, just like I'd done the year before; that's when she remembered. I asked if she was going to boil those nuts again.

This time she said no, she was going to soak them in alcohol.

I supposed the poultice hadn't worked. I mimed a gesture, as if knocking back a shot. "Horse-chestnut vodka?"

She said, "Not to drink." She told me she was going to rub it on her ankles. "Here, you want to see my ankles? I'll show you." She leaned against the tree, slipped off her shoe and rolled down one of her stockings. Her ankle was spongy and swollen, worse than I imagined, the pale skin netted with spidery veins. It hurt to look. I said I hoped the alcohol helped.

She pursed her lips and shrugged. I said using the alcohol as a rub was probably a good idea, because horse chestnuts aren't good to eat, and so probably no good to drink.

She said, "I ate."

Which stopped me cold; horse chestnuts are impossibly bitter. I asked her when she'd eaten them. "During the war." How did she prepare them? "You grind them up. You make flour for bread." I said horse-chestnut bread didn't sound very good. She touched her belly with the palm of her hand.

"When you're hungry, you eat."

I asked where she'd spent the war.

"Siberia; the Russians came through Poland. They rounded us up. Then they made us march all the way. I worked as a miner in a gold mine. Standing in cold water, always cold, hungry all the time."

And the way the Russians rounded up the Poles was not dissimilar to the way the Germans rounded up the Poles: they came down the streets in armoured cars, they blocked off the streets at the corners and they searched the houses, taking the men if there were any, taking the women, taking the older kids, taking any children, boys or girls, who looked big enough to work.

I looked at her hands. Her palms were rough and square. Her fingers were thicker than mine, curled and gnarled and knotted. She rolled her stocking up and stepped into her shoe, and as she did, she talked.

She said she lost four children during the war.

When she came to Toronto, she did all kinds of work in factories and on farms, picking tobacco, doing whatever she could to make some money, because she had three more children, because life goes on.

She'd got this arthritis from working in the mine, and she hurt all the time now, and the doctors were no help, useless, and now the kids were all grown, living in the suburbs, out of town, living lives of their own, always busy.

And she shrugged and went back to work picking up chestnuts.

SOCIOLOGY

KATHERINE GOVIER

On the porch Ellen stood without looking behind her, like a pack horse at a crossing where she'd stopped many times before. Alec came up the steps: she heard the clinking as his hands sorted the keys from the change in his pocket. Then she heard a low, drawling voice.

"You folks stay right where you are, and this gun ain't going off. You keep right on looking at that door."

She supposed it was time this happened. Their house was in what you called a transition area: you couldn't afford to buy there anymore, but you weren't supposed to live there yet. Ellen enjoyed living there, however. She was morbidly fascinated by the differences in circumstances between themselves and the next door neighbour who sat on his steps after dark and raised Newfoundland fishing songs to the sky. It fit with her view of the world, which was that as close as your hand were people who were not as lucky as you and therefore would like to kill you.

The man with the gun came up the stairs. He found Alec's wallet and took it. He took Ellen's purse. He asked for Alec's watch. The watch was gold with a gold band; it had been his father's, awarded for forty year's work in the factory in Quebec. Having died two months after retirement, his father had never worn it. When Alec reached twenty-one without a cigarette, his mother added the gold band and gave it to her only son. Wordlessly, Alec snapped it off his wrist and handed it over. Ellen groaned. Then the gunman got greedy.

"Your jewellery too," he said. He took a handful of Ellen's hair and pulled it back to see if she was wearing earrings. She wasn't. She had only a couple of rings, her wedding band and one other, which was a pearl she'd gotten for her sixteenth birthday. Earlier that month the pearl had become tight, and she had switched it to a smaller finger. Now she pulled and got it off. The wedding ring was hopeless.

"I can't get it off," she said to the mugger. "My fingers are swollen because I'm pregnant."

She looked him in the eye as she said the word pregnant. She felt she had never been in such danger; she had to enunciate the point of greatest risk. She was testing. It had been her fantasy during these last months that she would run into one of those maniacs who shot pregnant women in the belly or cut them open with a knife.

But the mugger looked back at her with a disinterested rage. Perhaps he would shoot her finger off and get the ring that way. It was still early in the evening, however, and a man was walking by only fifteen feet away, so the mugger just snarled and ran off.

Ellen and Alec attended pre-natal classes in a boys' club gymnasium in Cabbagetown. Alongside nine other pregnant women Ellen lay on the gym floor on a blanket brought from home and practised breathing patterns to prepare herself for labour. Her head on the pink- and blue-flowered pillowcase from their bedroom, she raised her hips and lowered them again; the water balloon that was her stomach went up and down. Then she got on hands and knees and Alec rolled tennis balls on her back as she humped it up and down like a dog trying to vomit. The idea was to make the birth natural.

They kept this up for six consecutive Thursdays. On the whole Ellen was disappointed in the classes. It was not the material so much as the other people. She'd thought their common predicament would promote instant friendship, but it had not. This was not for lack of effort on the part of the instructor, Riva, who used the word "share" frequently. By the end they would develop a limited closeness, like that of people stuck together in a train which is liable to go off the tracks. But where they came from, where they would go afterward would not be mentioned.

Ellen tried to pin down some information. She learned that Gloria and Ted were born-agains. She divined that Miriam was at least forty and was not married to the man she came with. She explained them to Alec, who disapproved of her curiosity. The only ones she could not explain were Robert and June.

June was tall with blond hair and moved hesitantly, but gracefully. Her eyes were cloudy blue. Sometimes the irises darted back and forth as if panicked, but Ellen did not believe she saw anything at all, not even light and shadow, because of the way she held her head. The way she held her head was the best part about her. Her carriage was like that of a large and elegant bird, her head alert and still as if she were listening for an alarm. Her seeing-eye dog lay at her feet, so devoted that he made the husband look like a redundancy. Robert was thickset, pimply, and sullen, and he watched June all the time.

June gave what the rest withheld; she laughed, she talked her fear. Ellen remembered best the day she sat on her metal stacking chair like an oracle, transparent eyelids showing the darting of sightless eyes, "I can't believe it's me who's pregnant," she said. "I suppose because I've never seen myself."

But isn't that what it's like, Ellen thought.

On the last night of class they watched a film of natural childbirth. Someone had brought popcorn, and they stared at the screen, silently passing the bucket. In the dark room Ellen could hear Robert's nasal voice very softly telling June what was being shown. "The baby is coming out of the mother's body," he said. Ellen and Alec both cried. Ellen thought that most of the other people in the class did too. She didn't know for sure though because when the lights went up, she didn't want to look too closely at their faces.

Riva packed the projector, and the women and their supporters made ready to leave. Swollen feet pushed back into bulging shoes; knees poked out to ten and two o'clock as legs strained to lift the immobile trunks. Stomachs first, they walked; the hard, heavy egg shapes pushing flesh away from the centre up to chest, arms, puffing the cheeks. Eyes red from strain, the ten making each other seem more grotesque than ever, the women made ready to go alone into the perilous future.

In the hospital, Ellen forgot all about her childbirth training and began screaming for an anesthetic. The baby was two weeks late and labour was being induced with a drug. "This baby must like you a lot," said the doctor, turning up the dose again. "He doesn't want to be born." When he came, he wasn't breathing, so the nurse grabbed him and ran down the hall. "My mother always said the cord around the neck meant they're lucky," said Alec. Ellen lay draped in green sheets, being stitched up by the doctor. She felt robbed, raped, aching, and empty. She told Alec it was just like being mugged, and they both began to laugh.

"Tell that to Riva," he said.

"But I don't feel bad. I feel – purified."

"Anyone who feels purified after a mugging has a bad case," said Alec.

In two hours they brought Alain back, cleaned up and swathed in a little white flannel blanket with a toque on his head to keep in the heat. Ellen began to think of the others in the class and how it would be for them. "I wonder what the odds are in ten births," she said, holding her son.

The party was at their place. There had been an RSVP on the invitation, but the evening before, Ellen had only heard from seven of the ten couples. They were bringing potluck, and she wanted to know how many paper plates to get. She found the class list with the telephone numbers.

The first thing she discovered was that Miriam's phone had been disconnected. Ellen began to feel superstitious. The idea of losing track of one of the group, of not knowing about one of Alain's peers, startled her. She called information and found Miriam's new listing. When she reached it, it turned out she had a new baby boy, and everything was perfectly all right.

Ellen's confidence returned. She decided to call the others she hadn't heard from. The Uruguayan woman had a girl, but Ellen didn't understand any of the details because of the language problem. She hung up and dialled June. The telephone rang seven times, and no one answered.

That was odd; there was always someone home when you have a new baby. She waited until after dinner and then tried again. This time Robert answered. Ellen felt irritated by the sound of his voice; that was when she realized how much she wanted to speak with June. But she said who she was to Robert and asked if they were coming to the party.

Robert cleared a rasp from his throat. Then he sucked in air. "I might as well be straight with you," he said. "We lost our baby."

"Oh my God," said Ellen. "I'm so sorry. I'm so sorry to intrude."

"We got the invitation," he said, continuing as if she hadn't spoken, "and we thought about coming. June wanted to, but I didn't."

Ellen was silent. "But anyway," he said, "it's kind of you to call."

"Oh no, no I shouldn't have. I had no idea."

"June didn't want to tell people. She wanted them just to find out," he said, "naturally." Oh of course it would be natural, thought Ellen, and at whose expense. She was ready to cry with embarrassment. She was dying to know what happened too, but she couldn't ask. "I am very sorry to intrude," she said again, more firmly. "It's a terrible thing."

"Yes," said Robert.

Then no one said anything. Robert started the conversation again with greater energy. "But that doesn't stop me from asking about your baby."

"We had a little boy," Ellen said, "and he's just fine." She didn't tell Robert about the fright they'd had when Alain didn't breathe. It didn't seem proper to have complaints when you had a live son.

"Congratulations," said Robert. "Your baby will bring you a lifetime of happiness." His tone was mean, humble but punishing. Ellen wanted to tell him that their lifetimes would never be so exclusive as he imagined, especially not now, but she didn't.

It was only as she told Alec that Ellen got mad. "Riva knew; she could have spared me that call; why didn't she tell me?"

"Maybe sparing you wasn't her concern," said Alec. He had not been in favour of holding this reunion. The incident only confirmed his belief that coming too close to strangers was asking for trouble. But he was sympathetic. He stood in the kitchen, holding Alain very tightly against his chest, and comforted his wife.

At noon the next day the new parents began to come up the narrow sidewalk. It was funny how nine babies looked like a mob. The oldest was three months, the youngest three weeks. Two of them had great swirls of black hair, but most were bald like Alain. One baby, born by caesarean to the born-agains, had an angelic, calm face, but most were pinched and worried, unused to life on the outside.

All through the house babies bounced on shoulders, slept on laps, sat propped in their infant seats. Now that it was all over, the parents could talk. They told birth stories about the heroism of wives, the callousness of physicians. Those whose babies slept through the night gloated over those whose babies didn't. It turned out one man was a lawyer like Alec and even had an office in the same block. One couple had a live-in already, and about half the women were going back to work.

Ellen got the sociology she wanted all along, and she was happy. Word had gone around about June, and everyone agreed it was better she hadn't come because it would have put such a damper on the party. The story was that she'd been two weeks overdue and had to go in for tests. At her second test the doctor told her the baby was dead. The worst part, all agreed, must have been having to carry the dead baby for another week. Finally June went through a difficult labour. There was nothing wrong with the baby that anyone could see.

When they told the story the women's eyes connected, and their lips pressed down. It was as if a train had crashed and the person in the next seat had been crushed. They could not help but feel relief, lucky to have been missed. But with luck came fear that luck would not last, and the long, hard oval of dread that had quickened in Ellen along with her offspring was born.

Ellen wanted a picture of the babies together. They put Alain out first, in the corner of the couch, propped on his blanket. Others followed with Lila, Andrew, Evelyn, Adam, Ashley, Orin, Jackson, and William, nine prizes all in a row. Their heads bobbed down or dropped to the side; their mouths were open in round O's of astonishment. They fell asleep, leaning on their neighbour or they struck out with spastic hands and hit his face without knowing.

The parents had their cameras ready. They began to shoot pictures, laughing all the while. The line of babies was the funniest thing people had seen in ages. No one had imagined how funny it would be. The babies were startled. They looked not at each other but at the roomful of hysterical adults. One toppled, and the one next to him fell over onto him. Then the whole line began to collapse. Strange creatures with faces like cabbages and changing goblin shapes, tightly rolled in blankets or drooping into puddles of chin and stomach, they could have come from an alien star. The parents laughed, with relief at their babies' safe landing, and wonder at who they might be. The flashbulbs kept popping as the nine silly little bodies toppled and began to run together into a heap, until one of them, Evelyn, Ellen thinks it was, began to cry.

THE GRINDER

Gwendolyn MacEwen

That summer, on Saturday afternoons at exactly twenty after one the rays of the sun turned everything golden; his hands, his shoes, his hair, time stood still and he learned all he needed to know of eternity. Then from down the street the clear tinkle of the old scissors-grinder's bell would summon him back to the fluid present, to world time. The scissors-grinder was one of those who came from places like Warsaw and Kiev to sharpen knives in the capitals of North America. He had pulled his little green contraption around the neighbourhood for forty years, and now you didn't often hear the whirring of the wheel at its work, only the bell's note growing louder, then softer, then dying.

LOST DOGS

Lisa Foad

Take me with you. I didn't say it. The television did. Just before we fell asleep.

You always have the TV on. You like the way its murmurs feel. Low hums that hug. Churn the air. Mark it with matter. Make it matter. There are words everywhere. They swirl and stick. Between your fingers, the clamp of your jaw, you feel letters like "*i*" and "*d*" slither and squish. Scream. You say sometimes it makes you dizzy. Sometimes it makes me dizzy.

When we wake, it's to the sound of breaking news, children gone missing.

From the knot that's our legs and arms, you disentangle. Rub at the sleep in your eyes. Prop yourself up on an elbow. Yawn.

Behind you, Mindy Lynn is missing. Seventeen hours. Last seen leaving school (gold-starred spelling test, Velcro sneakers that light up, bouncing red bursts). A blue Ford Taurus. Or was it a Toyota Corolla? It might have been a wagon. Witness this: Amber Alert. Amber Alert.

Eleven is an average age.

Strewn beneath us, the deck of cards. In particular, we've been sleeping on the suit of spades.

You stretch out one leg taut, then the other. An inadvertent scissor kick.

On the television, a fifth-grade picture day photo. Ringlets and red bows. Eyes, typically blue. Flush-cheeked, beaming. *Cheese.*

You fix two mossy green eyes upon me. Kohl-smoked. Real shiners.

Parents are pleading (a loose french braid, a purple hoodie, sequined blue jeans). *I can hardly breathe. I can hardly see.*

And you tell me that you are a missing child.

I find the seven of spades, use it as a visor.

Your hair is a waist-length swarm of long-legged spiders. Your t-shirt is thin and your throat is a runway.

I laugh.

You laugh.

I laugh again.

You arch your feet. "Well." Point your toes. "I was a missing child." Smile.

"What were you missing?"

You shoot me a wry look. Collect the strewn deck. Palm out for the seven of spades.

I surrender.

You shuffle slowly. Suggest, business.

I follow suit. "You're not missing anymore?"

You abandon the deck. Sit up and tail your hair to the side, drag your fingers through the knots. Say, "I'm twenty-six. I pay my rent. I have a Visa. A Bay card. I frequent bars and movie theatres, sign up for special deals. I exist above board. I'm evident. Evidence, in fact: When you're that visible, you can't still be missing, can you? At any rate, I still feel missing. And I've tried to recover. The things I missed out on, the things I miss. It's just not the same."

You were in search of your mother.

"Isn't everyone?"

"No."

Your mother left you. She left you at the grocery store, in aisle seven, canned fruit to your left, marmalades and jams and jellies to your right.

When you were discovered some time later, you were pale and fantastically silent, a cliff. Green eyes slush grey, cheeks icy. You clutched the handlebar of the shopping cart, two tiny pink knots. Your heels, wrapped in purple velveteen booties, knocked rhythmically at the cart's steel spine. Your lips trussed, a crimson bow. Inside the cart were Ritz crackers, two tins of tuna, diapers, Cream of Wheat. She never bought Cream of Wheat. You let out your first wail only after the woman with the red florets of hair, blue checkered vest, pin that promised, firmly, in ticker tape, MANAGER, pushed you past the instant potatoes, the soups that *eat like a meal*, to the courtesy desk.

You tell me this in a voice that churns. Your mouth's a tilt drum mixer. Slabs of sentence, sentencing. It's a matter of fact.

The day she left you, your mother wore the smart burgundy heels with the skinny spines, sharp toes. Matching leather purse, slender shoulder strap. The burgundy blouse with the classic high neck (wrap tie, collar knot), glossy buttons. Tight designer jeans, creative back-pocket stitch. Her hair fanned her face in soft, dusty waves.

"You remember all this?"

"It was in the police report."

Your father found you on the news. You were a purple velveteen ward of the Crown. In fluorescent-lit rooms with ecru-coloured walls, you'd been passed around. Fed strawberry puree. Offered apple juice, a sippy cup. At six o'clock, you were held tightly in the arms of a stranger. While you knocked your booties and gnawed on your fist, a man with a microphone pointed and *tsk*ed, pointed and *tsk*ed. The camera panned, zoomed. You buried your head in yellow silk, choked on the woody bouquet of Halston, and threw up a little. The camera tilted, zoomed. Caught the white-pink pulp as it dribbled down your chin, mashed against yellow silk, a wet scar.

The next day, the newspaper headlines boasted, MISSING CHILD, FOUND.

"So you weren't missing. You were left. Missing by default, maybe. More like misplaced."

"No." You flex your palms. Rattle your wrist, let your watch slip back into place. "I'm not done."

Your father picked you up immediately. Predictably, he couldn't even look at you. He began watching the news obsessively. Weather, especially. One night, he smashed the TV and never replaced it.

Before long, a busty woman named Marilyn with mudslide eyes was sitting at the kitchen table. Cloudy liquid wrestling with lemon slices, clunking cubes of ice. Skinny pastel cigarettes, lush strands of smoke streaming and pluming. Mounted under the corner cabinet, the mini black-and-white television (*Like sands through the hourglass... so are the Days of Our Lives*). *Non-negotiable*, she'd insisted. From the bedroom, soft murmurs. Low hums that hug, they fit together like spoons. He'd acquiesced.

She'd mix you fake drinks - oranges, reds, finger-swirl - and talk about art. Rubens, Kahlo, *The Garden of Earthly Delights*. One day, just drunk enough, she told you that your mother was either dead or in a big city with tall buildings and insufficient park space. Maybe somewhere on a television. She slid a shoebox across the table. Inside were old snapshots (honeymooning in Niagara, happy birthday from a mix), news clippings (bold headlines, MOTHER ABANDONS, and such), a wedding band, an engagement ring (pear-shaped solitaire, *vena amoris*). A letter. From a television station. Noting, *We were very impressed with your reel.* The location of the audition - weekend weathergirl - was blacked out. She left two days later. Whispered in your ear, on her way, *Today, the sun will suffocate beneath cloudy drifts, barely evade the drench, glassy shards of riling rain. Beam, some time later. I love you.*

"You remember this? That wasn't in the police report."

You left shortly thereafter. Eleven, average. Thumbed your way to a motel called MOTEL with a restaurant called RESTAURANT, a low-slung, brown-bricked, highway-side affair, fluorescents sizzling. You stood in the parking lot for a minute, mesmerized by the paved arteries, the barrelling headlights. Felt you'd fallen off the edge of something. You groped wildly, arms flailing. And fell. A man caught you. He was smoking a Dunhill. He told you his name was Dad and that your real name was Darling.

It was in the parking lot that you met Doe.

You heard her before you saw her. Laughing. It sounded like a song you'd heard somewhere before. It made your stomach hurt. You reeled. You reached. You found her. Standing in front of the restaurant, smoking a cigarette with one of the waitresses. She was the blonde in the tight stonewashed jeans, red scoop-neck t-shirt, a can of Tab and a pack of Players in hand. You tucked yourself in behind the jutting front wheel of a big rig and tried to remember the words.

Hers found you first. *Shit!* Eyes wide, sparkling green shadow. *Shit.* She picked at her cola-spattered t-shirt, dabbed at the droplets that glistened from the fleshy curves of her cleavage. She began to laugh. *You scared the shit out of me.* Her gold hoop earrings grazed her shoulders. *Excuse me, darling.* She nodded at the driver's door, turquoise rabbit's foot dangling from her key ring. *I've got to get going.*

You stuck out your thumb.

She studied you for a minute, and asked what kind of trouble you were in.

You told her you weren't in any, but that your mother might be. That she'd left you with your father who was not one. That you needed to get to a big city with insufficient park space, that you needed to find and be found.

She considered the pale yellow bruises that blotted your wrists, the whisky blear in your eyes. She said, *Hop in.* Bundled you in blue flannel and asked if you were hungry.

You were already asleep.

You rode with Doe for days. You rode with Doe for weeks. Derby City, Bull City, Motor City, The Swamp. Cigar City, Cow Town, The Nickel. You'd never have guessed there was so much to see. For a time, you forgot that you were looking for your mother. Doe fed you fruit pie and cherry soda at every stop. She let you use the CB and blast the air horn. She told you that *hammer down* meant go faster and that *clean shot* meant no cops. Sky everywhere, you'd never felt such boundlessness.

One day, over blueberry pie at a greying rest stop, you told Doe about the man in the motel. She got so angry that you started to cry. You wondered what you'd done wrong. She squeezed into your booth seat and held you so tightly you thought you might die. It felt almost as good as the motel bed. You would have been happy to die.

She said, *We've got to go to the cops.*

You bristled. You panicked. You said, *Please, Doe.* You said, *I'm sorry, Doe.* You gripped her arms and begged. *Clean shot. Clean shot.*

She said, *You're not in trouble, darling.* She brushed your bangs out of your eyes. She nuzzled your ear. She kissed your forehead.

You never saw Doe again.

While she was in the bathroom, you bolted out the door. Mudstone sky. You never looked back.

You thumbed your way through miles and miles. This car. That car. The men who picked you up gave you hits off their joints, sips of their king cans. *Do you like ZZ Top?* they'd ask. And turn up the volume. Push your head down between their legs. *How about Zeppelin?* they'd ask. And pull over. And pull you on top of them. *Oh, that's so good,* they'd say. And thrust faster and faster, harder and harder, while your tits bobbed at their hungry mouths.

When you finally saw the skyscrapers, your eyes lit up. He leaned past you, popped open the passenger side door. Put twenty bucks in your hand and told you to take care. Sped off, just as you were swinging the door shut.

You blinked. Disoriented.

The city was dark and ridden with reeds. Cobwebs stretched from spire to spire. Gun shots. Car alarms. Burglar alarms. The hookers yelled at you to get off their fucking corner. You got off the corner. Cars careening, you nearly got hit. Billboards. Flashing neon lights. People throwing bricks and the bones they'd broken through shop windows. There was shattered glass everywhere. Music pulsing. Women screaming. *Rape. Fire.* Then not screaming at all. The sidewalk spit up on your shoes. Teenage boys with black eyes and knife-scarred jaws leaned into you, said, *Hydro. Crystal. Ice.* Men grabbed at your ass, tugged at your tits and your hair, tried to shove you down alleys. Lead pipes. People bleeding. Begging. Shivering. A car slowed down. *Get the fuck in.*

You flattened yourself against the crumbling bricks of a building, covered your ears. And began to cry.

Someone snatched you.

You opened your eyes. The brightness burned, blinded you briefly. You blinked. She had thick chin-length curls, hot pink lips. And her nametag said Bev. She pulled you. Down the length of the diner with its black and white checked floor, its red vinyl counter stools. Past the men licking gravy off their fingers, shovelling forkfuls of lemon meringue pie into their mouths. And pushed hard at the door to the Ladies'.

Your t-shirt was stained. Your eyes were bloodshot. You stank of Budweiser. And your hair was tangled, sticky with come. She said, *I've been where you've been.* And amid the fizzle of the fluorescents and the ceaseless flush of a weepy toilet, she gently leaned you over the sink. She washed your face. She rinsed your hair. She ran hand lotion through its wet tips. She gave you leggings and a leotard, an off-the-shoulder sweatshirt. She said, *I'm sorry. It's all I've got.*

When you came out of the bathroom, Bev sat you down in a shiny red booth and gave you a plate of fries. You told her your name was Darling and that you were looking for your mother. You pulled out the tattered picture you'd been carrying and slid it across the table. *Have you seen this woman? Maybe on a television? Forecasting the weather?* She hadn't. But the diner had a satellite dish. Bev gave you the remote control and let you look for your mother for days.

You channel-surfed. You canvassed the customers. You played checkers with the waitresses - Annie and Della and Guinevere. You played cards with the cook, Vance. You modelled the sparkly boa Bev gave you. You ate peach pie and key lime pie, cherry pie. You got comfortable.

One day, the cops came looking. You spied them just as you were coming out of the restroom. Stroking their nightsticks. You dropped to your knees and hid behind the cigarette machine. Watched Bev hesitate, bite her lip. And point. To the booth in which you'd been sitting, the television you'd been watching.

You slipped quietly out the back door. And ran. Past the broken glass of bus shelters, the wild spurt of unruly fire hydrants, the televisions and toasters that had been hurled off balconies, the faded posters looking for lost dogs. You ran through alleys and backyards and junkyards, up and down skinny side streets, past thin houses with bed sheets for curtains, yellowed yards, spindly trees trimmed with toilet paper and underwear, faded holiday decorations. You ran until you couldn't run anymore and curbside, you doubled over, heaving.

Dizzy, you crawled through the grass towards chimes that tinkled. Marigolds stirred. You closed your eyes. You rang the bell.

She had long honey-coloured hair and the softest voice you'd ever heard. Tears welled in your eyes. She bent. The thick gold cross that hung from her neck stung your breast. She reached. You vaulted yourself into her arms and she carried you inside, her hands stroking your hair.

Inside, everything was plush. And gold. The couch. The drapes. The flocked wallpaper. The air smelled like lemons. And everywhere you turned, tiny crystal animals - swans and seahorses, tigers and unicorns - twinkled. She said, *In the paradise, you will have one of each for your very own.* You didn't know what she meant.

You crawled up through the soft spot between her thighs. She held you. You cried and cried. She rubbed your earlobes and told you that it was okay. She braided your hair and told you that it was okay.

She said that her name was Gail and that she loved you.

She kept you. You wanted to be kept.

She poured you a glass of flat ginger ale. She ladled you a bowl of chicken soup. It made you feel like you had the flu. You snuggled into her arms. And told her you were looking for your mother. You pulled out the photograph. She said, *Let me put this somewhere safe.* She gave you a book of bible stories. Closed the gold drapes. And said, *Don't answer the door for anyone.*

You didn't.

One day, you got a horrible cramping.

Gail stuck her fingers deep inside of you and pulled out a baby. The baby was you. The baby was yours.

"So you're missing a child?"

"The cycle is like any other," you declare. "Vicious."

There was blood everywhere. She gave the baby to you to hold. You didn't know how to love. You passed out.

When you woke, you were lying on the bathroom floor. Naked. Sunlight streamed through the skylight. You squinted. And saw Gail, her bare body pale and doughy. Cross gleaming. She bent over you, hoisted your limp body to hers. And plunged you both into the icy waters of the yellow bathtub. You screamed. She said, *I'm sorry.* And, palm to sternum, she pushed you underwater. You flailed and railed against her, came up gasping and crying. She slapped you hard. Your head spun. She said, *I'm so sorry.* And held you down until there was no more fight left in you. Lifted free of the water, your lips were blue. Your head lolled. In the distance, you heard her voice, soft and pale. She said, *I'm sorry. I'm so sorry. It had to be done.* You passed out.

When you woke, your tits were swollen, leaking milk. And your whole body ached. In your abdomen, a horrible cramping. The ballerina that sat atop the toilet tank stared. Arms reaching. Her gold tulle skirt concealed the extra roll of toilet paper.

Gail eyed your weeping breasts. She said, *Don't worry. They'll dry out in no time.*

The baby was gone.

Gail told you that it would be best if you didn't leave the house. That strangers would climb inside of you and lay eggs. That the eggs would hatch snakes, and that the snakes would writhe. And eat you from the inside out.

You were terrified.

Days passed. Weeks passed.

You grew restless and bored. There was no television. There was nothing in her cupboards and drawers but unsharpened pencils and rosary beads. There was nothing to read but your book of bible stories. You couldn't find yourself anywhere but right where you were standing.

One day, you asked Gail for the picture of your mother. She said, *I'm your mother now.*

Days passed. Weeks passed.

You thought about your father. You wondered if your mother missed being a mother.

Mostly, you missed Dad. You missed being Darling.

You began to stick things inside yourself. The thick handles of knives and hairbrushes and serving spoons. Mop handles and shampoo bottles. Eggplants. You reached for whatever you could fit. And with your hands at your clit, you came and came and came.

One day, Gail, home from work early, found you fucking yourself with jars from the spice rack. She tore the bottle of paprika from your pussy and threw it across the kitchen floor. She ripped the cross from her neck. And rammed it up inside of you, smacked you so hard across the face that you came. Enraged, she hit you harder. You passed out.

When you woke, you were in the basement. Gail was crying. Chanting. *Ab omni hoste visibili et invisibili et ubíque in hoc sáeculo liberetur. From every enemy both visible and invisible and everywhere in this lifetime be freed.* One hand on a bible, the other worrying her rosary beads. Your eyes burned and your skin crawled. Her voice got louder. *Ut quóties triúmphum divínae humnilitátis, quae supérbiam nostri hostis dejecit. How often the divine humility has triumphed casting out the pride of our enemy.* You began to gag. You gave up. You gave in. She said, *Good girl.*

She bound your breasts. She cut off your hair. She stuffed stale wafers into your mouth. She said, *I'm so sorry. It had to be done.* And then she locked the door.

Days passed. Weeks passed.

Every morning after Gail left for work, you tried the door. Defeated, you hauled yourself down the stairs, back into the blackness of the basement. One night, however, after she brought you your dinner, Gail forgot to turn the key. In the morning, the knob gave to your twist. You tiptoed through the house. In the bathroom, you looked in the mirror. You had no idea who was staring back at you. You pushed hard at the front door. Sky everywhere, your knees buckled. You remembered that you'd felt this feeling of boundlessness before.

You stole a pack of Dunhills. And walked for blocks and blocks.

Somehow, you wound up in front of the diner. Vance gave you a hug and told you that Bev was long gone. Something inside of you sank. He slid you a piece of pie and asked if you wanted a job. He said you could live at the diner. Your nametag said *Darling.* One day, Vance pulled you aside and said, *There's a way for you to make more money.* You already knew how to make more money. You did it on your breaks out back with the customers. Vance called you a slut. Hauled off and hit you. He said, *Some girls are just made for this.* And hit you again. He said that he deserved a cut. And left you bleeding on the floor.

You picked yourself up and you ran.

You slept on street corners and in bank machine vestibules. And with men who had daughters, men who had wives, men who had money. You slept with women who reminded you of your mother. You slept with women who reminded you of yourself. You spent holidays at the discount cinema watching second-run movies.

You phoned your father once. You could feel him groping for hope and his glasses. You didn't say a word. You held your breath and listened. Marilyn had left him. You could feel it. The empty space in which he was sitting was so loud. He said, *Diana? Is that you?* You were looking for her, too. You had nearly forgotten her name. You hung up. Hammered the receiver against the payphone. And turned on your heel.

You walked right into Bev. She had a black eye and was digging through a dumpster. She didn't recognize you. You were sure she was Bev. You couldn't be sure. You gave her a smoke and lit one for yourself.

You aged. One year. Two years. Three.

This is how you learned to love: *It will be over soon.* This is how you learned to love: under assumed names in small rooms with bad lighting; on street corners and in alleyways, on cat-pissed couches and in bathroom stalls; the word *sorry* in your ear, over and over, *It's over.* With a wooden spoon up your pussy, slick fingers that smelled like roses. Weather poetry. A hand around your neck, sticks in your ass. This is how you learned love.

You have never found your mother. Your father found you once.

You were working at a bar called BAR. It was small and dark and it smelled like sorrow. The tap beer was warm and pale. The hard liquors were fluorescent, blue and green. All along the walls, wildlife heads, mounted: moose and bison, elk and grizzly, bobcats and cougars. Your customers were named Clyde and Moe and Cheetah. You flashed your tits often and they tipped real well. Sometimes, you'd grind hard against the bar stool till you came. You didn't ever worry about the men getting out of line. A trio of yellow-eyed wolf dogs roamed the bar, guarded things.

One day, a man wearing a ragged overcoat came in. You knew he was your father. You could see it in his grey-green eyes, the dark circles that rimmed his sockets. You could see it in the wrinkles that creased his forehead, in the downturn curl of his lips, the way he took his glasses on and off.

You poured him a pint. You slid him a shot.

He said, *I used to love a lot of things. And I used to understand. But I've lost a lot of things. And nothing looks the same. I used to have a daughter. I used to have a wife. Now, I don't recognize myself. And I'm sorry for everything.* He swirled the beer in his glass, his eyes shiny and wet. He said, *I dream of paradise often, but when I wake, I can never remember what it looks like.*

Everything inside of you came crashing down.

At the end of the night, you locked him in and you fucked him hard up against the bar. The glasses rattled. The liquor bottles smashed. The wolf dogs howled. And in his ear, you came hard again and again and again. *Darling.* You knew he would come back, the next night and the night after that. You never went back. It satisfied you greatly to know that he would spend the rest of his life looking.

"Then what?"

"Then nothing."

You stopped looking for your mother. And you stopped looking for yourself. There was nothing to find. Things get boarded up and go black. There's nothing but weeds.

You look to me, your eyes narrowed, wet. And you reach.
This is called home. Love fuck. You say, "If I don't know any better, I can't do any better." I dry your eyes. I begin to cry. We are wet and dry. We fuck through it. You say that you want to protect me, me to protect you. From wind and yourself.

Blue-white, the television glows. Low hums that hug. *Take me with you.* We do it again.

KEYS

JOE FIORITO

There is a home for the elderly near a busy intersection in Parkdale where the young girls work the curb. One day, an old man in this building had his throat cut by a hooker. Here's what happened: every month, when the government cheques were delivered, the old men would stand on their balconies and drop their keys to the girls waiting below on the lawn. Perhaps the old man refused to pay, and things got out of hand. Afterward, the people who manage the building put a stop to girls on the lawn, and a stop to the dropping of the keys. But I somehow like the idea of those old men's flames flickering in the face of death; and the music of those keys dropping down on the grass.

NOISE OF TIME

B.W. Powe

Recording Human

Glenn Gould's essays ramble, his interviews are garrulous, his radio documentaries mix a variety of voices, his fragments fly off and flash like captions and advertisements.

"The microphone," he said, "is a great friend, because I was brought up with it."

A child of the speed of light, electricity in his bones and soul, he was one of the first of his generation to recognize the rewiring that had taken place. The electri-fried planet sends a jolt through our nerves. We are livid with input and output. Sleepless nights are encouraged. The fascination with telepathy rises. Suddenly, we have access to powers that most generations had simply dreamed about. Television, radio, hi-fi stereo recordings, and later digital tapes, compact discs, home terminals, and video recorders...

"In the electronic age," Gould wrote, "the art of music will become much more viably a part of our lives, much less an ornament to them, and that it will consequently change them much more profoundly."

Graffiti Wall

THE AUDIENCE WOULD BE THE ARTIST AND THEIR LIFE WOULD BE ART.

—Glenn Gould

TECHNOLOGY HAS THE CAPABILITY TO CREATE A CLIMATE OF ANONYMITY AND TO ALLOW THE ARTIST THE TIME AND THE FREEDOM TO PREPARE HIS CONCEPTION OF WORK TO THE BEST OF HIS ABILITY, TO PERFECT A STATEMENT WITHOUT HAVING TO WORRY ABOUT TRIVIA LIKE NERVES.

—Glenn Gould

Noise of Time

Crowds. Streets. Neon swarms and neon-modernism. People can swamp you, engulf you, catch up and carry you to places you don't want to go. Faces around you, in those city streets, wonder at the domes, boxes, and towers (the CN Tower looking, for an instant, like the world's biggest junkie's syringe), the galleries and monuments, the façades and mirrors, the gigantism and the construction. This is the time of noise, and noise of our time itself.

Toronto. It was this city that Gould carried in his memory, like a mirage.

Repetition Society

City streets set a stage. Electric lights turn the avenues and boulevards, corners and crescents, into platforms for performance. Punks and mimes, religious zealots and hookers, politicians and hot dog sellers, all understand the street is their soapbox and scaffold. After hours, in the dark, when Gould was fond of driving his Lincoln, the city is a showcase, a circus, an outdoor theatre and cinema; you can follow groups of people into bars and clubs, and you can be followed by groups who may be gangs or cops in disguise.

The street-sound is rock 'n' roll. It isn't Bach, Beethoven, and Brahms. (I could quibble: Wagner does, in a peculiar way, prepare you for Led Zeppelin.) Despite Gould's hope for an orchestrated city, a realm of New Listeners, the urban milieu is rock. We are shocked and lulled by the songs that pour out of car windows from tape decks and radios.

Gould watched his environment from inside a car (a Lincoln, built like an elegant tank), so that he could comment and observe and remain aloof. He could program his world: he could arrange other kinds of music on his tape deck; sing to himself; recite and rehearse a score.

The music merges with car rhythms. The principle is repetition. Exhaust pipes, horns, and wheels. These segue into crowd-sounds, the inarticulate him. On the street, conversation blurs into disconnected phrases and dissonant bits.

All of this is a great machine of noise. The machine threatens to drown our human voice, and leave us deafened. The machines of noise create the rhythms of hypnosis, the song of money and the song of new buildings.

THE BLUES

bpNICHOL

```
        l     e
        o   e
    l o v e
    o   e v o l
l o v e   o
    e v o l
  e   o
e     l
```

from *LOVE STREET* 1037 ON YOUR FM DIAL

SUSAN PERLY

Hey baby. Yeah. Uh-huh. You know who I'm talking to. You and me baby. That table for two – that private wavelength you've been hoping to dial up on that radio. Sure. You wondered what's she do in them off the air hours. Baby I'm going to do a little show just for you. Spin you some of my more private platters. This is going out to you know who I'm talking about who I hope you got my message – Say I sure hope you sure heard me there last night okay? (Was that a wasp or a love bug going into the wood?)...

a little Tao of the Blues.

MERCY MISTER PERCY

M.T. KELLY

I was born in a west-end area known as the Junction, just north of Parkdale, and trains were a factor in my childhood, even if I could not see, nor do I remember hearing them, from the one-bedroom apartment over a cigar store that I shared with my mother and father: 3103 Dundas Street West.

One of the memories I have of my father is his taking me to the Lambton roundhouse and putting me up in the cab of a steam locomotive. In a hallucinatory way I even remember being in one moving: fire, and the light of a very bright day, the men shifting about, a platform swaying. To this day trains reassure me in a profound way: I explain it now by describing trains as great benign beasts, monsters who will not hurt you: all this associated with my father.

That apartment was important. The apartment house was only two storeys, and as you entered our unit there was a bathroom to your right, a long hall with a living room and a bedroom side by side facing the streetcars of Dundas: opposite them a large kitchen leading out to the back and an iron fire escape enclosing a U-shaped court and facing "the lane." I once tried to go back and look at the place but was met by an old man nearly insane with anger and suspicion who would not let me in. I saw significance in the man's rudeness; he was an immigrant, and an echo from childhood came back: the "Maltese are driving us out." The "Maltese" were Poles and Ukrainians. Maybe the old man, a ruddy-cheeked, Anglo-Saxon, was nasty by nature but over the years he had sunk into mere paranoia.

In that apartment, I'd no room of my own, but only a cot at the foot of my parents' bed, beside the wall, near the door. After my father died, the cot disappeared and I shared my mother's bed. I had also shared it before he died, as I remember being in bed with my mother and his coming home one night and putting a wrestling hold, a leg lock, on her. He must have been drinking, and the kind of joking he intended was the kind that went with a grin with a White Owl nickel cigar stuck in it. I remember her whisper, "He'll kill us, he'll kill us," her nightgown, and a shriek.

Looking down the long hall of that apartment – railroad apartments, they called them after the lay-out of Pullman cars – coming home with my mother happy after Christmas shopping, the freshness of the outside still on us – I saw my father dialling for the ambulance that would take him away to die... fumbling at the phone, looking at us with what I thought then was unnecessary crisis – what I see now as shock and desperation. He'd known he was going to die: his eyes, looking at us. They were brown, dark, so big. I had forgotten his eyes. He and my mother used to talk and sing about eyes, hers were blue: "Beautiful beautiful brown eyes." My father's mouth, a thin Irish frog mouth: grim. So familiar now. How I remember things about my father, the optimism I had to make myself feel on a sunny September afternoon as he drummed his freckled hand on the arm of the car seat – we had a new car, a '54 Ford. He'd been sent home from the hospital for Christmas Day. I remember taking the turkey carcass into his bedroom after Christmas dinner. I know I wanted him to examine it with me in some happy scientific way: "Get it out, get it out, get it out, get it out!"

It's what comes back to you that can give a singular tone to a story: the phone table where my mother sat when she told me my father had died, on a brilliant January day; and somehow I thought I was going to receive news that he was having a bath. Then the crying and crying.

Baths. Because kettles had to be heated for bath water in that flat – and one of the few times I was left alone with my father he gave me a bath, and then he punished me – baths were significant. I recall the knobs of my mother's spine when I sat behind her in the bathtub and bathed with her. So many of my frantic feelings, so much of the agitation of that place, along with the grief and terror, come back. I remember walking down that long long dim corridor after the bath with my father. He was behind me and swinging his belt; then, lying across my parents' bed; the empty dark air, the space of the room above me: the detonating crack of the strap across the bedpost. He hit it repeatedly, not me.

My father had boxing gloves in the house and once he brought home a boy for me to box, to fight with in the living room. I half-remember the chesterfield, the furniture: I remember the swarm, the punching. He was a smaller boy, and I felt guilty about winning. The names of the boys I had to fight and fought are clear, I can recite them, like the ringing of a bell, but I will not list them here. After he died I found a book of my father's, a book about self-defence that had in it the technique for gouging out an eye.

At his death my father, who still smoked White Owl cigars, was fifty-eight, at least twenty years older than my mother. He could do "a hundred push-ups," swell out his chest so that milk bottles could be placed on it. He did this at parties, I was told, and every picture I have of myself in grade school shows a child, a year ahead in school because of his November birthday, small for his age, with his chest puffed out like a pouter pigeon. My father dressed "immaculately," and I do remember the smooth, nearly chamois-like quality of a beige sports shirt he had. Something of that shirt, a sliver of memory, still has in it weeping and love. When the loud weeping was done with after my father's death, I was sent to a Catholic school, De La Salle, located on an uptown hill and staffed by mostly strap-wielding Christian brothers who are now famous for their avuncular pedophilia.

I was nine. I was sick of our Junction apartment and neighbourhood – my special places were too small, and had no magic left in them. I was glad when we moved, although we moved to a similar one-bedroom apartment, this time a high-rise in Parkdale. The grief of my father's death, so intense, would last and last, and aspects of it must last still. I remember forming an imaginary club of always-victorious heroes, using his initials, the MTKs, and when I heard "Danny Boy" I would weep. But I grew and when I was about twelve or thirteen I got my own bed and my own room. The numbers of the apartments where we lived are like names to me, and I can tell them over and over again: at 60 Tyndall Avenue in Parkdale we went from apartment 302, one-bedroom, to 708, two-bedroom, to 901, two-bedroom. It was the same building my mother's boyfriend lived in. We were permanent. But transient! I did not live in a house until I was an adult.

Parkdale and the Junction were different neighbourhoods. Parkdale used to be connected to Lake Ontario through Sunnyside, that area south of Parkdale that bordered the lake and served as an amusement park, filled, as my old friend, Gwendolyn MacEwen said, with "dark musicians and dancers, green and purple monsters." This world of shore-front dance halls and Ferris wheels, so beloved by my pal Gwendolyn MacEwen, all ended in the fifties when the Gardiner Expressway's great trench and massive elevated concrete skyway cut the neighbourhood off from the lake.

Parkdale was also, in quite another way, a place apart in Toronto – because of our youthful enthusiasm for rhythm and blues, what many white boys sporting post-war "crew-cuts" or "flat-tops" called "nigger music."

In the late fifties and into the late sixties while other teenagers in town looked to Patti Page and then to the Beatles, "the boys" (and girls) of Parkdale listened to black "race records," to rhythm and blues, to *One scotch, one bourbon, one beer, so please mister bartender – listen here,* to the Buffalo radio stations, such as WUFO, and Randy's Blues from Nashville, and the Hound Dog from Niagara Falls: blues chirpers and shouters like Varetta Dillard and Ruth Brown and Dinah Washington and Solomon Burke and Bobby Blue Bland. For a decade we danced to the music at the Masaryk Hall (scene of many a Friday-night brawl and knife fight). We dressed in clothes which, as one of our girlfriends commented, "made us look like apprentice pimps": stovepipe pants, silk and wool suits. Because no one owned a car, the centre of our world was the Green Dolphin Restaurant on Queen Street and the Sound of the Hound on the radio:

I live on a lonely avenue,
My little girl wouldn't say I do,
I could cry, I could cry, I could cry...

from *1956: GLENN GOULD AND THELONIOUS SPHERE MONK*

SUSAN PERLY

The lake was clear and bottomless. It had not died yet. He came back to be with it, as he always came back. In the dark he thought about Goldberg, and he went out into the night and conducted him to the waves.

The lake breathed cold clouds out of itself. His hands were cold. Ten single icicles absorbing the loon and giving back the night canons.

He has been to New York. He has made his recording of Goldberg. It will be the best selling classical record of 1956. *Glenn Gould: The Goldberg Variations.* He is new. He is sure. He is unlike anything they have ever seen south of the 49th. Seen? – forget seen. He is unlike anything they have ever heard, that is the thing.

This creature can bend angels into notes, he can bend angels into angles no one has ever imagined before. Sacroiliacs asplendour, neck crooks, curvatures of cords, twists into you name it, and they all fit. Twists which call in a chaste and delicacy pings already in the air shaped to sound where he puts his icicles down.

It's not Petula Clark, but then – what is?

Now, you take Monk. Thelonious Sphere Monk on the keys. His hands flatten out, they are two flippers. They get in there. They slip on silence, silence is the gloves they wear. Evidence is considered, notes are taken, chords are suggested. He plays the piano.

They called Monk weird, they looked at his hats. Like with Glenn Gould, they went bananas over all the outerwear: scarves, sweaters, gloves, coats, caps, toques, skullcaps, grunts, groans. They called him *eccentric* as their riff in response to a mysterium tremendum's call at the keyboard. Monk's mumble, telling him he has some things to go see about...

But consider the iceberg theory of life. Consider the music heard as the tip of the iceberg, above water. Consider that Monk in a twirl away from the keys has gone to play for a while with the fishes in the water, consider that his is diving and biting off chunks of the iceberg under there, holding them in his hands and examining them for clues as to how he can tell in the tip of an iceberg the shape of what lies below and is invisible and is music in his hands...

Still busy checking out that iceberg. Still busy torqueing down on the ancient homage to the dance. He's working silence. How discrete it is. It's light. It's physics. What it plays at the part which has no need of notes. How it smiles: well, you needn't. And drives it back into time. Monk dances in the general direction of the piano. He sees a Monk already seated there, never gone. He moves towards his shape to make it true. He reinhabits his own outline, blood mumbles out of his mouth and crawls along the bones of his skeleton, his right foot dances to the time he has set himself, his flippers slip back into their gloves of quiet, and he knows he needn't but he does.

He was a Waldorf salad, as Cole Porter would say; he was a Berlin ballad;he was the nimble tread of the feet of Fred Astaire; he was an O'Neill drama; he was Whistler's mama; he was Canajun fare. A square so hip they turned Gotham green. Our boy Glenn Gould.

He played with his wrists below the keyboard; below or at – no higher. He sat on a special home-built seat built low to get those wrists right. Add a scarf add a mountain of sweaters add no circulation in your *jambes*, add an extra overcoat and momma! – they're gone ga-ga.

This c/o the Beaches, Anglican Hogtown magic, this genie caught inside an inn at the corner of Don Mills and suburbia, this c/o T.O.'s north of the Lawrence Plaza Brasilia poured-concrete stretch genius who might of a night bomb his car past concrete things flashing past instead of trees, listening to Streisand, pleased with the concrete which does not enter into the civilized discussion he is conducting with Goldberg the way lovely trees can and take you away from the point you are making inside a speeding vehicle which steams up nicely as you finish the point pulling into a donut shop for a coffee; as when over arborite in a booth used cars through a window are something to cast your eyes over, but never mind; as when a harvest of '56 Chevy Impalas don't enter your blood the way the sun coming up behind one of them could.

C/o that.

C/o phones; c/o edits; c/o a voice on a track talking to another voice on a track commented on by a third voice on a third track, though they have never met; c/o a night ride with Downtown. The sky you enter driving is large and violet. The orange light blurs to a shimmer above the violet. Around the orange on the violet comes a yellow all the way around, shimmering with white...

– Hey, wait a minute! What happened to the piano? Where's Monk? Where the hell did the piano go? Where did Monk go this time?

Below the surface of the water the iceberg is a hexagon. Monk is doing some geometry. He breaks off a piece of ice. He holds it in his left palm. He strokes it with his right. Out flows the beautiful uncut hair of graves. Monk winds it 'round his head. Voilà! – a fez of hisself c/o Walt Whitman, Esq.

Monk surfaces with a splash. He cats with his hat. He giggles a two-step or two. He gives an angel a smile. The future is jealous. It sidles up to the bar and stands him a round.

He takes notice; oh, he is aware; he dips delicious rubies, my dear, in the drink. He winks at the angels, he blows Walt a kiss, the future goes crazy and moves in close.

THE ARTISTS JAZZ BAND
COUGHTRY, RAYNER, MARKLE, 1965

JOHN REEVES

EATING THE BIRDS

MARGARET ATWOOD

We ate the birds. We ate them. We wanted their songs to flow up through our throats and burst out of our mouths, and so we ate them. We wanted their feathers to bud from our flesh. We wanted their wings, we wanted to fly as they did, soar freely among the treetops and the clouds, and so we ate them. We speared them, we clubbed them, we tangled their feet in glue, we netted them, we spitted them, we threw them onto hot coals, and all for love, because we loved them. We wanted to be one with them. We wanted to hatch out of clean, smooth, beautiful eggs, as they did, back when we were young and agile and innocent of cause and effect, we did not want the mess of being born, and so we crammed the birds into our gullets, feathers and all, but it was no use, we couldn't sing, not effortlessly as they do, we can't fly, not without smoke and metal, and as for eggs we didn't stand a chance. We're mired in gravity, we're earthbound. We're ankle-deep in blood, and all because we ate the birds, we ate them a long time ago, when we still had the power to say no.

WHAT HAPPENED TO RAVEL'S *BOLERO*?

HELEN WEINZWEIG

Sylvia sipped her martini from the plastic bathroom tumbler, not taking her eyes off the light patches of paint on the wall opposite. Her teeth chattered; she put the tumbler down on the bare floor. Richard said, "They haven't put the heat on yet." He poured himself another martini from the glass jar into a paper cup he held in his other hand. Some of the liquid spilled down the side of the jar, onto his bare thigh. Sylvia leaned over and licked his skin. He laughed like a boy and spilled a bit more. They were undressed and sat close together at the far end of the sofa. She picked up her drink. "Are you going back to your wife?" she asked. He lifted the glass jar and held it in the air and said, "Cheers." This time he gulped from the bottle. He began to undress her the moment she came through the door: he could never wait. She kicked off her shoes. On the wall opposite were two square patches of light grey paint. "The pictures, the ones I gave you?" she asked. "My sons came up in the station wagon over the weekend and took everything they could carry." Sylvia sipped from the tumbler. Her teeth chattered. He put his robe around her shoulders.

Richard lay stretched out the full length of the sofa, his long white legs muscular for his age. On the wall opposite, over the table where they often ate, there were two square patches of light grey paint. She got on top of him. "Are you going to sleep with your wife?" Sylvia wanted to know. In the darkening room she could not make out his expression. When she sat up the juices drained out of her on to the cushion, but she knew the stain would be absorbed by the rough brown cloth; even now she had to look closely to see an unevenness of colour in the middle cushion. He stood up and she put her face into the soft flesh of his belly; she smelled their sweat on his skin. Sylvia thought her purse felt heavier with the weight of the articles she had taken. She smiled up at him. Together they got up and started towards the bedroom.

Sylvia sipped from the plastic tumbler. The rugs were rolled up, her clothes were all over the bare floor, one shoe near the window, her dress in a heap. The rough brown cloth would absorb his ejaculation which dripped out of her when she sat up. Richard was wearing the wool tartan bathrobe she had given him that first Christmas. She had never seen him in house slippers. "What's wrong?" she asked immediately. "I think I'm catching a cold," Richard said. She could not find her other shoe. Her teeth chattered; she put the tumbler down on the bare floor. He gulped from the bottle. This time when she came in, having let herself into the apartment with a key she kept separate in a red leather case, she had to seek him out. He was in the kitchen; in front of him on the counter were a bottle of gin and a bottle of vermouth. He was wearing the bathrobe she had given him that first Christmas. He couldn't find anything to mix the martinis in; he opened and banged shut the cupboard doors. The cupboards were empty. The first desperate clutching, followed by sticky stuff seeping out of her all over the middle cushion when she sat up, but the rough brown synthetic material dried quickly. She stared at the empty hi-fi cabinet. "What's wrong?" Sylvia asked when she found him in the kitchen. "I've been asleep," Richard said. "I took the day off; I don't feel well." His wife will have the sofa cleaned, Sylvia thought. He was pale and kept his face averted. "The movers are coming in the morning," Richard said. He could never wait to make love to her. She put the palm of her hand against his forehead: it was hot. She got down on all fours and searched for the other shoe under the sofa. He looked at her finally and then away again. He couldn't find what he wanted in the empty cupboards and banged each door shut. Sylvia watched him consider an almost empty olive jar. He dumped a half-dozen olives on the counter. She brought out the ice cubes. "What's wrong?" Sylvia kept asking. "I've been transferred to New York. I'll be working out of Head Office." (His familiar bony face with the deep line down each cheek.) When he saw that she was not going to make a scene, he turned to face her. His brown eyes were clouded over. Side by side on the sofa, undressed, they drank martinis. He could never wait to make love to her. Across the room, against the wall opposite, at the oak table where they used to eat, she observed there was one chair and one place setting on the table in front of the chair. While he was under the shower she started to pick up her clothes. She couldn't find the other shoe.

Richard gulped the martini straight from the glass jar. "Does your wife still love you?" Sylvia asked. He moved to the end of the sofa, farthest from her, because the middle cushion was wet. (But the rough brown cloth would absorb the moisture.) Her teeth chattered; she put down the empty tumbler on the bare floor. He looked at her and away again. Together they got up and started towards the bedroom. She stopped at the corner to the little hall to look at the empty hi-fi cabinet. The second time, in his bed, was to be for her satisfaction. On top of the dresser were his wrist watch, wallet, keys and a Texaco bill. The dresser drawers were empty. He got under the covers. His feet were cold, as were hers, the heat had not come on yet in the apartment even though it was the middle of October. Together they got up and started towards the bedroom. She stopped to look at the empty hi-fi cabinet. The shelves were empty, the record compartments were empty. "What happened to Ravel's *Bolero*?" Sylvia asked. "Darling, I'm sorry, but my sons cleared out everything they could carry. I didn't dare say anything," Richard said. She turned and went first into the bathroom. She stretched out in the bed. She watched him go into the bathroom. When he returned she arched her back while he placed a towel under her. The second time, in the bed, where they could move more freely, was to be for her satisfaction. On top of the dresser were his wrist watch, wallet, keys and a Texaco bill. She picked up the bill and asked, "Is this where you live on Long Island?" He snatched the paper out of her hand.

Sylvia waited until he came out of the bathroom. "Will I see you again?" she asked. "We had to come to the end of the road sometime. This is it," Richard told her. Over the dresser where the mirror used to hang was an oblong patch of light grey paint in contrast with the darker paint. Richard snatched the bill out of her hand. She watched him go into the bathroom. Blowing his nose and shuffling in his slippers, Richard looked old. The bedroom was at the back of the building and was quiet, unlike the living room which echoed the constant noise of traffic on Avenue Road. She lay down on the towel. The second time was to be for her pleasure. "How old is your wife," Sylvia asked. "Same age as I am," Richard replied. He pulled the towel from under her and wiped his groin. All the same, their love-making was not entirely successful. She began to dress, picking up her garments one by one from the bare floor. He lay with his eyes shut. The dresser drawers were empty. She arched her back while he placed a towel under her. "Do you have twin beds or a double bed in your house on Long Island?" Sylvia wanted to know. In reply Richard said, "She is not like you in bed: she hasn't your energy." The elevators were still, everyone having gone out or decided to stay in for the evening. She had not been satisfied. His feet were cold, but his face when he kissed her was hot. He snatched the bill out of her hand. "It's a big promotion," he said later, "vice-president in charge of personnel. 82,000 employees, all over the world. I will have to live up to the job." He had small teeth that didn't suit his large features. She watched him go into the bathroom. On the oak table where they used to eat was a place setting for one. She couldn't find her other shoe. The dresser drawers were empty.

Sylvia pulled the drapes in the living room and lit the lamps. The sofa cushions were reversible. She began to pick up her clothes. On the oak table was set out a plate, a linen napkin in a sterling silver ring, a knife, fork and spoon, and sterling silver salt and pepper shakers. They went towards the bedroom. Where the mirror had hung opposite the bed there was an oblong patch of light grey paint on the wall. She would wait to comb her hair when he came out of the shower. "My sons took the records." She knew he referred to Ravel's *Bolero* which she had bought him for his birthday. Yet their love-making was not entirely successful. The dresser drawers were empty. "Where are my things?" Sylvia asked. "Darling, I'm sorry. The incinerator. I had no choice." His wrist watch, wallet and keys were on top of the dresser. She picked up the Texaco bill with his name and address imprinted in carbon from a credit card. "Is this where you live on Long Island?" she asked. Richard snatched the paper out of her hand; he put it in his wallet in front of the bills. He put the watch on his wrist and the keys in his pocket.

Sylvia let herself into the apartment with a key she kept separate in a red leather case. At first she thought he was out. Then she found him in the kitchen, looking for something in the cupboards. She saw the cupboards were empty. When she came in, he pulled his bathrobe together over his bare chest, tightening the sash. He looked at her, then away again. "What's wrong?" Sylvia asked. He kept his face averted. "The movers are coming in the morning." Richard replied. She brought out the ice cubes. He gulped from the bottle. "Cheers," he said, holding up the glass jar. When he saw that she was not going to make a scene he turned towards her. "I think I'm catching a cold," he said. His brown eyes were clouded over. They moved more freely in the bed. Before she went into the bathroom, she covered him with a blanket. The first thing his wife will do will be to have the sofa cleaned, Sylvia reflected. She noticed her purse where she had left it on the oak table where they sometimes ate. When he saw she was not going to make a scene, Richard began to undress her: he couldn't wait to make love to her. Some of the liquid spilled down the side of the jar onto his bare thigh. Sylvia bent over and licked his skin. He laughed like a boy. He snatched the bill out of her hand. Blowing his nose and shuffling in his slippers Richard looked old. She kicked off her shoes and one landed near the windows. "Listen," Richard said, "if you ever get to New York..."

He took off his robe and put it around her shoulders. Her teeth chattered. When she sat up the juices drained out of her onto the middle cushion, but the rough brown cloth absorbed the spill. His narrow white body was in sharp contrast with the dark cloth; she would forever remember the shape of him, she thought to herself. The bedroom was at the back of the building and was quiet. It faced the little gardens of the new condominiums on Oriole Road. She lay down on the towel and pulled the sheet up to her chin. He was apologetic. "My wife told my sons to start moving me back home. They left me with one towel." He never waited: he began to undress her the moment she came into the apartment. Their love-making was not entirely successful. He pulled the towel from under her and wiped his groin. "Hungry?" Richard asked. "We'll have to go out to eat. Let's go down to Pierre's. You'd like that, eh?" She began to dress. The evening traffic sounded loud in the living room. She went and stood outside the bathroom door to make sure he was still under the shower. She noticed her purse where she had left it on the oak table and picked up the sterling silver napkin ring and the sterling silver salt and pepper shakers and put them in her purse. She snapped the clasp shut. She went down on all fours to look for her other shoe under the sofa. When he strode back into the living room he was fully dressed. He looked distinguished in his dark blue suit, white shirt and dark blue tie with small flecks of red in it. His brown eyes were clear. "You must be hungry," he said, pulling on his cuffs, "we'll go down to Pierre's. You'd like that, Sylvia, eh?" She thought her purse felt heavier with the weight of the silver.

Sylvia remembered she hadn't combed her hair. When he came out of the shower she went into the bathroom and locked the door. She watched him go into the bathroom, admiring his long, lean back and small waist. He came back with a towel. "Does your wife still love you?" He stroked her legs and kissed her breast. He held her and said, "I have no choice. They're a very conservative company; a family firm run by family men. No private telephones." She began to dress. She got down on all fours to look for her shoe under the sofa. The evening traffic was loud in the living room. She stood outside the bathroom door to make sure he was still under the shower. She snapped the clasp shut. He held the door open. "Will you write?" she asked. "No promises," he replied, stepping backwards. "You're safe with me," she said. "No promises," he repeated. Blowing his nose and shuffling in his slippers he looked old. He held the door open for her. He was distinguished in his dark blue suit. The smell of his shaving cream and cologne was familiar. Sylvia was abstracted and silent. She shifted her purse to her other hand. Now that he knew she would not make a scene he smiled down at her.

EUGENIA

SARAH SHEARD

The smoke in the room was ferocious. In spite of that and my pre-party resolution not to, I cadged a cigarette from the stranger next to me and lit up in self-defence. *Defense de fumer.*

It was a Gitane. And suddenly I recalled Eugenia, the taste of that tobacco on her tongue, its incense clinging to her hair. She, who moved inside a pitchy Balkan aura, smudge pot of London train stations and Paris cafés. Each time I brought my hand to my mouth, our mad, bad school days were carried back to me...

Eugenia, standing before the mirror, turned this way and that to study her new shirt, a man's, very large. "What do you think?"

I shrugged. "Why so big?" She undid the buttons, one, two, three, until her breasts fell into view, then she doubled the shirt into pleats and tucked it into the waistband of her skirt, reaching up from underneath to pull the cloth taut. She dropped her crucifix over her head and the black beads rolled into the hollow between her breasts. The cross itself knocked inside her shirt like a heartbeat as she walked across the room and fell onto the bed beside me, exposing her flawless neck sliced into a V by the shirt, her face framed by a twist of hair as wiry and waxen as a horse's tail, that I caught and coiled into my hand. It was January but her skin still showed the faint striations left from a summer of halter tops and shorts.

Where'er she walks... To school and back. Branches of forsythia foaming into blossom at her approach, dropping seed in her wake.

Her hips sloped gracefully into a strong ass, curved and classic, womanly in spite of her age. The gores of her skirt clung to her haunches then flared out below like water pouring off a swimmer.

She enjoyed putting her clothes on me although our bodies were very different. We touched each other at first only as friends, in generic places, our hands instructing like mirrors. Look. This is how your hair should fall. Now tie this scarf around your waist. Knot it here, just once and let's see what the colour does for your skin. Good. Stand up straight. No, not that way. I'll show you. Let your breasts rise and part, now drop your shoulders a bit.

We took inventory of one another's bodies, composed the ideal collage of our best features – her breasts and hair, waist, her ass, my legs, her eyes, my shoulders and definitely her mouth. We went through a time of stealing small gifts for one another from cosmetic counters, indicating by signs what it was we wanted, then dropping the item inside our clothing, lingering a moment at the next counter before shamelessly strolling out.

We were never caught.

I liked to steal cigarettes just for the pleasure of watching Eugenia catch the tab of cellophane between her teeth and tear it apart, extract a tube with her nail and light it, her eyes on mine as she lifted her chin to exhale, lost in pleasure. I inhaled the forbidden in the air around her.

It was July. The last summer of high school.

Eugenia and I sat on my front porch cooling our feet in the night air. We'd missed the bus after our movie and had walked home instead, all the way across town. My father didn't come off shift for hours so I nipped a bottle of his beer from the fridge, opened it and carried it out to the porch where Eugenia sat tapping her ashes into a tiny cairn at her feet. We passed the bottle back and forth without talking, watch a bolus of midges swarm under the street lamp. In that hour something shifted inside me. The affection I was accustomed to feeling for Eugenia intensified into a kind of inexplicable yearning, like hunger but more urgent. I realized I was inhaling her breath.

"Eugenia, do you feel sleepy?" I whispered, my lips against her ear.

She shook her head. "Not yet."

We sat in silence. She lit another cigarette. It was all I could do to keep from wrapping myself around the lamppost and baying at the moon.

She took a last pull on the beer and then threw me a look with those heavy-lidded eyes – one with which I'd seen her drench strangers in movie lobbies, bus drivers, our gym teacher. I was struck dumb, my heart roaring inside my ears. I adored her, felt so tender I could have bitten her in tow. It was curious and confusing – I couldn't get out a sound, barely draw breath against the repressed excitement I felt.

She flicked her cigarette into the darkness, picked up the empty bottle and disappeared into the house. I followed, carrying our shoes. In the kitchen she turned and handed me the bottle and I dropped it into the carton of empties on the back stoop, making an effort to appear calm.

We were going upstairs to lie down. It was late. Eugenia was tired. She would stay the night. We'd often done that, shared the same bed together countless nights, chastely and without premeditation. But tonight she lit a candle and watched me from the bed as I undressed and when I undid my hair and sank onto the mattress beside her she pulled me tight to her, whispered my name and didn't turn away when I touched my mouth to hers, softly at first, not sure how to – but she opened her lips gently and the tip of her tongue slid out and touched mine and the wet taste of her, the tobacco and the ghost of beer flooded me with pleasure. I began to explore her mouth as her fingers slid down my back to steady me in the narrow bed, her ass against the cool plaster wall, I palmed it, suddenly realizing I'd longed to for months – and of course had, but only through cloth, brushing her skirt smooth, not like this, my hand sliding across her cool flesh, across the small of her back, her tiny waist ebbing away below the ribcage she was panting softly I could hear my own heart, the excitement in my clogged blood, my body a mattress of flesh thrown up against her, sharp fingernails across my back, coming up in front, claws sheathed to cup each breast she looked me straight in the eye then bent her head to crush each nipple against her teeth sending a scorching ache down between my legs I squeezed them tight, shuddering involuntarily and her hand moved over my belly and parted my legs she knew her own body, that was how she – and the liquid awaiting her drew a gasp. She seized my hand and directed it to the same place in her, thickly furred and also wet, there was a sound of my fingers sliding against her, the slick froth as she rocked against my hand, squeezing it between her thighs, letting out a moan, a shudder when a creak from downstairs—

Immediately we froze – ears cocked for footsteps on the stairs – but we had hours yet we were safe, her hip pressed to bring me back, my fingers so slippery I was losing her I blotted them against the sheet and slid them back quickly before she lost pleasure, her breasts pressed to mine, spreading, cool and so unimaginably soft – the bonelessness of her against me her fingers twisting my nipple my mouth anxious to taste her elsewhere but the rocking I didn't want it to stop, when suddenly –

She came, making sounds I'd never heard her – and then rolled onto her back with a sigh and I slid down and drew my cheek across her belly, her navel, following the line of hairs that divided her abdomen until my cheek came to rest on her pillowed bone the salty smell of her was – so sweetly intimate I opened her legs gently and began to tongue her there and both her hands clutched my head suddenly in a fury of sharp pleasure. I slid my tongue into her folds and she froze against my tongue, twisted aside for an instant, then brought herself back for more. I slid up and down its ridge, then off down one side into rain shadow and she moaned and arched, pulling my head up sharply by the hair. I torched her, broke off, lit her again until she began growling in her throat a purely animal sound and my own hips began to pulse against the bedclothes in time, blood rising just to think of her coming in my mouth like this, my Eugenia – she gasped once and I trilled my tongue against her then froze and in that instant she erupted, holding my head and jerking once, twice, spasms racking her in waves and I reached down and stroked myself quickly to climax, our spines fusing we locked hips until the convulsions melted away too small to count.

We drew apart from each other slightly to release our prickly heat, listening to the sounds of the house, the ticking of the room, our ears straining for the particular step of my father's below our window, muttering in search of the key, the slam and scrape as he came into the kitchen below, a grunt, as each boot was tugged off and flung behind the door.

He would undoubtedly notice Eugenia's cigarettes on the kitchen table, our shoes and satchels piled in the corner, would open the fridge, count the empties, note our theft...

I prayed we'd be asleep long before he returned and chanced upstairs, peered into our room and, God forbid, approached our bed, drawn by the mysterious scent of our passion to investigate, the ghostly imprint of the act hovering just above our sleeping bodies like a sneeze left by a leopard or a guardian angel.

THE DANFORTH

GWENDOLYN MACEWEN

He walked along Danforth Avenue a few days before the Greek Easter and everywhere in the butcher shops young lambs hung upside-down, dripping blood onto the steaks and veal chops and grinning pigs' heads. The Greeks were out promenading in their expensive tailored suits with loud ties and pastel shirts (their word for suit was *costume*), and huge gold rings and cufflinks. The women displayed their shining children, screaming at them shrilly, then grabbing and hugging them so they couldn't breathe. The children stared in rapture at the bonbons and toy bunnies and lambs in the store windows, the red and blue and green eggs in baskets lined with doilies and silver paper. In one window there was an egg the size of a football, and a four-foot-high City Hall modelled in dark chocolate. In another, a horse made of jelly beans, a cake shaped like a bible...

He passed the Medusa Beauty Salon, the Trojan Horse Coffee House, another meat store with more sacrificial animals – a counter full of slimy skinned rabbits lying on ice, their wild eyes staring into space. Then stores full of Kalamata olives and capers and sardines and feta cheese in huge stinky vats and bottles of golden oil. He went into a restaurant which had been an ice-cream parlour in days gone by and still had the old glittering chandeliers and high-backed wooden booths. Large jars full of Turkish delights and candy canes and horehound sticks lined the marble-topped counter. "You speak Grik?" asked the girl who served him coffee, and when he said no, she turned away and revealed a wonderful Minoan profile. The owner was behind the long iceberg of the counter, washing sundae dishes and rinsing out metal milkshake containers. Faded ads for Orange Crush and Vernor's Ginger Ale adorned the walls, a big old juke box gathered dust in a corner, dreaming of Jimmy Dorsey and Les Brown and His Band of Renown. A solitary cockroach climbed into an ashtray and died...

from *FUGITIVE PIECES*

ANNE MICHAELS

For years after my marriage ended, Maurice and Irena pretended to envy my freedom; secretly they amused themselves with the challenge of finding me a second wife. On my visits from old Salonika to Toronto, they connived like teenagers. Lunches, family parties, faculty dinners – every event a potential romantic minefield, with Maurice planting the bombshells. Maurice would make the introductions and then scram. I was accustomed to his refrain: "Now Jakob, I know this woman..." and remained unmoved.

But sometimes the world disrobes, slips its dress off a shoulder, stops time for a beat. If we look up at that moment, it's not due to any ability of ours to pierce the darkness, it's the world's brief bestowal. The catastrophe of grace.

She walks into Maurice and Irena's kitchen.

I don't know what to look at first. Her light-brown hair or her dark-brown eyes or her small hand disappearing into the shoulder of her dress to adjust a strap.

"Michaela is an administrator at the museum," says Maurice as he makes his exit.

Her mind is a palace. She moves through history with the fluency of a spirit, mourns the burning of the library at Alexandria as if it happened yesterday. She discussed the influence of trade routes on European architecture, while still noticing the pattern of light across a table...

There's no one left in the kitchen. All around us are glasses and small towers of dirty dishes. The noise of the party in the other room. Michaela's hips lean against the kitchen counter. Voluptuous scholar.

Michaela has only recently met Irena. She's asking after her.

I find myself telling Michaela a story that's a dozen years old, the story of Tomas's birth, about my experience of his soul.

"When Tomas was born, he was very premature. He weighed less than three pounds..."

I had put on a gown, scrubbed my hands and arms to the elbows, and Irena led me in to see him. I saw what I can only call a soul, for it was not yet a self, caught in that almost transparent body. I have never before been so close to such palpable evidence of the spirit, so close to the almost invisible musselman whose eyes in the photos show the faint stain of a soul. Without breath, the evidence would vanish instantly. Tomas in his clear plastic womb, barely bigger than a hand.

Michaela has been looking down at the floor. Her hair, glossy and heavy and parted on the side, covers her face. Now she looks up. Suddenly I'm embarrassed at having spoken so much.

Then she says: "I don't know what the soul is. But I imagine that somehow our bodies surround what has always been."

Standing together on the winter sidewalk, in the white darkness. I know even less than lamplight in a window, which knows how to pour itself into the street and arouse the longing of one who waits.

Her hair and hat circle her quiet face. She's young. There are twenty-five years between us. Looking at her I feel such pure regret, such clean sadness, it's almost like joy. Her hat, the snow, remind me of Akhmatova's poem where, in two lines, the poet shakes her fists then closes her hands in prayer: "You're many years late, / how happy I am to see you."

The winter street is a salt cave. The snow has stopped falling and it's very cold. The cold is spectacular, penetrating. The street has been silenced, a theatre of whiteness, drifts like frozen waves. Crystals glisten under the streetlights.

She points out her impractical boots, "party shoes," and then I feel her small leather glove around my arm.

Michaela lives above a bank. Her flat is a monastic cell of a sensuous order. I've entered an old world; the specifications of a dream. Magazines – *Nature, Archaeology, The Conservator* – and piles of books – novels, art history, children's stories – teeter on the floor next to the couch. Shoes left in the middle of the room; a shawl flung on the table. The clutter of hibernation.

Jumbled rooms breathe dimly in the shallow light. The dark autumn fabrics, the rugs and heavy furniture, a wall of small framed photographs, a child's lamp in the shape of a horse – all seem in defiance of the strict world of accounting in the bank below.

I'm a thief who has climbed in through a window only to find himself struck frozen by a feeling of homecoming. The impossibility of it; the luck.

I wait for Michaela to return with tea. I feel the malaise of the warm room, the peace of the immaculate snowfall. Michaela's crammed rooms have cast a spell. I'm already painted into the Rembrandt dimness.

She comes back, carrying a tray to the low living-room table; a silver pot, glasses edged in silver. Her shoes off, now wearing thick socks, she looks even younger. Now I see in Michaela's face the goodness of Beatrice de Luna, the Marrano angel of Ferrara, who reclaimed her faith and gave refuge to other exiles of the Inquisition.... In Michaela's face, the loyalty of generations, perhaps the devotion of a hundred Kievan women for a hundred faithful husbands, countless evenings in close rooms under the sheets, discussing family problems; a thousand intimacies, dreams of foreign lands, first nights of love, nights of love after long years of marriage. In Michaela's eyes, ten generations of history, in her hair the scents of fields and pines, her cold, smooth arms carrying water from springs...

"Tea?" she asks, pushing newspapers onto the rug, clearing a place.

She pauses in the middle of a family story; now she's the one uncomfortable at having spoken so much. About her parents, "like embassies" – Russian and Spanish soil under them – as they sat in their Montreal living room. About her grandmother, who told Michaela stories of her life that were actually fiction, either wishing Michaela to remember her in a certain light or wishing, herself, to believe in her longest-held fantasies. Michaela's grandmother described a huge house in St. Petersburg, the details of ornate fixtures, carved woodwork, even the personalities of servants. Drapery of green and gold, velvet dresses of wine and black. But mostly she insisted on her education, telling Michaela she'd been a student, a teacher, a writer for a newspaper.

Michaela offers her ancestors to me. I'm shocked at my hunger for her memories. Love feeds on the protein of detail, sucks fact to the marrow; just as there's no generality in the body, every particular speaking at once until there's such a crying out...

I am leaning forward on the sofa, she is sitting on the floor, the small table between us. It seems to be absolution simply to listen to her. But I know that if she touches me my shame will be exposed, she'll see my ugliness, my thinning hair, the teeth that aren't my own. She'll see in my body the terrible things that have marked me.

A last shudder of strangeness, a last flash of fear before longing pushes its blade into me, up to the hilt. Skinned alive. My hand reaches for hers and instantly I know I've made a mistake. I'm too old for her. Too old.

Now, impossibly – can it be without pity? – she is placing her cheek – soft sun-warmed peach – against my cold palm.

I begin to trace every line, her lengths and shapes, and realize suddenly that she's perfectly still, her hands clenched, and I'm appalled by my stupidity: my longing humiliates her. Too many years between us. Then I realize she's entirely concentrated, pinioned under my tongue, that she's giving me the most extravagant permission to roam the surface of her. Only after I explore her this way, so slowly, an animal outlining territory, does she burst into touch.

I'm paralyzed in the cave her hair makes. Then my hands move to feel her slim waist and suddenly I know how she would bend after a shower, twisting her hair into a wet turban, feel the shape her back would make, leaning over. I hear her small voice – long phrases of music and stillness like an oar balanced in its arc above the water, dripping silver. I hear her voice but not her words, so soft; the noise of her whole body is in my ears. Instead of the dead inhaling my breath with their closeness, I am deafened by the buzzing drone of Michaela's body, the power lines of blood, blue threads under her skin. Cables of tendons; the forests of bone in her wrists and feet. Each time she stops speaking, in each long pause, I renew the pressure of my grasp. I feel her slowly going heavy. How beautiful the blood's pull towards trust, the warm weight of the sleeper entering her orbit, pulling towards me, fragrant, heavy and still as apples in a bowl. Not the stillness of something broken, but of rest.

It's growing light when Michaela undresses, deliberate and dreamlike. Her clothes dissolve.

Even the wild molecules of objects in the room seem suddenly palpable. After years, at any moment, our bodies are ready to remember us.

She lies on top of me, the saddle of pelvis, the curve of skull, fibulas and femurs, sacrum and sternum. I feel the arches of her ribs, every breath flooding blood between the ossiicles of her ears and her feet.

But there is no tinge of death in Michaela's skin. Even as she sleeps, I see in her nakedness the invisible manifest, flooding the surface of her. I see my beloved's damp hair against her forehead, the stain of love like salt across her belly, the hipbone nudging the surface, complex with breath. I see the muscles pushing out her calves, firm as new pears. I see that she will again open her eyes and embrace me.

It's late, almost afternoon, when she says, though I may have dreamed it, though it's just something Michaela might ask: Are you hungry? No... Then perhaps we should eat so that hunger won't seem, even for a moment, the stronger feeling...

Michaela's hands above her head; I stroke the fragile place on the back of her smooth, soft arms. She is sobbing. She has heard everything – her heart an ear, her skin an ear. Michaela is crying for Bella.

The light and heat of her tears enter my bones.

The joy of being recognized and the stabbing loss: recognized for the first time.

When I finally fall asleep, the first sleep of my life, I dream of Michaela – young, glistening smooth as marble, sugary wet with sunlight. I feel the sun melting over my skin. Bella sits on the edge of the bed and asks Michaela to describe the feel of the bedcover under her bare legs, "because you see, just now I am without my body..." In the dream, tears stream down Michaela's face. I wake as if I've been dug out of the dream and lifted into the world, a floating exhaustion. My muscles ache from stretching into her, as I lie in sunlight across the bed.

Every cell in my body has been replaced, suffused with peace.

She sleeps, my face against her back, her breasts spilling from my hands. She sleeps deeply like a runner who's just emerged from the Samaria Gorge, who's heard only her own breathing for days. I drift and wake with my mouth on her belly, or on the small of her back, drawn home by the dream into her, her breasts soft loam, hard, sore seeds.

Each night heals gaps between us until we are joined by the scar of dreams. My desolation exhales in the breathing dark.

Our coming together is as unexpected, as accidental, as old Salonika itself, once a city of Castilian Spanish, Greek, Turkish, Bulgarian. Where before the war you could hear muezzins call from minarets across the city, while church bells rang, and the port went quiet on Friday afternoons for the Jewish Sabbath. Where streets were crowded with turbans, veils, *kippahs*, and the tall *sikkes* of the Mevlevis, the whirling dervishes. Where sixty minarets and thirty synagogues surrounded the *semahane*, the lodge where dervishes spun on their invisible axes, holy tornadoes, blessing drawn from heaven though the arms, brought to earth through the legs...

I grasp her arms, bury my brain in the perfume at her wrists. Bracelets of scent.

To be saved by such a small body.

THE BLOOR STREET VIADUCT

JOE FIORITO

The Bloor Street Viaduct crosses the Don Valley. There are sidewalks across the bridge. There were some four hundred jumpers since it was built in 1919, or roughly one every three weeks; that's fewer than the Golden Gate Bridge, but more than the Jacques Cartier, if you're keeping ghoulish score.

An Armenian teenager jumped; afterward, someone spray-painted his name and his dates on the footings down below, in that lovely cursive Armenian script which seems perfect for recording sadness.

The bridge was a magnet. It attracted, and it repelled.

A rumour: kids in a nearby school used to peer out the windows at the comings, in the hopes of seeing the goings.

A rumour: someone hailed a cab, stopped in the middle of the bridge, paid the driver, got out of the cab and jumped.

We put up a barrier to stop the jumpers. The barrier is made of metal rods which, seen from a distance, look not unlike the guts of a piano. We call it the Luminous Veil. Said the wag, I'd rather have voluminous ale than a luminous veil.

We jump elsewhere now.

The rods – there are some nine thousand of them – whisper in the high winds like an Aeolian harp. They were made, not across the bay in the steel mills of Hamilton, but around the world in Mumbai.

Signs at each end of the bridge advertise the telephone number of the suicide helpline. They take our calls in India when we need help with our computers, our printers, our electronic devices. Perhaps they ought to answer our suicide-prevention lines as well.

The Real Deal

by: NINA BUNJEVAC

THINGS USED TO BE SO GOOD BETWEEN US. WE WERE HAPPY AND CRAZY ABOUT EACH OTHER. AND THEN SUDDENLY THINGS BEGAN TO CHANGE...

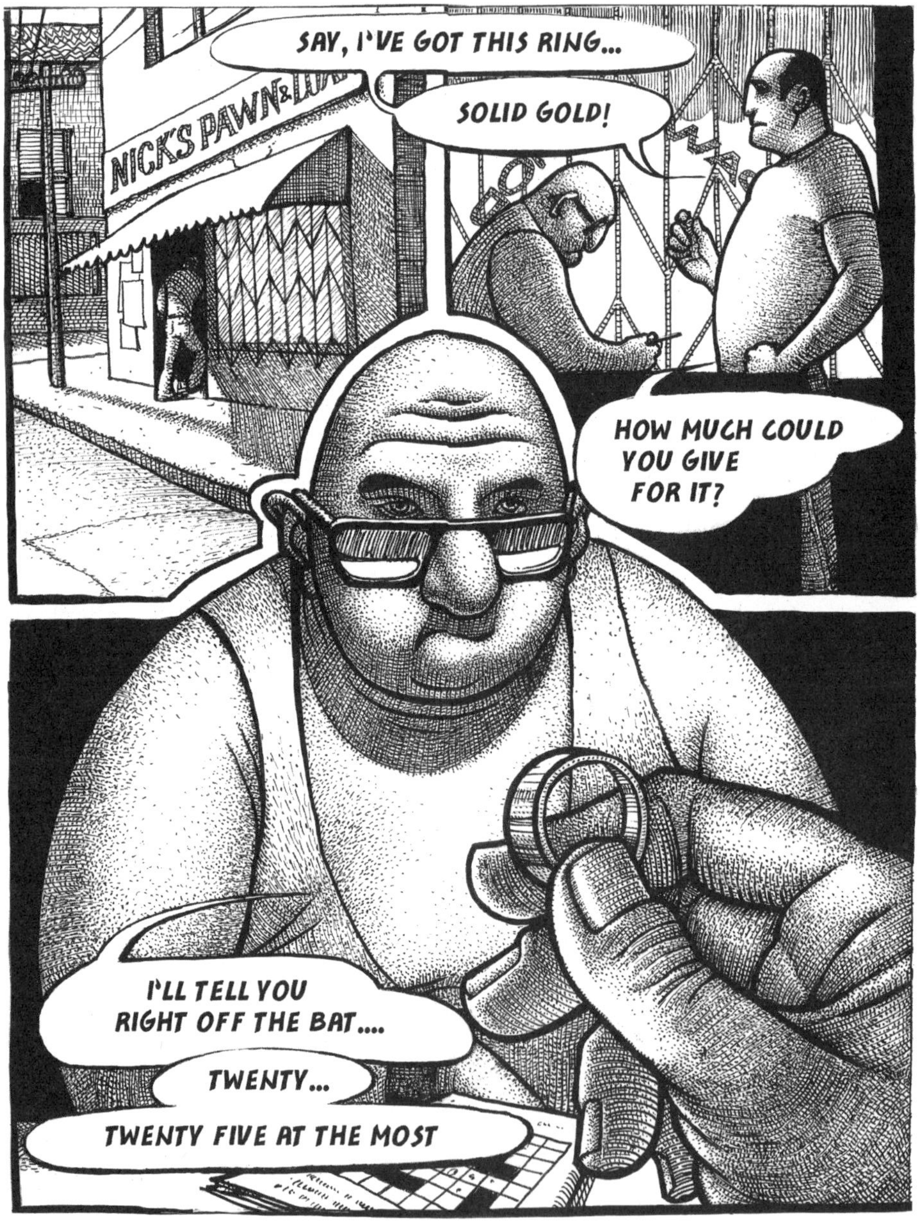

HE BECAME MOODY AND WITHDRAWN...

HE WOULD DISAPPEAR FOR DAYS AT A TIME AND WOULD NEVER TELL ME WHERE HE WENT.

HE BEGAN WITHHOLDING MONEY AND SEX.

HE WOULD COMPLAIN ABOUT MY HOUSEKEEPING FOR HOURS ON END. NOTHING I DID WAS GOOD ENOUGH FOR HIM.

I WAS DESPERATE AND LONGED FOR THINGS TO GO BACK TO THE WAY THEY WERE WHEN WE FIRST MET...

SOMETHING HAD TO BE DONE - I DECIDED TO CONSULT MADAM M.
I SEE THAT YOU ARE A GOOD PERSON...
OPEN
ADULT VIDEOS
MADAMME M SOLVES ALL LIFE PROBLEMS
DOWNSTAIRS
TAROT PALMISTRY TEA CUP
YOU HAVE HELPED MANY, MANY PEOPLE... BUT ALL PEOPLE DO IS TAKE ADVANTAGE OF YOU
YOU GIVE AND GIVE - NOTHING COMES BACK YOUR WAY
SHE WAS AMAZING - IT WAS LIKE SHE KNEW ME BETTER THAN I KNEW MYSELF...

SUDDENLY, MY ROTTEN LUCK BEGAN TO MAKE A WHOLE LOT OF SENSE...

I WANT YOU TO LISTEN TO ME...
...AND HEAR EVERY WORD I SAY.
I CAN HELP YOU...
...AS A SPIRITUALIST.
IT'S GONNA COST YOU THREE HUNDRED DOLLARS.
YOU SEE...
I DON'T DO THAT SORT OF THING HERE
I DO IT IN THE CHURCH!!!

I RUSHED OUT OF MADAM M.'S PARLOUR A DESPERATE WOMAN; HER LAST WORDS ECHOED IN MY MIND:

I WAS BROKE AND AFRAID TO ADMIT IT. THERE WAS NO OTHER OPTION BUT TO ASK TORVALD.

LATER ON THAT NIGHT TORVALD CAME HOME FROM WORK IN ONE OF HIS PECULIAR MOODS AND WENT STRAIGHT TO BED.

HE DIDN'T BOTHER SAYING GOOD NIGHT - HE DIDN'T EVEN LOOK AT ME.

I WAS SO UPSET THAT NIGHT...

BACK IN THE DAY, TORVALD WOULD HAVE HELD ME TIGHTLY IN HIS ARMS AT THE SLIGHTEST SIGN OF UPSET...

TEARS JUST KEPT COMING AND COMING...

I HAD RUN OUT OF AN ENTIRE BOX OF TISSUES. EVENTUALLY I FELL ASLEEP.

MY MIND MUST HAVE BEEN WORKING IN MY SLEEP BECAUSE THE SOLUTION TO MY PROBLEM FLASHED BEFORE MY EYES THE MINUTE I WOKE UP.
AN ASTRO-HUNGARIAN DUCAT - IT HAD BEEN GIVEN TO MY GRANDFATHER BY FRANZ FERDINAND HIMSELF...
I HEADED OFF TO THE PAWN DISTRICT...
THESE BLAHNICKS ARE KILLING ME...
AND WALKED INTO THE FIRST HALF-DECENT LOOKING SHOP.

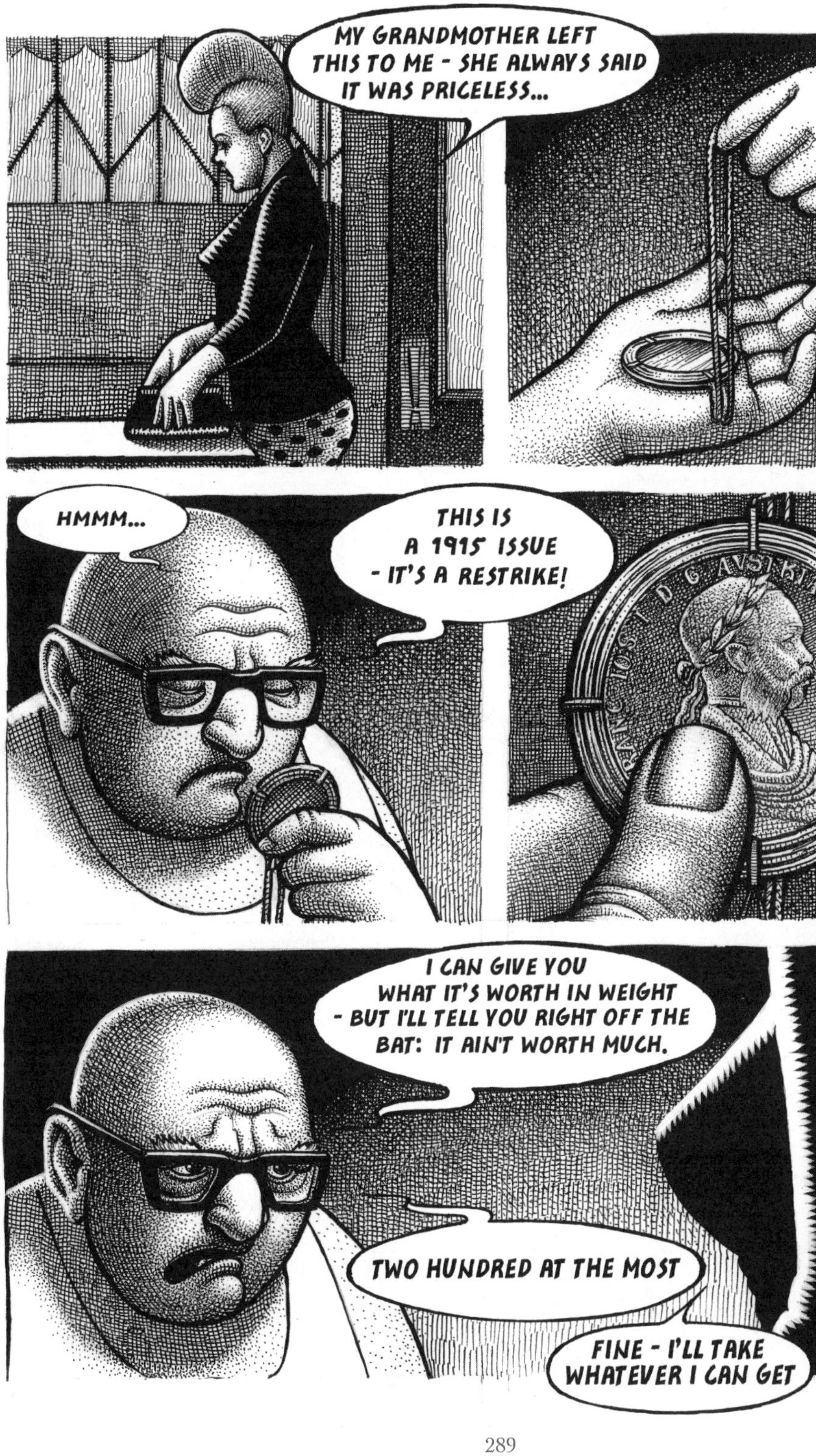
MY GRANDMOTHER LEFT THIS TO ME - SHE ALWAYS SAID IT WAS PRICELESS...
HMMM...
THIS IS A 1915 ISSUE - IT'S A RESTRIKE!
I CAN GIVE YOU WHAT IT'S WORTH IN WEIGHT - BUT I'LL TELL YOU RIGHT OFF THE BAT: IT AIN'T WORTH MUCH.
TWO HUNDRED AT THE MOST
FINE - I'LL TAKE WHATEVER I CAN GET

MADAM M. AGREED TO DO THE JOB FOR TWO HUNDRED DOLLARS - ALTHOUGH SHE SAID THAT THE MAGIC MIGHT TAKE A BIT LONGER TO TAKE EFFECT AS IT WOULD FOR THREE HUNDRED...

IF MADAM M. WAS RIGHT - I WAS TO HAVE MY OWN BUSINESS IN NO TIME, AND PLENTY OF CASH TO BUY THE DUCAT BACK FROM THE PAWN SHOP. IN THE MEANTIME, ALL I COULD DO WAS PRAY THAT TORVALD DIDN'T NOTICE IT WENT MISSING...

HER INSTRUCTIONS WERE SIMPLE - I WAS TO GO HOME AND GO ABOUT MY BUSINESS AS USUAL. AS I WAS GETTING READY FOR BED THAT NIGHT I NOTICED THE FIRST MIRACLE...

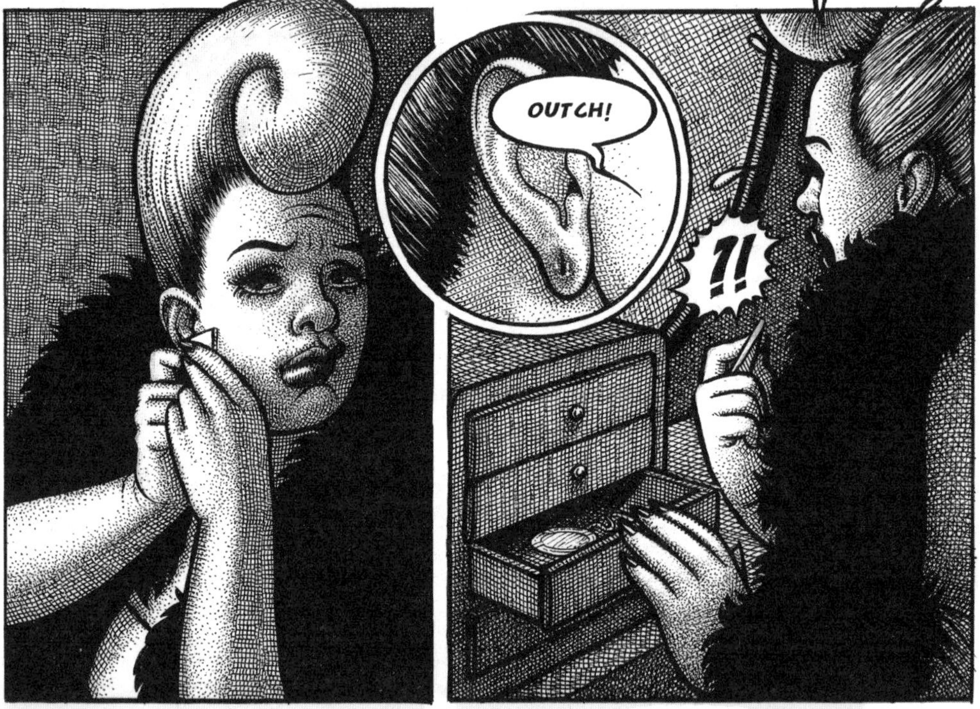

THE DUCAT WAS BACK IN THE JEWELRY BOX! AND THEN THE SECOND MIRACLE HAPPENED - I HEARD THE FRONT DOOR OPEN... TORVALD'S VOICE GREETED ME LOVINGLY LIKE IT USED TO.

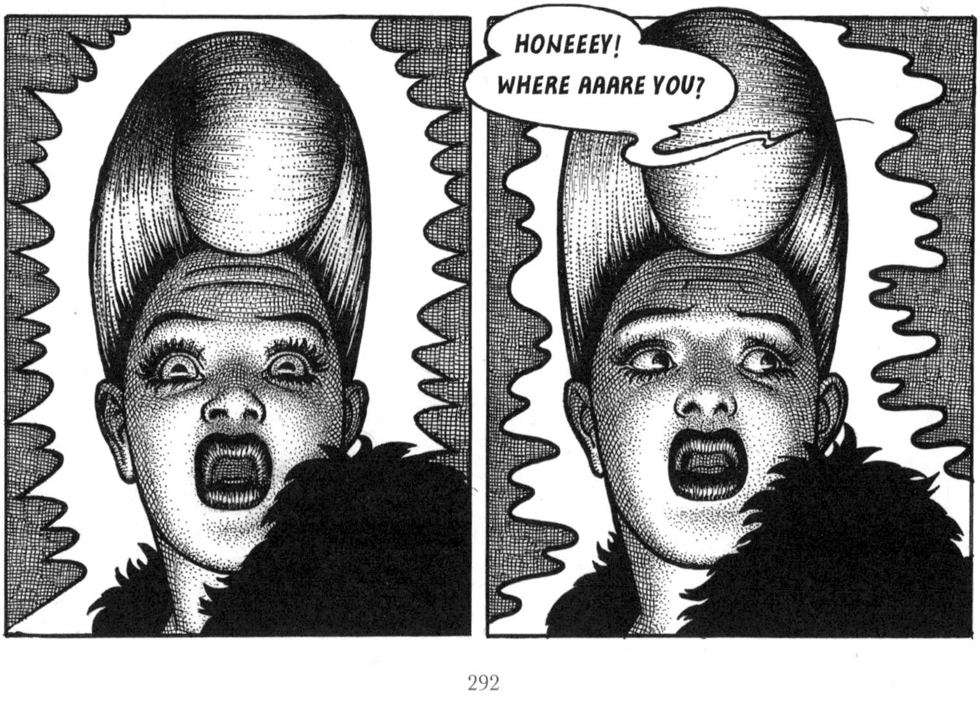

I RAN DOWN TO GREET HIM - AND THERE HE WAS - JUST LIKE WHEN WE FIRST MET - WITH GIFTS AND FLOWERS AND A LOVING SMILE...

I JUST KNEW THAT THINGS WERE GOING TO BE DIFFERENT FROM THEN ON - AND THAT IS HOW I KNEW - MADAM M WAS NO JOKE - SHE WAS THE REAL DEAL.

THE END

WINTER

Alice Boissonneau

At the height of January, the wind sweeps up the canal corridor of Spadina, driving the snow relentlessly into each narrow crevice. It is hard to see the dim light of the streetcar, working its way up, the shouts of the newsboy can barely be heard, jerked out through the wind.

The houses seem bound, frozen like reefs, forever.

Below the bridge it is worse, nothing to block the wind here. Smoke and steam boil up from the gulf where the trains are. It has a sort of deadly fascination, as if you asked yourself, and is this all then, is this the end? Here the city ends in the coal-yards and trains. Below the houses, everything rests suspended. Steam clings to the wires over the trains in streaming sheets. The line of burnt-brown brick houses seems least important of all, their stiff cindery washings flap forlorn.

What if the lake were to creep up here and freeze around the buildings?

OXTAILS WITH MUSHROOMS AND RICE

AUSTIN CLARKE

Winter bursting your arse. It cold. The thermostat won't get no higher than -5 degrees Celsius to give you a lil release from out o' the arms of snow and sleets. You wake up in darkness, get dress in darkness, and the road so slippery that you almost brekking a hip-bone every morning as you step outside to go to work in darkness.

It's Friday night. You need company and something to spice up your life.

"What you go-do?" as the Trinidadians say. Call up a few friends? Put on the calypso, Rahtee, rah: on your stereo? Plan a lil party? Do some wukking-up to keep the blood in your body circulating?

You should. Because if you don't find something to do, you'll get depress. Soon the ambulance going be coming straight to your apartment and tekking you away to the Madhouse, or else down to the Morgue, where they'll put you on a nice, clean white slab o' marble until your family back in the Wessindies hear and have to face the expense o' flying up to Toronto in a Bee-Wee to tek you home in a brown-painted walnut box 'pon a Air Canada plane. Oh, loss!

And when the black newspaper, *Share*, hear 'bout you and write a lil obituary, the only chorus they going sing over you is, "But I didn't know that she dead. In-true!" Or one o' your friends going say, "Wait! I rested my two eyes on that man not two days ago! Man, it was Thursday gone, when I butt-up on him in the subway. And you mean to tell me that in two-twos, in the twinkling of an eye, he *gone*? Wuh-loss!"

Yes, yuh gone. Yuh pass-away. Because it cold, and every day it dark, and you wukking all day and even with the fluorescent lights turn on, you still wukking in darkness. And you get depress, and yuh dead. Oh Lord!

Don't let this happen to you. Cut out this foolishness! Try cooking some oxtail with mushrooms, serve with plain rice.

You can get oxtails almost any place in Toronto – in a supermarket, where they does sell them wrap in plastic, or in any Wessindian store, where you does pay through your hat for them. Wessindian merchants don't call their shops "stores" or "shops for groceries"; Wessindian merchants does call their stores "specialty shops" nowadays, girl.

But a surer and more cheaper place to buy oxtails is down in the Kensington Market. Creep out o' your apartment and brave the cold. You have to make a little sacrifice to lay out a dinner for your best friends, even if the temperature is -40 Celsius and your fingers and toes get frostbitten. It can't really kill yuh.

Go down Spadina Avenue where they always tearing up the road, repairing it, and where traffics always driving so fast they look like they going lick yuh down; and you swing up Baldwin Street, where you will find the European Meat Market. Go in there, but keep in mind that once you cross that threshold you going stannup for at least thirty minutes before you get serve. And remember to pull out a piece o' paper from the dispenser, with a number writ-down on it.

Whilst you in there, all kinds o' people who think that they own the store going be pushing you and shoving you, while the cold wind bursting your arse every time the door open to let the next customer enter. And you pounding your boots 'pon the linoleum floor covered in sawdust, to drive warmth into your two foots and hope it travel up your two legs as you waiting and waiting for your number to be call.

But ignore that, and them. You are here on a mission, to buy two nice, big oxtails. So try to enjoy the waiting. Buy a hot dog or a cup o' coffee and listen to all the different languages that licking-down your ears. Try to pick up a word or two in Russian, Chinese or Italian. You might even get a lil advice 'bout sausages.

When they call out your number, and you manage to get to the front of the crowd and face the counter full o' meats, axe the woman to "Please give me *two* oxtails."

They does sell these nice clean oxtails whole, from the top part to the tail part. You may have to point to the exact pieces that you like, 'cause the woman serving you may not understand English too good, and you are not here in this noisy place, standing up in sawdust with all these people pushing you, to worry about speaking proper English – not even if you are a teacher in the English-as-a-Second-Language program in the George Brown College down the street. You here for one thing: oxtails.

Try to find a way to axe the girl, who may not understand English, to please cut the oxtails at the joints for you. You may have to point your fingers at the joints, and shake and nod your head, to make she put the oxtail under the power saw at the right place.

Don't follow them Jamaicans who does cut a oxtail between the joints and then cross-cut them, giving you four pieces from one joint o' oxtail. They know more 'bout how to cook jerk pork. (I, though, have a way of cooking jerk pork – which in truth and in fact was invented in Barbados – which have some Jamaicans trying to change their citizenship and become Barbadian!)

I actually prefer the oxtails sold in a ordinary supermarket. They have a nice thick ring o' fat round the bigger pieces, and the fat is the thing that does give the oxtails flavour. But the good thing about buying the oxtails in the European Meat Market is that it is close to them Wessindian specialty shops that does sell the other things that you need, like fresh thyme, bay leaves, hot red peppers, avocado pear, limes and lemons, cucumber, fresh parsley, a head o' lettuce, mushrooms, onions, garlic, tomatoes, a small-small can o' tomato paste, bags o' brown sugar from Demerara, cloves and coconut cream. And a sugarcake or a tamarind ball to eat whilst you freezing. These are the ingreasements you going need for this meal.

The next good thing about the European Meat Market is that it's 'cross the road from a liquor store. You don't want to have to walk all over Toronto, with winter bursting your arse, just to pick up a few ingreasements. It cold, so save some steps and get home to your warm apartment, where you can drink a cup o' tea and have some Peek Frean biscuits.

At the liquor store, get a cheap bottle o' red wine for the oxtails, or some Brights sherry. After all, you're having in friends, so put a little extra something in the food.

At last yuh get home, praise God! You have all the ingreasements for making the meal.

Now is the time to burn a stick o' incense that you buy from one of them Chinese stores near the Market. I find that the more Chinese characters the box have on, the more sweeter the incense going smell.

Light some candles. You have to create a festive atmosphere to take you mind offa the ice and the snow and the sleets and the cold... *brrrrrrr...* and take the chill offa life. Make the most of the days which the Lord, thy God, giveth thee – even if your days cold as arse.

A hot calypso by the Trinidadian calypsonian Crazy filling up your place and driving the neighbours up the wall, and driving them to call the police for you. You are listening and wukking-up to "Uh coming, Uh coming," blasting down the four walls. You are in such a good mood – like a real Spiritual Baptist! Let the malicious neighbours get on the telephone and call the police! They could all go to hell. You not disturbing no peace; you putting life into the winter of your discontent. But on second thought, you had better be a lil cautious, 'cause Canadians don't like no noise. They carries on their life as if they are mice in a church, quiet- quiet. You had better not turn up Crazy too loud. A cold jail cell isn't much different from being laid out on a cold slab o' marble.

So, the Chinese incense burning sweet in your apartment, and the fresh thyme, tomatoes and cucumber soaking in cold water. You ready to start.

Wash off the oxtails, 'cause sometimes they does have sawdust and other things on them. put the oxtails in a bowl with lil salt and fresh lime squeeze good. Swish them round for a minute or two, and leave them to soak for a lil while. Throw off the water, dry them off 'pon a towel and leave them on the counter.

Have a drink at this juncture. A lil red wine, preferable. But since this is Wessindian food, there isn't nothing better than a strong rum. Being a multicultural kind o' man, I myself would make a strong-strong, dry-dry martini to take the chill off my bones. Bombay Gin, no ice, and with four nice, big, green, juicy olives.

I don't lift a spoon or a pot cover unless I have a drink in my hand.

And music? I can't cook a sweet potato unless Crazy or some sweet Sparrow licking-down the place with calypso.

Making food is no different from making love. Axe any woman who know anything 'bout cooking!

But this is me. You might be a Christian-minded person, and you might have solemnly vowed to don't let any kind o' spirits pass your two lips, and guard against your body moving to any music with a beat. So, drink orange juice or bottle' water.

Now, getting back to the oxtails. Put the dry-off oxtails in a big saucepan with two bay leaves.

Christ, you know something? I forget to tell you to buy a package o' beef bouillon. *Beef.* Nothing but beef bouillon. This is very important. Don't experiment with any other kind o' bouillon.

Melt one beef bouillon in a cup o' boiling water.

Cut up two big-big onions and put them in the saucepan with the oxtails. Throw in some whole cloves, enough to full one teaspoon or a lil more; a lil salt; and as many hot red peppers as you or your friends could bear.

You don't want your Canadian friends to start asking for water, blowing their lips and making noise like when they're drinking hot coffee, or running too often to the bathroom while eating your oxtails. So, season them up in such a way that everybody is able to eat their belly full.

Bring the ingreasements that you just put in the saucepan to a boil. The minute it boil, turn down the heat. The whole apartment building is going be transform immediately with the aromas of your cooking.

Oxtails does take a long time to cook; and you want to cook them slow, till they get soft. Peel about six nice, juicy, fresh cloves o' garlic, and throw them in with the oxtails.

Now choose the amount o' rice you going cook. You need plain rice, or as some Barbadians call it, "white" rice.

"Boy, I cooking some white rice," a woman tell me once.

"You ever see rice that is black?" I axe her.

That was before I discover the basement of the Sin-Lawrence Market, where with my two eyes I see rice that was not only black, but brown and red too.

For this meal, though, I would cook basmati rice from India. Those Indians does grow good rice, and they know more 'bout rice than Wessindians. But you could also cook Chinese rice. The Chinese know 'bout rice too. And they know how to cook it. If you buy the rice in Chinatown, my foolish advice to you is, before you pay for the rice, make sure it isn't "sticky" rice. You need plain, perfume rice for this meal.

If you buy sticky rice by mistake, you will soon know; the rice going stick to the pot. But if you catch it before all the water boil out, add some ordinary rice, like Uncle Ben's, and the result won't be entirely like glue or Cream o' Wheat.

Put a slab o' butter in the bottom of a saucepan along with the rice, and water to suit the amount o' rice you are cooking. If you is a Wessindian or know how Wessindians does cook rice, drop a teaspoon o' coconut cream in the saucepan, and make sure that you stir she in good.

Put the rice over a medium-low heat – number 4 on the dial if you have one o' them pretty-pretty modern electric stoves. Whilst the water is getting hot, the rice grains are getting soaked, and in two-twos the rice cook, and you can count each and every grain.

Now, a few words about not serving the rice with peas of any kind. Peas-and-rice, as it is called in Barbados, or rice-and-peas, as it is known among Jamaicans, would be too much for this meal. By eating white rice, you would cut down on the richness of the oxtails cooked with mushrooms. Eating peas-and-rice with these oxtails would contradict the delicacy of the oxtails.

When the water in the oxtails boil-out and is reduced to about half the original amount, take the saucepan off the stove. Cut up another two or three big-big onions, in thick slices, and add them to the saucepan. Wash off and dry the mushrooms. Either cut-up each one in two or drop them in whole with the oxtails.

Uncork the bottle o' cheap red wine and empty at least one cup in the saucepan. Empty the small-small tin o' tomato paste in the saucepan. Bring all this to a boil, stirring from the bottom to make sure that nothing is sticking. Once it boil, turn-she-down immediately, to simmer.

All your troubles end. Most o' the hard work finish. All that is leff-back to do is make the salad. But yuh know, you don't have to make no damn salad, and tire-out yourself. We Wessindians aren't salad-eating people. I don't ever remember my mother using the word "salad" when I was growing up.

"Lettuce don't have-in no goodness. To-besides! I look like a sheep to you? Or a rabbit?"

Salad, or greens as some people does call it, was something that the stocks, the animals, in Barbados used to eat. White people over at the plantation used to eat salad too. But my mother's hand was twisted to make a salad to go with the main course (which she never called "the main course" but simply "the food"), she would shave a carrot.

I still hate carrots. Shaved or unshaved.

We used to grow lettuce in our kitchen garden, to put in sandwiches mostly; and I used to pretend to be a sheep and eat the lettuce straight outta the ground, sometimes without washing off the dirt. And sometimes, by accident, I would swallow a little green wirrum. But you couldn't tell the difference between lettuce out o' the ground and a fat green wirrum.

Now we living in Canada, where they say that salads are good for you. So, when in Rome...

I have a weakness for Romaine lettuce; and a more bigger weakness for Boston lettuce. So, wash some Boston lettuce in the sink. And since you going so far as to make a salad, why not wash some watercress, that the English like to make in sandwiches and take to the Epsoms Derby in picnic baskets?

Shake-off the water from the lettuce and the watercress hard-hard, but don't break the leaves. Since you don't possess one o' them things that does spin-round and dry lettuce leaves, you got to wrap-up the lettuce and sprigs o' watercress in paper towel, round and round and round. Leave them 'pon the counter to dry.

Get yuh salad bowl, one make-outta wood. Peel a nice clove o' garlic and, holding it in your hand, rub it all round the inside of the salad bowl. Rub and rub and rub, till the garlic rub-down to your fingernails or fingertips and nothing of the garlic left back.

Now sprig-up the dried-off lettuce into the bowl, in pieces big enough to stick with your fork and stuff inside your mouth. Sprig-up the watercress too, and drop the pieces on top the lettuce.

Get your tomatoes. Cut them in quarters and add to the lettuce. Sprinkle lil salt and lil white sugar.

Start stirring she up with your two hands. After you stir-she-up, pour in lil oil and squeeze half o' lemon through your fingers. Make sure no seeds fall in the salad, otherwise they might go down somebody's windpipe and choke her, and you'll have to spend your time pounding her on her back, to prevent her from strangulating and losing her breath and consciousness at your dinner table; and you may even have to neglect your other guesses, and take the person who swallow the seed o' lemon to the Emergency.

Get the salad fork and the salad spoon, and toss up your salad.

The very last thing to put in is the avocado pear. The avocado they sell here in Canada does get soft too quick; and soft avocado, like overripe tomatoes, does mash-up the crispness of your salad. So, wait and slice-up your avocado until just before you serving the salad.

By now, if you been taking your time, and not getting hot and sweaty like a racehorse, your oxtails will be done. They are going be soft – so soft that, if you taste one, all the meat going melt-off in your mouth. Some people like their meats soft-soft. Not me. I like to be able to bite into a piece o' meat and chew the meat between my teeth.

Only people who don't have their own teeth need oxtail to fall off the bone, so that they don't have to spend time chewing it. But you're not really suppose to suck meat. Meat is not a lollipop. Bite-in-it with your teeth, with the oil running down the two sides o' your mouth. Lick the oil from round your lips, from off your fingers. Feel the bone. Bite-in the meat again. And when all the meat gone off the bone, then, and only then, do you start sucking the bone, even if you make a lil noise. When you eat oxtail this way, you telling the person who cook the food and your host that it's damn sweet, and that you want some more.

Some people will tell you to take the oxtail off the heat to let she cool off before serving, but don't mind them, you're not going on a picnic, nor an outing. Food is to be eaten hot, particular in winter since Toronto so damn cold.

This kind o' food is going to taste even more sweeter heated up the next day, when all the ingreasements had a chance to work their magic into the oxtails.

To serve, all you got to do is place a little oxtail and a big oxtail on one plate. Ladle out a big heaping pot spoon o' rice and lay that beside the oxtails.

There is certainly nothing more better than piping-hot white rice. When you see all that steam rising, and you can smell the perfume of the basmati rice, and you place the first spoonful inside your mouth, Jesus Christ in heaven, you don't need nothing more better nor more healthier than this.

Stir-round in the bottom o' the saucepan with the oxtails for the thickness of the sauce, and pour a spoonful o' this goodness over the oxtails. If one of your guesses really know anything about eating this kind o' food, she going ask you to pour some more sauce over the rice too. And so asked, so do.

Don't serve the salad on the same plate as the oxtails and rice. This isn't no picnic; you don't have to pile-on everything on one plate! Keep back the salad till everybody done eating. I bet you that when you put the first plate o' oxtails and mushrooms and white rice in front o' your guesses, they going forget the damn salad.

Beer does go good with this food. If you cool, or playing cool, white wine is not bad. But if you really cool, a nice red wine will do the trick. If you are a "hard-seed," there is nothing more better with this kind o' food than a fair-sized shot o' rum in a long glass with a lot o' ice and a half-can o' soda water.

I bet anyone who eats these oxtails once will want to cook them more than once a week, from now on. But leave this meal for a Friday or Saturday night, in winter. This is special food, festive food. Food for making you feel good when you eat it.

"Man, this food is real Afro-dizziac!" a friend o' mine tell me once.

It does make you want to do certain things in bed. If you eat this kind o' food every day as the Lord send, imagine what would happen to your body, your mind, your energy, your heart and the person you living with?

WHEN JOHN LENNON DIED

SANG KIM

In the winter of 1980, when I was twelve and a police order kept my father away, Tom Chang, a deacon at my mother's church, visited our home every weekend. This was in Koreatown, near Bloor and Christie, and my father had put all of our savings into a convenience store because he believed that our luck was going to change and that fortune would finally come our way. My mother changed the locks after the last incident with my father and my five-year-old brother was sent to stay with my grandmother until things settled down.

Tom Chang was married with three children. One of them was a girl my own age, Sabrina, who was always so upbeat at our Sunday school that I had assumed she knew nothing about her father's weekend visits. I may have been wrong about this; maybe Sabrina did know, but as a good Christian she had faith that it was all a part of God's plan.

This was around the time John Lennon died and although I could not confirm it to be true, both my mother and Tom talked about him as though he was their friend. One night, they sat around the kitchen table listening to his music on the radio. My mother swirled whiskey in her glass while Tom kept time to the music by tapping his feet on the linoleum. And when he sang along to some of the tunes, his high-pitched voice was so different from my father's that I thought he sounded like a girl and not a real man.

My mother spoke in Korean to both of us, but Tom spoke to me only in English. He had studied in Canada and I remember my mother being very pleased when she told me this.

"He wrote this after he left the Beatles," Tom said during one song. The singer's voice had a raw and hurting feeling to it like he was crying out to somebody who was leaving him or had left him already. I asked Tom what the song was about.

"Oh, about loss," he said. My mother rose from her chair and stood at the kitchen window. Her arms were wrapped around her chest and she was looking at the drifting snow.

"It's late," my mother said. "Go to bed."

"But it's Saturday," I said. Tom laughed and put his hand behind my head and pulled me towards him like he was going to tell me a secret but, instead, he put a dollar bill in my hand.

"Go out and buy yourself a comic book," he said, and winked at me. We sold Archie comics at our convenience store, but I never liked reading them because there were no heroes in them.

It was also around this time that a brown Buick Riviera began to appear on our side street. I knew who owned all the cars on Euclid Avenue, at least the ones south of Bloor Street, and nobody owned a Buick Riviera. It would be there before I went to bed and be gone before I left for school the next morning. After dinner, I would watch from my bedroom window as the car pulled up slowly, like it was driving over broken glass, and park in front of Jake DiNardi's house just beyond the street lamp. In the weeks following Lennon's death, the car came around more than usual. Through my binoculars, I could see the outline of a man leaning forward in the driver's seat, looking up at my mother's room. I could tell it was a man by his body size; he was as big as my father and seemed to take up the whole front of the car.

When I went outside to buy the comic book with the money Tom had given me, the car was there as usual. The headlights were turned off but I could tell that the engine was still running from the white smoke coming out of the exhaust. I thought that the man inside must have been cold and had kept the engine on to stay warm. I crossed to the other side of the street. When the car was directly to my left, I took a quick look but could only see the back of the man's head.

I returned later with a copy of *G.I. Joe* tucked inside my coat and the car was still there, but the engine was shut off. A thin layer of snow covered the car, so I could not tell if someone was inside. A television set flickered in Jake's living room and I knew that he and his brothers were sitting around eating pizzas and watching *Hockey Night in Canada* like they did every Saturday night. I approached the car slowly and could hear the snow crunching under my boots. I wiped some snow off the passenger-side window and leaned in to look. On the seat there was what looked like a baseball bat and a pair of binoculars like my own, except they were much bigger. Suddenly, I felt someone standing behind me and was surprised to hear a sound like a drowning person coming out my mouth. I turned around to face him and recognized him as the owner of the car even though I had never seen his face before. He was a big white man wearing a bomber jacket and his leather gloves looked almost too small on his hands. The light in my mother's bedroom was on and I wanted to call out to her, but my mouth would not open.

"It's okay, kid," the man said. His breath was bluish in the air. "I'm not gonna hurt you. I just want to talk." He bent down to look into my eyes and I could see that his face was full of tiny craters. A scar the size of a caterpillar ran under his chin.

"You like my car?' he said. I shrugged my shoulders because I wasn't sure if I liked his car or not. "It's cold out here. Why don't we go in—" And before he could finish what he was saying, I made a run for the house. My *G.I. Joe* comic had slipped out of my jacket, but I just left it and kept running. When I reached my front door, I exhaled for the first time and looked back. The man was gone and his car was driving away, down our street. I saw the tail lights brightening at a stop sign before accelerating again.

Upstairs, the radio was still on in the kitchen but my mother and Tom were not there. I went down the narrow cold hallway toward my room and slowed down in front of my mother's bedroom. There was no light under her door and I could hear Tom saying something in a low voice and my mother giggling in a way I wasn't used to hearing from her. I went to my bedroom and lay on my bed. I wondered if the man and his Buick Riviera had anything to do with Tom being at our house all the time, and if the police were ever going to allow my father to return if he promised to never hurt my mother again.

In the morning, I could hear Tom walking past my room and down the staircase. When I looked out the window, he was not on the sidewalk and I heard a car squealing down the icy street but was not sure whose car it was. In the kitchen, my mother was frying eggs and humming to herself. She seemed happier than usual. I didn't tell her about meeting the man outside because I didn't want to ruin her mood. She put a plate of eggs in front of me and went downstairs to open the store. I went out into the street looking for my comic book and found it on the sidewalk buried in the snow. When I came back inside, the telephone was ringing. I picked up the receiver. It was a woman's voice speaking in Korean and she sounded upset about something.

"Where is she?" she said. I asked her if she was looking for my mother and she repeated herself, "Where is she?" I told her that my mother was downstairs watching the store. She hung up without saying goodbye. The woman sounded like an older version of Sabrina. And although I had never spoken to Sabrina's mother before, I thought that their voices would be similar because they were mother and daughter.

After an hour or so, I went downstairs to get a can of pop. The store was empty and my mother was sitting on a stool behind the counter. I could tell she had been crying and she turned away when she saw me.

"I have to go to the hospital," she said after a long time. "You stay here." Her eyes were red and her voice crackly just like it got when my father used to hit her. I had watched the store by myself before, but it was only for short periods of time like when my mother needed to take a washroom break. I sensed my mother would be gone much longer but I didn't bother mentioning that. She put on her coat and hurried out the door.

The neighbours were surprised to see me there by myself and helped me out whenever I didn't know the price of something, like canned tomatoes or shampoo. But I remembered the prices for most things like milk and bread and lottery tickets. Later, Jake dropped by because he had heard that I was alone and wanted to help. I knew he was just saying that and that he really wanted something for free, but I didn't mind because we could talk about things like the hockey game and superheroes and not about the kind of things that were going on in my house. When it was time for him to go home, Jake took a chocolate bar and a bag of chips with him. The store was slower at night because the snow was beginning to really come down.

I was refilling the milk fridge when the telephone rang. When I said "Hello," there was no answer on the other end, just loud music in the background. I was ready to hang up when someone finally spoke. It was my father and I was happy to hear his voice, although I could not tell whether he was happy to hear mine. He asked how I was and I told him I was fine and that I was watching the store by myself because my mother was at the hospital visiting a friend. He told me that he was proud of me and then asked about my younger brother, so I told him he was with our grandmother.

"When are you coming home?" I said.

"Soon," he said. I wanted to ask him if he knew anything about the man and the Buick Riviera but decided not to because I felt like his mind was somewhere else.

"I have to go," he said. "Everything is going to be okay." I didn't know what he meant by that or if I believed that everything was going to be okay or not. All I knew was that things were not like they used to be and might never be again and that I missed my brother, even though he bothered me sometimes.

When I got off the telephone with my father, I tore open a bag of chips and looked outside. It was like someone had dropped a white blanket over the storefront. I could not see any cars or people passing by, so I imagined everybody in their homes with people they loved and who loved them back. I wasn't sure if my mother was going to come back any time soon, so I walked myself through closing up the store. The most important part was to take the money out of the cash register and put it in the brown bag behind the ice freezer.

It was very late when my mother came home. I was at the kitchen table doing my homework. Her eyes were red and she looked tired. She went to the sink to pour herself a drink and asked me about my day. I told her everything went fine but not the part about Jake dropping by and taking food with him, even though I never said he could. I also wanted to tell her that my father had called, but I felt like she already knew.

"Get some sleep," she said. "You have school tomorrow." I asked her if Tom was going to come by. She turned away from me and took a big sip of her whiskey.

"No," she said. "He's not." She then asked me if I liked Tom.

"Yes." I lied because I knew it would make her feel better if I said that. She told me that he liked me too, liked me very much, but that he was probably never going to come to our house again. She was quiet for a long time and then she let out an exhaling sound, like the sound of a cat I had once heard when it was run over by a car. I could tell there was a lot on her mind so I got up to go to bed. I said good night to her from my bedroom door, but I don't think she heard me. She was sitting there at the table staring at the wall.

I awoke to banging on the front door. I got out of bed and looked out my window. It was very dark even though there was a lot of snow outside. I could not see anyone because the front door was on the same side as my window. When he raised his voice, I could tell it was my father and that he had been drinking, but I couldn't make out anything he was saying. Some lights came on in the houses across the street. I imagined my mother with her ear pressed against her bedroom door and holding the doorknob like a grenade ready to explode. My father sounded angry and he kept saying things to my mother as though she was standing in front of him but far away. I returned to my bed after the police came and took my father away. I lay there for a while thinking about my mother and whether or not I should go into her room. I knew that some bad things were happening to her now and that more bad things would happen to her again, but I did not feel sorry for her. As I began falling asleep, I thought about all the snow and my brother who was staying with my grandmother and how things didn't seem quite right in the world. John Lennon had died and I knew that it would be a long time before his death didn't mean anything to me anymore.

THE ART OF COOKING AND SERVING

MARGARET ATWOOD

The summer I was eleven I spent a lot of time knitting. I knitted doggedly, silently, crouched over the balls of wool and the steel needles and the lengthening swath of knitwear in a posture that was far from easy. I'd learned to knit too early in life to have mastered the trick of twisting the strand around my index finger – the finger had been too short – so I had to jab the right-hand needle in, hold it there with two left-hand fingers, then lift the entire right hand to loop the wool around the tip of the needle. I'd seen women who were able to knit and talk at the same time, barely glancing down, but I couldn't do it that way. My style of knitting required total concentration and caused my arms to ache, and irritated me a lot.

What I was knitting was a layette. A layette was a set of baby garments you were supposed to dress the newborn baby in so it would be warm when it was brought home from the hospital. At the very least you needed to have two thumbless mittens, two stubby booties, a pair of leggings, a jacket, and a bonnet, to which you could add a knitted blanket if you had the patience, as well as a thing called a soaker. The soaker looked like a pair of shorts with pumpkin-shaped legs, like the ones in pictures of Sir Francis Drake. Cloth diapers and rubber baby pants were prone to leaks: that's what the soaker was for. But I was not going to knit the soaker. I hadn't yet got around to visualizing the fountains, the streams, the rivers of pee a baby was likely to produce.

The blanket was tempting – there was one with rabbits on it that I longed to create – but I knew I had to draw the line somewhere because I didn't have all the time in the world. If I dawdled, the baby might arrive before I was ready for it and be forced to wear some sort of mismatched outfit put together out of hand-me-downs. I'd started on the leggings and the mittens, as being fairly simple – mostly alternate rows of knit and purl, with some ribbing thrown in. That way I could work up to the jacket, which was more complicated. I was saving the bonnet to the last: it was going to be my *chef-d'oeuvre*. It was to be ornamented with satin ribbons to tie under the baby's chin – the possibilities of strangulation through ties like this had not yet been considered – and with huge ribbon rosettes that would stick out on either side of the baby's face like small cabbages. Babies dressed in layettes, I knew from the pictures in the Beehive pattern book, were supposed to resemble confectionary – clean and sweet, delicious little cakelike bundles decorated with pastel icing.

The colour I'd chosen was white. It was the orthodox colour, though a few of the Beehive patterns were shown in an elfin pale green or a practical yellow. But white was best: after it was known whether the baby was a boy or a girl I could add the ribbons, blue or pink. I had a vision of how the entire set would look when finished – pristine, gleaming, admirable, a tribute to my own goodwill and kindness. I hadn't yet realized it might also be a substitute for them.

I was knitting this layette because my mother was expecting. I avoided the word *pregnant*, as did others: *pregnant* was a blunt, bulgy, pendulous word, it weighed you down to think about it, whereas *expecting* suggested a dog with its ears pricked, listening briskly and with happy anticipation to an approaching footstep. My mother was old for such a thing: I'd gathered this by eavesdropping while she talked with her friends in the city, and from the worried wrinkles on the foreheads of the friends, and from their compressed lips and tiny shakes of the head, and from their *Oh dear* tone, and from my mother saying she would just have to make the best of it. I gathered that something might be wrong with the baby because of my mother's age; but wrong how, exactly? I listened as much as I could, but I couldn't make it out, and there was no one I could ask. Would it have no hands, would it have a little pinhead; would it be a moron? *Moron* was a term of abuse, at school. I wasn't sure what it meant, but there were children you weren't supposed to stare at on the street, because it wasn't their fault, they had just been born that way.

I'd been told about the expectant state of my mother in May, by my father. It had made me very anxious, partly because I'd also been told that until my new baby brother or sister had arrived safely my mother would be in a dangerous condition. Something terrible might happen to her – something that might make her very ill – and it was all the more likely to happen if I myself did not pay proper attention. My father did not say what this thing was, but his gravity and terseness meant that it was a serious business.

My mother – said my father – was not supposed to sweep the floor, or carry anything heavy such as pails of water, or bend down much, or lift bulky objects. We would all have to pitch in, said my father, and do extra tasks. It would be my brother's job to mow the lawn, from now until June, when we would go up north. (Up north there was no lawn. In any case my brother wouldn't be there: he was heading off to a camp for boys, to do things with axes in the woods.) As for me, I would just have to be generally helpful. More helpful than usual, my father added in a manner that was meant to be encouraging. He himself would be helpful too, of course. But he couldn't be there all the time. He had some work to do, when we would be at what other people called *the cottage* but we called *the island.*

(Cottages had iceboxes and gas generators and water-skiing, all of which we lacked.) It was necessary for him to be away, which was unfortunate, he continued. But he would not be gone for very long, and he was sure I would be up to it.

I myself was not so sure. He always thought I knew more than I knew, and that I was bigger than I was, and older, and hardier. What he mistook for calmness and competence was actually fright: that was why I stared at him in silence, nodding my head. The danger that loomed was so vague, and therefore so large – how could I even prepare for it? At the back of my mind, my feat of knitting was a sort of charm, like the fairy-tale suits of nettles mute princesses were supposed to make for their swan-shaped brothers, to turn them back into human beings. If I could only complete the full set of baby garments, the baby that was supposed to fit inside them would be conjured into the world and thus out of my mother. Once outside, where I could see it – once it had a face – it could be dealt with. As it was, the thing was a menace.

Thus I knitted on, with single-minded concentration. I finished the mittens before we went up north; they were more or less flawless, except for the odd botched stitch. After I got to the island, I polished off the leggings – the leg that was shorter could be stretched, I felt. Without pause I started on the jacket, which was to have several bands of seed stitch on it – a challenge, but one I was determined to overcome.

Meanwhile my mother was being no use at all. At the beginning of my knitting marathon she'd undertaken to do the booties. She did know how to knit, she'd knitted in the past: the pattern book I was using had once been hers. She could turn heels, a skill I hadn't quite mastered. But despite her superior ability, she was slacking off: all she'd done so far was half a bootie. Her knitting lay neglected while she rested in a deck chair, her feet up on a log, reading historical romances with horseback riding and poisoning and swordplay in them – I knew, I'd read them myself – or else just dozing, her head lying slackly on a pillow, her face pale and moist, her hair damp and lank, her stomach sticking out in a way that made me feel dizzy, as I did when someone else had cut their finger. She'd taken to wearing an old smock she'd put away in a trunk, long ago; I remembered using it for dressing up at Halloween once, when I was being a fat lady with a purse. It made her look poor.

It was scary to watch her sleeping in the middle of the day. It was unlike her. Normally she was a person who went for swift, purposeful walks, or skated around rinks in winter at an impressive speed, or swam with a lot of kicking, or rattled up the dishes – she called it rattling them up. She always knew what to do in an emergency, she was methodical and cheerful, she took command. Now it was as if she had abdicated.

When I wasn't knitting, I swept the floor diligently. I pumped out pails and pails of water with the hand pump and lugged them up the hill one at a time, spilling water down my bare legs; I did the washing in the zinc washtub, scrubbing the clothes with Sunlight soap on the washboard, carting them down to the lake to rinse them out, hauling them up the hill again to hang them on the line. I weeded the garden, I carried in the wood, all against the background of my mother's alarming passivity.

Once a day she went for a swim, although she didn't swim energetically, not the way she used to, she just floated around; and I would go in too, whether I wanted to or not: I had to prevent her from drowning. I had a fear of her sinking down suddenly, down through the cold brownish water, with her hair fanning out like seaweed and her eyes gazing solemnly up at me. In that case I would have to dive down and get my arm around her neck and tow her to shore, but how could I do that? She was so big. But nothing like that had happened yet, and she liked going into the water; it seemed to wake her up. With only her head sticking out, she looked more like herself. At such times she would even smile, and I would have the illusion that everything was once again the way it was supposed to be.

But then she would emerge, dripping – there were varicose veins on the backs of her legs, I couldn't avoid seeing them, although they embarrassed me – and make her way with painful slowness up to our cabin, and put together our lunch. The lunch would be sardines, or peanut butter on crackers, or cheese if we had any, and tomatoes from the garden, and carrots I'd dug out and washed. She didn't appear much interested in eating this lunch, but she chewed away at it anyway. She would make an effort at conversation – how was my knitting coming along? – but I didn't know what to say to her. I couldn't understand why she'd chosen to do what she'd done – why she'd turned herself into this listless, bloated version of herself, thus changing the future – my future – into something shadow-filled and uncertain. I thought she'd done it on purpose. It didn't occur to me that she might have been ambushed.

It was mid-August: hot and oppressive. The cicadas sang in the trees, the dry pine needles crackled underfoot. The lake was ominously still, the way it was when thunder was gathering. My mother was dozing. I sat on the dock, slapping at the stable flies and worrying. I felt like crying, but I could not allow myself to do that. I was completely alone. What would I do if the dangerous thing – whatever it was – began to happen? I thought I knew what it might be: the baby would start to come out, too soon. And then what? I couldn't exactly stuff it back in.

We were on an island, there were no other people in sight, there was no telephone, it was seven miles by boat to the nearest village. I would have to start the outboard motor on our clunky old boat – I knew how to do this, though pulling the cord hard enough was almost beyond my strength – and go all the way to the village, which could take an hour. From there I could telephone for help. But what if the motor wouldn't start? That had been known to happen. Or what if it broke down on the way? There was a tool kit, but I'd learned only the most elementary operations. I could fix a shear pin, I could check a gas line; if those things didn't work I would have to row, or wave and yell at passing fishermen, if any.

Or I could use the canoe – put a stone in the stern to weight it down, paddle from the bow end, as I'd been taught. But that method would be useless in a wind, even a light wind: I wasn't strong enough to hold a course, I would be blown sideways.

I thought of a plan of last resort. I would take the canoe over to one of the small offshore islands – I could get that far, no matter what. Then I would set fire to the island. The smoke would be seen by a fire ranger, who would send a float plane, and I would stand on the dock in full view and jump up and down and wave a white pillowcase. This could not fail. The risk was that I would set the mainland on fire as well, by accident. Then I would end up in jail as an arsonist. But I would just have to do it anyway. It was either that, or my mother would... Would what?

Here my mind cut out, and I ran up the hill and walked softly past my sleeping mother and into the cabin, and got out the jar full of raisins, and made my way to the large poplar tree where I always went when I'd come to the edge of an unthinkable thought. I propped myself against the tree, crammed a handful of raisins into my mouth, and plunged into my favourite book.

This book was a cookbook. It was called *The Art of Cooking and Serving*, and I'd recently thrown over all novels and even *The Guide to Woodland Mushrooms* and devoted myself to it entirely. It was by a woman called Sarah Field Splint, a name I trusted. *Sarah* was old-fashioned and dependable, *Field* was pastoral and flowery, and *Splint* – well, there could be no nonsense and weeping and hysteria and doubts about the right course of action with a woman called Splint by your side. This book dated from the olden days, ten years before I was born; it had been put out by the Crisco company, a manufacturer of vegetable shortening, at the beginning of the Depression, when butter had become expensive – said my mother – so all the recipes in it had Crisco in them. We always had lots of Crisco on the island, because butter went bad in the heat. Crisco on the other hand was virtually indestructible. In the long ago, before she'd started expecting, my mother had used it to make pies, and her writing could be found here and there among the recipes: *Good*!! she'd written. Or, *Use half white, half brown.*

It wasn't the recipes that held me in thrall, however. It was the two chapters at the front of the book. The first was called "The Servantless House," the second "The House with a Servant." Both of them were windows into another world, and I peered through them eagerly. I knew they were windows, not doors: I couldn't get in. But what entrancing lives were being lived in there!

Sarah Field Splint had strict ideas on the proper conduct of life. She had rules, she imposed order. Hot foods must be served *hot*, cold foods *cold*. "It just has to be done, however it is accomplished," she said. That was the kind of advice I needed to hear. She was firm on the subject of clean linen and shining silver. "Better never to use anything but doilies, and keep *them* immaculately fresh, than to cover the table for even one meal with a cloth having a single spot on it," she ordered. We had oilcloth on our table, and stainless steel. As for doilies, they were something beyond my experience, but I thought it would be elegant to have some.

Despite her insistence on the basics, Sarah Field Splint had other, more flexible values. Mealtimes must be enjoyed; they must have charm. Every table must have a centrepiece: a few flowers, an arrangement of fruits. Failing that, "some tiny ferns combined with a bit of partridge vine or other coloured woodsy thing in a low bowl or delicate wicker basket" would do the trick.

How I longed for a breakfast tray with a couple of daffodils in a bud vase, as pictured, or a tea table at which to entertain "a few choice friends" – who would these friends be? – or, best of all, breakfast served on a side porch, with a lovely view of "the winding river and the white church spire sailing out of the trees on the opposite bank." *Sailing* – I liked that. It sounded so peaceful.

All of these things were available to the house with no servant. Then came the servant chapter. Here too Mrs. Splint was fastidious, and solidly informative. (You could tell she was *Mrs.* Splint; she was married, though without sloppy consequences, unlike my mother.) "One can transform an untidy, inexperienced girl into a well-groomed, professional servant if one is patient and kind and fair," she told me. *Transform* was the word I seized on. Did I want to transform, or to be transformed? Was I to be the kind homemaker, or the formerly untidy maid? I hardly knew.

There were two photographs of the maid, one in daytime dress, with white shoes and stockings and a white muslin apron – what was muslin? – and the other in an afternoon tea and dinner outfit, with black stockings and organdy collar and cuffs. Her expression in both pictures was the same: a gentle little half-smile, a straight-ahead, frank, but reserved gaze, as if she was waiting for instructions. There were faint dark circles under her eyes. I couldn't tell whether she looked amiable, or put-upon, or merely stupefied. She'd be the one to get blamed if there was a spot on the tablecloths or a piece of silver less than gleaming. All the same, I envied her. She was already transformed, and had no more decisions to make.

I finished the raisins, closed the book, wiped my sticky hands on my shorts. Now it was time for more knitting. Sometimes I forgot to wash my hands and got brown raisin stains on the white wool, but that could be corrected later. Ivory Soap was what Mrs. Splint always used; it was good to know such a thing. First I went down to the garden and broke off some pea vine and a handful of red flowers from the scarlet runner beans, for the centrepiece it was now my duty to arrange. The charm of my centrepiece would not however cancel out the shabbiness of our paper napkins: my mother insisted they be used at least twice, to avoid waste, and she wrote our initials on them in pencil. I could imagine what Mrs. Splint would think of this grubby practice.

How long did all of this go on? It seemed forever, but perhaps it was only a week or two. In due course my father returned; a few maple leaves turned orange, and then a few more; the loons gathered together, calling at night before their fall migration. Soon enough we went back to the city, and I could go to school again in the normal way.

I'd finished the layette, all except the one bootie that was the responsibility of my mother – would the baby have the foot of a swan? – and I wrapped it in white tissue paper and put it in a drawer. It was a bit lopsided and not entirely clean – the raisin smears lingered – but you couldn't tell when it was folded.

My baby sister was born in October, a couple of weeks before I turned twelve. She had all the right fingers and toes. I threaded the pink ribbon into the eyelets in the layette and sewed together the rosettes for the bonnet, and the baby came home from the hospital in the proper manner and style. My mother's friends came over to visit, and admired my handiwork, or so it appeared. "You did all this?" they said. "Almost all," I said modestly. I didn't mention my mother's failure to complete her own minor task.

My mother said she'd hardly had to lift a finger, I'd gone at the knitting just like a beaver. "What a good little worker," said the friends; but I got the impression they thought it was funny.

The baby was cute, though in no time flat she outgrew my layette. But she didn't sleep. As soon as you put her down she'd be wide awake and wailing: the clouds of anxiety that had surrounded her before she was born seemed to have entered into her and she would wake up six or seven or eight or nine times a night, crying plaintively. This didn't go away in a few months, as Dr. Spock's *Baby and Child Care* said it would. If anything, it got worse.

From having been too fat, my mother now became too thin. She was gaunt from lack of sleep, her hair dull, her eyes bruised-looking, her shoulders hunched over. I did my homework lying on my back with my feet up on the baby's crib, jiggling it and jiggling it so my mother could get some rest. Or I would come home from school and change the baby and bundle her up and take her out in her pram, or I would pace back and forth, pressing her warm, fragrant, wriggling flannelette body against my shoulder with one hand while holding a book up with the other, or I would take her into my room and rock her in my arms and sing to her. Singing was particularly effective. *Oh my darling Nellie Gray, they have taken you away, and I'll never see my darling any more*, I would sing. Or else the "Coventry Carol" from junior choir:

> *Herod the King, in his raging,*
> *Charged he hath this day,*
> *His men of might, in his own sight,*
> *All children young, to slay.*

The tune was mournful, but it put her right to sleep.

When I wasn't doing those things, I had to clean the bathroom or do the dishes.

My sister turned one, I became thirteen; now I was in high school. She turned two, I became fourteen. My girlfriends at school – some of them were fifteen already – were loitering on the way home, talking to boys. Some of them went to the movies, where they picked up boys from other schools; others did the same at skating rinks. They exchanged views on which boys were real dolls and which were pills, they went to drive-ins on double dates with their new steadies and ate popcorn and rolled around in the back seats of cars, they tried on strapless dresses, they attended dances where, drowning in swoony music and the blue light of darkened gymnasiums, they shuffled around mashed up against their partners, they necked on the couch in their rec rooms with the TV on.

I listened to the descriptions of all this at lunch hour, but I couldn't join in. I avoided the boys who approached me: somehow I had to turn away, I had to go home and look after the baby, who was still not sleeping. My mother dragged around the house as if she was ill, or starving. She'd been to the doctor about the baby's sleeplessness, but he'd been no help. All he said was, "You've got one of *those*."

From being worried, I now became surly. I escaped from the dinner table every night as soon as I could, I shut myself in my room and answered questions from my parents with grudging monosyllables. When I wasn't doing homework or chores or baby-tending I would lie on my bed with my head hanging over the edge, holding up a mirror to see what I looked like upside down.

One evening I was standing behind my mother. I must have been waiting for her to get out of the bathroom so I could try out something or other on myself, a different shampoo most likely. She was bending over the laundry hamper, hauling out the dirty clothes. The baby started to cry. "Could you go and put her to sleep?" she said, as she had done so often. Ordinarily, I would trudge off, soothe, sing, rock.

"Why should I? "She's not *my* baby. I didn't have her. You did." I'd never said anything this rude to her. Even as the words were coming out of my mouth I knew I'd gone too far, though all I'd done was spoken the truth, or part of it.

My mother stood up and whirled around, all in one movement, and slapped me hard across the face. She'd never done that before, or anything remotely like it. I didn't say anything. She didn't say anything. We were both shocked by ourselves, and also by each other.

I ought to have felt hurt, and I did. But I also felt set free, as if released from an enchantment. I was no longer compelled to do service. On the outside, I would still be helpful – I wouldn't be able to change that about myself. But another, more secret life spread out before me, unrolling like dark fabric. I too would soon go to the drive-in theatres, I too would eat popcorn. Already in spirit I was off and running – to the movies, to the skating rinks, to the swooning blue-lit dances, and to all sorts of other seductive and tawdry and frightening pleasures I could not yet begin to imagine.

DINGLES

Alice Boissonneau

The old grandmother sitting there in the sunlight, holding a baby on her knee, wears a black shawl around her head as in the Old Country. Smiles a warm radiant smile from her dark eyes as I pass, that rises like the first heat of spring coming up through the ground and thawing snow, melting the bones.

The street is grey with the plaster houses and the doorways, crowded, revealing dark interiors. Everyone lives close to the street, the flow of Italian is dark and warm, figures of people show black like beetles against the walls. Everything is close, the little tinkling bell of the grocery just a hand's-breadth away dingles in your mind...

THE CHISELLER

MORLEY CALLAGHAN

Old Poppa Tabb was never really cut out to be a manager for a fighter. He seemed too short and too fat, although he'd only got soft around the waist during the last year as Billy got a lot of work in the small clubs, fighting at the flyweight limit. If it hadn't been for his old man, Billy would have been a chesty little bum standing at night on street corners spitting after cops when they passed. The old man and Billy were both the same size – five foot two in their bare feet – only the old man weighed one hundred and thirty-five pounds and Billy one hundred and twelve.

Poppa Tabb had always wanted his son to amount to something and didn't like the stories he heard about his son being chased by policemen. It hurt him when Billy was sent down for three months for tripping a cop and putting the boots to him. So he thought his son might want to be a fighter and he made an arrangement with a man named Smooth Cassidy, who was very experienced with young fighters, to act as Billy's trainer and handler, and he himself held the contract as the manager. After Billy started fighting in the small clubs, Poppa Tabb bought two white sweaters with "Billy Tabb" on the back in black letters, one for himself and one for Smooth Cassidy. It was at this time that Poppa Tabb began to get a little fat around the waist. He used to sit over in the sunlight by the door of the fire hall and tell the firemen about Billy. He used to sit there and talk about "me and Billy," and have a warm glowing feeling down deep inside.

Late at night he used to wait for Billy to come home from drinking parties with fast white women. He waited, walking up and down the narrow hall of their flat, and he shook his head and imagined that Billy had gotten into an accident. When Billy came in and started to take off his shoes, Poppa Tabb, sitting opposite him, was so worried he said: "I don't want you strolling your stuff so late, Billy."

Billy looked at him. Standing up and coming closer, he said to his old man: "You tryin' to get on me?"

"No, only I know what's good for you, son."

"Yeah. Maybe I know what's good for me. Maybe I know you ain't so good for me."

"There're some things you got to do, Billy."

Billy raised his fist. "You want something? You want some of this?"

"You don't go hitting me, Billy."

"Say you want some and I smack you. Or get off me."

After that, when Billy came in late Poppa Tabb just looked at his bright sharp eyes and smelled the cologne on his clothes and couldn't say anything to him. He only wished that Billy would tell him everything. He wanted to share the exciting times of his life and have the same feeling, talking to him, that he got when he held up the water pail and handed the sponge to Smooth Cassidy when he was at ringside.

Billy did so well in the small clubs that bigger promoters offered him work. But they always talked business with Smooth Cassidy, and Poppa Tabb felt they were trying to leave him out. Just before Billy fought Frankie Genaro, the flyweight champion, who was willing to fight almost anyone in town because the purses for flyweights were so small, Poppa Tabb heard stories that Dick Hallam, who liked owning pieces of fighters, was getting interested in Billy and was taking him out to parties. At nights now Billy hardly ever talked to his old man, but still expected him to wait on him like a servant.

Old Poppa Tabb was thinking about it the afternoon of the Genaro fight and he was so worried he went downtown looking for Billy, asking the newsboys at the corner, old friends of Billy's, if they had seen him. In the afternoon, Billy usually passed by the newsstand and talked with the boys till smaller kids came along and whispered, staring at him. Poppa Tabb found Billy in a diner looking to see if his name had gotten into the papers, thrusting big forkfuls of chocolate cake into his wide mouth. The old man looked at him and wanted to rebuke him for eating the chocolate cake but was afraid, so he said: "What's happening Billy?"

"Uh," Billy said.

The old man said carefully: "I don't like this here talk about you stepping around too much with that Hallam guy."

"You don't?" Billy said, pushing his fine brown felt hat back on his narrow brow and wrinkling his forehead. "What you going do 'bout it?"

"Well, nothing, I guess, Billy."

"You damn right," Billy said flatly. Without looking up again he went on eating cake and reading the papers intently as if his old man hadn't spoken to him at all.

The Genaro fight was an extraordinary success for Billy. Of course, he didn't win. Genaro, who was in his late thirties, went into a kind of short waltz and then clutched and held on when he was tired, and when he was fresh and strong he used a swift pecking left hand that cut the eyes. But Billy liked a man to come in close and hold on, for he put his head on Genaro's chest and flailed with both hands, and no one could hold his arms. Once he got in close, his arms worked with a beautiful tireless precision, and the crowd, liking a great body-puncher, began to roar, and Poppa Tabb put his head down and jumped around, and then he looked up at Billy, whose eye was cut and whose lips were thick and swollen. It didn't matter whether he won the flyweight title, for soon he would be a bantamweight, and then a featherweight, the way he was growing.

Everybody was shouting when Billy left the ring, holding his bandaged hands up high over his head, and he rushed up the aisle to the dressing room, the crowd still roaring as he passed through the seats and the people who tried to touch him with their hands. His gown had fallen off his shoulders. His seconds were running on ahead shouting: "Out of the way! Out of the way!" and Billy, his face puffed, his brown body glistening under the lights, followed, looking straight ahead, his wild eyes bulging. The crowd closed in behind him at the door of the dressing room.

Poppa Tabb had a hard time getting through the crowd for he couldn't go up the aisle as fast as Billy and the seconds. He was holding his cap tightly in his hands. He had put on a coat over his white "Billy Tabb" sweater. His thin hair was wet as he lurched forward. The neckband of his shirt stuck up from under the sweater and a yellow collar button shone in the lamplight. "Let me in, let me in," he kept saying, almost hysterical with excitement. "It's my kid, that's my kid." The policeman at the door, who recognized him, said: "Come on in, Pop."

Billy Tabb was stretched out on the rubbing-table and his handlers were working over him. The room smelled of liniment. Everybody was talking. Smooth Cassidy was sitting at the end of the table, whispering with Dick Hallam, a tall thin man. Old Poppa Tabb stood there blinking and then moved closer to Billy. He did not like Hallam's gold rings and his pearl-grey felt hat and his sharp nose. Old Poppa Tabb was afraid of Hallam and stood fingering the yellow collar button.

"What's happening, Pop?" Hallam said, smiling expansively.

"Nothing," Pop said, hunching his shoulders and wishing Billy would look at him. They were working on Billy's back muscles and his face was flat against the board. His back rose and fell as he breathed deeply.

"Have a cigar, Pop!" Hallam said.

"No thanks."

"No? My man, I got some good news for you," he said, flicking the end of his nose with his forefinger.

"You got no good news for me," Poppa Tabb said, still wishing Billy would look up at him.

"Sure I do. Billy gonna be big in a few months and I'm gonna take his contract over – most of it, anyway – and have Cassidy look after him. So he won't be needing you no more."

"What you say?" Old Poppa Tabb said to Cassidy.

"It's entirely up to you, Poppa Tabb," Cassidy said, looking down at the floor.

"Yes sir, Billy made good tonight and I'm going to take a piece of him," Hallam said, glancing down at the shiny toes of his shoes. "The boy'll get on when I start looking after him. I'll get stuff for him you couldn't touch. He needs my influence. A guy like you can't expect to go on taking a big cut on Billy."

"So you going to butt in?" Poppa Tabb said.

"Me butt in? That's ripe, seeing you never did nothing but butt in on Billy."

"I'm sticking with Billy," Poppa Tabb said. "You ain't taking no piece of him."

"Shut your face," Billy said, looking up suddenly.

"Shut your face is right," Hallam said. "You're through buttin' in."

"You don't fool me none, Hallam. You just after a cut on Billy."

"You just another old guy trying to chisel on his son," Hallam said scornfully.

Billy was sitting up listening, his hands held loosely in his lap. The room was hot and smelled of sweat. Old Poppa Tabb, turning, went to put his hand on Billy's shoulder. "Tell him to beat it, Billy," he said.

"Keep your hands off. You know you been buttin' in all my life."

"Sure I have, Billy. I been there 'cause I'm your pop, Billy. You know how it's always been with me. I don't take nothing from you. I don't take a red cent. I just stick with you, Billy. See? We been big together."

"You never went so big with me," Billy said.

"Ain't nothing bigger with me than you, Billy. Tell this hustler to run." Again, he reached to touch Billy's shoulder.

"You insult my friend, you got no call," Billy said. He swung a short right to his father's chin. Poppa Tabb sat down on the floor. He was ready to cry but kept on looking at Billy, who was glaring at him.

"Goddamn, he your old man," Hallam said.

"He can get out. I done with him."

"Sure you are. He'll get out."

They watched Smooth Cassidy help Poppa Tabb get up.

"What you going to do about this?" Smooth Cassidy muttered to him. "You ought to be able to do something, Poppa."

Old Poppa Tabb shook his head awkwardly. "No, there's nothing, Smooth."

"But he your boy, and it's up to you."

"Nothing's up to me."

"It all right with you, Poppa, then it all right with me," Cassidy said, stepping back.

Old Poppa Tabb's jaw fell open. He did not move.

"Well, that be that," Hallam said. He took a cigar out of his pocket, looked at it and suddenly thrust it into Poppa Tabb's open mouth. "Have a cigar," he said.

Poppa Tabb's teeth closed down on the cigar. The crowd had gone and the big building was empty. It was dark down by the ring. He didn't look at anything. The unlighted cigar stuck out of his mouth as he went out the big door to the street.

IMPOSSIBLE TORONTO

H. MASUD TAJ

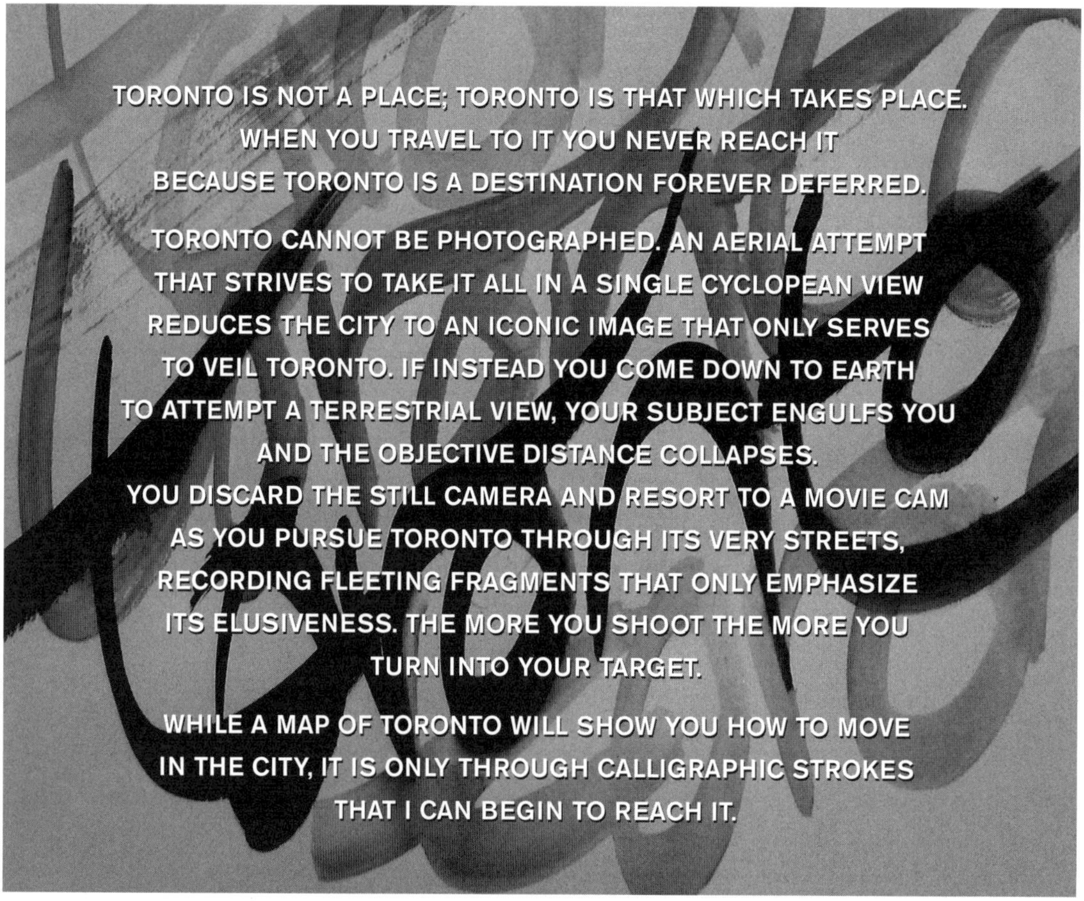

WHAT TO WEAR

Greg Kearney

I can't – I cannot – wear what I'm wearing to meet my sister.

I pivot in the mirror. I try different poses. Laconically slouched. Balletically balanced, chest out and shoulders back. It doesn't matter. I still look like hell.

From the neck up is okay. My hair is buzzed down to bristle. My face is angular, hollow-cheeked. So that's all fine and good. From the neck up, I look like an elite athlete. But from the neck down, well. That's another thing altogether.

This T-shirt exposes my thin, vascular arms. It clings to my round, hard gut that juts out at impossible angles. Looks like I'm smuggling an oven. I'm trying to think – do I own a poncho? Do I dare wear a poncho? Jutting gut or poncho? Jutting gut or poncho? It's such a "Sophie's Choice."

The last time my sister saw me, eight years ago, I had a perfect body, a waterfront condo, a daily column in the city's best and biggest newspaper, two nervous Weimaraners, and a beautiful Spanish boyfriend who was prone to rectal prolapse. I'm sure Sheila didn't know that last bit about the prolapse, unless Javier told her. They really hit it off, and Javier only knew a handful of English words and phrases. *That is interesting. I am fine. Herpes. How dare you!* And, of course, *rectal prolapse.* So I guess it might have slipped out in conversation. In any case, Sheila worshipped me, and was envious of all that I had.

Back then, Sheila was trying to be an actress. She had played the Diane Keaton part in *Crimes of the Heart,* her last year of theatre school. A talent agent saw her performance and took her on as a client. The agent sent her out on countless auditions, but Sheila never got work. Supposedly her agent said that the casting people invariably said that Sheila looked "too intellectual," even though she isn't intellectual. At all.

Floundering, Sheila asked if she could borrow some money. I immediately agreed. I always help her out. Our mother died young and our father is an iceberg, so I've always felt responsible for her.

I asked why she needed money. She said she *had* to get a nose job. She said her life would be worthless if she didn't get a nose job.

We were standing around the marble island in my old kitchen. "A nose job," I said aloud. Javier nodded understandingly, understanding nothing. I looked heavenward, pondering.

"I'm sorry," I said. "I can't facilitate self-mutilation."

"But it's not self-mutilation," Sheila said. "A doctor will be doing it, not me."

"I'm sorry. Way too many gay men have been responsible for making women look ridiculous. I have to buck the trend."

"It's not really a trend. It's my life. It's my livelihood."

"I'm sorry, Sheila. I don't agree with cosmetic surgery. Period."

"Fine. You can be a rich fag with everything, and I'll just fucking die. In the gutter."

She stormed out. I called and called, for several months. She never picked up, never called back. What more could I do? I was saddened, I missed her – perhaps total independence was for the best.

I got shingles, all down the right side of my chest, so bad it made my doctor wince. He tested me for HIV, it came back positive. And I only had 205 T-cells. He put me on the cocktail. It made me sick for months. I had no health insurance. I burned through all my savings. Javier literally went out for milk and never came back. I sold the condo.

An AIDS Committee volunteer, this nice older woman, ran errands for me and walked Ike and Tina, my dogs. I had never really bonded with them. They were always so yappy and frenetic, and now that I was sick I just wanted to drown them. So I asked the woman if she wanted them. They seemed to like her better anyway. She took them and renamed Ike Marty. Marty and Tina. They sound like Palm Springs swingers. But supposedly Marty comes when she calls.

So here I am, getting by on disability, living in a co-op that houses poor people with HIV. And I stand, before my mirror, assessing my body in fluorescent light. The meds caused lipodystrophy, sucking the fat from my face and arms and legs and plopping it on my midsection. I feel like a monster. I mean, I am glad that I survived. I just don't want to look so blatantly like a survivor.

I am a member of an internet dating site for men with HIV.

After months of silently lurking, a few weeks ago, I started chatting online with a guy in my area. Twenty-six, a chef, good grammar and spelling. He sent me a pic – cute as a button. I sent him a pic that I took of myself last year, black-and-white, head and shoulders. He wrote back right away, said I was handsome. We agreed to meet. At Woody's. I'll be the one in the black-and-white striped sweater, I wrote.

I was early. I had two pints before I saw him. He looked at me. Kept on walking. Seemed to circle the bar. I was sure he'd leave. But he came back to my table and said hello. He was wearing a pendant made from a hearing aid.

"Are you Ron?" he said.

"Hi," I said, "Kieran?"

"How's it going?"

"Good. Can I get you a drink?"

"Oh. No. That's okay. Thanks." He took a stool and sat. Smiled at me. Stopped smiling abruptly.

"So," I said. "I like your necklace. Where did you get it?"

"A friend made it."

"Oh. Anyone I might have heard of?"

He did his smiling/stop smiling thing again. "Listen," he said. "I'm a very candid person."

"Good," I said. "That's a good way to be."

"Yeah. So. I have to say. I'm looking for someone who's kind of... how do I say it?"

"Candidly?" I said.

"I'm looking for someone who's kind of at the same stage of the journey. You know?"

"Oh. You said in your ad that you were looking for someone older."

"Yeah. No. I am. I guess I should say I'm looking for someone at the same stage of HIV journey."

"Oh. What stage are you at?"

His eyes scanned the ceiling. "You know. I'm totally healthy. And happy. And, you know, unhindered. In any way. By HIV."

"Me, too."

"Right. But you've, I think, had it longer than me."

"Yeah. Probably."

"And you had to take some of the earlier drugs."

"I don't know. Yeah."

"Right. So I haven't had to deal with that. With the earlier drugs and the – you know. Deformity or whatever."

He said *deformity*. I tried to be radiant and smile sagely, inured to insult. But I wanted to kick his head in. I had perceived myself as weathered. Grizzled, maybe. But deformed?

Am I deformed?

Say I'm deformed. Am I unequivocally, empirically deformed? Or is deformity a mutable thing, its official definition changing over time? Is deformity sexy, sometimes?

This is the dreck that keeps me up at night. I was handsome. Now I wear a girdle and eye shadow. Somebody told me that eye shadow makes all your other features incidental. I wear lots and lots of eye shadow.

Kieran put his hand over mine and wished me luck. Then he left. I got very drunk and went home with an older guy. We did it in his garage so as not to wake his mother.

So last week, over the phone, I told my father that I had HIV. Not because I thought he should know, or for his support. It was just something to say. Something that might make him pause before he went on again about his riding lawnmower.

"I've got HIV, eh?" I said.

"Huh. What's that?"

"The virus that causes AIDS."

"Oh. Yeah. Hugh. How'd you get in that jackpot?"

"I don't know. The usual way."

"Well. Isn't that something."

"Yeah."

"You still got those skinny dogs?"

"No."

I thought that was the end of it. but my news must have made an impression on him, because he called Sheila and told her that I had AIDS. She called me yesterday. "Ron. Ron? Ron! How are you, my love?"

"I'm okay. How are you?"

"I'm good. Dad told me that you haven't been well." Sheila sounded like she was on speed. "Dad-told-me-that-you-haven't-been-well" – it was all one quick word, the way she said it.

"What?" I said. "Oh. No. I'm fine. You mean the HIV?"

"Yeah! Yeah-yeah-yeah. Dad said you're – you're living with AIDS."

"No. no. I'm just HIV-positive. I'm completely fine."

"And what about your – oh! You know what? This is craziness. I have to see you. Let me come over right now."

"Yeah! But I have company right now. So."

"That is so great. I'm glad you're not all alone. What about tomorrow? I'll pick you up for lunch. Are you still on the waterfront there?"

"No. I'm at the Margaret Laurence co-op. On Dalhousie."

"Oh. Is that an artists' co-op?"

"Kind of."

"That's so fun!"

I pick out a blousy T-shirt. I walk downstairs, check my mail, and then go outside to wait for Sheila. She drives up in a new yellow car. An ugly Nissan-something, but new nonetheless.

She waves. I wave. I remember to walk toward her car.

She's a twig. Ninety-five pounds, tops. Her lithe, little bicep flexes on the gearshift. Her hair is rotten-tomato red. She's wearing a tiny, orange terrycloth tank top and matching shorts. "Don't you look handsome!" she says.

"You look good too. You're so tiny."

"I know. I'm so busy. I never have me time. I just forget to eat."

"What are you – are you still acting?"

She lets out this long, fake laugh. The car swerves a little. "No! No. Didn't Dad tell you?"

"No. we don't really talk about anything. I'm surprised he told you about me."

"Hmm. I think he's a bit more forthcoming with me. But. Yeah. I'm a personal trainer now."

"Oh! Wow. That's great. Do you work out of a gym?"

"I do. Yes. But I also have established quite a client base. Including – do you know Jaclyn Smith?"

"Really? Wow. I didn't know she lived in Toronto."

"She doesn't. But her former housekeeper, Arlene, she now lives in Toronto and has a very successful custom-made jewellery business. I've helped her meet and exceed all of her fitness goals. My advanced Kegel exercises were so effective, she cancelled her vaginal rejuvenation surgery and actually complained that her vagina was *too* tight. I'm sure she was kidding. Although she does often look like she is in physical pain."

I don't know where we're going. We run an amber light.

"Should you be telling me all this?" I say.

"Oh, she wouldn't care. She's an open book. She's great. She is a dear, dear, dear, dear, dear friend."

We're in the right lane, about to turn right, when we're broadsided by a minivan. The Nissan is thrust up and over the curb and into a mailbox. We both buck to the side. I clutch my chest. Sheila is gasping and pounding her palms on the dash. "Oh my God," she says. "This is just perfect. Fuck me with a chainsaw! Fuck! Fuck! Fuck!"

"Are you alright?" I ask.

"Me? What about my fucking car? My fucking brand new Altima!" She kicks open her door. An elderly woman is slowly getting out of the other vehicle. She has a gash on her forehead.

"What the fuck are you doing, fuckface?" Sheila screams.

"I'm so sorry," the old woman says. "I don't know what happened."

"You fucked up my brand new car is what happened!"

"I have my chequebook with me," the lady says. "Let's go to the car, uh, repair and get an estimate. I'll write you a cheque."

By now I've gotten out of the car. I'm standing between Sheila and the old lady, whose blood is seeping from the forehead gash and is streaked across her brow zigzaggy like New Wave makeup.

"Oh no-no-no-no-no," Sheila says. "You fucked up my new car, I'm going to fuck up your insurance premiums. We're doing this by the book."

"Please. I'm so sorry. I lost my husband recently. I'm 78 years old. I'd – please, I can write you a cheque for whatever it will cost. I don't feel so good."

Sheila does an odd, shivering pivot on one foot. "You are not hearing me! Look what you have done! To my car!"

The old woman starts to cry.

"Yeah, you'd better cry. I'm gonna fuck you up!" Sheila starts rehearsing with some air karate. A high kick. A left chop. I grab her hands and pull her to me.

"What's wrong with you?" I say. "Are you on drugs?"

"No, I'm not on drugs! I'm – my car is wrecked. And I'm standing up for myself. Drug use is not an issue here. Everybody does a little meth now and then. Everybody does a little meth. And I'm pissed off. I want. Justice!"

The old lady is starting to sway. The blood no longer looks like New Wave makeup; the blood – streaming down her face, staining her Peter Pan collar – looks like car-crash blood.

And so I do what a gallant man would do: I incautiously whip off my shirt, bunch it up, and press it to the woman's wound. The sun stings my clammy, bluish-white chest and back.

"Thank you, that's helping," says the old lady. "You're a nice man. How can one be so kind and the other one be so..."

"So what?" snaps my sister. "So righteous? So strong? Fuck. Once again, male privilege wins out, the dude takes his fucking shirt off and he's a big hero. But me? Fuck. Just mail me to Iraq and cut off my clit, why don't ya?"

"Okay," I say. "We've just had a little accident. Nobody's a hero, nobody's getting their clit cut off."

Sheila hyperventilates for a spell, then starts to sob in tandem with the old lady.

I'm mediating here. I never used to mediate. I used to exacerbate. I used to tell one writer friend that another writer friend thought that the work of the first writer friend was puerile and uninspired, and then tell the second writer friend that the first writer friend said essentially the same thing about the second writer friend's work, even if nothing of the sort was said. All so I could watch them ignore each other aggressively at the next wine-and-cheese thing.

Now I am a man with his shirt off. Even before I was deformed, back when my body was empirically beautiful, I never took off my shirt in public, except for that one time I did GHB at the White Party in Miami. But right now, I am an oddly shaped, shirtless man with his sickly stick arms around two tearful women, northeast corner of Pape and Gerrard. I hold them close and whisper reassurance, the stuff a straight man would offer his panicked girlfriend. "'S okay, baby. We're all okay. We're so chill."

I kind of like this new, provisional persona. I will play it for all it's worth – beer-gutted, splay-legged, gruff, certain, burpy – at least until the ambulance arrives, when I will likely drape myself in an emergency blanket. Unless one of my "girls" needs the blanket more, of course.

HITTING THE CHARTS

LEON ROOKE

Last night I was out doing the boogie.

Nothing at The Ruptured Duck, not much at Teen Town or The Gypsy Moth, but at The Hot Wire I read the vibes, contemplated my juices, and determined I was all set to get lucky.

My hour had been a long time coming.

It was a case of *Go Daddy Go*, or *macho macho* and *Disco Duck*, or give your heart to Old Mother Nature and *let the cool lady sink you on down.*

I got no money
and I got no friend.
Me by my lonely
and nearing the end.
I got no wife
and I got no love.
Me by my lonely
Living push and shove.

I located a lovely person, foxy # with drooping head, sitting alone at a table in a far corner the minute my eyelids cooled. This is the life, Dad, I told myself – and putting on my Ready For Anything face I hiked up my Truckstop Designer jeans and motored over.

"*Dance with me, Henry,*" I cried, and gave her The Look.

Without giving me a glance or saying a word she hoisted herself up and like a stately breeze headed out to the floor. I followed fast behind, chasing the scent of Wing Song by Prince Matchabelli, as the music wheeled into the high screech like a thousand jibjabs finally let out into the garden.

Ta-ta-tum ta-ta-tum, let the beat go on, I gave my hips their first twist and was off and running like a nag bolting the gate, throwing out my arms in a propeller spin so that no one could doubt which part of the floor was mine.

"I'm Jake," I told my partner on the up-breath, "how you making out?"

Nothing. Under her bangs her moon face looked like an opening cut out of a deep hedge. Never mind. I went up on first one toe and then the other, bending like green timber. In my high school days Jake B. Carlyle had been known as the eagle of the dance floor and it was all coming back after ninety-nine years.

Wang Wang Blues, I thought, and *Begin the Beguine, gonna take a sentimental journey.*

"You come here often?" I shouted.

No reply. Her sight was always on someone just behind me, never any movement up or down. Her noble head slid from shoulder to shoulder like a thing on tails.

"That's pretty groovy," I joked, "you pick that up in India?"

Not a flicker. Yet her very essence told me I was getting somewhere.

Butter in my hands, *yeah-yeah-yeah*!

I had come a long way in only a few hours. At the start of the evening the music had been like a rhino herd having a singalong with Mitch; I had left The Ruptured Duck and Teen Town a hippo on skateboards, but now I was hitting my stride. Jake, I told myself, your azimuth is in its five moons, Jupiter is high, and the time is yours! I had come through four repeat years at the Transcendental Meditation Centre, gone fourteen months with the Technocracy crowd, for twenty-seven years had been a devout Rosicrucian, and for one season had been a scrub guard for the House of David. Had spent half a lifetime kicking pigeons or just generally floundering about, but now my head was in place.

Daddy don't step on my Dr. Scholl's shoes because my clock has turned and the hour is ripe! I have weathered Frankie Laine's "Jezebel" and Spike Jones' "Beatlebomb" and my ears no longer extended to my feet. I was Fritz the Cat and purring out loud over all of discoland *Oh Mama we are the most, we are hot to trot tonight, your feet are on fire and Bo Diddley I ain't.*

The platter ripped to its demise. Strobe lights blinked and for an instant they let the tape deck cool. "Buy you a drink?" I said, and fifty arms shot up – though my own sweet dancing partner was nowhere to be seen.

I was bathed in black mud, a sightless knave. *Frail*, I thought, *oh frail is thy hand in mine, my fair Caithleeene*!

"Open the door, Richard," I cried, "oh Richard, open that door!"

Never mind. I was at home with these hard-to-get types and felt confident that before the evening ended I'd have her licking from my hands. Already I loved her air of indifferent and placid mystery, her aura of divine and mystic depth; I loved the way her hair bounced above expressionless ears and how her chin never dropped and how the light wheel grazed like sheep on her face. She was mine all mine and just the kind of sweet perfection I was looking for. *Mama Mama Mama*, I cried to the rafters, *treat me good*!

The platter spun anew and I quivered in my tracks, going solo for a while. Two or three of those I bumped gave me dirty looks and one in a feather-duster skirt and a strontium 90 smile murmured in my ear, "You better slow down, Pops, your face is snow-white, you definitely got lily-pad gills."

"I'm cooking with gas," I told this smiler, "no need to worry," and gave her a toad-footed spin that had her eyes tattling in her head.

Oh Jelly Roll roll, cream me no cream and butter me no butter.

I was beginning to get the feel of my digs. Beginning to realize what I had been missing out on by not doing the boogie scene long before. Beginning to regret all my tortured years of Monday Night Baseball and Friday Night poker and Saturday Night blues and the thousand bleak evenings sitting on my elbows.

Jake, I told myself, this is the high life, the real life, this is where it's at, old fossil-heart of mine, you're to turn over a new leaf dating from now.

No more 4 a.m. movies for me, with the final blip dropping like man's last breath across the snow-balled screen. No more weeping in the solitude of all my betrayals and longing for dawn's tender mercy to tuck me up in my drunken bed.

Oh frail is thy hand in mine, oh frail is your touch, my darling Caithleeene.

I was clearly cut out for this fine night-life. It was *Groovy Greybeard Groovy* and proper time I took off my age-old bib.

I grabbed a spin with loose flotsam whose date was spewing up Labatt's 50 in a corner, and kept her there for a full ten minutes while the gyroscopes wooed us with powerpack song and the smoke of cigarettes dropped from the black ceiling inch by inch and wrote death in the air with a thousand white signatures, and when finally she wiped off the sweat and said "Um tarred" I took my cues and hurried her back to her tongue-tied mate, murmuring *merci* and *toute la guerre* as a gentleman would, in the meantime keeping a wary eye out for my Dream Girl, the one fair lady in the whole of The Hot Wire whom I would woo and be wooed by and whom I would have.

But man is an island even at The Hot Wire and my Dream Girl was nowhere to be seen and it was all Lover's Lullaby for me.

I'll love her in the attic,
I'll love her in the cellar
I'll love her wherever
She's clearly ecstatic.

Oh frail your hand, Caithleeene. Oh your time was long time a-coming, Willie Mays.

I elbowed my way up to the black marble bar and told the cherub behind it to splash down in front of me whatever poison was nearest to hand, hang the expense, my son.

Set'um up Joe.

A man in a trench coat wide as a flag gave me a hearty slap on the shoulder and asked if I was from out of town, footloose and fancy-free the same as him. "Buffalo myself," he shouted, "USofA, city, county and nation built by God." But now and then, he confessed, he had to unwind. He fished out a card and waved it in front of me: CHARTERED ACCOUNTANTS, it read, FITZ, DIBBS AND SLIDE – We Have What Counts… "Dibbs," he said, throwing out a hand, "put'er there." He laughed, the joker, and went into a quick crouch, all better to goose a young lady just then passing by. The lady shrieked and spun, though not before Dibbs was again upright and innocently staring off into the dim yonder. The lady stared at my outstretched hand which Dibbs had refused, then reared back and smacked her mighty fist against my face.

"Reprobate," she snarled, and scooted on.

Oh Daddy shoot me with novocaine! Oh Mama, tell me the news!

"Works every time," snickered Dibbs. "I pulled that trick on Fitz one time and he lost three teeth." He grabbed at my arm, pulled me along: "Let's go visit the Men's. In this sumphole I can't hear myself think."

I was grateful, once reaching the Men's, for my Life by Riley platform heels. They let me tower over Dibbs, shorter than a barber pole and about as cool, and moreover kept my flared cuffs dry.

"Buffalo's all right," ventured Dibbs, looking for a high spot to perch, "but there are things a man can't do in his own home town. Too many Twinkies he has to look out for. In Buffalo, city of God, you wouldn't find me coming within a mile of a dump like this."

"Time waits for no man," I told this snake. "Shake, rattle, and roll." Scratches in the door behind which Dibbs hid himself told me to CALL GLORIA, first with the latest, last with the most. Stickers on the wall said NO NUKES and SAVE OUR SEALS AND REMEMBER PEARL HARBOR and GOD ADORES A TURKEY.

"A man's got to break out of a rut," Dibbs was telling me. "Got to get his arms around something unfamiliar now and then. You got a paper I could read? Mind you," he said, "the wife don't understand, but I say what the hell, a quick poke never hurt anyone. These young people now, not worth a crap, but they have the right idea. I tell you it's places like this that's keeping old Dibbs feeling young."

I sloshed down my gin, hardly listening to Dibbs, floating back to the action of wings of song, thinking how I had found and lost my thrill on Blueberry Hill, on Mood Indigo and Rock Island Line. Sock it to me, baby, I told old Dibbs, these shoes were made for walking, now who's got the smack?

"My daughter, seventeen," Dibbs went on. "Precious lamb, she's hot to trot for experience, can't wait to run off with the first dogcatcher sniffs up her skirt. Last week I caught her writing Ann Landers, complaining how her parents kept her penned up, 'they don't trust me,' she said. Oh I lit into her, I really told her where she stood. I smelt smoke the other day walking into her room, and my fist nearly took off her head. She'll think twice next time. She sees me taking a drink at home, asks 'Why can't I have one?' I tell you I've got blisters from the times I've had to smack that child. My daddy smacked me around, what do you think, that I'd disapprove? How else you imagine I got where I am?

Not long ago I came home, found some squirt kid trying to sneak away through the backyard. I pulled him back inside, punched his nose, kicked him in my den. My den is redwood panelled, most beautiful stuff you ever saw. I got fourteen rifles mounted, collector's items, every one in working order. Blow the head off a moose, great weapons, I tell you a person don't even have to aim. I said, 'There they are, kid, take your pick.' 'Whut, huh?' he said – I tell you kids today don't even know human speech. 'You got it, kid,' I told this squirt, 'the next time you come nosing round my daughter you going to get my .12 ought right between your eyes.' Oh that kid scrammed, I tell you we're raising nothing but chickens these days. In my day I'm proud to say I was mauling cherries all over town, me and jailbait had a natural attraction for each other. You think I don't know what's going on? What kids have in mind? Now the kooks you find in here, these laid-back dope fiends living off my tax if I actually lived here – if I found my daughter sleeping around like these kooks I'd choke her, no questions asked. She knows it too. Oh she toes the line. A sweet girl, a precious angel. You should have seen that letter she was writing Ann, just as proper as you please. Me, I'd spend a week on it and still not have the commas right. That's education, that's what I'm paying for. I mean, a parent's got to contribute, right? Out here, out in the real world, well it's all going to hell in a handbasket quicker than the eye can blink, wouldn't you say? But I've got faith, I'm a bundle of love, none of that negative crap for me."

Groovy, I thought, Oh Daddio, show me the way.

"Oh boy!" Dibbs said, jacking up his pants, "that felt good, third time I been today, healthy sign, wouldn't you say?" – and without a sprinkle of water over his hands but with time to slick back his receding hair he was off and running, leaping back into the fray. "I can still git it up," he shouted back, "don't think I can't." He crowded a friendly neighbour off a bar stool and scrambled up huffing, his brow shining with sweat, while a multitude of white gulls dipped their wings in a slow circle overhead, part of the décor that gave The Hot Wire its classy name. The beat was whining out of a half-dozen ceiling vents with a kamikaze craze and the floor was pounding and at the tables a hundred good-time voices were screeching in gratitude. It was meal time at the Oasis and I was with it, baby, I was Johnny on the Spot, old Johnnie B. Kool.

"Long may your willy ream," shouted Dibbs, now off to the dance floor, grabbing at every feline shape, "I've got more notches than Billy the Kid and I mean to dip it while the dippin's good."

Oh Mama, I thought, *Oh hunter home from the hill. Oh man in the Grey Flannel Suit. Oh make me a pallet on the floor. Oh it ain't me, babe*! Gyrating couples shook past under waves of yellow mauve and blue. I yearned to step forward and embrace each of them, to say *Oh you spinning swingers, what you see here is a man who takes his lessons from Father Time, from the Mole People who burrow every year in my yard.* September Song *and* Autumn Leaves *and* Some Enchanted Evening, *all that is smoke in my eyes. Shoot Tchaikovsky, give the mickey to Mahler, old B. is bleeding on the floor. I emerge each year newborn and ripe for action. I have shucked Paul Harvey's Decade of News, I'm Johnny Belinda On-the-Spot. Butter me no butter and Yule me no Yule, I want all your wooden nickels, old Dibbs and I will talk them into gold.*

Hubba-hubba, babe, wake up little Suzy, take me to the hop!

Oh frail is they hand in mine, how frail,

My fair Caithleeene.

A man with an undertaker's face, seated by the woman next on his list, leaned into my shoulder, said, "I'm from Saskatoon, that's my wife Munchie I'm with. Say hello to the nice man, Munchie." Munchie glowered, then showed her red tongue, pulling at my sleeve. "What a character," she said. "I was wed once and that was enough." I sank down beside this wind-swept pair, yearning for Saskatoon where I've never been, for the Mom and Pop I'd have there waiting for me to make something of my life. No doubt the woman I should have married was still waiting for me, waiting in Saskatoon. Her life had been ruined, mine too, because I hadn't had the good sense to stay where I was born and with what was good for me, this dream-time Saskatoon. She would have lived next door, would have initiated me gently into sex, would have urged me to put my life back together and not commit suicide after losing the race for high school presidency by 900 votes. *You can do it, Jake, I've always believed in you. Oh Jake, there's always next year. Oh Jake, you did this when they dropped you from the checkers team.* Happy kids, a sound business of my own, all waiting in Saskatoon. Big warm house, couple of cars, a good snowblower to keep our driveways clear.

I could have made it big in Saskatoon.

"Look at him," the undertaker man said. "Saskatoon's got him. Happens every time."

"Buy me some peanuts," his Munchie said, "how do you like my hair?"

Adios, Saskatoon.

When I hear you call... my love song... to me...

I went in search of my dream girl. I tapped the wrong beauty on the shoulder and the boyfriend rose up from his chair to stand on my toes. The music was loud and I didn't take in the advice he was giving, though his beauty's voice left no room for any misunderstanding: "Go suck eggs," she said. "Cock your leg up to a fire hydrant, buzz off, me and him are here to have us fun." Under these scrofulous urgings, I chuglugged on.

Oh broken-hearted melody, oh melancholy baby, I'm coming round the mountain yes I am.

The floor was solid concrete but I could feel it vibrating. Before the place became The Hot Wire it had been Elmo's Body & Fender Shop. Under this very ceiling where gulls circled and lights flashed 3000 times to the single blink Elmo's drab crew had put on a new grill and bumper, new radiator, new hood and paint job after my erstwhile wife, unable to give up sweets and tormented by broken fingernails, had tried to drive her Volkswagen through our very own front door. Lovely woman, she'd sat on the red seat screeching out through broken glass that there "*was not power enough under the hood!*" Then to back up and come again, knowing I was in there somewhere.

I'm all for you, body and soul.

Where was old Elmo now, I wondered. And erstwhile wife, where was she? They too ought to be here doing the boogie, didn't know what they were missing.

Dibbs punched me on the arm, shoved me back against a wall.

"Got change?" he demanded. "Any change?"

"Oh yeah, yeah," I said, and commenced digging.

"A dollar? Two dollars? My old lady don't take collect calls any more not since our oldest went yo-yo and cut out on us. Calls all the time, wants to speak to God. A fruitcake, can you imagine, my son!"

He scratched at my palm, took what change I had.

"Got to report in, you know," he explained, going. "Conference, you know! Midnight oil, what Dibbs won't do to keep together house and home!" He smacked his brow, came back at me again. "How you fixed? Anything to spare? A loan? Woman over there with the navel cut, skinny as a playing card, I asked her how much, she gave me the wink. Let you have seconds, what do you say?"

I plonked down a dollar into his hand. Added another.

"Go for quality tonight," I told him, "it's all on me."

Ah, your hand in mine, Caithleeene.

Dibbs was insulted, then thought better of it and gave me another of his bosomy slaps on the shoulder. "Great guy," he said. "I knew you were a great guy. One of the gang." Grinning, he tucked my two bucks inside his fat wallet, and strode off to make his call.

Ah, frail, Caithleeene, but a champion of love as we set off across endless dunes.

Up a lazy river, Caithleeene...

Rocky Mountain river fever, Caithleeene.

Rock of Ages, Caithleeene.

My erstwhile wife Rebecca June, driven into fits on account of my drivel and my habit of bending precious silverware and my eternal bad moods and my insistence on calling her *my frail Caithleeene.*

"Munchie's going!" someone shouted from across the room, and I looked up and there through air more shaded than the ocean floor was Saskatoon waving both arms, now pulling Munchie in front of me, shouting, "Munchie, say goodbye, Munchie, to the nice man!"

Munchie put her hands under her breasts and lifted them and blew me a kiss: "Goodbye, nice man!"

And I was moved, I was genuinely moved. I wept, and for the promise, even the promise, of a second kiss I would have followed her even *past* Saskatoon.

So much for your hand in mine, Caithleeene.

Dibbs came back. "No answer," he said.

"Ten o'clock, twelve o'clock," I told him. "Blue Moon, Standing on the Corner, Mercy, mercy, Mr. Percy."

"Guess she's out visiting her mother."

"Swing low," I said. "Looking over Jordan."

He spilled the coins back into my pocket. Slumped his shoulders. Ah yes, old Dibbs was subdued.

"Takes all the joy out," he said. "You never know what those bitches will do! Oh well, I'm turning in."

I took the door with him.

On the street, breathing fresh air, he shrugged and I shrugged, and each turned and headed off our separate ways.

Ah, frail your hand in mine, Caithleeene. Yours and Dibbs'. Sisters and brothers on the lam.

Shh-boom, shhh-boom... old buttermilk sky... Boo-boo-ba-boo of the night...

I got no money
and I got no friend.
Me by my lonely
and nearing the end.
I got no wife
and I got no love,
Me by my lonely
Living push and shove...

Two old ladies, arm in arm and peck-pecking their canes, looking straight ahead, were approaching me on the sidewalk.

Black glasses.

Blind.

I steered over, hugged back against a street-front door. Held my breath.

"Good evening, young man," the two together said.

They passed on.

Ah, frail, Caithleeene. Frail. But still here. Still mine.

CROW JANE'S BLUES

BARRY CALLAGHAN

Crow Jane, who was a singer in the local after-hours clubs, was walking down Spadina Avenue, her hands in her pockets. There were chrome studs on the lapels and cuffs of her jean jacket. It was nearly midnight but there were five bandy-legged boys playing stickball on the sidewalk in front of the Silver Dollar Show Bar and across the street, in the doorway beside the Crescent Lunch some immigrant women, probably cleaning-women, were huddled around a homeland newspaper. Their warm laughter touched the loneliness that Crow Jane had felt all week, a loneliness that left her with a listless sense of loss, but she wasn't sure about loss of what, and that was why she was out walking around her old haunts, looking into the show bars from the old days, threading her way through the late-night street hustlers who were standing half out in the street between the parked cars, and for a moment she felt good, seeing herself years ago the way she used to slow-walk down the street knowing where everything was, the upstairs bootlegger who kept the beautiful Chinese twin-sister hookers who put on a show every midnight, and over on Augusta Street, behind the fruit stalls, there was heavy-jowled Lambchops, the Polish-Jewish giant who hired himself out as muscle to the after-hours clubs. But then, watching a tall white girl in front of a hat shop, the way she primped her hair with pleasure as she caught her reflection in the glass, Crow Jane hunched up and put her head down, suddenly disconsolate. When she looked up, the girl was gone.

An empty bus pulled away from the curb and she turned and wandered back up the street, into the Silver Dollar Show Bar where a lithe black girl wearing a silver sequin halter dress was on the stand. Crow Jane sat in a darkened corner drawing circles on the tabletop in the dampness from ice-cold beer bottles, and as she sat listening, the revolving coloured lights made the singer look like several women at once, all of them afloat in a wash of light, and Crow Jane thought, *She's light, lighter than me, and I bet some slicker salesman gave her momma an old black and white TV to see those black breasts and this here's the daughter of that old black and white TV*, singing with her head back, eyes shut, opening memories up inside Crow Jane, the night long ago that she wore a dust-rose shirt and had gone up the two flights of stairs on College Street to the small dance hall where two big old women wearing sweatbands and bloated by bad food took tickets at the door. She'd danced with a narrow-hipped, long-legged white girl called EveLynn, and in the lingering light the white girl had said after they'd gone home and Crow Jane had sung for her in a moaning whisper just like this girl singing here in the Show Bar, *And yes,* she'd said, *in the lingering light is where I do like to touch, touch you, ten years ago almost, lying back on the white sheets of the big cannonball bed, her nipples small, the pinky-brown of white women, and yours are plum-coloured she'd said, lying in that bed every night, with her legs spread like a wishbone and, Baby,* I said, *I got sweetening's, I mean in my time I've sung the song, I been lying up with the shades down just holding on to holding on, but you come high-heel sneaking in your sling-backs into my life and now I got high on sunshine,* and the singer on the stand was isolated in a small spotlight, just her face, a black face on a white moon suspended for a moment in the noisy room, *But sunshine don't get it all the time 'cause a long time ago it was that I was with you, my little sweetenings, an' we got to always come home to the cabbage, which is why I always to this day every night sing the song how you were my love who brought me the cherry that had no stone, 'cause stones and cabbage is how I most remember my old beat-up hand-me-down days, when I be a little girl pedalling my fool self on my tricycle along the long hallway, dead end, man, I learned early to make the tight turn when you come to the end, so I see this girl so sharp up there in her spotlight of silver sequins looks like me in all the places I already been and turned back from, 'cause you see even my mind got hallways, I mean sometimes I lean back singing a song or lying up with another woman, all the good womens in this world, or poppin' pills, and them pills look like lemon-yellow bowling balls rolling down inside my head, an' sometimes when I get scared, when some sucker comes at me leering with the big hard-on in his eyes, I just sit there talking baby talk we used to talk, me an' EveLynn looking at each other side by side in the mirror, we used to prop the mirror on the bed, that blond hair of yours on my shoulder an' ever since then I got all the cabbages and none of the kings, an' I been down along the long hallway, pedalling on my tricycle with the bell on the handlebar that don't work, just goes fhzz fhzz like my daddy's old Ronson lighter that got no flint, railroad halls we called 'em, but nobody knows that no more 'cause nobody rides them trains, which is why I like the mouth harp sound, harmonica you called it, white words for black birds, lonesome trains and pain, that was my daddy since back then the onliest work a black man bagged was Pullman porter which my daddy was for a while till insomnia set him down, the clickity-clack inside his head he said, an' I mean he had the light on the whole time, he put pennies on his eyes when he went to sleep an' said I ain't dead, the light jess don't go out,* and Crow Jane, listening to the voice on the stand in the small room of the Show Bar, was reminded so much of herself that she decided she wanted to talk to the younger singer, thinking she'd buy the girl a drink, hold her hand a little like she was holding hands with herself, and scribbled a note inviting her to the table. Crow Jane gave it to the waiter. The singer read the note and with a shrug flicked it back behind the piano, *and that too is cabbage, boiled cabbage heads, the state of shredded stink, which is bigger than big, all the cabbage-stinking long halls of the world with a Raggedy-Ann kid on a tricycle going fhzz fhzz at the dead-end dirty window that don't look out on nothing but back alleys, mean mealy living, man, like Daddy drinking whisky which kept his eyeballs on all the time, bulbed outta his headbone before he died, looking on the lookout for what never was, only him always sitting on an afternoon with his hair konked to get it straight, looking at me he'd say, Sweet Thing, when you're black stay back an' if you're brown stick aroun' but if you're white you're right, all that sour self-laughter of him, an' sometimes when I was with that white girl, I think he did tell it true 'cause I loved her an' black weren't beautiful then, baby, nigger heaven was nowhere, there was just my old daddy sitting on his rusty dusty listening to the "Salt Pork Blues" on the old 78s, his hair straight with lye under the stocking cap and even then, me only being a little girl on the downside of ten, I saw that a grown man sitting with a woman's ugly rolled stocking like a circle of surgical tube on his head was weird, trying to dude himself into the land of seersucker soul, arctic power, whitener was what he was up to an' drove himself stone blind on booze an' left me, little girl sucking wind the day he died, gone down like the light comes up, always the lights come up, ole young girl up there singing so pretty, I got a baby way 'cross town who's good to me,* and then she stepped down, taking the hand of a lean black man wearing a knitted wool cap, strutting a silver-handled cane and a T-shirt that said SPADE POWER. Crow Jane liked that. *I can dig it, I can dig it,* and she laughed, wishing that she knew them but it was closing time and people rose and straggled out and Crow Jane suddenly had the feeling that all her past was emptying out of her head, leaving her alone at her table in the corner, staring at the rough ceiling painted black, the water pipes and heating ducts all exposed in the light, *And that one time, I don't know why me, but they put my picture in the paper, big, full-face, singing at a festival over on the island, an' I felt good an' I said, Daddy, you may be dead and down but there I be, I is, big as lightning on the page for all to see who I am 'cause I am, Crow Jane has sung the song, the fhzz, fhzz is finished an' I took that clipping from the paper, an' I said to myself, EveLynn, wherever you are hiding in this here old city with your kids or whatever, I'm looking you in the eyeball, big, and I am the queen of darktown and I may not be having a ball but I'm still strutting, an' I wanted it bigger, so I scissored out that head of myself and took it down to one of them blow-up-yourself picture places an' I say, man, I want this big for framing, hang myself over my head in my bed, two feet by three I said an' he shrugs, and when I come back there I am, mounted on cardboard, an' I can't find myself for the looking, my whole face just gone to great big grey and dark dots an' I say, where'd I go, man, I don't see myself at all, an' he says that's what happens when you blow yourself up outta some newspaper, you disappear into dots, 'cause if you look close that's all you was in the first place,* and so the only thing to do was go home, still wanting to take the singer's hand and hold it to her cheek, sweat and perfume on the woman's neck, and to look into the other woman's eyes like she was looking into a mirror, but when Crow Jane went by, walking slowly, it was like there was no silver on the glass, nothing there, and the singer looked right through her, leaving Crow Jane suddenly alone in the doorway, facing the darkness of the street in the cool early morning air. She walked up Spadina. A big milk transport truck rumbled by. She went past a closed restaurant in which a fat-bellied man was all alone swabbing the floors, wearing a stringy undershirt and torn pants, and he waved a grubby hand and when she shrugged with disdain he mouthed a curse at her through the glass. Fog had come in off the lake and she could hear her own footsteps in the empty street.

LOV

Ludwig

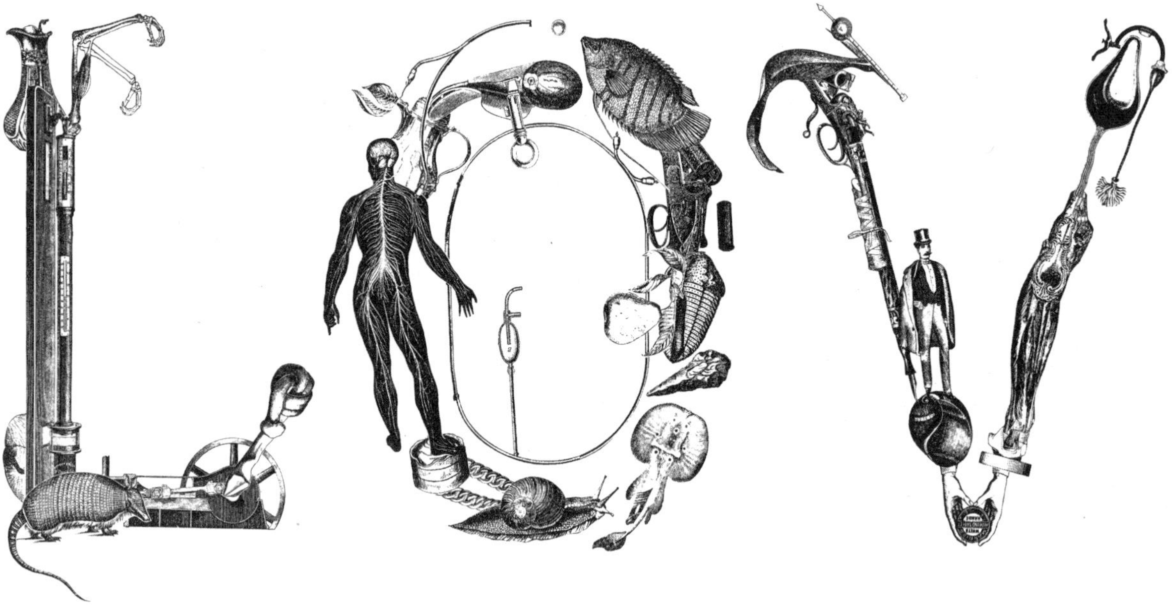

ERS

ZELLER

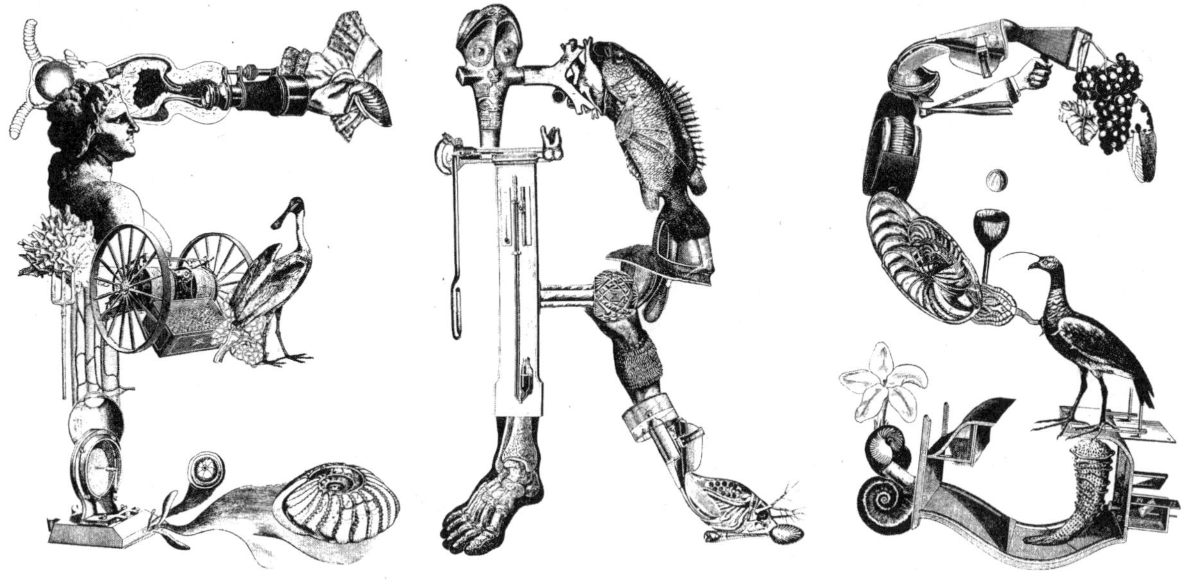

MRS. PUTNAM AT THE PLANETARIUM

JANICE KULYK KEEFER

Tuesdays Mrs. Putnam locked her flat, walked three city blocks to the subway; passed, with the sombre airiness of a ghost, through grilles and spokes and greedy-mouthed machines, and rode from Jane and Bloor to Museum. Rode in summer, when the cars were full of tourists with cameras clotting their necks and the pale yellow tiles made the station seem a morgue, ice under the hammer heat of asphalt overhead. Rode in winter when the closeness of the cars made Mrs. Putnam, in her Merino wool coat, her black mink toque, clammy, dizzy, ravaged like a book with pages razored out. Did not ride in spring and autumn since those flighty seasons no longer existed for her now. Once there had been day trips to Niagara-on-the-Lake in tulip time, or autumn splendour in Muskoka with the boarders from St. Radigonde's or, more rarely, much more rarely, outings with Adam to the Island in late May, early September. Long before there'd even been a planetarium, back when the museum walls had been the colour of greased soot, and stone lions snarled in the Tomb Garden.

On this Tuesday – mid-November, snowless, skyless – Mrs. Putnam claimed the seat reserved for veterans, pregnant women and old-age pensioners and started for the planetarium. Across the aisle from her were advertisements for office temps, notices for putting your newborn through university, and pamphlets about "Careers without College." Mrs. Putnam glued milky brown eyes to them. For the past ten years she had been retired on a pension sufficient for her to maintain her flat, though not to repair the cracks in the plaster or buy poison enough to terminate the roaches. She had neither nieces nor nephews with babies requiring to be sent to Victoria or Trinity College, and since she'd come by her post as English Mistress and later Language Specialist with only a Grade 13 diploma from Harbord Collegiate, Mrs. Putnam had no need to consult pamphlets at all. Yet it was imperative to do so – otherwise she would have had to look upon her fellow travellers, and Mrs. Putnam had no interest in anybody else's story but her own.

Twelve-year-olds with pink or green or orange hair, Jamaicans looking resolutely uncolourful in raincoats, Lebanese waiters mournful as blank television screens, Pakistanis with babies on their laps, babies with perfectly round faces and eyes like black moons in the dank heat or chill of the subway car. Arms sweating, legs jolting, Mrs. Putnam holding tight and tighter to the silver pole in front of doors out which her stop would show as welcome as the ram to Abraham, and in another sort of thicket altogether.

Changing trains she noted men at the newspaper kiosks who reminded her of Adam – no similarity whatsoever in colour of hair or lack of it, no slightest resemblance in build or height, but perhaps the cut of the overcoat, the precise indentation of the fedora. She was not the sort who would have held a lover's hand or gazed into his eyes, but often after he had left her side and was safely showering she would take up his hat from her dresser and press her fingertips along the crease his own hand made in the felt. His wife had the vexing habit of presenting him with a new fedora every Christmas. She ordered them by telephone from Creeds; it was one of the few things she could do for him. The little else she could do Althea had told while waiting in Mrs. Putnam's office one rainy Sunday afternoon for Uncle Adam to take her to tea with Aunt Rosamund.

"She's awfully pale, of course, being an invalid, but it's amazing how strong her hands are – she does yards of crochet and knits scarves and vests and things, none of which Uncle Adam can wear, since he's allergic to wool (*though he wore cashmere mufflers and Harris tweeds, as Mrs. Putnam could have told her*) but he does have his office filled with crocheted doilies and coasters everywhere, even under the secretary's typewriter, which shows how devoted they are to one another. Aunt Rosamund's made me all kinds of tablecloths and comforters for my own hope chest – she says I'm like a daughter to her, since she hasn't any children of her own, which is sad, don't you think Mrs. Putnam? Maybe you feel the same – I mean, having no children, not even a husband even. I mean, of course you did have a husband once, at least you say you did, I mean – no offence Mrs. Putnam –"

Mrs. Putnam took none. Pimply, placid Althea, who hadn't the imagination of a pincushion and thus, any notion of the fact that while Aunt Rosamund was crocheting quiet mounds of doilies, Uncle Adam was taking more than tea with Hilary Putnam. Althea, thick as three planks, who couldn't recite a line of poetry to save her soul (*a soul the colour and consistency of clotted cream,* thought Mrs. Putnam) but who nevertheless passed all of Mrs. Putnam's classes for the six years she was at St. Radigonde's and her uncle at Mrs. Putnam's. Tuesday and Thursday evenings, from six to ten, and, perhaps half a dozen times a year, an entire Saturday or Sunday when Rosamund could be persuaded there was pressing work to be done at the trust company of which her husband was vice-president. Kind Althea, who hadn't meant anything by her remarks, since she hadn't the intelligence to think ill of anyone's peculiarities, but who merely parroted schoolgirl gossip about the English Mistress' marriage, which, as Mrs. Putnam knew extremely well, all the girls and over half the staff believed to be a harmless fiction, if not an outright lie.

Southbound to Museum Mrs. Putnam stared at her reflection in the window as the train racketed through a tunnel. The mink toque had been a present from Adam, the last she'd ever had from him. The first had been a ring – one topaz in a (twelve-carat) band. To match her eyes, he'd said – and her hair, which was a watered blond, definitely not twenty-two-carat, but then, all her own at least, and hadn't it made the first grey hair scarcely noticeable? Though he'd not been there to notice anything the night that Mrs. Putnam's mirror finally ambushed her. A massive coronary at his desk, or so Althea had announced the day after the funeral to which, of course, his niece's English teacher had not been summoned. Rosamund – Rosamund was still sipping the small beer of invalid life in Rosedale, having, to counterbalance her fringed nerves, an amazingly strong heart. Althea had vouched for it – of all her former pupils, Althea was the only one who still sent Christmas cards to Mrs. Putnam, rang her up on shopping trips to town, and never sounded disconcerted by the minute and peculiar questions put to her – not on the subjects of how many children she had, and of which sex, but of whether there had been any change in her aunt's condition. There never was.

Mrs. Putnam's was a different case. She had been a carelessly handsome, strong-blooded young woman and it had been to her the strictest form of punishment to watch as, year by year, the slow blue veins that Adam had once traced along her arms and breasts struggled up to the very surface of her skin like drowning swimmers. Liver spots over her hands, the peevish slouch of skin, cracks in her lips which, in the caustic light over the bathroom mirror, seemed to be fissures or crevasses down which her very soul might slip – these were to Mrs. Putnam stages of a cross made of real and not symbolic wood; they left scars and splinters in her shoulders. Her colleagues at St. Radigonde's would not have noticed – she had no friends among them and no confidantes; they, for their part, regarded her merely as an English Mistress renowned for the strict discipline she kept within her class, and for the tedium of the material she set her students. Not even Adam had known that, while she buried his niece under slabs of Pope and all of Milton's *Aereopagitica*, at home, alone, she'd finger a vellum Swinburne, recite from memory the lusher lyrics of Tennyson or read aloud from Keats in a special edition, gilt-edged with plump, fawn-coloured, soft suede covers.

Pigeons were wheeling over the Museum steps, or skittering after bits of popcorn that schoolchildren, on their way home from a session with dinosaurs or dusty Indians in the anthropologist's bargain basement, had bought from the Italian vendors. At their yellow-painted cars, crenellated with candy apples, fragrant with the steam from roasting chestnuts, Mrs. Putnam did not so much as glance – nor at the faces of the children, flushed against the chill of this grey air outside, sharp as icicles against her cheeks. Mrs. Putnam liked neither popcorn nor children overmuch – on the one she had lost a quarter of a tooth some twenty years ago; on the other she had wasted 40 years. In none of her students had she bred a love of Shelley, Scott or Swift, though she had done a creditable job in teaching them what sentence fragments, comma splices, and malapropisms were. For, some fifteen years ago, the Headmistress of St. Radigonde's had decided that English literature would have to be hatcheted and contemporary culture (plus remedial grammar) put in its place if the school were to hold its own against the more prestigious, if less venerable, private girls' schools in Toronto. Mrs. Putnam had lately read that no-one taught *Edwin Drood* or *Silas Marner* to schoolchildren these days – it was all contemporary song lyrics and Shakespeare comic books. A colleague of hers, retired now from Weatherstone School, had got up a petition against it and asked Mrs. Putnam to sign, but she hadn't. *I do not care. I do not care*, was all that Mrs. Putnam had written in reply.

No one asked Mrs. Putnam for the extravagant sum it cost to get a ticket to the planetarium: on Tuesdays old-age pensioners were admitted free – into the museum as well, though Mrs. Putnam refused to set so much as the toe of her ankle boots inside the place, now that they'd changed everything round and destroyed the garden. On Sunday afternoons after Adam's death Mrs. Putnam had walked under the arches and the stone lions, listening to snow or leaves fall as if they'd been the bells that had hung from the roofs of the tombs. Once a man not much older than herself had watched her from the window of the garden door and asked her, after she'd returned, to have tea with him downtown. From his accent she had diagnosed him as Eastern European, and refused, not out of loyalty to Adam's memory, but because she'd been raised in the belief that people whose names ended in *off* or *ski* or *vich* might be high-school janitors but hardly the social equals of a Stuart or Jones or Putnam – she'd had visions of the man's stirring his tea with his index finger. Foreigners had been barred from St. Radigonde's since its founding by an interim Anglican bishop in 1833, though somewhere in the middle of Mrs. Putnam's term at the school *that* had changed as it had everywhere – Mrs. Putnam understood that the country's prime minister was married to an immigrant from that country whose flag looked like a checkerboard.

Once inside the planetarium she walked up and down corridors painted the colour of milk frozen in the bottle, ignoring the displays of information on the walls and joining the small queue in front of the projection room. Waiting for the doors to open she looked down at her hands, then lifted them a little cautiously to her face, stroking her cheek with the leather, inhaling its rich, almost meaty scent. Real kid, none of that pigskin business – though she had to eat macaroni and skimp on the cheese four days a week, Mrs. Putnam would have her necessary luxuries, mere tokens of the things she could have had if Adam hadn't betrayed her at his desk that Tuesday morning, or, at the very least, if Rosamund's nerves had done her in before he had to die.

Particles of rouge-like motes of rosy dust clung to Mrs. Putnam's gloves; all the heating and air-cleaning machines whirring through the foyer made her eyes feel papery, her skin crisp under the powder she had pressed on that morning. Why wouldn't they open the doors, why must they make her wait – 70 years old and with the dignity, the presence of a dowager queen, yet they kept her in line as if she were queuing up for cigarettes at the five and ten. Where on earth was the manager, he would have to be talked to, he would have to—. Someone in front of her began to whistle – further down the line she heard, distinctly, a belch. Mrs. Putnam drew tighter the collar of her good, her *excellent* cloth coat, pulled the mink toque down so it covered her earlobes – shrivelled, hard now like dried apricots – and waited. If Adam had been with her, if ever he could have been with her... But then, if there was anything she detested it was whining women, watering their tea with tears over the mistakes they'd made. *She* had made up her mind when she was thirteen – just after her mother had died – that she would marry well or never marry at all, having learned from her parents' case that life as or with a bank clerk was no great addendum to the sum of human happiness.

Adam had been charming to her – it hadn't been his fault that Rosamund had had the tenacity of a wirehaired terrier in her grip on life, on Adam, and on the president of Adam's company: Rosamund's father. And yet if desire, need and hope had anything to do with our lot on earth; if there were justice under the stars... The subjunctive mood, Miss Putnam had drilled into her students' heads, is always used for things that one merely wishes or hypothesizes to be true.

But now it was as if the gates of a post-modernist heaven had been opened for the pensioners and straggling students. The inner doors of the planetarium swung slowly apart and gathered them in like the great skirts of a *Mater Misericordia.* As quickly as her dignity and arthritic hip would let her, Mrs. Putnam found her customary seat, three rows back from the front, and at right angles from a certain twist in the crumpled metal that projected stars on the egg-shaped dome over her head. She drooped into the chair like a bird to its nest on a darkening winter afternoon; back she tilted, closing her eyes until her head had found its cradling place and the low music rising from the projector crept across her like a hand stroking her brow. And then she looked up at the great black bowl, not hard and blank as the subway window but soft, dewy, gelid – like a membrane to which Mrs. Putnam could raise up her hands, poking fingers through to touch the stars.

Lights dimmed, the music faded and a voice fountained from the projector, talking about Pole stars and Betelgeuse and Charles' Wain. The names didn't matter to Mrs. Putnam; she was lying in the grass on the Island with Adam – they had rented one of the small canoes and paddled out to the hand's breadth of land that was now a bird sanctuary; they had beached the canoe and were lying on their backs in wild, tall grass, watching the stars. For once he was not wearing his fedora; she had on her finger a ring with one diamond and a band of twenty-four-carat gold. Rosamund was in Mt. Pleasant and even Althea had been sent back home to Thunder Bay, to parents who had at last decided that the advantages of a private education did not outweigh the loving kindness to be found only in the bosom of one's family. Softly Hilary opened lips that time had not so much as crumpled:

Now sleeps the crimson petal, now the white... Now lies the earth all Danae to the stars...

and the stars sang back to her. They were not crystal splinters as children imagined them, but round, fragrant as water lilies you might pick off the mirror of a lake and hold up to your face, breathing in their succulence and fragrance—

Across the table from her someone began to snore, with all the violence of a chainsaw massacre. It was hot in the darkened room, the leatherette under Mrs. Putnam's hands began to feel like fur and she was floating somewhere between floor and stars. The voice was talking now about satellites and lasers. Mrs. Putnam remembered hearing on the radio that before long man would be able to orbit messages in space – celestial billboards advertising Pepsi or the other cola, *billet-doux* or messages of condolence that could circle earth forever, forcing their stories down peoples' very eyes. If it were possible, floating through a darkness cut to ribboned light – what would they say were she to chisel it into the night sky: *Rosamund, detested of Adam who loved Hilary alone,* Hilary who loved Keats and Tennyson and silk against her skin, and all the powders and perfumes of Araby she could not wear to St. Radigonde's, but which she would apply each evening upon coming home, whether Adam was coming or not, whether she believed in him or not, coming or going, leaving or loving, Betelgeuse and Charles' Wain, Miss or Mrs. Putnam, Althea and detested Rosamund and petalled stars in the night sky, looking down where she lay, in her story, nobody else's story – head lolling against the squashed leatherette as a voice explained the simulated stars shifting, blooming, exploding on the painted ceiling over the sleeping dark in which Mrs. Putnam lies curled tight, a newborn's fist around some fiction of a finger to grab onto, climbing steep, black spaces in between the stars.

NIGHTCHILD

Gwendolyn MacEwen

...he threw himself over Niagara Falls in a barrel, he walked across the Grand Canyon on a tightrope, he sat on the top of a flagpole eating nothing but raisins and sunflower seeds and defying the world, he flung himself through one of the windows at Casa Loma, brandishing a sword and proclaiming to the dancers on the ballroom floor that he was the man in the iron mask. He composed music and played baseball...

A GAME OF INCHES

LINDA GRIFFITHS

It's the bottom of the ninth and I'm standing at the plate, and thousands of people are chanting "Hit that ball! Hit that ball! Hit that ball!" My teammates behind me in the dugout are chanting, "Hit that ball! Hit that ball! Hit that ball!" It's all resting on me. And I know I'm not going to hit that ball. As I lay there alone in my bed, I realized I'd had my very first baseball nightmare. And I thought, surely now he'll call.

The light changed that day. There was the wet rain and the damp and the sliding about on the packed icy surface, but it did seem that an almost imperceptible change occurred, like the turning up of a dial of light. The turning of the season. The time when John used to look for the very first baseball magazines. You know what I mean? They're not very good, they're made of newsprint and they herald the later abstracts and larger tomes that come out throughout the season. These magazines were like daffodils or tulips to him, because, of course, they meant spring training.

I knew he wouldn't call in winter. I knew he wouldn't call Valentine's Day. Ridiculous, the way it comes right in the armpit of winter. There's no more depressing time of year. No, he has no use for those kinds of occasions, the bleeding hearts in the store windows, the silly, humorous cards, "If you break my heart, I'll break your face," and so on. No, I knew he wouldn't call then. He'll call in the spring. Or the summer. Or at the very latest, fall.

I'm aware that it's ridiculous, being a virgin at my age. I should have just gone out and done it a long time ago and got it over with. But oh no, I had to wait. Still, I don't know why everything has to be done at once. Painters don't paint masterpieces all at once. They begin with a triangle, a circle, a square. They move onto a bowl of fruit, an apple, a pear, eventually a banana and then they go on to paint *Boy Blue* and *Pinkie*. Of course it's possible that some people just aren't very highly sexed. As if there was a kind of gauge with "nymphomaniacs" on the top, then "highly sexed," "very sexed," just plain "sexed," "lightly sexed," all the way down to "barely sexed."

When I told my psychiatrist my baseball nightmare, he said something I know he's been dying to say for a very long time. He said that this dream might mean that I was gay. This disturbed me, not because of any prejudice, but because I've never felt particularly gay. But I told him that I'd be willing to seek a second medical opinion and if they concurred, I would be willing to work on becoming gay, with qualified professionals, for several years if necessary. Still, it didn't feel quite right.

It's true, I never had boyfriends as such. Of course, I had the experience of "that dance." You know the one I mean. My mother spent three hundred dollars on a dress. In the fifties they had those dresses with the crinolines that stuck straight out. In bright green taffeta and I weighed two hundred and four pounds. Then came the snow boots, large brown galoshes with soles as thick as bricks. I clomped into that dance carrying my shoes in a little bag. I saw the girls, batting their eyelashes and giggling and listening to the boys talk about sports, pretending interest the way women do. I wasn't going to do that. I made for the couch and sat there watching like a giant frog. I wasn't going to eat anything. I wasn't going to drink anything. I wasn't going to take my boots off. I just sat there and waited until it was over and then I went home.

This is all that's left: a giant house, some mouldy antiques, a small annuity. I've always liked to keep a room in my house empty; actually, not a room, an entire floor. I thought that if I filled up the whole house with things – with my voluminous collection of books on the female orgasm, the works of the modern French feminists – *Angst, Volumes One Two and Three* – with lamps and tables and things, then there would be no room for *him* when *he* came. I thought a lot about it that spring three years ago, inviting John to come and stay. I'd had my eye on him, but then I'd had my eye on other fish before. I thought, "This is the way it's done. The woman has the nest and provides, and the man is in between things, he doesn't have much money, he moves in and that's the way it's done." So I said to John, "Well, if you don't have a place to stay, you can always stay at my house, you can pay me two hundred and fifty dollars or nothing." And he said, "Sure." The way they do. "Sure."

I sat in my kitchen waiting for him to come and I wish I had known then about Sadaharu Oh. Sadaharu Oh was perhaps the most successful hitter ever. He hit more home runs than Hank Aaron or Babe Ruth. A Japanese man, he was a high-school star until he made the major leagues and went into a giant slump. He just couldn't hit the ball. He's in despair. Finally his teacher comes to him and says, "Oh, you must learn to concentrate on *ki. Ki* is the point of spirit energy in the body." Now, I would have thought that this point of *ki* would have been located somewhere at the top of the head, or the forehead or the mouth or, at the lowest, the chest. But no, it appears this point of *ki* is located all the way down, about two inches below the navel. Sadaharu Oh learned to concentrate on his point of *ki* and balance his spirit energy and still he couldn't hit the ball. His teacher came to him and said, "Oh, you must understand and eliminate the *mah. Mah* is energy between opponents." In this case the pitcher and the batter. Sadaharu Oh had to learn never to think of the pitcher as his enemy. He had to think into the eyes of the pitcher, through his own eyes in a giant circle, thus eliminating the *mah* between them. And he learned to do this and still he couldn't hit the ball. Then, it's terrible, they're about to throw him off the team and he has one last game. He's in despair and his teacher comes to him and says, "Oh, you are a piece of shit," the way they do. "You have one last chance. You must hit the ball standing on one leg." Sadaharu Oh thinks he's crazy but he doesn't have anything to lose, so he agrees.

He goes out to the stadium to face the fans. They are so used to him striking out that every time he comes up to bat, they chant, "Oh, strike out! Oh, strike out! Oh, strike out!" But he quiets them in his mind, concentrates on his point of *ki*, eliminates the *mah* between himself and the pitcher, and raises himself on one leg in the now familiar "flamingo stance." He waits for the perfect moment, hits the ball with a resounding crack, it arches up and out of the park! He runs around the bases, hits home plate, and flings his arms up in his only gesture of emotion for the next twenty-two years. And the crowd chants, "Oh! Oh! Oh! Oh! Oh... Oh... Oh... Ohh... Ohhhhhhh... Ohhh... Oh."

I sat in my kitchen, waiting for John to come, with some lapsang suchong tea in a perfect china cup, and a fresh strawberry tart with whole-wheat crust, of course made from scratch, and I heard the doorbell ring. I looked down the long hallway and saw him through the glass, a huge black shadow with a suitcase. I waved him in and he walked down the hallway, coming closer and closer, looming larger and larger, seeming to cut out all the light behind him and all of a sudden all I can see is the enemy!

A man a man a man! With his man smell smell smell, his penis penis penis! A rapist! A warmonger! An oppressor, a brute! I know all I'll want to do is serve and serve and serve. I see forty-five years in one fell swoop. He is old and bald and has cancer and I'm changing his colostomy bag. I want to take a piece of chalk and draw a giant circle around me and say, "No! You can't come here. This is me! This is my mind, I fought for it! This is me, you can't come here!"

Instead, I say, "Come on in. Take a beer from the fridge." I've stocked the fridge and the cupboards and the freezer with enough food to last seven nuclear wars. I know that he must feel my panic and yes, my revulsion. But how could I tell him that although these things are true, he is also my beloved?

He moves in up to the third floor where he creates unbelievable devastation. I seem pulled by my very genes up to the third floor just to do a bit of dusting, not to move anything around. I see his dirty laundry scattered on the floor. I'm tempted to pick up one of his shirts and smell that unbelievable combination of polyester blend and sweat. Just to get used to him, you understand. I'm further tempted to gather up the shirts, not the socks, only the shirts, and carry them downstairs and wash them and then say casually, "Yes, no trouble really, I had to do a black wash anyway."

It is as if we've lived together for forty years, it's that comfortable, that ordinary, at the same time there is an unspeakable tension between us. Then one day he comes in and says, "Do you mind if I watch the game?" Game? What game? "The Blue Jays and the White Sox." I say, "Sure," the way I do now. "Sure."

We are in the living room and as I turn on "the game," I hear that hard-edged announcer's voice. The sound of all little girls being separated from their fathers. The voice says, "The Blue Jays are in the Skydome and they've opened the roof, they've closed the roof, and they're opening, they've closed, yes they've opened, no they've closed the roof..." But I can't watch the game. I am only aware of him behind me on the couch, it's as if the back of my head has eyes. I know he's wondering whether or not he can put his boots up on the couch. I want to beam out to him, that I dearly want him to feel comfortable enough to put his boots up on the couch. At the same time, I feel that if he does, I'll chop his feet off. Finally he gives a contented sigh, stretches himself out on the couch, and puts his boots up. I tell myself, "You see, the world hasn't fallen apart, the boots are up, so what?" But I still can't watch the game. All I can think of is, "Does he want tea, coffee, pound cake, lemon meringue? Any of the enormous meal I've prepared and hidden in the back of the fridge?" No, I can't watch the game. Then I think, "Is it possible that perhaps at this moment, he is also thinking of me?" I glance at him. Wrong, wrong, wrong. He, of course, is watching the game.

I don't know how many games went on like that, without my seeing a single one. I began to plot and plan the way women do, checking ahead in the television guide to see when the games were on, so that when he came in, he wouldn't have to say, "Do you mind if I watch the game?" Because the game would already be on. But we were, maybe only I was, exhausted with the tension of the unspoken between us. Then one night I was just fed up. He wasn't home but I put the game on anyway and sat staring blankly at the screen. I heard him come in and get a beer from the fridge and I thought, "No, everything's fine. This is how they do things. They come in, they get beers from fridges, they crack them open, they flop on the couch, they fart, and they watch the game."

But this night, for some reason, I wasn't thinking so much of him. It was as if a glow of light began to illuminate my mind and for the first time I saw these players, these White Sox. A bunch of men dressed in what looks like long underwear with numbers on them, loping about chewing wads of cud that stick out of their mouths like tumours, scratching and spitting gobs of phlegm and tobacco juice and spit into some kind of trough that must be in front of them. A gang of fairly ordinary fellows, all shapes and sizes. Then, in come the Toronto Blue Jays – warped and introverted and miserable. I think, "What's wrong with them? What have we done to them? What have they done to themselves?" The entire team looks like it's in its second year of psychotherapy.

As the game progresses, I understand more and more, until finally I know that it's the top of the ninth. All baseball stories begin with, "It's the bottom of the ninth" or "It's the top of the ninth." It's the top of the ninth and the game is tied and the bases are loaded and there are two down and the White Sox are up to bat and the Blue Jays are in the field. The Blue Jays' pitcher appears to be losing his mind, quite literally coming apart at the seams. He gets a tragic, haunted look in his eyes and starts to twitch and shake in an almost Parkinsonian manner. Then he starts to pull at himself. And as if on cue, all the other players start to pull at themselves too. The other players are more circumspect, they pull down and a little to one side, but this Dave Steib, he goes right for it. Then he starts to talk to himself and it appears everything is going to disintegrate until a calm comes over the entire stadium. The coach, Cito Gaston, the classiest man in baseball, has come out to talk Dave down. He gets to the mound, but before he begins to speak, you can see the tension start to drain away from Dave's face. He begins to regain control of his limbs, and to do fairly ordinary things with his hands, like play with the ball. We don't know what Cito has said. We only know it's perfect. A job well done, Cito goes back to the dugout, sitting like Yul Brynner in *The King and I.*

Dave strikes the batter out. The Blue Jays are up, and out comes George Bell, the Butcher of San Pedro, the most hated man in baseball. Clearly, George is a man used to boos. Booo booo booo! "Eeeef the Canadian faaans don't like me, they can keees my purple butt!" "Booo. Booo. Booo." But today, the fans aren't booing. They're quiet, almost kind. It's not putting George in a good mood at all. He looks like he wants to eat the plate, the bat, the ball and the pitcher. He swings, misses, and his statistics come up on the television set before you. You know everything. You know he's been in a giant slump, that he needs an eye operation, that his shoulder's gone, his elbows are gone, his knees are gone, his ankles aren't very good either, we know his contract is up, that he'll ask for too much money. Meanwhile the announcers are saying, "Perhaps George will get a single today." And George raises his bat, big as a fence post, hacks and hews the empty air, strikes out, throws his bat to the ground and stalks off in a snit.

Then in comes a large chin followed by curling blond hair coming to the nape of the neck, Kelly Gruber. Most young boys want to be baseball players and end up being policemen. Kelly wanted to be a policeman and became a baseball player. He's holding his pinkie finger at an unusual angle and his skin is stretched thin and taut over his cheekbones. It seems he's also been in a slump and the fans are booing him too. With the black chalk marks smeared under his eyes, he looks like that rock singer, Alice Cooper. He bends over the plate, his lips thin with tension, and cracks the ball for a stand-up triple. As he arrives on third base, you can hear him thinking, "Just let them call me 'Mrs. Gruber' now."

Then there is a curious dragging sound, a player appears to be dragging a giant cross onto the field and on his face are tears from his latest appearance on Vision TV. Tony Fernandez is a man clearly tormented by the wounds of Christ. And I want to beam into the television set, "Tony, of course it's all right to believe in Jesus and be tormented by the wounds of Christ. Just not right now, it's the bottom of the ninth." He clearly hears me because he seems to solidify. Underneath his torment we see a body as neat and graceful as a young gazelle. He comes to the plate with no unnecessary panache, waits for the perfect moment, almost invisibly whacks the ball and drives Gruber in!

We win! We win! At least, they win. The Blue Jays win. I win. John and I win. Yeah, team! We're very excited, John and I, because of the game of course, and it's ten o'clock at night and it seems that something more could happen, that the evening could extend. But we don't seem to be able to engineer it and I get almost Dave Steibian in my twitches as I say, "Coffee?" "No." "Tea?" "No." "Pound cake?" "No." "Chicken breasts? Broccoli with hollandaise sauce?" "No." Things are about to come apart at the seams when a calm comes over the living room. I turn and there is Cito Gaston, handing me a pack of cards. And Kelly Gruber has found the candles. And Tony Fernandez wipes the coffee table clean. John and I play Crazy Eights by candlelight till four o'clock in the morning. Then dawn starts to alter the light, we are tired, yet it seems that something more could happen with the evening, something more. A long silence. I look at John, of course I don't speak. Finally he says, "Well, I guess I'd better crash."

"Yes. You should crash." I should crash. We all should crash. We say goodnight, he goes down the hallway to the bathroom to leave the toilet seat up, then climbs the stairs to the third floor. Lying alone in my bed, I hear his heavy body fall on the mattress on the floor above me and I ache the way women ache when they want something they can't ask for.

Then I hear a very curious sound. Like ice cracking. I follow the sound into the living room, and there, sitting on the couch, is George Bell. He's crying in a heartbroken manner and burbling, "Sheeet, man. Sheeet. Everyone knows, man. They think I'm feeneeesh. I'm not feeneeesh. I got two years left in me, two years, and my contract is up. I gotta go out there and act like a king. My eyes are gone. My shoulder is gone. My knees gone. My ankles aren't very good. Cito, he says, keep our eye on the ball. I can't see the goddamn ball."

Smooth as silk, I go up to him and help him take the chips off his shoulders. First the left one then the right, which is even larger. Then I am in his arms, his hands are huge and calloused like bear paws and they are travelling over me, finding places I didn't know existed. All the moves I thought I would have to learn by rote or with professionals are coming through me in waves. He is no longer the Butcher of San Pedro, these are not butcher's arms, but blacksmith's arms and they are holding me so gently. He touches me with the sweetest part of his bat and we are at first base, we are at second base, at third base, *oh ohhhhhh* home. Then I am curled in his arms and he is tickling me with his moustache.

Now I don't know if that was a proper orgasm. I don't think anyone really knows what an orgasm is, certainly not in all the books I've read. All I know is that I was very pleased and I didn't want to do it anymore.

As I helped George strap the chips back on his shoulders, he said, "Pamela, they say I'm a pretty shitty guy, maybe that's true, maybe that's not true. But I tell you one thing, don't you worry about this John. Just play your natural game." And he was gone.

I had such a moment of peace, even the French feminists within were peaceful. Yes, of course, just play your natural game. But how to be natural with *him*? I was becoming more and more unnatural. Seemingly unbidden, I was giggling, batting my eyelashes, wiggling odd parts of my body in coy ways. My voice had gone up octaves, I was running around like Betty Crocker in heat.

Natural? It seems natural when he goes out to say, "When are you coming home?" Just like that, "When are you coming home?" But when I say it, it comes out like an order born of brutality and desperation. I want to grab the words back. If I don't say, "When are you coming home?" there is a unnatural conversational gap. There is no natural left. I'm just a schemer now. I think, "What he needs is a good shirt. It would look just like his other shirts, except it would cost two hundred and fifty dollars. He wouldn't be able to tell, they can't, you know. But fifteen years down the road, when he's with someone a little closer to his own age, all the things from this time will have disintegrated, except for that one shirt and he will think of me."

Just after the all-star game, John said that he was "getting it together" to look for a place again and that pretty soon he would be off my hands. Again there was that silence. I just wanted to say, "Oh don't be so ridiculous. Marry me. Marry me. Marry me. I'll nail your feet to a perch. I'll nail mine to one. We'll stay there frozen forever, locked in this beautiful prison!" But then I thought, "No, that can't be quite right." Sometime after the Blue Jays lost the playoffs, he said that he was a little closer to getting a place and he pretty well had a line on one.

It's the bottom on the ninth. Joe DiMaggio is standing at the plate. It's all resting on him. If he hits, the team will win the World Series, he will break all the records. The crowd is electric, insane. The ball comes toward him, he waits for the perfect moment, swings, hits it with a resounding crack and it arches high over the park. He's done it! The crowd cheers wildly, everybody gets up to leave, the game is over... except for one outfielder standing by the wall. The ball's already travelled over the wall several feet when this outfielder makes the most astounding leap. He jumps up, arches back, reaches out that extra impossible quarter of an inch and catches the ball! The photograph of this moment shows the fans with their jaws dropped open, with their coats and hats half on. That outfielder never played baseball again. He opened a bar. Baseball stories are like that. They always seem to have that twist of lemon.

Just after the World Series, which was hard to watch because, of course, the Jays had "choked in the clutch," an expression I truly despise, John said that he had found a place and he couldn't thank me enough and he owed me dinner. Even as he spoke I thought I caught something out of the corner of his eye, something that seemed to ask for something, but no, I was probably wrong.

He is standing in the hallway with his suitcase and I am standing in front of him. It's an awkward moment. I see this nose coming toward me, looming larger and larger. I get what's supposed to happen. I do understand the physics of it. Something has to occur so that our lips can touch. He comes closer and closer, and then, I don't why I did it, but I turned my head. I turned my head just a quarter of an inch and his lips brushed my ear awkwardly and a wall went up between us. A wall as cold and as grey as a Toronto sky in February. We try to reach our hands over the wall. I say, "Don't worry about the rent." He says, "I'll give you a call."

I am standing under the ball. It's one of those moments when there's no question the outfielder will make the catch. The ball comes closer and closer, looming larger and larger, and then, for some reason, it slips between the mitt and my hands. It's one of those ridiculous bloopers. There I am with my bum in the air, searching for the ball between my legs. I finally find it, too late to throw to third base. A couple of inches, one way or another. I hear the door close gently behind him.

You can imagine what a meal the French feminist would make of such a moment. They're very good in the politics, but about male/female relations, very dicey, very dicey indeed. You can just hear them. "Oh, Philippe, Philippe, I am woman. You are man. I am cunt. You are penis. I am penis, You are cunt. Oh, please fuck me. Oh, don't fuck me. I hate you, I love you. I hate you. Ooooh, I will die if you leave. You will die if you stay. You must come, come, go, go, oh fuck me."

Well, I am not like that. I didn't get hysterical, instead I hid for a year, never leaving the house. My hibernation ended one morning when I woke up, threw open the window and smelled mud under the frost. I turned on the radio and heard that George Bell was signing copies of his book – imagine George writing a book – at the World's Biggest Bookstore. I knew I had to see him again. The World's Biggest Bookstore is not where I usually buy my books, but I ventured into a warehouse-like building, with screaming bargain signs and hideous lighting. There were crowds of schoolchildren milling about but it was easy to see George. At the end of a long line, there he was, a nattily dressed Dominican man with a moustache and large sunglasses, flanked on one hand by a security guard with a gun, on the other hand by an overwrought, overachieving woman publicist. The schoolchildren were waving bits of paper, chanting "I got his autograph. I got his autograph."

A stack of books announced the apt title of George's book, *Hardball.* I clutched a copy to my chest and lined up, the one adult in a mass of children. When I finally got to George, I waited for some sign of recognition but it was impossible to see his eyes behind the shades. To ignite his memory, even though my voice was shaking, I boldly asked, "Would you mind writing 'to Pamela' in my book?" I wanted something personal after all. The overwrought, overachieving woman publicist screeched, "No! He's only going to write his name!" George flexed his gold-ringed fingers and signed his name, smiling at me in an innocuous way. I retreated to a vantage point near a large section on the royal family. The Queen and her corgis were everywhere. George knew I was watching him. A lumpy fourteen-year-old, who'd wanted to have his baseball signed but wasn't allowed, joined me, recognizing a good spot when he saw one. The two of us stood in companionable silence as George signed his way to the end of the line. Still no acknowledgement. I intuited that the lumpy lad was living in some suburban hell, camped out in his parents' basement, trying to keep his mind alive by quoting baseball statistics. Our bond grew as the clock struck 12:30, the hour when the book signing was to end. As George left he had to walk right by us. As he came closer and closer, I began to fear he would leave without any signal of our past acquaintance when at the last moment he leaned towards me and said, "If you're ever in the Windy City, look me up." Windy city? My lumpy friend explained that George had been traded to the Chicago Cubs. Traded? Not a Blue Jay? "Yeah, didn't you know? A whole bunch of last year's team are gone, like Tony Fernandez." Tony of the cross? Gone? I felt as if the ground beneath my feet was dissolving. What can it mean? They were our team, those particular Blue Jays, not just any jays flying about the city. Is there no loyalty? Can this mean John won't call? I am ten years old again and my best friend has moved away and the world is cracking and there's nothing left nothing left. But somehow I pull myself together. My only refuge is knowledge. I resolve to learn, to research, to be practical and thereby come to an understanding as to how the game was played in all its aspects. The lumpy fourteen-year-old takes me over to the baseball section and I buy three hundred and fifty-seven dollars worth of baseball books, give him my signed copy of *Hardball* to begin training.

In the spring of my training, I watched the Blue Jays build their new team. As I saw them bring in Joe Carter, his face splitting with an enormous smile that filled up the Skydome whether the roof was open or not, I worked on balancing the spirit energy of my *ki.* I was still having considerable difficulty eliminating the *mah* between myself and just about everybody else as I watched a peculiar energy begin to take hold of our Jays. By midsummer I was speed-reading through the wisdom of Yogi Berra who once said, "Baseball is ninety percent mental, the other half is physical."

He didn't call.

I intensified my training. Halfway through the season I could stand on one leg for considerable lengths of time. My knowledge increased. I knew Babe Ruth once ate a hat. Lou Gehrig was obsessed with his mother. Walter "The Big Train" Johnson, master of the fastball, used to give young batters a break, the catcher whispering, "The Big Train likes you today," and somehow the ball would be right over the plate. All of this was in tandem with the strengthening of the new team. I didn't forget those players who had gone and missed them deeply, but still I welcomed the sight of Roberto Alamar, like a young bear cub, playing the game with such ease it made me want to weep. Alomar took over Dave Steib's position as the player most likely to pull at himself. Nineteen times in one game, I noted.

And still he didn't call. Even though I felt fairly certain that the *mah* between myself and the world had significantly diminished.

A World Series win began to be a tangible goal, one that fuelled the imagination and inspired sold-out games. The stands were full, the team moving together like a dream. Veteran Dave Winfield was brought in to clinch the win. The Jays management was spending money, critics said they were buying a World Series rather than building a true team from within. Big Dave Winfield didn't care. One night he strode to the front of the stands, raised his mighty hands like a conductor and yelled, "More noise!" The crowd roared back. I managed a yell myself, all the while maintaining my flamingo stance.

There was a *soupçon* of a frenzy or what passes for one in this city and of course the detractors were doing their best to squash it. Journalists droned on with macabre delight about "choking in the clutch" and the "curse of the Blue Jays." I sensed that this was a delicate moment and called Cito Gaston into the living room for a chat. "Cito, we all know what you're trying to go. You want the big win, the World Series, entry into the Hall of Fame. We all do. But it can't all be about winning and losing, it must be about how you play the game. If it isn't, then I am a loser and I won't accept that. Take it from me, no one ever won by thinking about winning all the time. You can't play your natural game then. You can't push to win, pray to win, think to win, plan to win – you can only be ready to win. Prepared. Tell them it's about waiting for the perfect moment, balancing your spirit energy, eliminating the *mah*, playing your natural game, and having the courage to...the courage to...

Only then does the obvious occur to me. Daringly, carelessly, I pick up the phone and dial the number I'd carried on my back like a cross for two seasons. Of course he was home, of course he was. "Hello John? It's Pamela. Yes, I've been watching. I think they just might take the World Series this year. Next year too? Oh, don't be silly." And I laugh my natural laugh.

Note. The Toronto Blue Jays won The World Series in back-to-back years, 1992 and 1993.

from DREAM CHAMBER

Sorel Etrog

SOD'S BROOD, BE ME FEAR!

SANGLORIANS

S A V E

ARMS APEAL WITH LARMS, APPALLING

KILLYKILLKILLY!

A TOLL A TOLL

ENDONATIONAL CALAMITIES

GAYLEGS TO RIOT OF US! GALLOCKS TO LAFFT!

ALL THE ANCIENT GODS AND THE RESIDUE OF RITES AND FOLKLORE UNCONSCIOUSLY CONNECTED WITH THEM BECAME A PART OF AN ANCESTRAL DREAM - WORLD.

Insignificant, oppressed, dispersed, forced exiles joined self exiles. The Dadaists and Joyce were like the Celts on their wanderings through Europe:

BRAVE FOOTSORE HAUN !
WORK YOUR PROGRESS !
HOLD TO ! NOW !
WIN OUT, YE DIVIL YE !

The social and cultural foundations of the west were shattered; Fixed points of established order were destroyed; Radical departures from familiar logic were taken: Words, colours, and shapes were accepted as products of the unconscious. They got rid of the intoxication of the past, put experience into motion, and created 'Anti-art', 'Anticulture'.

EVERY PAGE MUST EXPLODE, WHETHER THROUGH SERIOUSNESS, PROFUNDITY, TURBULENCE, NAUSEA, THE NEW, THE ETERNAL, ANNHILATING NONSENSE, ENTHUSIASM FOR PRINCIPLES, OR THE WAY IT IS PRINTED.

AN AVIATOR IN INK

Talking to that 'ideal reader suffering from that ideal insomnia', shaking the prestige of culture, Immuning yourself from the *bons mots*, from 'the amenities of the amenities with all their amenities', drumming 'literature into the ground,' so that a new humanity can rise, merely to fall once again.

THE FALL (BABABADALGHARAGHTAKAMMINARRONNKONNBRONNTONNERRONNTUONNTHUNNTROVARRHOUNAWNSKAWNTOOHOOHOORDENENTHURNUK!)

OF A ONCE WALLSTRAIT

The great fall of the offwall

NOW TELL ME

TELL ME

TELL ME THEN!

W H A T W A S I T ?
A .... !
? .... O!

What might have been is an abstraction
Remaining a perpetual possibility
Only in a world of speculation...
Footfalls echo in the memory

IN THE DREAM CHAMBER

...one clings still.
I'll bear it on me.
To remind me of

IT IS NOT ABOUT SOMETHING
IT IS THAT SOMETHING ITSELF.

THEY NEVER TOLD ME

AUSTIN CLARKE

I am getting old. And I hate it. I use swear words to stem the silent flow of years that overtake my actions, and even the flow of my speech. My first recognition of this malady of old age is the stumbling, and the climbing of stairs. And after many trials, the stammering to find the word that does not come easily into my mind, and that remains on the tip of my tongue. And they never told me how to be cool and decent about this slowing down of speech; the lengthening struggles to find the correct word, remembering it until I match the thought to the written word itself... the fading of faces, the disappearance of names from the faces that my eyes move over, like an usher's flashlight in a crowded cinema; and from the pages of names in my pocket diary. I am old. But I hide it. I hide my fear of old age; and my shame of it. I do not want to get old; do not want to be recognized; to be greeted by old friends, precisely because they are old; or, to be pointed out by a smiling young woman, with her eyes, and a nod, and a smile, that illustrates her question, and her concern, "Would you like my seat, sir?"

But I take the offer and take her seat; and my indignation swells, and smells like stale perspiration. I take the seat. I am very close to this young woman as she stands up. I can see the thin outline of her panties through the summer-thin dress. I become ashamed of myself. Of my desire. And I want to scream my indignation out, to everyone on this crowded bus, "Do I look so old to you?"

But shame and reality keep my lips shut.

And when I return to my house, two hours after my encounter with the kind young woman, I confront myself in the small unframed, rectangular glass over the white washbasin. The washbasin is made of smooth white enamel. The small bathroom is painted white. The paint shines. There are large brown bottles and a damp washcloth in the sink; and bottles of pills for headache, and pills for earache; and pills to pacify the cough that rumbles in my chest; and pills for head colds. And pills for losing weight; large pills, colourful pills, pills that I have left untouched, left in a bulbous green bottle. And then a round tin, flat like a puck slapped around in a hockey game. Kiwi Black Shoe Polish! And around the tin are the words, "noir, kiwi, black, kiwi, noir, kiwi, black, kiwi." I had not known that "kiwi" was another name for "black." I turn the catch, the little metal wings on the tin. "Water resistant. Leather nourishing." And round the diameter of the tin is the reassurance: "By appointment to H.R.H. the Duke of Edinburgh. Makers of shoe polish." The picture of a kiwi bird is drawn in yellow.

As I twist the catch, the full power of the shoe polish strikes my nostrils; and I dig my middle finger deep into the thick, silky blackness, moving my three fingers covered in the black soil of thick shoe polish over my face – I think of Negro minstrels, and of white men who wanted to turn themselves into black men. The hand that holds the black shoe polish is black. And nervous. And shaking in the horror of the act I am committing; turning myself into a black-face black man; while all I wanted to do was to slick my hair with black shoe polish, to make myself look sleek and younger; to make young women stop getting up to offer me their seat. I want to look young. I rub the black shoe polish into my skin. I look at my reflection. And I see the laughing face of a man. The face of Al Jolson. The face of a white man who sang like a cantor who is Negro, whose hand is black, and I imagine myself singing a song written by a white man, by Stephen Foster pretending to be a down home country boy black man,

Way down upon de Swanee Ribber,
Far far away,
Dere's whu my heart is turning ebber,
Dere's whu de old folks stay...

I am an old man still, and I am mouthing the words of this song; and my back takes on the shape of an old man moving to the slow beat of the song. My back is bent. The song overcomes me. My lips are large; and red. My eyes droop. My hands shake. I am Al Jolson. I am singing the minstrel blues,

Way down upon de Swanee Ribber,
Far far away,

and my face is by appointment to H.R.H. the Duke, and I feel comfortable with my new darkness, and I move my body slow. And I dance, and I laugh and my teeth become pearly white, and my eyeballs lose their pupils; and are now completely white. And I am rocking from one side to another side. And my voice has become deep, and I roar with laughter at my antics.

I sometimes come to my home and climb the forty-seven steps to this bathroom, and after I close the door behind me, I find I'm lost in my head, I've forgotten completely why I climbed those steps. So I retrace my forty-seven steps, counting out loud their number. The count becomes everything, mindful that one false step will send me hurtling down to smash myself against zero, the bronze panel in the front door; and then, I will have to rouse myself and re-climb and re-count the forty-seven steps, and enter the bathroom a second time... and then try to remember why I had entered it the first time. But now it comes back to me. I had wanted to get a tissue of white Kleenex to polish my reading glasses with so I could see *whu my heart is turning ebber...*

In the bathroom, I look at my blackened hair, not so black as I had wanted it to be, and I turn the tin of shoe polish over, and I see it is a tin of Canadian shoe polish made at the Kiwi Polish Company (Canada) Limited, in Hamilton, just a few miles west of Toronto; and this closeness, like family, makes the black paint on my face more acceptable. I like being black-faced. In safety and security beneath the "black, kiwi, noir" of my new complexion, behind the mask that is painted black on my face. I can now wallow in the peace of being lost in a place where I will take a seat beside a young woman, where I will inhale her alluring perfume; and when the bus stops, enjoy the touch of her arm, and wonder if at my age – which nobody knows for certain – if her sweet, soft arm, and the whiff of her auburn hair against the blackened, curled hairs on my unshaven chin, could ever reawaken that dormant, once sweet sensuality which... "dream on, old man!... " might come alive, stand as erect as the first bursts of spring flowers, with me now travelling in peace; buried deep in the deeper tranquility of forgetfulness.

Riding up and down on a bus, the Rosedale route down to the waterfront on Sherbourne Street. I even stop and get off at the large LCBO liquor store. And buy a mickey of rum, fifteen-year-old El Dorado Rum, made in Demerara. And back on the bus, I sneak a sip from the shaking bottle, caused by the hard driving over a broken pot-holed road, and caused by the strength of the rum. I hold the bottle under my winter coat. Nobody sees me. Nobody looks at me. Nobody cares. I am an old black man with my face painted black at the back of the bus.

And the bus turns around, going north from the waterfront along this same Sherbourne Street where it touches Queen Street East; past the multitudes of bums and beggars; and the homeless; and drunks; and no one knows me. I have become one of them. No one has to be kind to me, to offer me a seat. I can hum. I can sing, under my breath, like Al Jolson, the whole entire song...

Way down upon de Swanee Ribber,
Far far away,
Dere's whu my heart is turning ebber,
Dere's whu de old folks stay...

I have to admit, however, with some embarrassment, and more shame, sitting on the rough-riding bus, that the call of the bathroom has become urgent oftener now and no longer do I have the urge that I used to have to pacify my urge to pee. With a mind that no longer distinguishes amongst faces and nor does it recognize one address from the other, a mind that does not place a face against a telephone number, I watch my own sloughing off of habits of cleanliness, I watch my own deterioration, my own incapacities; the increasing difficulty to unscrew the cap of a plastic bottle; trying to unscrew the cap of the gin bottle; reaching up to take frozen food from the refrigerator; or to accept the offer of space in a line-up at the cinema; and beneath it all, there is my increasing urge to pee, to empty, to void myself. Would those who offer me such consideration want to help me pee? To help me into the void? Full of good-willed unawareness. I resent all such gestures, especially when they come from young women. Not many women my age express these pleasantries. No woman of my age has ever offered me her seat. I presume it is because we are in the same boat, a boat that more and more refuses to float.

In the Sixties, I lived in many cities in America: in New Haven, Williamstown, and in Boston; and in the South, in Durham, North Carolina; in Bloomington, Indiana, and in Austin, Texas. In those cities and towns, in America, not many people got up to offer any black person their seat. I lived through the years of the determination of that black woman, Rosa Parks, who refused to surrender her seat in the "white section" of a bus in Selma, Alabama. Not being in blackface or in anybody's face back then, I chose to sit, voluntarily, in the "black section."

Here in Toronto in those self-same Sixties, I was crossing Hoskin Avenue from Trinity College and I was wearing the College's soccer colours and I took up my position as centre forward. I did not score a goal; but I was called "off-side" three times during the match; and when the final whistle was blown, and the game was over on the Front Campus pasture, I wallowed in the cheers of the cheerleaders chosen from the beautiful first-year women students; and I headed back to Trinity College with victory in my muscles and in my loins, to the dining room at the college; and as a new resident in the college, halfway to my new home, I turned right instead of left, and after I reached Yonge Street, that was the name on the telephone pole, I guessed that I had made the wrong turn. I corrected that and turned right but it was long after the last plate of white fish and mashed potatoes in a white thin sauce had been served and eaten in the dining hall that I realized that I was lost. I began in this town by being lost, standing at the corner of Bloor and Yonge in my football uniform.

And here I am, fifty-nine years later on this same corner on a cold November evening peeling back the years ever further than Trinity College to a time still in Barbados when I was strong enough to run four races – the 100 yards, the 220 yards, the 440 yards and the 880 yards – and the long jump, in one afternoon and come first in each and then to be crowned "Victor Ludorum," Champion of the Games, who now finds himself on Bloor Street, meeting himself face to Kiwi face, in the show window of a specialty men's clothing store, Harry Rosen's, and I find it natural to think of T.S. Eliot who we studied during those school days and what he said about trousers and old men:

I grow old... I grow old...
I shall wear the bottoms of my trousers rolled.
Shall I part my hair behind? Do I dare to eat a peach?

I ate two peaches this morning. A ladies' magazine had told me that peaches would lengthen my life but they are my favourite fruit anyway. I like the sweet sensual tickle of hairs kissing my mouth, but now I have to wonder what Eliot's caution meant and still means, the way we look so eagerly, with such yearning, for our future before we have even got a decent look at our present, this present where in blackface I eat a peach and wear my trousers rolled and mount a stair hoping to see a face above the stair, hoping for fairness if not friendliness, as I did back in my college days, when I stood at the top of a stairs on a stoop in a complete silence, hearing the creaking of startled shoes; the heavy sound of a dead lock, as I managed to read a well-written notice, not much larger than a tea-time calling card, stuck with Scotch tape to the inside pane of glass in the heavy, grand mahogany double door: NO COLOREDS.

On the door itself, written in an uneven hand, the assertion, or the wish: JESUS BLESS THIS HOME.

Having come through such disappointments, having lived through flushes of, if not constant, anger and disdain for more than fifty years, having taken my place on the back of the bus and then gracefully accepted my place at the front, I have witnessed my share of deterioration of the spirit, of the body. I have seen deterioration and disintegration not only in other men, those dark pouches of disappointment beneath the eyes that they blame on their livers, but increasing fragility, as a stake in itself, a fragility in my leg, my leg like life itself, covered by an infestation of scabs. And scabs that hatch. And the bone seen peeping through the flesh. And the flesh has become paper beneath my grey trousers that are loose and baggy, three sizes too large for my body, my shrunken body. It is an act of faith, this determination to stay alive while we watch ourselves shrink, doing my best, as an act of the denial of death and dying by assertively wearing my paisley scarf that catches the sunlight of the mid-afternoon, brown, grey, maroon, gold dots, commas in the design of this scarf, a silk scarf glorious and aristocratic, which is still easy for me, for I used to be a man who was studied in the taking of time, even in my years of schooling, to arrive at an aristocratic bearing; for I always wore for public appearances charcoal grey trousers with an almost indiscernible thin vertical stripe in them; a white shirt with the front stiffened by starch, and a very hot iron, a white shirt worn in dress attire with mother-of-pearl studs; and a black silk jacket, single-breasted, custom-made, in a conservative English cut, being a practising gentleman of letters, of which I knew there were and are none too many in our time, bedecking myself in such an outfit and variations of it to assert the relishing of this aristocratic self, which makes me now feel the full weight of my bladder upon me, feel the apprehension of wetness, the apprehension of the stench of pure pee and the loss of all such earned dignity as I have, earned in the deepest sense, as one earns day to day a living. I shift from foot to foot, trying to take the weight off my bladder, which suddenly has the weight of all my past years, while at the same time I try to tighten my legs, to tense my whole body, to tense my mind, try to think of elsewhere; I go over the alphabet, from A to ZED... from A to ZEE... refusing to surrender to my body, to fragility, refusing incontinence, refusing to give in to any sign that all is lost, trying to remember so simple a thing as balance, the perfect balance that accrues to being young, along, of course, with the unknowingness that also accrues to being young; but now, being old, being one of *de old folks*, no matter where I rest or reside I have lost nearly all sense of balance, have lost my focus, lost even the quickness of the eye required to read the number on my house from inside a moving taxi, that number that I myself screwed into my green-painted front door, emerald green so I can alert some driver who has picked me up, who cannot speak my language, to the fact that We are Here, I am Here! "Here-here!" Home! As I shout, "Green," and we keep going, passing by the door, having to stop and back up, being fortunate for me that there is only one door on this street that is painted green, such taxi drivers telling me, "You? Sure? Okay? If you know where it is you going..."

The last time the driver letting me out to stand on the sidewalk like a lord, a landlord, outside my own door as I revised the muddle of my thoughts by revisiting the number of steps up the staircase inside the house that climbs from the front door, up... up... up... up... up... up... up... up... up... up... up... up... up... thirteen steps... an unlucky number!... and at the first floor top step turn right; and up... and I do this each time that I return home; and I wonder if the young woman who offered me her seat climbs an exact number of steps to reach her bedroom every night? High-stepping. I am tormented by yearned-for memories of my own high-stepping, tormented because everything remembered that gives me pleasure also becomes a torment to this black man who I admit is myself, absurd in blackface, toying with the metal wing opener to his Kiwi can, who only wants, when all is said and done, to sit for an hour in a large single bathtub, to soak, in hot suds, in contentment, in comfort and ease of heart, a heart that is beating hard, having climbed another fourteen steps, having gone round a corner in a hallway in order to get to my third-floor bedroom; and although the bones in my knees do not creak and crack, I am aware that so much time is passing so quickly; each stair reminding me of time, a step, a stair, an inch gained, an inch lost; all things being equal, I like my stairs. These stairs are my country. My country for an old man. I like the dignity that comes from having had the will to set my body straight, in an erect posture, if only for a moment, in order to climb...

To where I lie on my back on my bed; and I make myself raise each leg; and count to thirty, for each leg, and I huff and puff during these calisthenics that I've come to believe in as being good for me, and then my legs plop down on the bed, a remembrance of when I ran four races, meanwhile forgetting where my cell-phone is so's to call in case of emergency alone so high up in my house... But even so, if I had my cellular phone, all the names in my pocket diary are the names of friends dead, or nearly all of them dead. Dark casualties:

"...and Tom? Whu' happen to Tom?"

"He dead."

"...and when last you see Dick?"

"Dick gone, too."

"That is life. That is the life bequeath to all o' we."

"To all o' we!"

"I hate like arse getting old..."

"Who-else dead? One foot in the grave...?"

I dial a number, and a deep-throated hum, a misplayed bass note on an organ, takes over...

"...the number you have dialled, is no longer in service."

But I am still here, yes, still in service; and glad to be, even if I am *way down upon the ribber* in this land of the living where I one day lately, on a whim, went searching through old letters and older pocket diaries determined to seek out evidence of the living, to seek out all those still whinnying with us, their names in alphabetical order, the names of men and women with whom I grew up and also men and women in this alien country of silent people who do not open their front windows and say, "Mawnin, neighbour!" And so, as if the day I did this seeking out of names was actually the Day of Dead Souls, Ash Wednesday, I called their names, one-by-one. Down upon a river, up a creek they came, to let me mark the foreheads of my friends as each appeared before me in my bathroom mirror. I marked their brows with a penitential thumb smear of Kiwi black polish: Grace Sin-Hill. Dalton Guiler. Superintendent Boyce. Mewreel Sealey. Judy Thomas. Rudolph Hinds... I remember him, one of the best of tenors in Barbados. D. Parris. Everton Weekes (now Sir Everton Weekes). Richie Haynes (now Sir Richard Haynes). Jill Shephard. Bruce LaPorte, former Director of Black Studies at Yale University, Edward Cumberbatch, one of the best half-milers on the island, during my time, running on a hot afternoon track, marked in staggered lanes... and Malcolm X, Roy McMurtry (Judge of the Supreme Court), Norman Mailer, Morley, wagging his cane at me, telling me, "First, you outlive the bastards, then you outwrite them"... all such as these rising up in my mirror full of pride but marked by penitence, standing in their youth like standing in a river to surrender their seats to me, singing along with me, *dere's whu de old folks stay*, and among them, many beautiful women. Yes, beautiful. Surrendering. Yes, but on what grounds was this surrender made in my favour? Grounds that made me and still make me suspicious. Why does this unalloyed kindness bring out in me such suspicion?

It is the raw suspicion that I am a mere hindrance, to be helped as a way of avoidance, a suspicion that I do not seem to be an elderly, well-dressed West Indian gentleman... "an older man," a phrase used and regarded as a term of dignity and respect back in Barbados but here, in Toronto, there is no doff of the hat, no pleasant smile on the face, no wave of the hand. Suspicion that here in this country, in the privacy of the heart, I am regarded as "an old piece o' shit!" as my feet stumble and slip and slide on the moving steps of an escalator, or, upon my walking into a revolving door, being caught in the door by the rude disregard of the person ahead of me, so that, given the cautiousness common to old men, I freeze and become stiff, and I look as if I am dead – a corpse in a revolving door – and I go round two times more, against my will, sometimes three more carousel times!... before I dare to slip out and disappear in a silence of self-accusation and shame, completely bewildered as I hear from a distance the lazy lapping of waves at the edge of a beach where there is the smell of saltiness after a wave has died and the soft whisper of that dying breath touches my own lips with the fire of an unexpected kiss. A kiss that tells me that I love life. I love life even as I embrace wishes of the way I would like to die, to die in my sleep, in the embrace of sleep, where I would be insensitive to what is going on around me... But in the meantime... it is this "meantime" my God, that kills me. This meantime state of slow-moving uselessness like a sudden slap of blindness, this meantime in which so it seems I am having to re-learn, like a child, all the things I have taken for granted, that I take for granted on Bloor Street on this damp November Saturday late afternoon when I look up warily to see who is walking directly in my path and I pick a man, with my warning antennae out of the strolling crowd. He too is slow. He too is shaking. He tries to control two walking sticks. They wobble as he walks. He's hardly walking. Shuffling and stumbling. He raises the walking stick in his left hand, to greet me. Something like crazed glee, huge relief in his eye at seeing me. Certainly I recognize the man. But I do not understand why, of all the people to slip in and out of my memory, I should be confronted by this man. The stick in his left hand waves. I do not know if this is enthusiasm. Or threat. "Dave, short for Davenport. My name is Davenport. Windsor-hyphen-Britain." Dave! Oh God, oh God! From Trinidad. We were at U of T together. 1955. The stick in his right hand joins the other stick, waving his greeting. I pretend I do not recognize him. I am in blackface. Shining face. Shining with youngness. Doing my imitation of Al Jolson. He stops in my path. He is smiling. He is happy to see me. He is blocking me. I read his happiness at meeting his old friend. But I move around him. Out of his path. *My heart is turning ebber.* His mouth is open. I raise my right arm and say, like I used to in those civil right days, "Do you know what time it is?" His mouth hangs more open.

I have spotted a taxi. The taxi stops. "Where you going, old man?" the taxi driver calls out to me in a foreign accent, leaning across the front seat. I guess he is from Somalia. Or Nigeria. Or Niger. Or Zimbabwe. Or another country in Africa where they held the slaves before they packed them into small holds. Before they were shipped out on the passage to America and the West Indies.

Immediately, I resent this African, calling me an old man, when I am trying to cut years off my life; in protest against girls and women who offer me their seats on crowded buses, and in the subway; and in long lineups; and such meetings as this, meeting up, unsuspecting, with old lost friends, who, immediately in their flesh, in their deterioration held up by two walking sticks, remind me of how inevitably and finally lost I am. *Swanee*, I tell the driver. Take me to Swanee.

NATASHA

David Bezmozgis

It is the opposite which is good to us.
—Heraclitus

When I was sixteen I was high most of the time. That year my parents bought a new house at the edge of Toronto's sprawl. A few miles north were cows; south the city. I spent most of my time in basements. The suburbs offered nothing and so I lived a subterranean life. At home, separated from my parents by door and stairs, I smoke hash, watched television, read, and masturbated. In other basements I smoked, watched television, and refined my style with girls.

In the spring, my uncle Fima, my grandmother's youngest brother, married his second wife. She arrived from Moscow for two weeks to get acquainted with him and the rest of the family. Dusa, our dentist, had known the woman in Russia and recommended her. She was almost forty and my uncle was forty-four. The woman was the latest in a string of last chances. A previous last chance had led to his first marriage. That marriage, to a fellow Russian immigrant, had failed within six months. My uncle was a good man, a hard worker, and a polymath. He read books, newspapers, and travel brochures. He could speak with equal authority about the Crimean War and the Toronto Maple Leafs. Short months after arriving in Toronto he took a job giving tours of the city to visiting Russians. But he wasn't rich and never would be. He was also honest to a fault and nervous with people. My grandmother's greatest fear was that he would always be alone in the world.

Zina, the woman, had greasy brown hair cut in a mannish style. She was thin, her body almost without contour. The first time I saw her was when my uncle brought her to our house for dinner. She wore tight blue pants, high heels, and a yellow silk blouse which accentuated her conspicuously long nipples. The top buttons of her blouse were undone and a thin gold chain with a Star of David clung to her breastbone. When she kissed me in greeting she smelled of sweat and lilac.

Zina strode into our house as if she were on familiar territory, and her confidence had the effect of making my uncle act as though he were the stranger. He stumbled through the introductions and almost knocked over his chair. He faltered as he tried to explain how they had spent the day and Zina chided him and finished his sentences. When my mother served the raspberry torte, Zina fed my uncle from her fork. In Russia she was a "teacher of English" and she sprinkled her conversation with English words and phrases. The soup my mother served was "tasty," our dining room "divine," and my father "charming." After dinner, in the living room, she placed her hand on my uncle's knee. I was, as usual, high, and I became fixated on the hand. It rested on my uncle's knee like a small pale animal. Sometimes it would arch or rise completely to make a point, always to settle back on the knee. Under her hand, my uncle's knee barely moved.

After her two weeks in Canada, Zina returned to Moscow. Before she left, my mother and aunt took her shopping and bought her a new wardrobe. They believed that Zina would be good for my uncle. The last thing he needed was a timid wife. Maybe she was a little aggressive, but to make it in this country you couldn't apologize at every step like him. My grandmother was anxious because Zina had a young daughter in Moscow, but she conceded that at this age to find a woman without a child probably meant there was something wrong with her. My uncle did not disagree. There were positives and negatives, he said.

The decision was made quickly and days after Zina's departure my uncle wrote her a letter inviting her to return and become his wife. One month later, Zina was back in Toronto. This time, my entire family went to the airport to greet her. We stood at the gate and waited as a stream of Russian faces filtered by. Near the end of the stream, Zina appeared. She was wearing an outfit my mother had purchased for her. She carried a heavy suitcase. When she saw my uncle she dropped the suitcase and ran to him and kissed him on his cheeks and on his mouth. A thin blond girl, also carrying a suitcase, picked up Zina's abandoned bag and dragged both suitcases through the gate. The girl had large blue eyes and her straight blond hair was cut into bangs. She strained toward us with the bags and stopped behind Zina. She waited patiently, her face without expression, for her mother to introduce her. Her name was Natasha. She was fourteen. My mother said, Meet your new cousin. Later, as we drove my grandparents' home, my grandmother despaired that the girl's father was obviously a *shaygets.*

One week after their arrival, everyone went down to North York City Hall for the civil ceremony. A retired judge administered the vows and we took photos in the atrium. There was no rabbi, no chuppah, no stomping of the glass. Afterward, we all went to our house for a barbecue. One after another people made toasts. My uncle and Zina sat at the head of the table like a real married couple. For a wedding gift they were given money to help them rent a larger apartment. My uncle's one-bedroom would not do. This wasn't Russia and the girl couldn't continue to sleep in the living room. The one time my grandparents had gone to visit, Natasha emerged from the shower naked and, without so much as acknowledging their presence, went into the kitchen for an apple. While my grandparents tried to listen to my uncle and Zina talk about Zina's plans to get her teaching certificate, Natasha stood in the kitchen and ate the apple.

At the barbecue, my mother seated Natasha between me and my cousin, Jana. It was our duty to make her feel welcome. She was new to the country, she had no friends, she spoke no English, she was now family. Jana, almost two years my senior, had no interest in a fourteen-year-old girl. Especially one who dressed like a Polish hooker, didn't speak English, and wasn't saying anything in Russian either. Midway through the barbecue, a car full of girls came for Jana and Natasha became my responsibility. My mother encouraged me to show her around the house.

Without enthusiasm I led Natasha around the house. Without enthusiasm she followed. For lack of anything else to say, I would enter a room and announce its name in Russian. We entered the kitchen and I said kitchen, my parents' bedroom and I said bedroom, the living room, which I called the room where we watch television since I had no idea what it was called in Russian. Then I walked her down into the basement. Through the blinds we could see the backyard and the legs of our newly incarnated family. I said, That's it, the whole house. Natasha looked around the room and then shut the blinds, rendering the already dim basement almost dark. She dropped down into one of the two velour beanbag chairs I had in front of the television. Chairs that I had been earnestly and consistently humping since the age of twelve.

—You have all of this to yourself?

—Yes.

—It must be nice.

—It is.

—What do you do here?

—Watch television, read.

—That's it?

—That's most of it.

—Do you bring girls here?

—Not really.

—Have you had sex down here?

—What?

—You don't have to say if you don't want to. I don't really care. It doesn't mean anything.

—You're fourteen.

—So what? That doesn't mean anything either. I've done it a hundred times. If you want, I'll do it with you.

—We're cousins.

—No we're not.

—Your mother married my uncle. It's too bad. He's nice.

—He is.

—I feel sorry for him. She'll ruin his life.

—It's hard to imagine his life getting worse.

—She'll make it worse.

—She's your mother.

—She's a whore. Do you want to know how it sounds when they do it?

—Not particularly.

—They do it at least three times a day. He groans like he is being killed and she screams like she is killing him.

A month after the wedding. My uncle, Zina and Natasha rented a new two-bedroom apartment ten minutes' walk from our house. This was in the early summer and I was on vacation from school. Instead of going off to camp I made an arrangement to work for Rufus, my dealer. Over the course of the year we had become friends. He was twenty and, while keeping up his business, was also studying philosophy at the University of Toronto. Aside from providing me with drugs, he also recommended books. Because of him I graduated from John Irving and Mordecai Richler to Camus, Heraclitus, Catullus, and Kafka. That summer, in exchange for doing the deliveries, I got free dope - plus whatever I shorted off potheads - and a little money. I also got to borrow the books Rufus had been reading over the course of the year. This, to me, was a perfectly legitimate way to spend two months, although my parents insisted that I had to find a job. Telling them about the job I already had was out of the question, and so the summer started off on a point of conflict.

A week into my summer vacation, my mother resolved our conflict. If I had no intention of finding a job, she would put me to good use. Since I was home by myself I would be conscripted into performing an essential service. I was alone and Natasha was alone. She didn't know anyone in the city and was making a nuisance of herself. From what I could understand, she wasn't actually doing anything to be a nuisance, but her mere presence in the apartment was inconvenient. My family felt that my uncle needed time alone with his new wife and having Natasha around made him uncomfortable. Besides, she was difficult. My uncle reported that she refused to speak to her mother and literally hadn't said a word in weeks.

The morning after my mother decided that I would keep Natasha company I was on my way to my uncle's new apartment. I hadn't seen him, Zina, or Natasha since the wedding and the barbecue. They hadn't been back to our house and I had had no reason to go there. In fact, in all the years that my uncle lived in Toronto I had never been to his apartment. I preferred not to see how he lived.

By the time I arrived, my uncle had already left for work. Zina met me at the door wearing a blue Soviet housedress that could have passed for a hospital gown. Again, she wore no bra. I was greeted by nipples, then Zina. She put her hand on my arm and ushered me into the kitchen, where she was filling out forms to obtain credentials from the school board. A stack of forms was laid out on the table along with black bread and cucumbers. She made me a sandwich I did not want and told me what a wonderful man my uncle was. How she was very fortunate to find such a man and how good things would be as soon as Natasha became accustomed to their new life. We were co-conspirators, she and I, both working for Natasha's well-being. She was convinced that I would be able to help her. She sensed that Natasha liked me. Natasha didn't like many people.

—I'm her mother, and not matter what she says, I would cut off my right arm for her. But she has always been different. Even as a baby she hardly smiled.

Zina led me to Natasha's door and knocked. Through the door she announced that I was here. After a brief pause Natasha opened the door. She was wearing blue jeans and a souvenir T-shirt from Niagara Falls. I could see behind her into the room. There was a small bed and a table. On one wall was an old poster of Michael Jackson circa *Thriller*. In bold red letters a phonetic approximation of Michal Jackson's name was written in Cyrillic. I read the name slowly letter by letter since I was effectively illiterate. It gave me something to do while Natasha and Zina glared at each other in acrimonious silence.

—I'm an enemy because I took her away from her criminal friends. I'm an enemy because I wanted to give her a better life. Now she won't say a word, but one day she'll thank me.

Without breaking her silence, Natasha grabbed my hand and led me out of the apartment. As we went past the door Zina called after us telling me to watch out for Natasha. I was to make sure that she didn't do anything stupid. Natasha should remember what it would do to my uncle if something were to happen to her. Even if she didn't care about how Zina felt, she should at least consider my uncle, for whom she was now like a daughter.

In the stairway Natasha released my hand and we descended to the back of the building and the parking lot. Outside, she turned and spoke what must have been her first words in weeks.

—I can't stand looking at her. I want to scratch out my eyes. In Moscow I never had to see her. Now she's always there.

We wound our way out of the parking lot and toward the subdivisions leading back to my house. On the way I decided to stop at Rufus's and pick up an eighth for one of our regular heads. Rufus had a house not far from us, and since it was still early in the morning I knew that he would be home. I walked ahead and Natasha trailed along, more interested in the uniform lawns and houses than the specifics of where we were going. Aside from the odd Filipina nanny wheeling a little white kid, the streets were quiet. The sun was neither bright nor hot and the outdoors felt conveniently like the indoors: God's thermostat set to "suburban basement."

—In Moscow, everyone lives in apartments. The only time you see houses like this is in the country, where people have their dachas.

—Three years ago this was the country.

We found Rufus on his backyard deck listening to Led Zeppelin, eating an omelette. Although he was alone the table was set for four with a complete set of linen napkins and matching cutlery. Rufus didn't seem at all surprised to see us. That was part of his persona. Rufus never appeared surprised about anything. At twenty years old he had already accomplished more than most men twice his age. It was rumoured that aside from dealing Rufus was also a partner in a used car lot/body shop and various other ventures. Nobody who knew him had ever seen him sleep.

Even though I had only intended to see Rufus for as long as it took to get the eighth, he insisted on cooking us breakfast. Natasha and I sat at the kitchen counter as Rufus made more omelettes. He explained that even when he ate alone he liked to set a full table. The mere act of setting extra places prevented him from receding into solipsism. It also made for good karma, so that even when he was not expecting guests there existed tangible evidence announcing that he was open to the possibility.

While Rufus spoke Natasha's eyes roamed around the house, taking in the spotless kitchen, the copper cookware, the living room with matching leather sofas, the abstract art on the walls. If not for the contents of the basement refrigerator, the house gave no indication that it was owned and inhabited by a drug dealer barely out of his teens. This was no accident. Rufus believed that it helped his business. His clients were all middle-class suburban kids, and despite his bohemian inclinations, a nice house in the suburbs was the perfect location. It kept him local and it meant that, for his customers, a visit to their dealer felt just like coming home.

Back on the deck I explained to Rufus about Natasha, leaving out certain details I didn't think he needed to know. As Rufus and I talked, Natasha sat contentedly with her omelette and orange juice. Since we'd left my uncle's apartment her attitude toward everything had taken a form of benign detachment. She was calibrated somewhere between resignation and joy.

I noticed Rufus looking at her.

—Did I mention she was fourteen?

—My interest, I assure you, is purely anthropological.

—The anthropology of jailbait.

—She's an intense little chick.

—She's Russian. We're born intense.

—With all due respect, Berman, you and her aren't even the same species.

To get her attention Rufus leaned across the table and tapped Natasha on the arm. She looked up from her omelette and returned Rufus's smile. He asked me to translate for him. His own family, he said, could be traced back to Russia. He wanted to know what Russia was like now. What it was really like.

With a shrug Natasha answered.

—Russia is shit but people enjoy themselves.

After that first day, Natasha started coming to our house regularly. I no longer went to pick her up but waited instead for her to arrive. Through my basement window I could see her as she appeared in our backyard and wandered around inspecting my mother's peonies or the raspberry and red currant bushes. If I was in a certain mood I would watch her for a while before going upstairs and opening the sliding glass door in the kitchen. Other times I would just go and open the door. We spent most of our days in the basement. I read and Natasha studied television English. When I had a delivery to make she accompanied me. Between reading, television English, and deliveries, I taught Natasha how to get high. I showed her how to roll a joint, to light a pipe, or, in a pinch, where to cut the holes in a Coke can or Gatorade bottle. In exchange, Natasha taught me other things. Many of these things had nothing to do with sex.

After our days in the basement we would listen for my mother to arrive home from work. To avoid some serious unpleasantness I made a habit of setting my alarm for five o'clock. If we weren't sleeping, the alarm simply reminded us to open a window or get dressed. By the time my mother came home we were usually in the kitchen or out in the backyard. Chores that had been assigned to me were usually done at this time. It pleased my mother to come home and find me, spade in hand, turning over the earth around the berry bushes. Also, once it was established that Natasha much preferred to stay at our house, my mother grew more than accustomed to having her around. Unlike me and my father, Natasha volunteered to help her in the kitchen. The two of them would stand at the sink peeling potatoes and slicing up radishes and cucumbers for salad. I often came in to overhear my mother telling stories about her childhood in postwar Latvia – a land of outhouses, horse-drawn wagons, and friendly neighbours. In Natasha she found a receptive audience. They spoke the same language – Russian girl to Russian girl. This despite the fact that, in too many ways, Natasha's childhood couldn't have been more different from my mother's if she had been raised by Peruvian cannibals, but there was never any indication of this in our kitchen. Only my mother telling stories and Natasha listening.

Very quickly, our family of three became a family of four. No more than two weeks after I picked her up at my uncle's apartment Natasha became a fixture at our house. It was a situation that, for different and even perversely conflicting reasons, suited everyone. It solved the Natasha problem for my uncle. It solved the Zina problem for Natasha. It made my mother feel like she was protecting my uncle's last chance at happiness and also satisfying her own latent desire for a daughter. It absolved me of the need to find a job and cast me in a generally favorable light with the rest of my family. And, strangely enough, Natasha's incorporation into the household made the things we did in the basement seem less bad. Or not bad at all. What we did in the basement became only a part of who we were. There were layers upon layers. Which was why, at any one moment, I felt for Natasha the most natural and unusual feelings; to explain the feelings would be impossible, but whatever they were they were never bad.

Since I had been conditioned to approach sex as negotiation, I was amazed to discover that it could be as perfunctory as brushing your teeth. One day, after some but not too many days together, Natasha simply slid out of her jeans and removed her shirt. We were sitting inches apart, each on our own beanbag. Moments before, we had finished smoking a joint and I had gone back to Kafka's diaries. I became aware of what she was doing slower than a sixteen-year-old should have. I looked over as she was wriggling out of her pants. That she saw me looking changed nothing. On the beanbag, naked, she turned to me and said, very simply, as if it were as insignificant to her as it was significant to me: Do you want to? At sixteen, no expert but no virgin, I lived in a permanent state of want to. But for everything I knew, I knew almost nothing. In the middle of the day, Natasha in the basement, was the first time I had seen a live naked girl. All the parts available for viewing. Nothing in my previous dimly lit gropings compared. In my teenage life, what was more elusive than a properly illuminated naked girl? And the fact that it was Natasha – my nominal cousin, fourteen, strange – no longer mattered. After spending days with her and thinking about her at night, I knew very well how I felt. And so, when she asked if I wanted to, I wanted to.

That day was the first of many firsts. With the house to ourselves and no threat of being disturbed, we did everything I had ever dreamed of doing – including some things that hadn't even occurred to me. We showered together, we slept in the same bed, I watched her walk across the room, I watched her pee. These prosaic things, being new, were as exciting as the sex. And for me the sex was as much about the variation as the pleasure. Much of the pleasure was in the variation. I kept a mental list from position to position, crossing off one accomplishment after another. Nothing was repeated until everything was attempted. That way, in the event that I was struck by a bus, I would feel as though I had lived a full life. Most of the things we did Natasha had already done, but she was perfectly happy to oblige. If she was doing it as a favour, she never expected gratitude and demanded nothing in return.

In our quieter moments Natasha told me about the men who had taken her picture. She had never minded any of it, but she never understood why they couldn't explain why they liked one thing over another. They had always known exactly how they wanted her to look but none of them could give her a reason. Why did they prefer her leg raised this way and not that, why squatting from behind or holding her hand in a certain position? Some of the positions had been practically identical, and yet they had insisted on them. The only explanation they offered was that it looked good, or that it was sexy. And yet she never felt that way about men. she never cared how they looked, or what side she was viewing them from.

—You don't care how I look?

—You look how you look. If you bent over it wouldn't make any difference to me.

I bent over.

—That doesn't make any difference?

—It looks stupid. But what if I bend over? Does it look stupid?

—No, it looks good.

—Why is that?

—It just does.

—You can't explain it?

I thought it had to do with the forbidden. The attraction to the forbidden in the forbidden. The forbiddenest. But it still wasn't much of an answer.

At the same time that things with Natasha were improving my mother started to hear the first rumblings of trouble in my uncle's marriage. My grandparents, who had been accustomed to visiting my uncle frequently, were informed that maybe they shouldn't come over quite so often. Their habit of arriving unannounced was aggravating Zina, who insisted that she had too much to worry about without always having to accommodate my grandparents. My grandmother, although hurt, naturally made excuses for both my uncle and Zina. We were a close family, she said, but not all people can be expected to be the same way. Also, with time, as Zina became more comfortable, she was certain that she would feel differently. In any case, as long as my uncle was happy she was prepared to respect Zina's wishes. My uncle, for his part, said nothing. The signals were mixed. There was what my grandmother said, but my mother also knew that he and Zina took a weekend trip together to Niagara-on-the-Lake and another to Quebec City. After Quebec City my uncle sported a new leather jacket and a grey Stetson. Whatever was happening between them, he wasn't complaining.

I heard all of these things through my mother, but I also heard other things from Natasha. I now knew more about my uncle's life than I ever had, and certainly more than anyone else in my family. I knew, for instance, that he now spent as many nights on the living room couch as he did in the bedroom. I knew that Zina was racking up long-distance bills to Moscow, calling Natasha's father, a drunk who had effectively abandoned them years ago. She called in the mornings as soon as my uncle left for work and made various and emphatic promises. Natasha had seen her father only infrequently as a child, and was perfectly content to go the rest of her life without seeing him again. She could say the same thing about her mother. Essentially, since the age of eight, she had been on her own. Going to school, coming home cooking her own dinners, running around with friends. Zina, when not at work, was chasing after Natasha's father or bringing random men into the apartment. As much as possible, Natasha avoided her.

When Natasha was twelve a friend of hers told her about a man who paid ten dollars for some pictures of her. The girl had gone and taken a shower in the man's bathroom and he had not only paid her but also bought her dinner. He had promised her the same again if she could bring a friend. Ten dollars each for taking a shower. Natasha remembered thinking that the man had to be an idiot. She went, took her shower, and collected her ten dollars. There wasn't much to it and it wasn't as boring as hanging out at her friend's apartment. And ten dollars was ten dollars. Zina hardly gave her anything, and so it was good to have some of her own money.

After that man was another who took pictures of her and some friends in the forest. He had them climb birch trees and lie down in a meadow. He asked some of the girls to hold hands and kiss each other. Another man took some photos of her in her school uniform. None of these men touched her, but she wouldn't have care if they had. They were nice and she felt sorry for them.

All of this led eventually to a Soviet director who had gone from working at the Moscow studios to making pornographic movies for Western businessmen. The man had a dacha on the outskirts of the city and would send a car around to pick up Natasha and her friends. Some of these friends were girls, some boys. They would spend the day at the dacha eating, drinking, having a good time. At some point the director would shoot some movies of them. Aside from teenagers there were also older women. On the first day, Natasha watched the women have sex. She understood that doing it or not doing it was not a serious consideration. In the end, everyone did it. If not in movies, then somewhere else, and it made absolutely no difference one way or the other. The only thing about having sex at the dacha was that it was much more pleasant. The house was beautiful and there was a large lawn and a forest. There was also a *banya* and a Jacuzzi. The filming itself didn't even take very long. The rest of the time they just relaxed. She was never asked to do anything she didn't want to, and she never saw anyone else do something that she wouldn't have done herself. Even though she and her friends knew they wouldn't be at the dacha if it weren't for the movies, the sex never felt as though it were the focus. The director and the other men became their friends. They treated them very well. And if they wanted to sleep with the girls, the girls could see no reason why not. At the end of the day everyone got twenty-five dollars.

Natasha didn't have any of the pictures or movies, which was disappointing since I wanted to see them. But it wasn't like she was a model. She didn't keep an album of pictures to show to prospective photographers. She was the album. They looked at her and preferred not to know about her past. And without having pictures around there was no risk of Zina finding out what Natasha was doing. Not that she thought Zina would care, instead it was that Natasha suspected Zina would want the money. In any case, when Zina did finally find out it was only because she heard something from another girl's mother. And much as Natasha expected, Zina told her that if she was going to be a whore she could at least help out with the rent. Natasha never felt like a whore. She didn't do it for the money, but she also wasn't so stupid as to turn it down. If anyone was a whore, it was Zina. And she came cheap. She sold herself to Natasha's father for nothing, and the men she brought to the apartment treated her like filth. They paid her with curses and bruises.

I carried all this information around like a prize. It was my connection to a larger darker world. At Rufus's parties it allowed me to feel superior to the other stoner acolytes comparing Nietzsche to Bob Marley. I took Natasha to these parties and she stood quietly listening to our incoherent and impassioned conversations. Later she would surprise me with just how much she had understood. By midsummer, if called upon, Natasha could answer basic questions and had learned enough to know when to tell someone to fuck off. The other stoners liked more than anything to hear Natasha say fuck off in her crisp Moscow accent. In crude canine fashion, they accepted Natasha as one of their own. Natasha was cool.

We coasted this way into August when Zina appeared in our backyard one evening during dinner. The way she looked, it was clear that something horrible was about to happen. My mother opened the sliding door and Zina burst into our kitchen and inaccurately described what Natasha and I had been doing. Then screams, sobbing, and hysterics. I watched as my father wrenched Natasha from her mother, her teeth leaving a bloody wound on Zina's hand. Zina let fly a torrent of invective, most of which I couldn't understand. But I understood enough to know that what was happening in the kitchen was nothing compared with what was to come. Zina threatened to call the police, to place an ad in the Russian newspaper, to personally knock on all of our neighbours' doors. Natasha thrashed in my father's grip and freed herself enough to lunge unsuccessfully for a bread knife. She shrieked that her mother was a liar. I sat in my chair, nauseated, contemplating lies and escape.

After my father bandaged Zina's hand she waited outside while my mother talked with Natasha and me. With Zina outside my mother fumbled for the proper way to pose the question. It was hard to believe that what Zina was saying was true, but why would she make something like this up? Natasha said that it was because her mother hated her and never wanted her to be happy. She was jealous that Natasha was happy with us and wanted to ruin it, just as she had dragged Natasha from Moscow even though she hadn't wanted to go. Zina hated her and wanted to ruin her life, that was all. When my mother turned to me I denied everything. Unless Zina produced pictures or video I wasn't admitting a thing. I was terrified but I wasn't a moron.

When it became obvious that we had reached an impasse, my mother called my uncle. He came to our house in a state of anxiety that was remarkable even for him. He sat down between my mother and Zina on the living room couch. I was beside my father, who was in his armchair, and Natasha stood rigidly with her back against the door. My uncle confessed that he didn't know what was happening. Everything had been fine. What situation doesn't have problems, but on the whole he was content. The only explanation he could propose was that all of this might have had to do with a fight between Zina and Natasha over a phone bill. There had been a very expensive bill to Russia, almost six hundred dollars, which Zina had said were calls to her mother. He would understand that while getting used to a new life Zina would want to talk to her mother. Also, her mother was alone in Moscow and missed her. It was only natural that there would be calls. That there were so many was unfortunately a financial and not a personal problem. If it was within his means, he would be happy if Zina talked to her mother as much as she liked. But as it was, he had suggested that she try to be more careful about the amount of time she spent on the phone. They talked about it and she said she understood. It was then that Natasha accused Zina of lying to him and said she wanted her mother to tell him the truth about who she had been calling. This started a fight. But at no point did he hear anything about me and Natasha. He was certain it wasn't true and was just something between a mother and daughter. Everyone was still getting used to things and it would be a mistake to make too much of it. In a day or so everyone would calm down and it would be forgotten.

That night my uncle, Zina, and Natasha slept at our house. Natasha in the guest room, Zina on the downstairs couch, and my uncle on the floor beside her. Zina refused to leave the house without Natasha and Natasha refused to leave with Zina. I was relegated to my basement. In the morning Natasha had indeed calmed down and she agreed to return home with Zina and my uncle. Forgoing breakfast, the three of them walked out the door neither looking at or touching one another. As we watched them go my mother announced that she had now seen enough craziness to last a lifetime. Whatever the truth, she knew one thing for certain: Natasha and I were kaput.

The following day, after hours of waiting, I left the house and headed for Rufus's. Books, bong, television; no distraction could eclipse the greater distraction of Natasha's absence. I was alone in my basement, she was up eleven floors with Zina – I couldn't understand why she didn't come. Our afternoons could still be ours. My mother's proscription didn't have to be obeyed between nine and five. Had the situation been reversed, I would not have disappointed her. Despite everything that had happened the previous night. I couldn't see why anything needed to change. Clearly, judging from the teeth marks on Zina's hand, Natasha wasn't Zina's source of information. And even though Zina's accusation happened to be most true than not, it appeared to be an unfortunate raving coincidence rather than something she could confirm. I didn't see why I had to suffer because of a lunatic.

A pool company's van was parked outside Rufus's and I followed the sound of voices into the backyard. In the middle of the yard, Rufus stood with two men from the pool company. Guys in jeans and gold shirts with the pool company's logo stitched on the breast pocket. The three were talking like old friends, each with a beer in hand, discussing the possible dimensions of a possible pool. Rufus invited me to contribute to the deliberations. If the price was right they could start digging tomorrow.

I had never known Rufus to be much of a swimmer; on nights when some of the other stoners and I would hop the fences of neighbourhood pools, he rarely participated.

—Do you even swim?

—Berman, nobody swims in these things. They're for floating. Fill them up with plastic inflatables and free-associate. Gentle swaying stimulates the brainpan.

I watched the pool guys pacing off most of his yard.

—Why not start with a hammock and work your way up?

—Sometimes I'm out here and I need to take a leak. But I don't want to go inside. The weather's nice. I want to stay out but I need to pee. Just for that the pool would be worth the investment.

—You could pee on the bushes.

—I'm a suburban homeowner, there's a social contract. Pissing in the pool is fine but whipping out your dick and irrigating the shrubbery is bad news. It's all about property value.

I settled back on Rufus's deck and waited for the pool guys to leave. I had no deliveries to make that morning and I had neglected to bring along the books I was supposed to return to him. I was there without the veneer of pretext. After escorting the pool guys back to their van Rufus joined me on the deck.

—Where's the girl?

—With her mother.

—I thought she hated her mother.

—She does.

—So what are you doing here? Go liberate her.

—It's forbidden.

—You're sixteen, everything is forbidden. The world expects you to disobey.

—I've been accused of unnatural acts.

—Society was founded on unnatural acts. Read the Bible. You start with Adam and Eve, after that if somebody doesn't boink a sibling it's end of story.

—You mind if I use that argument with my mother?

Rufus got up and looked out across his yard.

—What do you think about a hot tub?

—Instead of the pool?

—With the pool. Do everything in mosaic tile. Give it a real Greek feel. Put up some Doric columns. Get a little fountain. Eat grapes. Play Socrates.

He descended from the deck and walked to the corner of his yard and struck a pose that was either Socrates or the fountain. Our conversation was over.

From Rufus's I walked to my uncle's building and lurked until an old man was buzzed in by another old man. Romeo climbed a trellis, so I took the stairs. Eleven flights later I was in the hallway, passing the smells of other apartments. With one or two exceptions all the doorposts had mezuzahs, just like the hallways above and below. Everyone conveniently assembled for UJA solicitors and neo-Nazis.

I knocked and Zina opened the door. She was wearing the same blue housedress. She blocked the doorway so that it was hard to see beyond her into the apartment. At first she said nothing. I had prepared myself for the worst, but she seemed pleased to see me.

—I wanted to apologize to you myself. I don't blame you for what happened. It wasn't your fault. She has turned grown men inside out and you're just a boy. It was crazy to expect anything else. I know how weak men are. I am to blame. The life in Russia was like a disease to children. Natasha is a very sick girl.

Behind Zina I noticed a movement. It was Natasha. I could see her over Zina's shoulder. She stood at the far end of the apartment, leaning against the living room couch. When I caught her eyes they reflected nothing. They were no less remote than the first time I saw her at the airport. She continued looking in my direction, but I couldn't discern if she was looking at me or the back of Zina's head. Zina, sensing Natasha's presence, turned to look at her daughter. When she looked back at me, her turning was a motion that included the closing of the door.

—It will be best for everybody if you didn't see Natasha anymore.

Late that night, after a day spent missing Natasha, despairing over the black void that was the remainder of my summer and my life in general, Natasha knocked on my basement window. I woke up and cupped my hands against the glass to see out. By the sound of the knock I knew it was her. I looked out and saw her squatting like a Vietnamese peasant in front of the window. In the dark it was hard to see her face. Upstairs in the kitchen I opened the sliding glass door and went into the yard to join her. She was hugging her knees at the base of our pine tree; her suitcase, the same one I had seen at the airport, was lying on the grass beside her. When I got close enough I could see that she had been crying.

I joined her on the grass. Already, after only one day apart and remembering the way she had looked at me over Zina's shoulder, I didn't feel as though I could touch her.

—You listened to her lies. Why did you listen to her lies?

—What was I supposed to do?

—You could have knocked her down. You could have broken down the door.

—And what then?

—I don't know. Something. Something else would have happened. But you left me alone with her.

—You looked right at me. Why didn't you say anything?

—But I already told you everything. You saw how she tried to ruin my life and your life and how she was killing your uncle. You knew all of this but you didn't do anything. You're like your uncle. You want people to make decisions for you.

Natasha picked at the grass. Tears welled up in her eyes. She let them fall. I got up and picked up her suitcase. It felt empty and weighed almost nothing. I made a move toward the house.

—What are you doing?

—Taking it inside.

—I can't go inside. I can't stay here. I have to leave.

—You have to leave tonight?

—Do you want to come with me?

—Where?

—Florida. One of the businessmen who came to the dacha lives there. He is very rich. He promised that if I ever came to Florida he would give me a job. He'll give you one too.

—We have to decide this tonight?

—Yes. I can't stay here and I can't go home. There is no more home. My mother has left your uncle. I can't live with her and I can't stay with him. I have nowhere to go.

—What do you mean your mother left my uncle?

—I forced them to decide.

I put the suitcase back down.

—She made him sleep on the couch again. I went out to the living room. At first he was asleep but when he woke up and understood what was happening he didn't stop me. He knew whose mouth it was. And then she heard and came out of the bedroom. He needed me to do it that way or he would never have gotten away from her. I wasn't going to let her ruin his life. I wasn't going to let her win.

Strangely, my first thought was about my grandmother. My next thought was that my uncle would kill himself.

—He let her insult him, embarrass him, steal his money. But he wouldn't leave her. He was a coward. So I gave him a coward's reason to leave. It's funny, other men would have felt the opposite way. They would have taken it as a reason to stay and spent the next two years fucking me.

I helped Natasha back down into the basement and promised her that I would wake her before my parents got up. I gave her my bed and slept on the floor. When the alarm rang I dug out all the money I had and gave it to her. It amounted to a little more than a hundred dollars. I watched her drag her suitcase down our street, heading in the direction of the bus station and Florida.

When my parents woke up the phones were already ringing. My uncle had arrived on my grandparents' doorstep at seven in the morning. His marriage was over. This confirmed my grandmother's suspicions. From the first she had felt something wasn't right with Zina. That her daughter was the product of a *shaygets* should have been enough. Now my uncle was without an apartment and he was financially obligated for Zina and Natasha because of the sponsorship papers he had signed. As to why the separation had to be so drastic, why he couldn't stay in the apartment until he found a new place, my uncle was vague. They could no longer live together. Nobody in my family asked about Natasha or even knew that she had left home. As far as the family was concerned, once my uncle severed his relationship with Zina, she and Natasha ceased to exist.

For days afterward I stayed in my basement. I had no interest in going out, seeing my friends, making deliveries. I was compromised by everything I knew. I knew too much about my uncle. I knew things about him that a sixteen-year-old nephew should not have known. And when my mother invited him to our house for dinner – in an effort to bolster his spirits – I sat across the table from him and tried to suppress the feeling of an awkward bond. The bond two men have when they have been with the same woman. It wasn't the sort of bond I wanted to share with my forty-four-year-old uncle, especially under the circumstances. But the feeling was more powerful than my desire not to feel it. It was too easy to picture him with her. Everything my uncle did during dinner – talking, eating, drinking – reminded me that he had been with Natasha. The mouth he spoke with, the hands he ate with, his physical self, were the same mouth, hands, self that had been with Natasha.

Of those first few depressing days after Natasha left, the dinner with my uncle was the worst. During that dinner he avoided the subject of Zina and Natasha entirely. It was the only thing on everyone's mind and so, characteristically, it was the only thing nobody mentioned. Instead my uncle gave a very long and detailed history of the Israeli-Palestinian conflict. Arafat, Rabin, Ben-Gurion, Balfour, Begin, Nasser, Sadat. I wondered what kept my uncle going. What life offered him. Why he didn't kill himself. Watching him, listening to him talk, I realized that there was nothing I could do for him. I felt better.

The following morning I ended my self-imposed seclusion and took the familiar walk to Rufus's. Weeks remained in my summer. There were books to read and whatever else the summer still had to offer. During my seclusion I had avoided all phone calls. Rufus had left typically cryptic messages, as did some of my other friends. Something in their voices intimated that there was excitement in our world. Activity was taking place without me. Conversations, discoveries, all sorts of important new things. Because of Natasha, I had removed myself from the common equation, and I was ready to return and accept my place within the social order.

Approaching Rufus's house, I wasn't surprised to see the pool company's van as well as a large truck brimming with dirt. Guys with wheelbarrows were carting dirt out from Rufus's yard and shovelling it into the truck. Teams of six landscapers shouldered ten-foot-long Doric columns in the opposite direction. The strains of Bizet's *Carmen* wafted from the backyard. The neighbourhood had never seen anything like it.

In the backyard, I spotted most of my friends. Guys that had never held down a real job, guys like me who spent their days in basements reading, smoking, and engaging in self-abuse. They were fanned out across Rufus's yard, straining, digging, smoothing, lifting, side by side with the landscapers and pool installers. They looked very happy. Intimately involved. And already they had succeeded in transforming Rufus's yard. A massive hole, many feet deep, dominated the property. An orange plastic fence had been erected around the hole's circumference to keep the workmen and stoners from accidentally falling in.

Up on the deck, seated with one of the pool guys I had seen on my last visit, was Rufus. A blueprint was laid out on the table and both of them were hunched over it as though it were a battle plan. I mounted the steps to the deck and stood behind Rufus and waited for him to acknowledge me. Over his shoulder I could see the detail of the blueprint. There were columns, cypress trees, a fountain, and Rufus's hot tub. Rufus looked up as I bent closer to get a better look. For the briefest instant his face assumed an expression I had never seen before. At that moment I didn't understand what it meant, but I later recognized it as pity.

—Berman, what's the matter, you don't return calls anymore?

He rose and had me follow him down into the yard. I felt the onset of dread. Something about Rufus's posture alerted me to tragedy. It was then that I also realized that none of my friends had said anything to me. The yard was busy, but not so busy that none of them would have seen me. I had, after all, seen them. the sum of these impressions began to register. I knew that whatever it was, it was very bad and that I was trapped and helpless to avoid the damage. I sensed all of this as I descended from the deck and heard the screen door open. Using her hip, Natasha slid the door closed. She was carrying a tray with a pitcher of water and multicolored plastic glasses. Rufus watched me for a reaction and then took me gently by the shoulder and out to the front of the house.

—Berman, this is why I asked you to call. I wanted to tell you on the phone, but it wasn't exactly the sort of thing I could leave on an answering machine.

Another team of landscapers passed us with a Doric column. I felt a compulsion to stick out my foot and trip them, to start a brawl, draw blood, break bones.

—She doesn't want to see you. I'm sorry about this, Berman. It's just the way it is.

—How much do those things weigh?

I made way for the Doric column.

—Not as much as you'd think. They're masonry and plaster, not marble. If they were marble I'd need slaves.

—I thought she was going to Florida.

—Come on, Berman, she's a fucking kid. How is she supposed to get to Florida? She barely speaks English. Either she's here or she's on the street.

—Right.

—She thinks you betrayed her. She's very principled. Anyway, she'll be safe here.

—That's one way to look at it.

—I hope you're not mad. It's not personal.

—I still have some of your books and maybe a few grams of weed.

—That's cool. Don't sweat it. Consider them yours.

—What a great deal for me.

—That's a shitty attitude, Berman. You're smarter than that.

—I'm a fucking genius.

—Take care of yourself, Berman.

I lingered in front of Rufus's house after he left and watched the wheelbarrows come and go. I waited for the workmen to bring in the last of the Doric columns and then walked home. In another country, under another code, it would have been my duty to return to Rufus's with a gun. But in the suburbs, at the end of my sixteenth summer, this was not an option. Instead, I resorted to a form of civilized murder. By the time I reached my house everyone in Rufus's yard was dead. Rufus, Natasha, my stoner friends. I would never see them again. By the time I got home I had already crafted a new identity. I would switch schools, change my wardrobe, move to another city. Later I would avenge myself with beautiful women, learn martial arts, and cultivate exotic experiences. I saw my future clearly. I had it all planned out. And yet, standing in our backyard, drawn by a strange impulse, I crouched and peered through the window into my basement. I had never seen it from this perspective. I saw what Natasha must have seen every time she came to the house. In the full light of summer, I looked into darkness. It was the end of my subterranean life.

GRIEF

ELIZABETH PHINNEY

I be alone now with the corrupt energy needed to survive strange places, though it was not always so. I be livin in a city where no right-minded creature should be, in a system so huge, I'll never be seein it one end to the other. I got digs under the concession stand at a drive-in movie theatre. It be dry and there be a field of puny plants adjoinin upon which to feed, but it be one helluva comedown from the glories I been livin. Clover be far and thievery be next. It be smellin bad; the stench from machines, movement without life, the stink of life that ain't life poisons everything within range.

There be many lost creatures about, haunted souls makin home in the bleakness. Skeletal cats hiss and yowl, rangy dogs shiver and howl at shadows, startin at any motion. There's one old codger I be seein, city man, diggin in the junk bins for treasure. He be shunned in his time, it be there in his eyes; he be seein what he can afford to. I followed him a ways on one mild day, through the screechin and the cryin and the cars and the riot that this place be made of. Down alleys, between buildings, his own kin reekin of fear, flyin by steerin clear like he be made of something dreadful, unearthly. He be queer lookin, smellin fusty. Collected bags of cans and bottles, torn old clothin, wire hangers. Whatever value he placed on them, I not be knowin. He got no home to keep these things. He got no place at all. He just keeps movin. I've got to dig my own den deeper, move on, or die.

I be havin a past like every livin thing and it clogs my days like a storm drain makin stagnant cesses of rainwater. Some days be so sweet the whole damn place shines and those be the days I indulge to no good end. Spinnin the reel of my life, freezin on beauty. Isabel be brushin her hair or pullin off old rubber boots too big by far, or maybe sittin in the sunshine, something simple and heart-stoppin and I could die rememberin but damned if I'll die with her forgotten. Memory be powerful.

It be a fine morning
(Knowin ye be somewhere in't)
I be seein nothing but car and stone
Hearin air rushin through city portals
Keenin and cryin;

But the clouds be racin and the wind be knowin me
Tellin

Flowin fury of greyed water roarin
Ripplin rhythm of long grass hissin
Swayin stand of forest hushin
Streamin silk of yer hair whisperin

I be cliff edge, embraced
Wind and I
Partners in Grace
And ye be the song of the tallest tree standin.

Black days I remember William. He be Isabel's dad and the man I would have called Father had I been born a human. He be a farmer, workin nature. Many days I chirped beside him in the fields as his will was wrought. He be something to see, liftin rocks ten times the size of my body and hurlin them away. He be so tall he comforted like a movin oak and I thought him as solid. I looked up, not knowin he shot my ma and any other pups she had with her, not rememberin Isabel's hands reachin down and scoopin me into her pocket, startin life between us.

Her ma be dead before I became and where she be learnin love is something only the earth be knowin. That is as it should be. Mystery be something I believe in. I knew the sweet bush and soft meadows framin the world and I knew the centre, the house, her room. I slept in a little hollow she could see from her window all the winters of my days, but never for long. Spring send me boundin in, weightless and happy. She be a fine companion. Every moment together be sweet; playin and laughin and chasin and singin. What be time? Ever and ever meant nothing. I be. Joy be simple. But change be the nature of all things and a big storm cloud moved in, swift and slick and full of hurt.

I be learnin then. Learnin groundhog and man. Learnin hurtin that ain't to defend but to possess, pleasure so dark with violence not one mote of light be shinin. Big black day when the sun be hid and time flowed in, corruptin me, cuttin my being in two like an axe. I be a witness. Blood and pleas in Isabel's soft room, William be hurtin her, takin his pleasure; twisted roots tangled never to stand true.

I still got no name for that day. Life before life after. She be blood and stillness and lonesomeness and I be erased in the face of that hurt. I froze with time until she rose up and told me my past, sobbed out the truth of my ma, of William, how I be *groundhog*. I skittered away with blanket of grief, draggin, with dead weight of knowledge pressin my brain, my heart. Flight away from the whole tremblin world; I ran blind, losin my shadow.

I walked on. To this place of deadness, this place of life that ain't life, though it be full of humans. My days be haunted. I be wantin to believe in William still, need to believe he be only weak, not evil. But faith be power and I got none. I dug this den shallow. Let the predators come, I'd like a fight. Let the fur fly. I run into kin, them brave enough, hungry enough, so sick with city they don't care whose turf they slink onto. I whistle waming (comeonyebastards) and they turn tail.

I remember only when I can't stop the reel from slowin, from snickin tight on frame of loss. I've got to dig my den deeper, move on, or die.

Today I be missin ye.
It be the warm weather, I be thinkin;
Soft grey air of spring lost on fall day.

It be so cold here 'midst many skin be
Pullin tighter holdin heat of hurt
Like life savings.
Eyes pink, filterin rose, but I not be cryin;
I be colder now than winter's breath
But I not be cryin, missin ye.

The editors wish to acknowledge their appreciation for all the work and concern given to this project by Marilyn Di Florio and Susan Walker

PERMISSIONS

Margaret Atwood

THE ART OF COOKING AND SERVING © O.W. Toad, 2006. From *Moral Disorder*, McClelland & Stewart Ltd., 2006. Reprinted by permission of the author and Random House of Canada Ltd.

EATING THE BIRDS © O.W. Toad, 2007. From *The Tent*, McClelland & Stewart Ltd., 2007. Reprinted by permission of the author and Random House of Canada Ltd.

THE MAN FROM MARS © O.W. Toad, 1998. From *Dancing Girls and Other Stories*, Emblem Editions, 2008. Reprinted by permission of the author and Random House of Canada Ltd.

THE VICTORY BURLESK © O.W. Toad, 1983. From *Murder in the Dark*, McClelland & Stewart, 1997. Reprinted by permission of the author and Random House of Canada Ltd.

David Bezmozgis

NATASHA © David Bezmozgis, 2005. From *Natasha and Other Stories*, Harper Perennial Canada, 2005. Reprinted by permission of Harper Perennial Canada.

Alice Boissonneau

DINGLES © Alice Boissonneau, 1991. From *There Will Be Gardens*, Exile Editions, 1991. Reprinted by permission of Exile Editions.

EARLY MORNING © Alice Boissonneau, 1991. From *There Will Be Gardens*, Exile Editions, 1991. Reprinted by permission of Exile Editions.

SHADOWS © Alice Boissonneau, 1991. From *There Will Be Gardens*, Exile Editions, 1991. Reprinted by permission of Exile Editions.

WINTER © Alice Boissonneau, 1991. From *There Will Be Gardens*, Exile Editions, 1991. Reprinted by permission of Exile Editions.

Joseph Boyden

PAINTED TONGUE © Joseph Boyden, 2001. From *Born with a Tooth*, Cormorant Books Inc., 2008. Reprinted by permission of the author.

Dionne Brand

AT THE LISBON PLATE © Dionne Brand, 1994. From *Sans Souci and Other Stories*, Women's Press Literary, 1994. Reprinted by permission of the author.

Nina Bunjevac

THE REAL DEAL © Nina Bunjevac, 2012. From *Heartless*, Conundrum Press, 2012. Reprinted by permission of the author.

Barry Callaghan

THE BLACK QUEEN © Barry Callaghan, 1982. From *The Black Queen Stories*, Little Brown and Company Canada, 1994. Reprinted by permission of the author.

CROW JANE'S BLUES © Barry Callaghan, 1982. From *The Black Queen Stories*, Little Brown and Company Canada, 1994. Reprinted by permission of the author.

OUR THIRTEENTH SUMMER © Barry Callaghan, 1995. From *A Kiss Is Still a Kiss*, Little Brown and Company, 1995. Reprinted by permission of the author.

Morley Callaghan

THE CHISELLER © Estate of Morley Callaghan, 2012. From From *The Collected Stories of Morley Callaghan, Volume One*, The Exile Classics Series Number 22, Exile Editions, 2012. Reprinted by permission of the Estate of Morley Callaghan.

LAST SPRING THEY CAME OVER © Estate of Morley Callaghan, 2012. From *The Collected Stories of Morley Callaghan, Volume Two* The Exile Classics Series Number 23, Exile Editions, 2012. Reprinted by permission of the Estate of Morley Callaghan.

A SICK CALL © Estate of Morley Callaghan, 2012. From *The Collected Stories of Morley Callaghan, Volume One*, The Exile Classics Series Number 22, Exile Editions, 2012. Reprinted by permission of the Estate of Morley Callaghan.

STRANGE FUGITIVE © Estate of Morley Callaghan, 2011, The Exile Classics Series Number 19. From *Strange Fugitive*, Exile Editions, 2011. Reprinted by permission of the Estate of Morley Callaghan.

Austin Clarke

GALAXIE © Austin Clarke, 2013. From *They Never Told Me and Other Stories*, Exile Editions, 2013. Reprinted by permission of the author.

OXTAILS WITH MUSHROOMS AND RICE © Austin Clarke, 1999. From *Pig Tails 'n Breadfruit*, Random House Canada, 1999. Reprinted by permission of the author.

THEY NEVER TOLD ME © Austin Clarke, 2013. From *They Never Told Me and Other Stories*, Exile Editions, 2013. Reprinted by permission of the author.

Matt Cohen

AFTER DINNER BUTTERFLIES © 1972, 2013 Stickland Ltd. From *Columbus and the Fat Lady, and Other Stories,* House of Anansi, 1972. Reprinted by permission of Stickland Limited.

David Cronenberg & Norman Snider

DEAD RINGERS © David Cronenberg, Norman Snider, 1988. Reprinted by permission of the authors.

Robertson Davies

WHAT'S BRED IN THE BONE © Robertson Davies, 1985. From *What's Bred in the Bone*, Macmillan of Canada, 1985. Reprinted by permission of Pendragon Ink.

Mazo de la Roche

THE CURE © Mazo de la Roche, 1928. From *Selected Stories of Mazo de la Roche*, University of Ottawa Press, 1979. Reprinted by permission of Peters Fraser & Dunlop on behalf of the Estate of Mazo de la Roche.

Sorel Etrog

DREAM CHAMBER © Sorel Etrog, 1986. From *Dream Chamber*, Exile Editions, 1986. Reprinted by permission of the artist.

GLOBAL VILLAGE © Sorel Etrog, 1980. Printed by permission of the artist.

Timothy Findley

THE WARS © Timothy Findley, 1977. From *The Wars*, Clarke, Irwin & Company Ltd., 1977. Reprinted by permission of the Estate of Timothy Findley.

Joe Fiorito

THE BLOOR STREET VIADUCT © Joe Fiorito, 2006. From *Union Station*, McClelland & Stewart Ltd., 2006. Reprinted by permission of the author.

CHESTNUTS © Joe Fiorito, 2006. From *Union Station*, McClelland & Stewart Ltd., 2006. Reprinted by permission of the author.

GO, GO, GO ON © Joe Fiorito, 2006. From *Union Station*, McClelland & Stewart Ltd., 2006. Reprinted by permission of the author.

KEYS © Joe Fiorito, 2006. From *Union Station*, McClelland & Stewart Ltd., 2006. Reprinted by permission of the author.

Lisa Foad

LOST DOGS © Lisa Foad, 2008. From *The Night Is a Mouth*, Exile Editions, 2009. Reprinted by permission of the author.

Vera Frenkel

ONCE NEAR WATER © Vera Frenkel, 2008. Stills sequence from *ONCE NEAR WATER: Notes from the Scaffolding Archive*, video, 15:25 minutes r.t., 2008. Printed by permission of the artist.

Hugh Garner

CABBAGETOWN © Hugh Garner, 1968. From *Cabbagetown*, The Ryerson University Press, 1968. Reprinted by permission of the Estate of Hugh Garner.

Katherine Govier

THE IMMACULATE CONCEPTION PHOTOGRAPHY GALLERY © Katherine Govier, 1994. From *The Immaculate Conception Photography Gallery*, Little, Brown Canada, 1994. Reprinted by permission of the author.

SOCIOLOGY © Katharine Govier, 1985. From *Fables of Brunswick Avenue*, Harper Perennial Canada, 2006. Reprinted by permission of the author.

Barbara Gowdy

WE SO SELDOM LOOK ON LOVE © Barbara Gowdy, 1992. From *We So Seldom Look on Love: Stories*, Somerville House Publishing, 1992. Reprinted by permission of the author.

Linda Griffiths

A GAME OF INCHES © Linda Griffiths, 2009. First appeared in *Exile: The Literary Quarterly*, Vol. 33 No. 1, 2009. Reprinted by permission of the author.

Max Haines

THE RINGER © Max Haines. First appeared in the *Toronto Sun*, 1989. Reprinted by permission of the author.

Steven Hayward

AUGUST 7, 1921 © Steven Hayward, 2000. From *Buddha Stevens and Other Stories*, Exile Editions, 2000. Reprinted by permission of the author.

Sheila Heti

HOW SHOULD A PERSON BE? : WHAT IS DESTINY? © Sheila Heti, 2011. From *How Should A Person Be?*, House of Anansi, 2011. Reprinted by permission of House of Anansi Press.

Greg Kearney

WHAT TO WEAR © Greg Kearney, 2011. From *Pretty*, Exile Editions, 2011. Reprinted by permission of the author.

M.T. Kelly

MERCY MISTER PERCY © M.T. Kelly, 2013. Printed by permission of the author.

Sang Kim

WHEN JOHN LENNON DIED © Sang Kim, 2013. From *Carter V. Cooper Short Fiction Anthology Series*, Book Three, Exile Editions, 2013. Reprinted by permission of the author.

Janice Kulyk Keefer

MRS. PUTNAM AT THE PLANETARIUM © Janice Kulyk Keefer, 1986. From *The Paris-Napoli Express*, Oberon Press, 1986. Reprinted by permission of the author.

Gwendolyn MacEwen

DANCING © Gwendolyn MacEwen, 1972. From *Noman's land*, Oberon Press, 1972. Reprinted by permission of the Estate of Gwendolyn MacEwen.

THE DANFORTH © Gwendolyn MacEwen, 1972. From *Noman's land*, Oberon Press, 1972. Reprinted by permission of the Estate of Gwendolyn MacEwen.

THE GRINDER © Gwendolyn MacEwen, 1972. From *Noman's land*, Oberon Press, 1972. Reprinted by permission of the Estate of Gwendolyn MacEwen.

THE MINNIES © Gwendolyn MacEwen, 1972. From *Noman's land*, Oberon Press, 1972. Reprinted by permission of the Estate of Gwendolyn MacEwen.

NIGHTCHILD © Gwendolyn MacEwen, 1972. From *Noman's land*, Oberon Press, 1972. Reprinted by permission of the Estate of Gwendolyn MacEwen.

SHORESIDE © Gwendolyn MacEwen, 1972. From *Noman's land*, Oberon Press, 1972. Reprinted by permission of the Estate of Gwendolyn MacEwen.

THE TOWER © Gwendolyn MacEwen, 1972. From *Noman's land*, Oberon Press, 1972. Reprinted by permission of the Estate of Gwendolyn MacEwen.

Robert Markle

BLAZING FIGURES © Robert Markle. From *15 Years in Exile, Volume 1*, Exile Editions, 1992. Reprinted by permission of the Estate of Robert Markle.

Bruce Meyer

THE STALLION AND THE SULTAN OF SWAT: A TRUE STORY © Bruce Meyer. First appeared in *Exile: The Literary Quarterly*, Vol. 35 No. 2. Reprinted by permission of the author.

Anne Michaels

FUGITIVE PIECES © Anne Michaels, 1996. From *Fugitive Pieces*, McClelland & Stewart Inc., 1996. Reprinted by permission of the author.

Christine Miscione

SKIN, JUST © Christine Miscione, 2013. From *Auxiliary Skins*, Exile Editions, 2013. Reprinted by permission of the author.

bpNichol

BLUES © bpNichol, 1974. From *love: a book of remembrances*, Talonbooks, 1974. Reprinted by permission of the Estate of bpNichol.

Michael Ondaatje

IN THE SKIN OF A LION: THE BRIDGE © Michael Ondaatje, 1987. From *In the Skin of a Lion*, McClelland & Stewart, 1987. Reprinted by permission of Trident Media Group.

Charles Pachter

FAMILY,1970 © Charles Pachter. Lithograph printed by permission of the artist.

Susan Perly

LOVE STREET: 1037 ON YOUR FM DIAL © Susan Perly, 2001. From *Love Street*, The Porcupine's Quill, 2001. Reprinted by permission of the author.

1956: GLENN GOULD AND THELONIOUS SPHERE MONK © Susan Perly, 1990. From *Hard Times*, The Mercury Press, 1990. Reprinted by permission of the author.

Elizabeth Phinney

GRIEF © Elizabeth Phinney, 2008. From *Exile: A Literary Quarterly*, Vol. 15 No. 1, 2008. Reprinted by permission of the author.

B.W. Powe

THE NOISE OF TIME © B.W. Powe, 1989. From *The Glenn Gould Profile*, Collections Canada, National Library Archives. Reprinted by permission of the author.

Paul Quarrington

KING LEARY © Paul Quarrington, 1987. From *King Leary*, Doubleday Canada Limited, 1987. Reprinted by permission of the Estate of Paul Quarrington.

John Reeves

THE ARTISTS JAZZ BAND: COUGHTRY, RAYNER, MARKLE, 1965 © John Reeves. Printed by permission of the artist.

Leon Rooke

HITTING THE CHARTS © Leon Rooke, 2006. From *Hitting the Charts*, Biblioasis, 2006. Reprinted by permission of the author.

Joe Rosenblatt

STORMED BY SUNLIGHT © Joe Rosenblatt, 1985. From *Escape from the Glue Factory,* Exile Editions, 1987. Reprinted by permission of the author.

R. Murray Schafer

ARIADNE © R. Murray Schafer, 1985. From *Ariadne,* The Porcupine's Quill, 1985. Reprinted by permission of the author.

Matt Shaw

MATCHBOOK FOR A MOTHER'S HAIR © Matt Shaw, 2007. From *The Obvious Child,* Exile Editions, 2007. Reprinted by permission of the author.

Sarah Sheard

EUGENIA © Sarah Sheard, 1992. Reprinted by permission of the author.

Michael Snow

WALKING WOMAN © Michael Snow. A still photo from *New York Eye and Ear Control,* 1964 – 16mm film, 35 minutes r.t., B&W, sound. Printed by permission of the artist.

Helen Weinzweig

WHAT HAPPENED TO RAVEL'S *BOLERO*? © Helen Weinzweig, 1989. From *A View from the Roof,* Goose Lane Editions, 1989. Reprinted by permission of the Estate of Helen Weinzweig.

H. Masud Taj

IMPOSSIBLE TORONTO © H. Masud Taj, 2013. Printed by permission of the author/calligrapher.

Ludwig Zeller

EPONA AT HER MIRROR © Ludwig Zeller. Reproduced in *To Saw the Beloved to Pieces Only When Necessary,* Exile Edition, 1990 (original title: Rearview Mirror). Reprinted by permission of Susana Wald.

L,O,V,E,R,S © Ludwig Zeller, 1979. Six letters from *Alphacollage,* The Porcupine's Quill, 1979. Reprinted by permission of Susana Wald.

THE SPHINX IN TORONTO © Ludwig Zeller, illustration to the homonymous poem, published in *When the Animal Rises from the Deep the Head Explodes,* Mosaic Press/Valley Editions, 1976. Reprinted by permission of Susana Wald.

BIOGRAPHICAL NOTES

Atwood, Margaret (1939–). Born in Toronto, Atwood's 15 novels include *The Edible Woman* (1969), *Surfacing* (1972), *Life Before Man* (1979), *The Handmaid's Tale* (1985), *Cat's Eye* (1988), *The Robber Bride* (1993), *Alias Grace* (1996), *Oryx and Crake* (2003), *The Penelopiad* (2005) and *The Year of the Flood* (2009). Her poetry collections include *The Circle Game* (1964), *You Are Happy* (1974), *Interlunar* (1984), *Morning in the Burned House* (1995), and *Maddaddam* (2013). She has received many of literature's most prestigious awards, including the Governor General's Award (1966, 1985), the Trillium Book Award (1991, 1993, 1995) and the Booker Prize (2000).

Bezmozgis, David (1973–). Born in Riga, Latvia, Bezmozgis lives in Toronto. His published works include *The Free World* (2011) and the story collection, *Natasha and Other Stories* (2004), which won the Commonwealth Writers' Prize for Best First Book (Canada and Caribbean Region) and the Reform Judaism Prize for Jewish Fiction. Bezmozgis' first feature film, *Victoria Day* (2009), debuted at the Sundance Film Festival. In 2012, he was named one of the *New Yorker*'s "20 Under 40."

Boissonneau, Alice (1918–2007). Born in Walkerton, Ontario, Boissonneau was a novelist and short story writer who also published a memoir of life in Toronto, *There Will Be Gardens* (1991). Her stories have appeared in *Canadian Forum*, *Alphabet*, and *Exile*, and she also wrote for the *Anthology* series on CBC Radio. She is the author of two novels, *Eileen McCullough* (1983) and *A Sudden Brightness* (1994).

Boyden, Joseph (1966–). Born and raised in Willowdale, Boyden is the author of three novels: *Three Day Road* (2005), which won the Amazon/Books in Canada First Novel Award and the Rogers Writers' Trust Fiction Prize, *Through Black Spruce* (2008), which won the Giller Prize, and *The Orenda* (2013). His short fiction collection, *Born with a Tooth*, was published in 2001.

Brand, Dionne (1953–). Born in Guayguayare, Trinidad, Brand moved to Toronto in 1970. She has published several volumes of poetry, including *Land to Light On*, which won the Governor General's Award in 1997, *thirsty* (2002, shortlisted for the Griffin Poetry Prize), and *Ossuaries* (2010). Brand's fiction includes the short story collection *San Souci and Other Stories* (1989), and the novels *At the Full and Change of the Moon* (1999), and *What We All Long For* (2004). Her non-fiction publications include *No Burden to Carry* (1991), *Bread Out of Stone* (1994), and *A Map to the Door of No Return* (2001). She currently lives in Toronto and teaches at the University of Guelph.

Bunjevac, Nina. (1973–) A comic book artist, illustrator and art teacher, Bunjevac's work has been published in a variety of literary magazines and comic anthologies in Europe, the United States and Canada, including *Exile, Mineshaft, Black, Giuda, Le Dernier Cri, Komikaze* and *Broken Pencil.* Her comics collection, *Heartless*, was released in 2012. She lives in Toronto.

Callaghan, Barry (1937–). Born in Toronto, the son of Morley Callaghan, Callaghan became an English professor at York University and also founded the journal *Exile* and the publishing house Exile Editions. Callaghan is a poet, novelist, journalist and translator. His books include *The Hogg Poems and Drawings* (1978), *The Black*

Queen Stories (1982), *When Things Get Worse* (1993), *A Kiss Is Still a Kiss* (1995), *Between Trains: stories* (2008), *Beside Still Waters* (2009), the memoir *Barrelhouse Kings* (1998) and three volumes of collected non-fiction, *Raise You Five* (2005), *Raise You Ten* (2006), and *Raise You Twenty* (2011).

Callaghan, Morley (1903–1990). Born in Toronto, his earliest stories appeared in the Paris literary magazines *Transition* and *This Quarter.* His novels include *Strange Fugitive* (1928; new in 2011), *Such Is My Beloved* (1934), *More Joy in Heaven* (1937), *The Loved and the Lost* (1951; new in 2012), *A Time for Judas* (1983) and *Our Lady of the Snows* (1985). His short story collections include *Now That April's Here* (1936), *Morley Callaghan's Stories* (1959) and *The Complete Stories of Morley Callaghan: Volumes One - Four* (2012). He is also the author of a memoir about his youthful literary adventures with Hemingway, Fitzgerald and other literary notables, *That Summer in Paris* (1963; new expanded edition 2013).

Clarke, Austin (1934–). Clarke emigrated to Toronto from Barbados in 1955 to study economics and political science at the University of Toronto. Best known for his trilogy of novels about immigrant life in Toronto and *The Polished Hoe* (2002), winner of the Giller Prize, Clarke has also written six volumes of short stories including *In This City* (1992), *There Are No Elders* (1993), *Choosing His Coffin* (2003) and *They Never Told Me and Other Stories* (2013), and several works of non-fiction, including *Growing Up Stupid Under the Union Jack* (1980), *A Passage Back Home* (1994) and *Pig Tails 'n Breadfruit* (1999).

Cohen, Matt (1942–1999). Born in Kingston and raised in Ottawa, Cohen received the Governor General's Award for his novel, *Elizabeth and After.* His work includes the novels *Korsoniloff* (1969), *The Disinherited* (1974), *The Sweet Second Summer of Kitty Malone* (1979), *Nadine* (1987), and *Emotional Arithmetic* (1990); the short story collections *Columbus and the Fat Lady* (1972), *Night Flights* (1978), *The Expatriate* (1982), *Racial Memories* (1990) and *Getting Lucky* (2011); 10 childrens' books; and the memoir, *Typing: A Life in 26 Keys* (2000).

Cronenberg, David (1943–). Born in Toronto, Cronenberg is an internationally acclaimed filmmaker, screenwriter and actor. An Officer of the Order of Canada and a Fellow of the Royal Society of Canada, his films include *Stereo* (1969), *Shivers* (1975), *Rabid* (1977), *Scanners* (1981), *The Fly* (1986), *Dead Ringers* (1988), *A History of Violence* (2005), *Eastern Promises* (2007), *A Dangerous Method* (2011) and *Cosmopolis* (2012).

Davies, Robertson (1913–1995). A novelist, playwright, critic, journalist and professor, Davies was among Canada's best-known writers and men of letters. His 11 novels include *Fifth Business* (1970), *The Manticore* (1972), *What's Bred in the Bone* (1985), *The Lyre of Orpheus* (1988) and *The Cunning Man* (1994). A recipient of many awards, Davies received the Governor General's Literary Award in 1972, was shortlisted for the Booker Prize in 1986 and was inducted as Companion of the Order of Canada in 1973.

de la Roche, Mazo (1879–1961). Born in Newmarket, Ontario, de la Roche is remembered for her *Jalna* novels – which became international bestsellers in the 1930s – about a grand house in a fictional town based on Clarkson, Ontario. Among her books in the series are *Jalna* (1927), *Whiteoaks of Jalna* (1929), *The Master of Jalna* (1933), *Young Renny* (1935), *Return to Jalna* (1946) and *Morning at Jalna* (1960). She was also the author of short stories and a memoir, *Ringing the Changes* (1957).

Etrog, Sorel (1933–). Born in Romania, Sorel Etrog is a Canadian sculptor and writer. His artwork has been widely exhibited in Canada and abroad, and has been commissioned in major international cities around the world. As a writer, he is best known for *Spiral,* his collaboration with Marshall McLuhan, and for his illustrations for such writers as Samuel Beckett and Eugene Ionesco. Sorel Etrog was appointed a member of the Order of Canada in 1994 and was made a Chevalier de l'Ordre des Arts et des Lettres by the Government of France in 1996.

Findley, Timothy (1930–2002). Born in Toronto, Findley had a successful career as an actor before he began writing. His novels include *The Last of the Crazy People* (1967), *The Wars* (1977), *Famous Last Words* (1981), *Not Wanted on the Voyage* (1984), *The Piano Man's Daughter* (1995), *Pilgrim* (1999) and *Spadework* (2001). His short stories have been collected in three volumes, *Dinner Along the Amazon* (1984), *Stones* (1988) and *Dust to Dust* (1997). His non-fiction includes *Inside Memory* (1990), *From Stone Orchard* (1998) and *Journeyman: Travels of a Writer* (2004).

Fiorito, Joe (1948–). Born in Thunder Bay, Ontario, Joe Fiorito is a city columnist for the *Toronto Star.* He is the author of a best-selling memoir, *The Closer We Are to Dying* (1999), and the novels *Tango on the Main* (1996), *Comfort Me with Apples: Considering the Pleasures of the Table* (2000), *The Song Beneath the Ice* (2003), which won the City of Toronto Book Award, and *Union Station: Love, Madness, Sex, and Survival on the Streets of New Toronto* (2007).

Foad, Lisa (1976–). A Canadian short story writer and journalist, Foad lives in Toronto. Her debut collection, *The Night Is a Mouth* (2008) won the 2009 ReLit Award for short fiction, as well as an Honour of Distinction citation from the Writers' Trust of Canada 2010 Dayne Ogilvie Grant for an emerging lesbian, gay, bisexual or transgender writer.

Frenkel, Vera (1938–). One of Canada's most renowned multidisciplinary artists, respected both internationally and at home, Frenkel's installations, videotapes, performances and new media projects address the forces at work in human migration, the learning and unlearning of cultural memory and the ever-increasing bureaucratization of experience. She lives in Toronto.

Garner, Hugh (1913–1979). Born in Cabbagetown in Toronto, Garner is best known for his novel by that name, *Cabbagetown* (1950). His other books include *Storm Below* (1949), *Waste No Tears* (1950), *The Yellow Sweater* (1952), *Hugh Garner's Best Short Stories* (1963), which received the Governor General's Award for Fiction, *Author, Author!* (1964), *Men and Women* (1966) and *One Damned Thing After Another!* (1973).

Govier, Katherine (1948–). Born in Edmonton and now living in Toronto, Govier writes fiction and non-fiction. She has published nine novels and three collections of short fiction, including *Random Descent* (1979), *Going Through the Motions* (1982), *Fables of Brunswick Avenue* (1985), *Angel Walk* (1996), *The Truth Teller* (2000), *Creation* (2002) and *Three Views of Crystal Water* (2005). She has been a visiting lecturer in Canadian and British universities and received the Marion Engel Award in 1997.

Griffiths, Linda (1956–). Born in Montreal, Griffiths lives and works in Toronto. A writer, actress and playwright, her dramatic works include the plays *Maggie and Pierre* (1981), *Jessica* (1987), *Brother Andre's Heart* (1992), *The Darling Family* (1992), *The Duchess* (1998), *Alien Creature* (2000) and *Age of Arousal* (2007). In 1989 she published the non-fiction book, *The Book of Jessica: A Theatrical Transformation.* She is the winner of numerous awards, including five Dora Mavor Moore Awards and a Gemini Award.

Gowdy, Barbara (1950–). Born in Toronto, Gowdy is the author of six novels, *Through the Green Valley* (1988), *Falling Angels* (1989), *Mister Sandman* (1995), *The White Bone* (1999), *The Romantic* (2003) and *Helpless* (2007), and a collection of short stories, *We So Seldom Look on Love* (1996).

Haines, Max (1931–). Born in Nova Scotia, Max Haines is the author of 27 books. He is best known for his "Crime Flashback" column, appearing in the *Toronto Sun* and syndicated across Canada, and Latin and South America. He lives in Toronto with his wife.

Hayward, Stephen. Born in Toronto, Hayward is the author of two novels, *The Secret Mitzvah of Lucio Burke* (2005) and *Don't Be Afraid* (2011), and a short story collection, *Buddah Stevens and Other Stories* (2000) which won the $10,000 Upper Canada Writers' Craft Award in 2001.

Heti, Sheila (1976–). Heti was born in Toronto and is the author of a collection of fiction, *The Middle Stories* (2001), the novels *Ticknor* (2005) and *How Should a Person Be?: A Novel from Life* (2012), and co-author of *The Chairs Are Where the People Go* (2011), with Misha Glouberman.

Kearney, Greg (1973–). Born in Kenora, Ontario, Kearney has lived in Toronto since 1993. He is the author of the story collections *Mommy Daddy Baby* (2004) and *Pretty* (2011), and playwright of *The Cry Sisters*, *The Betty Dean Fanzine*, and *Cancun.* He was resident humour columnist for *Xtra!* from 1999 to 2004.

Kelly, M.T. (1946–). Born in Toronto, Kelly's first novel, *I Do Remember the Fall* (1977) was nominated for the Books in Canada First Novel Award. He is the author of five novels, including *The Ruined Season* (1982), *A Dream Like Mine* (1987; 2009), which received the Governor General's Award for Fiction, and *Save Me, Joe Louis* (1998). He has also written two story collections, *The More Loving One* (1980) and *Breath Dances Between Them* (1991), and two poetry collection, *Country You Can't Walk In* (1983) and *Downriver* (2009).

Kim, Sang. A Toronto restaurateur and writer, Sang Kim is the author of *A Dream Called Laundry* (2006) and *Ballad of a Karaoke Cowboy* (2007), and the forthcoming *Woody Allen Ate My Kimchi.* He is the recipient of the $10,000 Best Story Award in the emerging writer category of the 2013 $15,000 Vanderbilt/Exile Short Fiction Competition.

Kulyk Keefer, Janice (1953–). Born and living in Toronto, Kulyk Keefer is professor of English at the University of Guelph. Her books include the poetry collections *White of the Lesser Angels* (1986) and *Marrying the Sea* (1998), non-fiction works *Reading Mavis Gallant* (1989) and *Honey and Ashes: A Story of Family* (1999), and short stories and novels such as *The Paris-Napoli Express* (1986), *Transfigurations* (1987), *Travelling Ladies* (1990), *The Ladies' Lending Library* (2002) and *Thieves: A Novel of Katherine Mansfield* (2004).

MacEwen, Gwendolyn (1941–1987). A poet, novelist, storyteller and playwright, MacEwen published more than 20 books in her short lifetime. The definitive volume of her work, *The Selected Gwendolyn MacEwen*, appeared in 2007, reprinting in 2013. Her novels include *Julian the Magician* (1963) and *King of Egypt, King of Dreams* (1971). Her short stories – selections appear in this anthology – include *Noman* (1972) and *Noman's Land* (1985). She is the author of two plays, *The Trojan Women* (1979; new in 2009) and *The Birds* (1983).

Markle, Robert (1936–1990). Markle was born on the Six Nations reserve near Brantford, just outside of Toronto. He was a distinguished painter and sculptor – his work is collected in all the major museums of the country – journalist for the *Toronto Telegram* and *Toronto Life*, man of letters, and maker of idiosyncratic whirly-gigs. His published work appeared in *Exile: A Literary Quarterly.*

Meyer, Bruce (1957–). A Canadian educator and author of more than 30 books, Meyer teaches English at Laurentian University in Barrie, Ontario, and has taught at the University of Windsor, McMaster University, Trinity College at the University of Toronto, Humber College and Seneca College. His published works include the story collections, *Goodbye Mr. Spalding* (1996) and *The Stories* (1997), and the poetry collections *The Presence* (1999), *Anywhere* (2000), *The Spirit Bride* (2002), *Oceans* (2004), *A Book of Bread* (2011), and co-authored with H. Masud Taj the poetry-emblem book *Alphabestiary* (2011).

Michaels, Anne (1958–). A Canadian poet and novelist born in Toronto, Michaels is best known for novels *Fugitive Pieces* (1996) – which received the Orange Prize for Fiction, the Trillium Book Award, the Chapters/Books in Canada First Novel Award, and the Guardian Fiction Award – and *The Winter Vault* (2009). Michaels is also the author of three poetry collections, *The Weight of Oranges* (1986), *Miner's Pond* (1991) and *Skin Divers* (1999). Her most recent work is her single book-length poem, *Correspondences* (2013).

Miscione, Christine (1986–). Christine Miscione is a fiction writer, with an MA in English Literature from Queen's University. Her work has appeared in the literary journals *ELQ/Exile: The Literary Quarterly*, *This Magazine*, and *The Puritan*. In 2012, her short story, "Skin, Just," won the Emerging Writer category of the Vanderbilt/Exile Short Fiction Awards. Her first collection of short stories, *Auxiliary Skins*, was published with Exile Editions in 2013.

bpNichol (1944–1988). Born in Vancouver, but a long time resident of Toronto, bpNichol was an internationally renowned Canadian poet. Prolific in a number of genres, including poetry, fiction, musical theatre, spoken word and television writing, his most famous published work is *The Martyrology*, a long poem of nine books in six volumes published between 1972 and 1987. His other poetry collections include *Konfessions of an Elizabethan Fan Dancer* (1967), *Still Water* (1970), *Monotones* (1971), *The Captain Poetry Poems* (1971), *Selected Writing: As Elected* (1980), and *Zygal* (1985). "bpNichol Lane" in Toronto is named in his honour.

Ondaatje, Michael (1943–). The Sri-Lankan-born author's work includes fiction, autobiography, poetry and film. Best known for his novels, *Coming Through Slaughter* (1976), *The English Patient* (1992), *Anil's Ghost* (2000), *Divisadero* (2007) and *The Cat's Table* (2011), he has also published over 10 books of poetry, receiving the Governor General's Award for Poetry for *The Collected Works of Billy the Kid* (1970) and *There's a Trick With a Knife I'm Learning to Do* (1979), and has received the Giller Prize, the Booker Prize, the Scotiabank Giller Prize, the Prix Médicis and the Governor General's Award for Fiction.

Pachter, Charles (1942–). Born in Toronto, Pachter is an internationally renowned painter, printmaker, sculptor, designer and lecturer. An Officer of the Order of Canada and Chevalier de l'Ordre des Arts et des Lettres, his work has been displayed at the Art Gallery of Ontario, the Royal Ontario Museum and the McMichael Canadian Gallery, among many others.

Perly, Susan. Born in Toronto, in the early 1980s her *Letters from Latin America* was broadcast on CBC. During the Iraq War she broadcasted *Letters from Baghdad.* Her short stories have appeared in *Impulse, Friction 1* and *Friction 2,* and in an anthology, *Hard Times.* Her novel, *Love Street,* appeared in 2001.

Powe, B.W. (1955–). A poet, novelist, essayist, philosopher and teacher, Powe's published works include *Outage* (1995), *The Unsaid Passing* (2006) and *These Shadows Remain* (2011).

Phinney, Elizabeth (1958–). A writer and freelance book editor who currently resides in Toronto, Phinney's work has appeared in *Exile* and in *Blood + Aphorisms.*

Quarrington, Paul (1953–2010). Born and raised in Toronto, Quarrington was a novelist, playwright, screenwriter, filmmaker, musician and educator best known for his novels, including *King Leary* (1987), *Whale Music* (1989), *Galveston* (2004) and *The Ravine* (2008). His memoir and final book, *Cigar Box Banjo: Notes on Music and Life,* appeared in 2010.

Reeves, John (1938–). Born in Burlington, Ontario, Reeves' work has appeared in every major Canadian magazine extant since the launch of his freelance photographic practice in 1962. In 2002, he received the Canadian Association of Photographers & Illustrators Award for Lifetime Achievement. He has also worked as a radio and television broadcaster. His photography is represented in the nation's major institutions and archives. He has published *God's Big Acre: Life In 401 Country,* with George Elliott (1986) and *About Face* (1990).

Rooke, Leon (1934–). Born in Roanoke Rapids, North Carolina, Rooke lived in Victoria before moving to Toronto. His numerous novels and short story collections include *Last One Home Sleeps in the Yellow Bed* (1968), *Cry Evil* (1980), *A Bolt of White Cloth* (1984), *Who Do You Love?* (1992), *Oh! Twenty-seven Stories* (1997), *Who Goes There* (1998), *The Fall of Gravity* (2000), *Painting the Dog: The Best Stories of Leon Rooke* (2001), *The Beautiful Wife* (2005), *Hitting the Charts* (2006), *Pope and Her Lady* (2010) and *Wide World in Celebration and Sorrow: Acts of Kamikaze Fiction* (2012). Also an artist, his paintings and sculptures show at Toronto's Fran Hill gallery. His prizes include a Governor General's Award, the Canada-Australia prize, the W.O. Mitchell prize, a CBC Fiction Award, the North Carolina Literature Award, and two ReLits (poetry and short fiction).

Rosenblatt, Joe (1933–). Born and raised in Toronto, Rosenblatt has published many volumes of poetry, including *The LSD Leacock* (1966), *The Bumblebee Dithyramb* (1970), *Dream Craters* (1975), *Top Soil* (1976), *The Sleeping Lady* (1980), *Brides of the Stream* (1983), *A Tentacled Mother* (1995), *The Voluptuous Garden* (1996), *Parrot Fever* (2002), *The Lunatic Muse* (2007) and *Dog* with Catherine Owen and Karen Moe (2008), and the prose works, *Escape from the Glue Factory* (1985) and *The Kissing Goldfish of Siam* (1989). The *Joe Rosenblatt Reader* appeared in 1995.

Schafer, R. Murray (1933–). Born in Sarnia, Ontario, Schafer is a Canadian composer, writer, music educator and environmentalist globally renowned for his theories on music and music education. He is the author of more than 25 books, including a novel, *Smoke* (1976), reprinted in 1987 as *Ariadne*, as well as such publications as *Ezra Pound and Music* (1961), *The New Soundscape* (1968), *When Words Sing* (1970), *Music in the Cold* (1977), *R. Murray Schafer: A Collection* (1979), *On Canadian Music* (1984), *Shadowgraphs and Legends* (2004), and *A Little Sound Education* (2009). He was the first recipient of the Glenn Gould Prize (1987), and has received the Walter Carsen Prize (2005) and the Governor General's Performing Arts Award for Lifetime Artistic Achievement (2009).

Shaw, Matt (1982–). Raised in southwestern Ontario, Shaw now lives in Toronto. He received the $10,000 Journey Prize in 2005 and is the author of a collection of short stories, *The Obvious Child* (2007).

Sheard, Sarah (1953–). Born in Toronto, Sheard is the author of three novels: *Almost Japanese* (1985), *The Swing Era* (1993), and *The Hypnotist* (1999). A practicing psychotherapist and writing coach, she also owns a horse and is writing a non-fiction book about the western reining scene.

Snider, Norman (1945–). A screenwriter, journalist, lecturer and fiction writer, Snider lives in Toronto. His most recent screenplay was for the film *Casino Jack,* starring Kevin Spacey, which premiered at the 2010 Toronto International Film Festival. He has also published *Smokescreen: One Man Against the Underworld* (2004), *The Roaring Eighties and Other Good Times* (2007), *Casino Jack* (2010) and *How To Make Love To A Movie Star* (2012).

Snow, Michael (1929–). Born in Toronto, Snow is a Canadian artist working in painting, sculpture, video, films, photography, holography, drawing, books and music. *Walking Women* was first exhibited at Expo 67 in Montreal; in 2004, a photo collection of his most well-known work, *BIOGRAPHIE of the Walking Woman / de la femme qui marche 1961-1967*, was published in 2004. His many citations include a Guggenheim Fellowship (1972), Chevalier de l'Ordre des Arts et des Lettres (1995) and the Queen's Golden Jubilee Medal (2002) and the Gershon Iskowitz Prize (2011).

H. Masud Taj (1956–). Born in India, Taj is an oral poet in both Urdu and English, a calligrapher, and an architect. His on-the-page poems have been featured in anthologies of Indian poets as well as Canadian poets, and are archived in the *Special Poetry Collection* of Carleton University, where he is Adjunct Professor of Architecture. He co-authored with Bruce Meyer the poetry-emblem book *Alphabestiary* (2011). Taj lives with his family in Ottawa.

Weinzweig, Helen (1915–2010). Born in Poland, Weinzweig emigrated to Canada when she was nine. She is the author of two novels, *Passing Ceremony* (1973) and *Basic Black with Pearls* (1980), winner of the Toronto Book Award. Her fiction collection, *A View from the Roof* (1989), was nominated for a Governor General's Award.

Zeller, Ludwig (1927–). Born in Chile, Ludwig Zeller, a poet and visual artist, emigrated to Toronto in 1971, and lived there until moving to Mexico with his family in 1993. His published works include more than 50 volumes of poetry, visual art, fiction and criticism, published in Spanish and translated around the world.

The Exile Book of... Anthology Series ~ books to date

Diverse Voices: *Showcasing the Best of Canadian Writing*

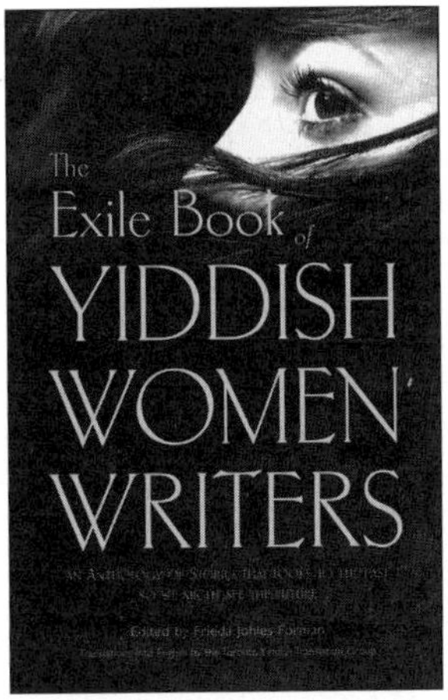

YIDDISH WOMEN WRITERS

Fiction/Prose/Memoir 306 pages ~ $19.95

This important book, which includes various texts never before translated into English, and most of which originally appeared in books, journals and newspapers, is the first to emphasize the work of so many Canadian-Yiddish women writers, like Chava Rosenfarb, Rachel Korn and Ida Maze.

Major anthologies of Yiddish prose in translation concentrate on popular male writers. By their exclusion from these anthologies, Yiddish women writers were denied their place in history, and important voices were never heard. Yiddish women writers provide the vital link to understanding Jewish experience in Europe, North America, Israel and other parts of the world. This anthology represents a transformation of Yiddish literature and with it a fresh understanding of Ashkenazi and Sefardi life.

DEAD NORTH

Fiction 336 pages ~ $19.95

An enjoyable and rollicking ride, this collection of Canadian Zombie Fiction contains 20 stories exploring a broad spectrum of the undead, from Romero-style corpses to those inspired by Aboriginal mythology, all shambling against the background of the Great White North. The anthology's specific focus on Canadian settings distinguishes it from the pack, and its exploration of many types of zombies weaves a vast compendium of fiction. Strong writing and imagination are showcased in clever stories that take readers through thrills, chills, kills, carnage, horror, and havoc wreaked across the country.

NATIVE CANADIAN FICTION AND DRAMA

Fiction 396 pages ~ $26.95

A wide-ranging anthology of contemporary Native literature, the work of men and women of many tribal affiliations, startling in their reinvention of traditional material and their invention of a modern life that is authentic.

• Tomson Highway, Lauren B. Davis, Niigonwedom James Sinclair, Joseph Boyden, Joseph A. Dandurand, Alootook Ipellie, Thomas King, Yvette Nolan, Richard Van Camp, Floyd Favel, Robert Arthur Alexie, Daniel David Moses, Katharina Vermette.

purchase at: www.ExileEditions.com, Amazon, online retailers

CANADIAN DOG STORIES

Fiction 368 pages ~ $24.95

"Twenty-eight exceptional dog tales by some of Canada's most notable fiction writers have been compiled in this feast of short stories. The stories run the breadth of adventure, drama, satire, and even fantasy, and will appeal to dog lovers on both sides of the [Canada/US] border."–*Modern Dog* magazine

• Marie-Claire Blais, Barry Callaghan, Morley Callaghan, Lynn Coady, Mazo de la Roche, Claire Dé, Stan Dragland, Jacques Ferron, Mavis Gallant, Douglas Glover, Katherine Govier, Kenneth J. Harvey, E. Pauline Johnson, Janice Kulyk Keefer, Stephen Leacock, Alistair Macleod, L.M. Montgomery, P.K. Page, Charles G.D. Roberts, Leon Rooke, Jane Rule, Duncan Campbell Scott, Ernest Thompson Seton, Matt Shaw, Mark Strand, Timothy Taylor, Sheila Watson, Ethel Wilson.

CANADIAN SPORTS STORIES

Fiction 376 pages ~ $24.95

"Most of the stories weren't so much about sports per se than they were a study of personalities and how they react to or deal with extreme situation... all were great reading." –4/5 Star Review, *goodreads.com*

• Clarke Blaise, George Bowering, Dionne Brand, Barry Callaghan, Morley Callaghan, Roch Carrier, Matt Cohen, Craig Davidson, Brian Fawcett, Katherine Govier, Linda Griffiths, Steven Heighton, Mark Jarman, W.P. Kinsella, Stephen Leacock, Barry Milliken, L.M. Montgomery, Susanna Moodie, Lisa Moore, Margaret Pigeon, Mordecai Richler, Diane Schoemperlen, Rudy Thauberger, Priscila Uppal, Guy Vanderhaeghe, Jordan Wheeler.

PRIESTS, PASTORS, NUNS AND PENTECOSTALS

STORIES OF PREACHERS AND PREACHING

Fiction 288 pages ~ $22.95

The Word of the Lord is alive and consoling, alive and riotous, righteous and retributive, playful and provocative throughout the land. Sometimes it is the priest who is the confessional ear to the Lord, sometimes the Lord is hollering in the ear of the baffled believer, sometimes He appears naked in His agonies, sometimes He stands in the agony of His nakedness. However He appears, He appears again and again in the lives of priests, pastors, nuns and Pentecostals in these great stories of a kind never collected before.

• Mary Frances Coady, Barry Callaghan, Leon Rooke, Roch Carrier, Seán Virgo, Jacques Ferron, Marie-Claire Blais, Hugh Hood, Morley Callaghan, Hugh Garner, Diane Keating, Alden Nowlan, Alexandre Amprimoz, Gloria Sawai, Eric McCormack, Yves Thériault, Margaret Laurence, Alice Munro.

EXILE
editions
Fiction, Poetry, Translation, Drama and Nonfiction

20 CANADIAN POETS TAKE ON THE WORLD

Poetry 300 pages ~ $24.95

Canadian poets translate their favourite international poet, and each translating poet provides an introduction to the translated work. Oana Avasilichioaei, Ken Babstock, Christian Bök, Dionne Brand, Nicole Brossard, Barry Callaghan, George Elliott Clarke, Geoffrey Cook, Rishma Dunlop, Christopher Doda, Steven Heighton, Andréa Jarmai, Evan Jones, Sonnet L'Abbé, A.F. Moritz, Erín Moure, Goran Simic, Priscila Uppal, Paul Vermeersch, and Darren Wershler, translating the works of Nobel laureates, classic favourites, and more, including Jan-Willem Anker, Herman de Coninck, María Elena Cruz Varela, Kiki Dimoula, George Faludy, Horace, Juan Ramón Jiménez, Pablo Neruda, Chus Pato, Ezra Pound, Alexander Pushkin, Rainer Maria Rilke, Arthur Rimbaud, Elisa Sampedrín, João da Cruz e Sousa, Leopold Staff, Nichita Stănescu, Stevan Tontić, Ko Un, and Andrei Voznesensky.

From our Exile Classics Series ~ *27 books to date*

Dedicated to keeping culturally important works in print!

LAWREN HARRIS: CONTRASTS ~ $24.95

Group of Seven painter Lawren Harris' poetry and paintings take the reader on a unique historical journey that offers a glimpse of our country's past as it was during early urbanization. 168 pages, includes 16 colour paintings by Harris. Introduction and Walking Tour by Gregory Betts.

New Fiction for Autumn 2013

THEY NEVER TOLD ME ~ $19.95

Winner of the Giller, Commonwealth, Trillium and Writers' Trust prizes, Clarke has crafted great stories of an alchemical wit and hard-earned wisdom in this collection, his best and most provocative to date. 216 pages. Eight stories – concludes with a prose portrait of Austin Clarke by author Barry Callaghan.

THE SECOND ~ $29.95 (hc)

A NOVEL ABOUT SPIRITUALITY, RELIGION AND POLITICS

An erudite work of secular fiction in which a trinity of characters clash over the complex ideologies that shape politics, religion, and spirituality, ultimately confronting their individual identities through the realization of just how hard it is to make belief believable. 580 pages.

$15,000 Short Fiction Competition

(The Carter V. Cooper~Exile Short Fiction Competition, sponsored by Gloria Vanderbilt) : for Canadian writers only

$10,000 best story by an emerging writer, $5,000 best story by a writer at any career point

The 12 shortlisted are published in the annual *CVC Short Fiction Anthology* series, and *ELQ/Exile: the Literary Quarterly*

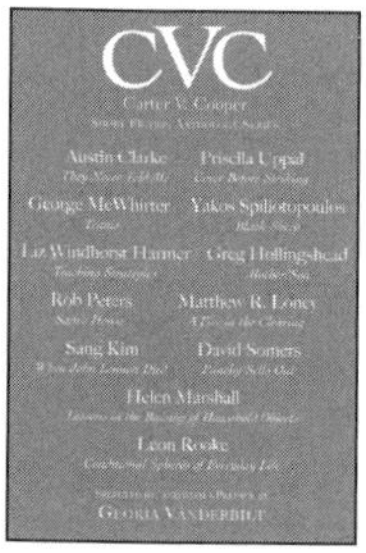

CVC Anthology One: Frank Westcott, Richard Van Camp, Gregory Betts, Kristi-Ly Green, Rishma Dunlop, Zoe Stikeman, Silvia Moreno-Garcia, Leigh Nash, Hugh Graham, Ken Stange

CVC Anthology Two: Christine Miscione, Leon Rooke , Kelly Watt, Darlene Madott, Linda Rogers, Daniel Perry, Amy Stuart, Phil Della, Jacqueline Windh, Kris Bertin, Martha Bátiz, Seán Virgo

CVC Anthology Three: Sang Kim, George McWhirter, David Somers, Leon Rooke, Helen Marshall, Priscila Uppal, Yakos Spiliotopoulos, Greg Hollingshead, Matthew R. Loney, Rob Peters, Liz Windhorst Harmer, Austin Clarke

EXILE editions

$2,500 Poetry Competition

(The Gwendolyn MacEwen~Exile Poetry Competition) : for Canadian and U.S. writers

$2,000 for the best suite of poetry – $500 for the best poem

Winners are published in *ELQ/Exile: the Literary Quarterly*

Both competitions open in October ~ Guidelines/forms at www.TheExileWriters.com

AUXILIARY SKINS

"NEW GENERATION" FICTION

Christine Miscione's debut collection illumines all that's perilous, beautiful and raw about being human. From the surgically gutted, to the racially transformed, to a story of self-excision that won year two of Exile's $15,000 Short Fiction Competition, this collection is chock-full of razor blades masquerading as lemon tarts and everything in between. "No one writes stories or sentences quite like these, and her originality is as strong as her imagination.... This is honest, impressive, visceral writing, stylistically polished and full of punch."—*Telegraph-Journal*

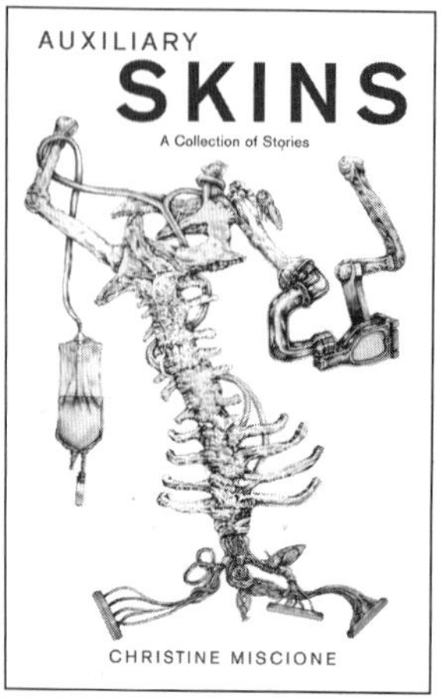

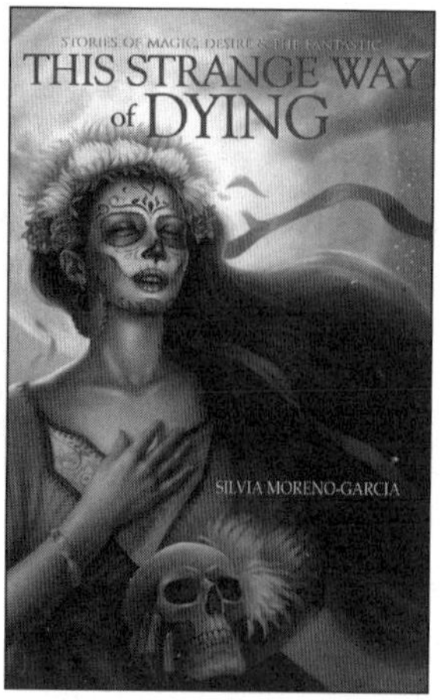

THIS STRANGE WAY OF DYING

Spanning a variety of genres – fantasy, science fiction, horror – and time periods, Silvia Moreno-Garcia's debut collection features short stories infused with Mexican folklore yet firmly rooted in a reality that transforms as the fantastic erodes the rational. Moreno-Garcia was the year one winner of Exile's $15,000 Short Fiction Competition.

www.ExileEditions.com or Amazon

EXILE editions
Fiction, Poetry, Translation, Drama and Nonfiction